graham brice

bagatelle

graham brice

bagatelle

Published in 1993 by
Images Publishing (Malvern) Ltd,
Upton-Upon Severn.

British Library Cataloguing in Publication Data

A catalogue record for this book is available
from the British Library

ISBN 1 897817 18 5

Designed and Produced by Images Publishing (Malvern) Ltd.
Printed and Bound by Bookcraft Ltd, Midsomer Norton, Bath, Avon.

For Sheila who made the
impossible possible.

acknowledgements

This book came about because in January 1979 I left England bound for Saudi Arabia. Those fourteen years of experience are now crammed within these pages. One year ago I met Tony Harold and Cath Whiting who have edited, argued and fine-tuned the words. Without them this book would never have been published. Thanks also to Chris Redman for the striking cover design, and everybody else at Images who touched the book at some time but who I did not meet due to the fact that we live four thousand miles apart.

part one

1968 – 1981

chapter 1

It had rained for most of the night. In fact it had been raining on and off for most of the past three days. But as midnight chimed and December 9th, 1968, became December 10th, the clouds began to disperse. By 12.30 a.m. the sky was crystal clear and the first signs of frost were evident on the ground. The temperature continued to fall for the remainder of the night until by early morning everything in the town of Yeovil and the surrounding countryside was covered in a glistening blanket of white.

Yeovil, a town of some 25,000 people in the county of Somerset, prospered on helicopters and leather. Nestled in the heart of a rural environment, its inhabitants were for the most part born and bred there, or had gravitated there from outlying villages. Yeovil was also a growing community. Small housing estates encroached ever further into fields that until recently had formed the boundary of the town. One such estate was the Avalon. The streets, which formed small closes off a main road, were named after other Somerset towns; so you would drive along Bridgwater Road to gain access to Glastonbury Drive or Wellington Drive or one of the other half dozen or so drives that had been built. The houses were all of a similar design, the only noticeable difference being that Taunton and Ilchester, the first two drives, which were on opposite sides of the main road, contained detached houses. The remaining drives contained more modest semis.

By 6.30 a.m. there were signs of life in at least half of the houses on Ilchester Drive, but at number 7 it would be another ten minutes before the alarm clock, which rested on the bed-side table beside the sleeping figure of David Whittle, would ring.

When the shrill noise finally broke the early morning calm David Whittle moved quickly to silence it. He pulled himself out of bed, resting for a moment on the edge before reaching down in the dark and picking up his dressing-gown which he folded and placed there every evening. His feet slipped automatically into his slippers, which were placed under the dressing gown, and he moved silently out of the bedroom. He turned on the light on the landing and, before closing the bedroom door gently behind him, he looked back at the sleeping form of his wife, Olive.

His early morning ritual was well established – downstairs to put the kettle on, back upstairs to the bathroom to wash and shave, downstairs again to make the tea and then another trip back upstairs with a cup of tea for his wife. A kiss on the cheek to ensure she was awake and finally, just before descending the stairs again, he would knock on the door of one of the other two bedrooms and inform his son, Simon, that it was seven o'clock and time to get up.

The methodical approach that David Whittle brought to his early morning activities pervaded his life. He was forty-five years old and for as long as he could remember his actions had been dictated by routine. He had finished his schooling at eighteen and after completing two years national service had entered the accounting profession. Both his educational years and national service had, to a great extent, been superfluous. He was naturally gifted at maths so a career working with numbers was inevitable, and he already carried a military bearing and discipline long before he entered the enforced service.

Half an inch under six feet tall, his erect, pencil-thin stature gave the impression of someone much taller. His hair, which was trimmed every second Tuesday on his way home from work, was parted with a razor-sharp divide; a small, neatly-trimmed moustache was inspected every day to ensure that errant hairs were clipped.

Those who knew David Whittle described him as a pleasant if somewhat remote individual who doted on his wife and son. Indeed, the only thing that he had done throughout his life that could in any way be described as unusual was his marriage to Olive James. Until then he had little time for socialising and women, preferring to spend his early working years in establishing himself with a local firm of accountants; it was therefore somewhat surprising that in the space of six months he met and married Olive James. More surprising was the fact that, at twenty, she was ten years his junior.

Olive James was the only daughter of a local farming family.

They had met through a mutual acquaintance and for both it had been love at first sight. He had been drawn to her simple beauty and delicate build, and saw in her the perfect qualities of a mother to raise his children. She had been attracted by the security of his lifestyle and background. One year after they married she had given birth to a son, Simon. He was to be the first member of a planned family of three children but nature would not comply and, although doctors could find nothing wrong with either of them, Olive did not become pregnant again. At first this caused a slight ripple in their relationship but, in time, they both came to accept that Simon would be their only child and they directed all their love and attention towards him.

For thirteen years little of note had happened to the Whittle family. The most momentous decision that David Whittle made was to move from the security of his accountancy practice to become the assistant chief accountant of a large leather goods manufacturing firm that had opened a factory on the outskirts of the town. The move brought with it a company car and a significant increase in salary that had enabled them to purchase the detached house in Ilchester Drive.

The only other event of importance that had taken place had been seven months earlier when Olive Whittle had announced that, thirteen years after giving birth, she was once again pregnant.

"Simon."

The call provoked no response from the sleeping figure.

"Simon. If you're not down here in five minutes, young man, breakfast will be cleared and you'll go without."

Simon yawned and climbed slowly out of bed. He walked over to the bedroom mirror and stared at the reflected image. He ran his hand across his chin, looking for traces of stubble or acne. The examination was cut short by a more plaintive appeal.

"Simon, are you up yet?"

Simon pulled open the door. "I'm up, Dad. I'll be there in a couple of minutes."

He dressed quickly, discarding the pyjama trousers in a bundle at the foot of the bed. As he pulled open the door he was framed once more in the mirror. He stared quizzically at the reflection, leaning forward until he was nose to nose with the image. His facial muscles relaxed and a large grin split his features. He winked, laughed and bounded down the stairs two at a time.

"Morning, Dad." Simon Whittle pulled a high-backed chair from the dining room table and seated himself. His father slowly folded the paper that he had been reading and placed it beside his plate. He looked up at his son, a faint smile creasing the corners of his mouth. The look was a mixture of adulation and expectation. His son had inherited his stature and his mother's looks. He was tall for his age, although his shoulders tended to stoop forwards when he was worried or upset about something. The delicate facial features, which in early years had led to the mistaken belief by some that he was in fact a girl, were now darkened by the shadow of facial hair. His hair, dark brown in colour, was collar length and hung in an inverted "U" shape framing his face.

"Morning, son. Looks like a good day for a . . ."

Whatever he was about to say was drowned out by a truncated scream from the kitchen. Simon beat his father to the door and was greeted by the sight of his mother holding her side with one hand and supporting herself against the sink with the other, her face contorted in pain.

"Olive, are you alright? Is it the baby?" Simon's father stepped from behind him.

There was no need for a reply as another jolt of pain visibly wracked her. Simon stood transfixed as his father rushed to place a chair beneath his helpless wife. She sat heavily, her legs splayed in an ugly, almost obscene fashion. The room was cool, but perspiration plastered her hair to her forehead.

David Whittle knelt beside his wife and, unsure of what to do, patted her hand as an affectionate distraction.

"David, I think I need to get to the hospital." The voice was weak and came from behind partially clenched teeth.

"Hospital? But the baby's not due for another month yet."

"David, my love, I'm not sure I can hold out for another minute let alone a month. Please call the hospital, tell them we are on our way."

He released his wife's hand and hurried from the room with a new sense of purpose to make the phone call.

Olive Whittle noticed her son for the first time. "Simon, darling, it looks like your baby brother or sister can't wait to join the family." She saw the look of concern on her son's face. "Don't worry, I'm alright. Remember, this little bundle is as much for you as it is for us." She rested her hands on top of the stretched fabric of her maternity dress.

Simon seemed unsure of what to say.

"They're expecting you." David Whittle walked back into the room and stood by his wife's side, his face a mixture of concern and excitement. "They said to remember the overnight bag. Have you packed a bag?"

"No, I thought I had more time. Give me a hand up and I'll show you what I need."

Olive Whittle struggled to her feet and leaned on her husband's arm as they made their way unsteadily out of the room. Simon stood just inside the kitchen door and watched it close behind him. He moved to the tiled counter, picked up a glass that was drying there and filled it with water from the tap. He drank slowly, his eyes gazing out on the frost-covered garden. He was still standing there several minutes later when his father pushed the door open, carrying a small suitcase in his left hand.

"Simon, I need you to help your mother into the car, it's icy out there this morning. I'll bring it round to the front door." He waited but Simon did not move. "Simon, did you hear me? Come on, we're in a hurry." A touch of impatience had entered his voice.

Simon turned and faced his father. Their eyes met and David Whittle immediately felt guilty. He placed the suitcase on the floor and walked towards his son.

"I'm sorry, I know this must be hard for you. It's going to take a little getting used to for all of us after all these years." He reached out and put his arm around his son's shoulder. "You don't need to worry. Once the baby's born and we're all back home, life will return to normal." He kept his arm around Simon's shoulder as he gently coaxed him towards the door.

"Sure, Dad. Come on, let's help Mum." The words were softly spoken but his face had lost the animated expression that had been there only a few minutes before.

Olive Whittle was leaning against the wall in the entrance hall. The front door was open but she seemed oblivious to the cold wind. Simon disengaged himself from his father and moved forward protectively towards his mother.

"You need your coat, Mum."

He pulled a large blue quilted coat off a peg and attempted to get his mother's arms into it but finally settled for placing it around her shoulders.

A few minutes later she was in the car. Her face was a deep purple colour, her breathing hard and rasping; and it was with great difficulty she managed to speak.

"Can you get yourself off to school? I'm not sure what's going to happen or how long it's going to take. Why don't you ring Dad at lunch-time?"

Simon looked at his mother and nodded.

"Wish me luck."

He mumbled good luck and closed the door. The car pulled away and he walked slowly back into the empty house, his shoulders slouching forward.

Simon stared at the dining room table, but his eyes seemed not to focus on the china or table-cloth with matching table-mats. With calculated precision he moved around the table pushing the chairs back into place. As he lifted his mother's chair something fell against his leg. He looked down and saw a blue envelope and a small package with a large red bow in the middle. He reached down and picked up the two items. Placing the package on the table he studied the envelope, turning it over several times in his hands, before he slid his finger under one corner and ripped it open. The card inside contained the clear, neat script of his mother's hand which was instantly recognisable "For the best son ever, Happy Fourteenth Birthday, Love Mum & Dad."

Simon went through the motions of school. He was distracted all day. He was normally a lively, animated pupil, quick to state his point of view, but today he was withdrawn. In the normal bustle of school-life it was over-looked. The morning drifted away and although many of his friends congratulated him on his birthday his response was unenthusiastic and brief. He felt no desire to be dragged into conversation that might lead him to inform anyone that his mother was in labour.

There was no news at lunch-time when he telephoned, but when Simon arrived home after school he found his father stretched out in one of the armchairs, his feet on the coffee table. Thinking his father was asleep, he turned to leave the room.

"Simon, you're back. Great news. You have a healthy baby sister, Karen Louise, born at 2.33 this afternoon. I've just got back from the hospital."

David Whittle's face told the story. He jumped up and strode around the room, filled with a frenetic energy; a fixed smile added to the almost manic demeanour. The normally controlled and precise man was missing; in his place was an animated caricature with an impish, child-like grin. He started to speak, his words coming in short bursts.

"Who would have thought it? Fourteen years! A new beginning. Unbelievable. Fatherhood all over again. Unbelievable."

Simon remained standing while his father walked around him; he had not spoken since he had entered the room.

"She was premature, of course. But healthy. We can go and see them together tonight. Six o'clock. They should be home within a week."

He stopped speaking and moving; a frown furrowed his brow as if he was having difficulty grasping a thought.

"Wait here." He pointed a finger at Simon and left the room.

He returned a few seconds later carrying the package with the red bow and the birthday card.

"Happy Birthday, son. You seem to have found the card." He extended his hand with the package in it. "With all the excitement this morning . . . " Unsure of what to say he let the words hang in the air. He watched as Simon slowly unwrapped the present. "Imagine you having the same birthday as Karen. Unbelievable."

Simon looked at the gift, a watch. "It's lovely, Dad, just what I wanted. Thanks." His voice lacked emotion or conviction but his father didn't notice.

Olive Whittle looked tired. Her normally lively face was drained and pale and when Simon leaned over the bed and kissed her lightly on the cheek, the cold dampness of the skin caused him to pull away quickly.

"How are you, son? Happy Birthday."

"Fine, Mum. How are you?"

"Contented."

David Whittle fussed around the bed. He looked ill at ease, uncertain about his role in this alien environment. He placed the flowers he was holding on the small cabinet at the side of the bed but they looked as if they would fall off, so he retrieved them and put them on the foot of the bed instead.

"So, where is she? Not out on her first date yet, I hope?" David Whittle laughed at his own humour.

"She's in an incubator." David Whittle's face froze. "It's okay, nothing to worry about; she had a slight problem feeding, so they put her on a drip feed and, as an added precaution, placed her in an incubator. It should only be for a few days; remember she wasn't due for another month." David Whittle's face relaxed but did not resume its former smile.

A nurse walked by the end of the bed.

"Oh, Nurse Carey, this is my son, Simon. Can he see his sister Karen, please?"

"Of course. Follow me."

Both Simon and his father followed the nurse. They passed a large glass window behind which could be heard the sound of crying. Twenty or so small, clear plastic cots were placed in two rows. Just under half were occupied by small wrapped bundles. The nurse led them on past the window and through a door marked "Private Staff Only". The room was silent. There were two plastic cots similar to the ones they had just passed but these were fully enclosed. There were wires and tubes leading into both of them. David Whittle looked at the small figures contained in each bubble. He moved towards the incubator on his right, stopped and looked to his left. A look of consternation crossed his face as he realised that he did not know which one was his daughter. The nurse moved to his left.

"Here she is." Seeing the look of concern on David Whittle's face she sought to assure him that everything was alright. "Don't worry about the fact that she is in an incubator, Mr Whittle, it's standard procedure for underweight babies. She'll probably be out in a couple of days."

Simon was hanging back. He seemed reluctant to move at first but, finally, curiosity got the better of him and he joined his father and peered into the incubator. The tiny figure looked so vulnerable. She stretched one arm slowly above her head and her mouth opened to yawn. The fingers of the extended arm opened slightly, grasped, and finding nothing, withdrew. Her arm and hand quickly folded back into her body which had maintained its foetal position. She appeared to be asleep but suddenly her eyes opened. Simon's face was level with hers and he looked directly into deep blue eyes. Just as quickly as they had opened the eyes closed. Simon backed away. His body, rigid, did not betray his emotions; but for a moment his face held a look that could have been fear, hate, or a mixture of both.

"So, Simon, what do you make of your little baby sister? Something special, isn't she?"

Simon turned away; he coughed slightly and ran his hand across his face. "She certainly is, Dad."

When they returned to Olive Whittle a few minutes later David Whittle was once again smiling.

"She looks so peaceful and so small. I don't remember Simon being that small."

"Well that's because he wasn't. Simon was over nine pounds." She turned her attention to her son. "You're very quiet. Is everything alright?" His mother reached out and took his hand.

"I'm fine, Mum, it's just a bit of a shock. It's the first time I've ever seen you in hospital. You look very tired. Perhaps we should leave and let you get some sleep."

She thought for a few seconds, as if weighing up what would be best for Simon.

"You're right. It has been something of an unusual day, and I am exhausted." Turning to her husband, who was standing on the other side of the bed, she asked him to pass her handbag. She pulled out a folded piece of paper. "This is a list of telephone numbers of the people you must telephone. Don't forget anyone, please."

They said their farewells and headed out into the cold, crisp evening air. Driving home the only noise in the car was David Whittle whistling very softly, but once back in the house the frenetic energy seemed to invade his body again. He took a bottle of champagne from the fridge and two champagne flutes from the drinks cabinet. He struggled with the cork and when it finally popped a spume of foam shot across the carpet. He looked around and noticed for the first time that his son was not in the room with him.

"Simon." He waited for a reply; none was forthcoming. "Simon, come and join me in a celebratory drink."

Simon walked into the living-room. He was still wearing his outdoor coat and shoes. His father handed him one of the glasses.

"A toast. To Karen Louise and her mother Olive."

He took a long drink from his glass. Simon took a tentative sip. His father quickly finished the glass of champagne and wasted no time in refilling it.

"Now, where did I put that list Olive gave me?" He began searching his jacket pockets. "Here it is." He moved around Simon who was standing in front of the coffee table. "I have to make some phone-calls, keep spreading the good news."

Simon's face remained impassive. He put the almost full glass of champagne on the table and followed his father into the hallway.

"Dad, I'm going to walk down to the youth club. I'll see you later."

David Whittle was holding the phone receiver in his left hand and had just finished dialling. "Oh, are you sure?" Someone at the other end of the phone line spoke. "Margaret? Hello, it's David. Can you just hold on a minute." He placed his hand over the mouthpiece and spoke to Simon. "I thought you might want to . . ." The words or lack of them tapered off.

"Look, Dad, you're busy, why don't I just get out of your way for a while." He moved towards the front door.

"Well, if you insist. Don't be late." He returned his attention to the phone. "Margaret. It's a girl."

Simon walked the mile or so to the youth-club. The church hall stood out like a beacon beside the dark foreboding structure of the church itself. He stood by the door for a few seconds; laughter and warmth hung invitingly in the air. Then, turning slowly, he pulled up his collar and walked away, his scarf flapping in the brisk north-easterly wind.

He seemed impervious to the elements. Head bowed, he strode forward, his tall stooping frame moving purposefully. He walked for a few minutes before raising his hand to his eye and brushing away the liquid that had formed there.

The tears streaked across his face. The fourteen-year-old youth was a child again, and had never felt more alone.

Simon walked for over an hour. The housing became less dense and he was surprised when he looked up and found he was at the outskirts of the opposite side of town, by the entrance to a popular wooded area. He walked along the short path that led to the old rusted gate that gave entrance into the woods. The gate squeaked on its hinges as he pushed it open. The main path followed a circular route to the top of a hill which afforded a view of the valley in which Yeovil lay. Simon strode out along the path and began labouring upwards.

He stopped once to look back at the view below, his eyes focusing beyond the symmetrical beauty of the yellow lights set against the black night. The wind had dropped and the air was still. It was then he heard the sound: a muffled cry, the type of cry a rabbit or a small animal might make if it was trapped. It came from above him and he set off up the path with the aim of finding the source of the intrusion into his solitude.

He found her standing in the middle of the path, not ten feet from him, head bowed, statue-like. She was crying softly, the sound muffled by a large, brightly-coloured scarf that hung on either side of her face. Absorbed in her grief, she was unaware of his presence.

Simon's breathing, which seconds previously had been loud and sporadic, now became silent and methodical. He stared at her, a silent rage growing until it consumed his body. He moved forward until he was standing in front of her, then stopped as if unsure of himself. She sensed his presence and looked up. Her face was wet from her tears and her eyes sparkled. Momentarily they looked pleased, but quickly refocused into confusion when she saw she did not recognise the person standing in front of her.

He moved swiftly. His hands reached out and grabbed firmly around her neck. He stared into her eyes looking for acceptance. He saw only fear.

She struggled in vain. The crying stopped.

Long after she was dead he still held her in a vice-like grip. The

Long after she was dead he still held her in a vice-like grip. The expression on his face was one of contentment, the colour generated from an inner warmth and pleasure that had replaced the pain.

He finally let the body fall. As he walked away, head held high, the sense of desolation that had engulfed him since that morning disappeared into the cold night air.

CHAPTER 2

Somewhere in the deep recesses of my mind, in that grey area between asleep and awake, lay a thought which I was unable to grasp. I chased it around as it bounced at random. My eyes stayed firmly closed, ensuring that nothing interrupted the chase. Finally, as my senses awakened, I was able to pull into consciousness the outlines of a number.

Seven.

Two times seven, fourteen, three times seven, twenty-one.

Fourteen, twenty-one, seven. Seven, fourteen, twenty-one.

The jumble of numbers was persistently intrusive, and my mind, dulled by sleep, fought them resentfully. Then, in an instant, I was awake and I understood. It was seven days to my twenty-first birthday. It was seven years since my fourteenth birthday.

Fourteen was, in hindsight, the milestone that changed me forever, but it was the announcement of the pregnancy, seven months earlier, that had set the scene for the change.

I never understood why they wanted another child. We were a happy, contented family. Just the three of us. As a small boy I had once asked my mother why I had no brothers or sisters, but that was childish curiosity, not a request.

When they first told me about the baby they never asked me what I thought; they simply assumed that I would share in their happiness. But to me their happiness was a betrayal.

I prayed that night that she would die. I could grieve for her and mourn her loss if she was dead. Alive, I knew, instinctively, that I would lose her to this unborn intruder. I would be reminded it of it every waking moment and be expected to be pleased.

She did not die but she, as did everything, changed.

The changes didn't happen overnight. They were gradual, but they were real. There was now another presence in the house with us. As my mother grew in size I found I was unable to look at her. She had always been a thing of beauty, delicate and slight, warm and loving; but the growth within her consumed her beauty and took over her body; it bloated her and drained her. We had always been close but now I was uncomfortable in her presence. I could not explain it and became moody and reserved. She noticed; I know she did, but she said nothing. Father of course, noticed nothing. He was self-absorbed.

Ultimately I felt cheated by their irresponsible actions. They had no right to inflict this upon me; they had duties and obligations as parents, and yet, by their thoughtlessness, they were neglecting those duties. The rules of life, which they had laid down, had been adhered to for thirteen years. Now they had chosen not just to break those rules but to disregard them. We had always shared everything; now I was excluded from their private love. Even in the womb the unborn stranger had all of their time, attention and love. I would try to share news of my day with them – my hopes, my problems – but my words were continually pushed aside for news of a visit to the clinic, the baby's first movement or any one of a thousand more important things. I wondered, if I killed myself, would that hurt them? Would they feel guilty? Would they miss me? I concluded not, or if they did, the feelings would only last until it was born and then it would really have won – totally replaced me.

It is easy for a teenager to distance himself from his parents; it's all part of the ritual of growing up, but this was different. A wedge was driven between us, and slowly I began to retreat into my inner-self. It was there that I discovered the voices.

Seven years on, I still cannot accurately describe the voices; they were simply there, soft and mellow. I had always known of their existence, but until my fourteenth birthday had not needed them, had not depended on them. They grew in volume, but not in intensity, the closer we came to the birth.

December 10th was always my day. When the baby came she even took that from me. It was almost as if that tiny fragment of flesh bore me malice from the moment of her conception, and her ultimate act was to choose December 10th on which to be born. I knew when I left home that night that something terminal had happened but I did not set out with the intent to kill anybody. It just happened. An accident. I am not sure I ever understood it. It was not like a dream; it was far too real, and yet months afterwards, seven years afterwards, the whole picture rarely comes into focus.

The sexual content was the one most analysed and least understood. I was a virgin; indeed, had never seen a naked woman. She died so easily, no fight and I ran. She was mine for a time, warm to the touch; she could have been my first. It was some fifteen minutes after I left her that I became aware of the damp feeling around my groin and I realised that I had ejaculated.

And over everything was spread the comforting blanket of the voices; they protected me and shielded me, not from outsiders, but from the loneliness and fear that was myself.

The morning after there was nothing on the news about a murder, and for one fleeting moment I wondered if I had dreamt the whole episode. The fear of this – of losing what I had achieved – was greater than the fear of discovery. But I knew it had happened. I had my freedom to prove it.

Finally, on the lunch-time news, the radio confirmed the result of my actions – a body had been found in a small Somerset town. A murder investigation had been launched. The school buzzed with rumours of sexual assault and mutilated bodies. Comfort turned to the stirrings of panic. I fully expected an authoritarian figure to stride into the classroom, point an accusing finger and shout, "Guilty". Yet nothing happened and the panic sank deep into my soul.

The following morning's paper revealed the details.

> The body of twenty-year-old Tracey Gates was found early yesterday morning in a local beauty spot known as Hollow Woods. The discovery was made by Mrs Ann Wilson, who was walking her dog along a popular footpath. The cause of death was strangulation.
>
> Police Inspector Charles of the Somerset constabulary has commented that a person is assisting with their inquiries. Despite further questioning, Inspector Charles would only elaborate by saying that the time of death was between ten-thirty and midnight. There had been no sexual assault, and robbery does not appear to have been the motive.

The accompanying photograph meant nothing. The grain of newsprint left it difficult to decipher who she had been; a sad ignominy, as I never knew either. The column inches ran on but little more was said.

The evening brought further news that twenty-two-year old labourer Andy Simms had been charged with the murder. Mr Simms, it was reported, was believed to have been the boyfriend of the deceased. At the trial, the story slowly emerged that the couple had entered the woods together. An argument ensued and he left. When he returned some twenty minutes later, he found her dead, panicked, and ran.

The defence rests its case. The prosecution dismisses his story. The foreman pronounces guilty and the judge sentences an innocent man to life imprisonment.

In the days and weeks that followed these events the voices became such an integral part of my life that I ceased to question their existence. They never spoke in words that I could hear or comprehend but they were soothing in a methodical, almost harmonic way. In time, they disappeared. I neither missed them nor needed them.

Life for me never did return to the "normal" my father had spoken about. It was impossible to ignore the new member of the family or the impact of her presence. I had to share, or more accurately, learn to share, and I was not good at it. I was unable to reconcile myself to the new lifestyle. I found my father's view on almost every subject unacceptable, and my mother had become a stranger – indeed, someone else's mother. I withdrew from my family, became insular and independent. I grew to enjoy my solitude. I did not need their love or even their understanding. I had found my strength from another source.

All this happened over a period of several years. It may have gone unchallenged, but for the question of university. I had always excelled at school, and my father assumed, incorrectly, that I would welcome and embrace the opportunity to expand my academic horizons. I suppose it was partly because of the certainty of his views that I fought him; but, more importantly, I was bored with academic learning, and could see nothing to be gained by simply learning more. The outcome was the commencement of a career in insurance, and whilst this did not quite cause an estrangement from my family, I did move from home to the sanctuary of my own accommodation, in Taunton.

On December 10th, 1968, I came close to understanding the real Simon Whittle. At the time I believed that I had seen the full person. Now seven years on, on the verge of my twenty-first birthday, I know that I was wrong. This is a journey – a marathon, not a sprint. In time I may come to appreciate who or what I really am, but for now, I am merely content to ease the pain.

I sense a change. The voices have returned. I don't understand their significance, but neither do I question their existence. To me, they signal peace and tranquillity, and yet I cannot focus on their message without being aware of their impact, and so I am wary but excited.

chapter 3

Peter Wells' strong northern accent was constantly at odds with the rural Somerset tones that he dealt with everyday. During his twenty plus years in insurance he had moved frequently, always heading south. From Durham he moved to Coventry, and from there to Worcester, to Cardiff, and now, Taunton. He was a gregarious person with a strong tenor voice that he often demonstrated in pubs and private parties when he had had a bit too much to drink. He was a solid insurance professional and when Simon Whittle joined the world of insurance in Taunton and needed a mentor, Peter was the obvious choice.

Insurance does not have apprenticeships nor tutelage but effectively Simon served as Peter's pupil for two years. As with his academic work at school Simon was a quick and avid student. He learnt insurance from the ground up, not just the policy language but the human side that is intrinsically involved with selling someone a policy or settling a claim. He carried the title of trainee inspector and spent much of his time travelling throughout the county with Peter Wells, insuring homes, farms and small businesses through a network of brokers, solicitors and banks. He saw the fires, the dead livestock, the floods. He had abuse hurled at him and shared many a laugh. He was like a sponge absorbing everything around him. But his claim to fame in such a short time was his ability to win people over, to gain their confidence to the extent that they felt secure when they insured their business or home with him.

He was, however, still low in the pecking order, and was given many of the irritating and menial jobs that other inspectors either thought were beneath them or were simply too idle to do. Simon saw these as opportunities, and often built what appeared to be a dead-end lead into new business. If nothing else, each call meant a new challenge and a chance to learn.

It was one such opportunity that had a profound effect on his life.

"Simon, next Wednesday, the tenth, are you doing anything in the afternoon, around 4.30?"

There were three of them in the inspectors' office, a large basement room which provided the five inspectors and Simon with a base. It was invariably a place of chaos and generated an atmosphere all of its own.

Peter Wells looked up from his report writing and was about to say something to Dick Parker when Parker winked at him. Simon was busily turning the pages of his diary.

"I was anticipating buying you lot a few beers at lunch time, but I can put that off until the evening. Why, what did you have in mind?"

"There's an old dear, Mrs Butterworth, lives in Curry Rivel. She doesn't drive and she wants someone to visit her and review her household insurances. Plus, she said something about going on holiday and wanting some travel insurance. You interested?"

"Sure, unless Peter needs me for anything else." Simon looked towards Peter Wells who shook his head.

"Okay, Dick, no problem. Can you let me have the details sometime tomorrow? I'm already late for an appointment."

After Whittle had left the office Peter Wells spoke. "You've set him up, haven't you?"

"Me? Peter, I am offended that you should think such a thing. According to my diary, next Wednesday is our Mr Whittle's birthday, his 21st birthday no less, and from the goodness of my heart I have just arranged a small birthday present for him."

"Do I learn more now or do I have to await the outcome of this little prank?"

Parker had stood up and was putting on his coat in preparation for leaving. "Let us just say that I may have told a small white lie about Mrs Butterworth's needs." With that final comment he left the office. Peter Wells shook his head slowly, before returning to his report.

One week later, at precisely four-thirty, Simon Whittle knocked on the door of Rose Cottage, a small, inelegant dwelling set back from the main road that ran through Curry Rivel. The door was eventually answered by a dishevelled, middle-aged lady in a night-dress with her left leg in a plastercast. Simon was no good at guessing people's ages, but it was obvious that this was not the woman that he had come to see.

"Good afternoon. I was looking for Mrs Butterworth. Is she at home?"

Without speaking the woman gestured with her hand for Simon to come inside. Moving somewhat unsteadily, she hauled herself upstairs, before collapsing inelegantly on the bed. Simon followed and watched in confusion as she struggled to pull herself upright. He attempted to address the situation.

"I'm sorry, there appears to be some mistake. I was expecting to meet Mrs Butterworth. If she isn't in perhaps I can come back at a later date." Simon started to move towards the bedroom door.

"I'm Mrs Butterworth. What the hell were you expecting and who the hell are you?"

Mrs Butterworth's speech was slightly slurred and a half-empty bottle of gin confirmed Whittle's suspicions that she had not just woken from a sleep, but was in fact fairly well anaesthetised.

Simon was now more confused than ever and he was having difficulty thinking straight. The room was oppressively hot and he was acutely embarrassed by the manner of the woman lying on the bed.

"I'm Simon Whittle. I've come about the home insurances." He stopped, but Mrs Butterworth showed no signs of recognition. "You arranged the appointment with Dick Parker and he asked me to call on you."

A smile spread slowly across her face as recognition dawned.

"It's your birthday, isn't it?"

The question took Simon by surprise but before he could reply Mrs Butterworth continued.

"Now I remember." She seemed to become more animated and regain some of her composure. "Come and sit down here, keep me company." She patted the covers of the bed by her side.

Simon opted instead for an upright chair that he pulled into the middle of the room. He took off his overcoat and placed it over the back but it did nothing to reduce his temperature. He reached down for his briefcase and pulled out a clipboard to which some papers were attached.

Mrs Butterworth watched in amusement, the smile never quite leaving her face. She proceeded to tell Simon her life story, the essence of which was that her doctor husband had departed for greener pastures and she found drink helped to deaden the pain. It transpired that it was her ankle that was broken. She had slipped recently and fallen.

Simon suspected that gin had played a part in the fall. He tried to interrupt the one-way conversation and steer it around to the purpose of his visit, but Mrs Butterworth, in full flow, was not to be halted.

She was dramatically theatrical in her conversation and her movements were causing her to part company with her night-dress. Although on occasions she did see fit to heave it back on, most of the conversation was now taking place with Mrs Butterworth semi-topless.

With growing embarrassment Simon looked for a quick exit. Part of his embarrassment was caused by the fact that Mrs Butterworth was not unattractive. He could imagine that in the right clothes and surroundings she would have looked very presentable for her age. However, in her current drunken stupor and disarray the only adjective to describe her was pathetic.

Hauling the night-dress back in place again she asked Simon to adjust her pillows. He walked towards her and leaned forward. As he did so she gripped his hand and placed it on her breast. Before he could move he felt the nipple stiffen beneath the fabric. Propelled backwards in revulsion and panic, he reached for his coat and briefcase, intending to depart, but Mrs Butterworth had other ideas.

She let the night-dress fall from her shoulders to reveal large pendulous breasts, with nipples red and engorged. Tauntingly, she started to caress herself. Simon watched in fascination. He walked towards her, arms extended, and saw the glint of victory in her eyes.

He stopped at the edge of the bed as if debating whether or not to sit down. Mrs Butterworth was breathing heavily. She reached out her hands and slowly began to unbuckle his trousers. Despite her incapacity she led him expertly with her lips and thighs, and, when he climaxed early, she lay back with a satisfied smile on her face.

Simon, his face half hidden in the pillows, remained inside her, unsure of what to do. After several minutes of silence she moved to disengage herself. The effect on Simon was almost instant as he became erect again. He began to move slowly, but more firmly and confidently, within her. He moved above her, and raising himself on his elbows, looked down at the face below him. Mrs Butterworth, with eyes closed, jerked her head from side to side as loud guttural noises escaped from beneath her lips. Simon moved his hand and placed it beneath her chin; he held her head still. Her eyes opened, a mocking smile danced across her face and sparkled deep within her eyes. Simon thrust deep within her; at the same time he moved both hands up to her neck, caressing the flesh, squeezing until he could feel the Adam's apple raised and firm. Her body began to rock spasmodically. He pressed the hands firmer, spreading his fingers to increase the pressure.

Suddenly the bedroom door opened. A young man stood in the doorway; he seemed to take an age to fully comprehend the scene in front of him, but finally, he turned and left, slamming the door behind him.

Simon moved away from Mrs Butterworth quickly. He sat on the edge of the bed and held his head in hands.

"That was my son."

Further sickened by this revelation Simon moved quickly. He dressed and collected his papers. He avoided looking at the bed and did not speak. As he reached the door to leave she finally spoke.

"What, no words? Just a quick fuck and goodbye?"

Simon turned and looked towards her. She was sitting up in bed, naked, holding the bottle of gin in one hand and the glass in the other. He tried to think of something to say but his mind wouldn't function. He turned and left. As he closed the door behind him he heard the sound of shattering glass as the bottle was hurled at the door.

Simon left the house and drove quickly away, putting as much distance as he could between himself and Mrs Butterworth. On the outskirts of Taunton he pulled into a deserted lay-by and threw up in a hedgerow. He rested against the door of the car gulping in quantities of cold crisp air. Some minutes later he felt able to continue, and drove back to the office.

The office was in darkness when he arrived. He had arranged to meet his colleagues at the Ring of Bells. Concluding that they must already be there he decided to leave his briefcase in the office before joining them. He unlocked the rear door of the building and walked along the long corridor that led to the office. The lights from the car park outside illuminated the passageway, but as he entered the darkened office he reached out to switch on the light.

"Surprise."

For the second time that day Simon was completely taken aback. Some twenty of his colleagues were squeezed into the office. A large cake in the Roman numerals of twenty-one sat on top of his desk, together with a pile of gifts. He stood, briefcase in hand, too stunned by the scene to respond.

"A first, I've never seen Simon stumped for words before." Laughter rang out. The candles on the cake were lit, a glass of champagne placed in Simon's hand and a chorus of "Happy Birthday" struck up.

Simon still hadn't moved. His face slowly changed from a look of surprise to a large grin.

"Come on, birthday boy, blow out the candles."

"Hang on, before we lose the moment, I would like to propose a toast." Peter Wells moved forward and stood by the side of Simon. "To a unique character who, if he ever gets his hair cut and shaves, has a real chance of making it in this business. Congratulations on making it this far – here's hoping your future will be as bright as the present. Happy birthday."

Glasses were raised and drained.

Dick Parker was standing at the back of the room. "Hey Simon, how was Mrs Butterworth? I told you she was a dear, sweet old lady."

Those who were in on the joke, and that seemed to be most of them, laughed. Simon finally found his voice. He raised his hand with the empty glass in it and the room fell silent.

"Firstly, I am totally underwhelmed by your choice of location for a party, but be that as it may I thank you for your kindness. And secondly, I refuse to do any more favours for Parker on the basis that he can lead a young man into temptation. Let the drinking begin."

The party wound its way from the office to the Ring of Bells and ended close to midnight. Simon, by this stage, was incapable of driving and Peter Wells drove him home. As they pulled up outside of the entrance to his flat Peter offered an apology about the Butterworth affair.

"Sorry, Simon, I knew what was happening, but I was sworn to secrecy. Knowing Parker's fascination with chasing anything in a skirt I think I can guess what happened. You okay about it?"

Simon thought for a few moments before answering. "I doubt if you can guess, but don't worry about it. An ability to laugh at yourself appears to be a pre-requisite to survival around here. Thanks for the party, Peter, it meant a lot."

Once inside Simon poured himself another drink and sat down in the darkness to reflect on the day. Its significance was not so much the fact that Simon turned twenty-one or that he lost his virginity, but the fact that one year later, on December 10th 1976, Mrs Janice Butterworth was murdered.

chapter 4

By the time the police car pulled up in front of the house, a small group of onlookers had formed on the pavement outside. Ghouls pretending concern, they parted deferentially to let Inspector Daniels and Detective Constable Rogers through. Daniels flashed his ID and walked straight past the young PC stationed at the gate.

"What have we got?" Daniels asked brusquely of an unshaven form that stood in the hallway.

"And good morning to you, Inspector Daniels," replied the form.

"Sorry. Good morning, Doctor Jones. What have we got?"

"A corpse, female, mid to late forties, huge knockers." Daniels stared at Jones who smiled and continued, "Death by strangulation, approximately eight to twelve hours ago."

"Do we have a name?"

Jones suppressed the urge to say "Yes, Ivan Jones," and instead pronounced, "Mrs Janice Butterworth," as if he were announcing her grand entrance at the local Hunt Ball.

Daniels walked forward, addressing Jones as he went: "Post-mortem by four o'clock today." It was not a request, it was a command.

Jones, who resembled a Victorian grave robber that enjoyed handling dead bodies, facetiously saluted the Inspector's retreating back. Rogers followed, notebook in hand. In the kitchen a white sheet covered a good portion of the floor and the irregular contours left little doubt as to what was underneath. Daniels lifted the corner of the sheet, stared for a few seconds, then turned away. Two plainclothes policemen were dusting for fingerprints and a further two uniformed officers were scouring the garden.

Daniels surveyed the scene, rotating on his heels to take in the whole 360 degrees. Rogers, unsure, stood his ground and waited. Moving to the garden, Daniels seemed to remember the younger man's presence.

"What do you think?"

"It would appear, sir, that the intruder entered through the back door after it had been opened by the deceased." Realising the stupidity of what he had just said Rogers attempted to correct himself, but Daniels indicated that he should keep going. "It would appear that the intruder came across the fields and probably departed the same way."

Daniels, taciturn as ever, barked, "Deductions need facts. Explain."

"Sir, the back door has mud on the frame about eighteen inches from the ground. There are no traces of mud in the hallway nor on the front path, but there is considerable mud on the kitchen floor and indications on the path round the back of more than one set of feet. Conclusion – one person going back the same way as he came." Rogers halted, breathless, aware of the cold chapping his lips.

Daniels smiled to himself, "Why 'him' and why only one?"

Rogers' face creased in puzzlement realising that he had no basis for these assumptions. Before he could reply Daniels was off talking to Sergeant Price who, as the first officer on the scene, was able to bring him up to date on what had happened.

The sergeant, a non-descript whiling away time until retirement, told Daniels that the body had been discovered by a friend from the village, Miss Martha Tibbs, a spinster who had called on Mrs Butterworth at 9.30 that morning to ask if she was intending to shop in Taunton that day. Receiving no reply to her knocking at the front door she had walked around to the back of the house, found the door open, and the body. Her call from the house to 999 had been logged at 9.37. Without being asked, Price told them that a policewoman had accompanied Miss Tibbs back to her house which was three doors down on the left.

Back in the kitchen, Daniels looked in disgust at Jones who was quietly sipping a cup of tea, totally unconcerned by the corpse some three feet away.

"Right, Jones, get her out of here."

"Excuse me," Rogers asked self consciously, "but are there any signs of sexual assault?"

"Look for yourself, boyo." Jones pulled the sheet off the body.

Rogers forced himself to look down and was surprised, and relieved, to find that Mrs Butterworth was not only fully clad in night-dress and dressing gown but that there was no trace of blood. She looked asleep. The only tell tale sign of her condition was the purple hue around her mouth and eyes.

Jones leaned forward and pulled up the night-dress to reveal white thighs with two vivid bruises on the inside of the left one. Without pulling the night-dress down, he lifted both arms and pointed at similar marks on the inside of both arms. Rogers waited for Jones to speak, but the man with the ever present smirk played dumb. Daniels looked at Rogers who hesitantly began another thesis.

"Intruder forces his was in, the decea . . . umm, Mrs Butterworth falls backwards, intruder jumps or falls on top of the deceased causing bruises to the thigh, strangles her where she falls, pinning her arms down with his legs to prevent her from scratching him. No sexual assault."

"Very good, boyo. Not a pubic hair out of place. No sexual assault, no broken nails, a very clean murder."

Daniels, unable to suppress his look of contempt, watched in silence as the body was removed. His silences were the things that got Rogers most. He had only been in Taunton for a few months and although he was appreciative of the time and interest that Daniels was taking in him, he was still uncomfortable in Daniels' presence.

Alan Rogers was one of the new breed of policemen. University educated, he had found the transfer from theoretical knowledge to practical application relatively easy but had been somewhat surprised when he had learned that his first appointment was to be in Somerset. Apart from it being significantly different from the Birmingham area where he had grown up, it was also somewhat of a backwater from the police work perspective. He reasoned that there must be logic somewhere in the system and at twenty-four, with age on his side, he had quickly set about establishing himself within the Taunton force, working as closely as possible with Daniels.

The work to date was interesting, if not dynamic, and as such he had expected the investigation of a burglary or some such similar matter when he heard Daniels calling his name earlier that morning. It wasn't until they were halfway to the scene of the crime that Daniels had told him of the murder. It took some moments for the knowledge to sink in and then he had no idea what to say. You could hardly thank someone for taking you to the scene of a murder.

A quick inspection of the house took place with Rogers following three steps behind Daniels. During their brief tour Rogers concluded that theft did not appear to be the motive. The house was comfortably disorganised, lived in, not deranged. Coming down the stairs Daniels finally spoke.

"I'm off to see Miss Tibbs. Follow the path across the fields and see where it leads and then meet me at her house. And Rogers, learn to speak your mind authoritatively. Half-arsed notions produce half-arsed solutions."

Rogers moved off into the garden, the sting of criticism tempered by the advice. At the end of the flagstone path at the rear of the house, a small gate gave direct access into the field. The grass was flattened as if someone walked this way regularly and there was little to see. The path diagonally bisected the field and led to a stile, the wood of which was worn smooth by the hands and feet of time. Crossing the stile the path skirted a second field but there were signs that someone recently had chosen to go straight through the ankle-high grass. The length of stride did not indicate that someone was running, more a casual saunter. Reaching the far side of the field Rogers leaned against a five-bar gate and surveyed a deserted country lane. A mud deposit on the lower rung indicated that someone had recently climbed over the gate or used a foot to push it open. Hauling himself over the gate he looked for any tyre tracks that would indicate how the murderer had made his getaway. The road was clear in both directions – not even a trail of muddy footprints to indicate that the murderer had walked away from the scene. Having checked the road for a couple of hundred yards in both directions, Rogers set off back across the fields to join Daniels.

Miss Tibbs was a frail, elderly spinster. As no attempt was made to introduce him, Rogers stood with his back against a wall and observed the scene. He listened to the brief dialogue. Daniels was being subtly persuasive, encouraging Miss Tibbs to recall anything unusual about last night. Miss Tibbs appeared confused and was somewhat tearful. The teacup she held in her left hand shook with a gentle rocking motion, the contents cold and untouched. Her answers for the most part were monosyllabic and added nothing to their limited store of knowledge.

Outside, Daniels looked skyward before suggesting an adjournment for lunch. Seated in the lounge bar of The Angel Rogers reflected that life was seldom like the movies. This was the work he had dreamt of doing for as long as he could remember and yet instead of being hot on the heels of a murderer he was sipping a beer, with Daniels' blessing, and eating a pork pie. However, not wishing to waste this opportunity, and recalling Daniels' advice about speaking out, he told Daniels about his walk across the fields. As usual Daniels made no comment but Rogers was sure the information had been stored away to be recalled at a later date.

"What about footprints?" Daniels' eyebrows raised questioningly.

"Sorry, sir, I don't believe there were any that were distinct enough to take a cast of."

"Doesn't that strike you as odd? It rained most of yesterday. There's plenty of mud about and yet no footprints."

Rogers chose to bite his pork pie as a means of buying time and eventually volunteered, "Perhaps the murderer wore something flat and smooth like a carpet slipper, which is unlikely, or he somehow managed to mask the tread of his footwear." He paused to collect his thoughts and let Daniels speak, but Daniels stared instead at a fixed spot on the wall, forcing Rogers to continue. "Following that line of thought implies that the murderer set out intentionally to murder Mrs Butterworth and that by default he knew the deceased."

"Very good, boyo." Nervously fingering the dimples on his beer glass, Rogers was surprised more than amused by Daniels' attempt to imitate Jones. Reverting to form he continued, "But how did he get out of the field?" The question was rhetorical and Daniels left the thought hanging as he went on to explain the rarity of such crimes in these parts and stressed heavily that it was almost inevitable that it would turn out to be a member of the family or at least someone with whom the deceased was familiar. He stressed the importance of interviewing everybody in the village and the immediate vicinity, and most importantly being able to identify the difference between what people had actually heard and seen as opposed to what they thought, or hoped, they had heard and seen. Daniels told Rogers that be would be working with him on the murder investigation. His first job was to conduct a thorough search of the cottage with PC Bragg from the Taunton station.

"Remember," Daniels said, wiping away the crumbs from the end of his moustache, "this is Somerset. Murders do not go unsolved in small country villages."

Daniels dropped Rogers off at the front of Rose Cottage and left to see Sergeant Price at the other end of the village. As Price was the only policeman in Curry Rivel, the small police station and his home were one and the same place.

Rogers found Bragg drinking tea in the kitchen.

"Well, well, it's the Inspector's blue-eyed boy. What would you like me to do now, sir? Can I polish your badge for you, sir? Oh yes, sir, please sir." Bragg's booming laughter at his own joke split the silence of the house.

"Cut it out, Ian, we have work to do."

Ian Bragg and Alan Rogers had struck up an easy-going friendship since Rogers had arrived in Taunton. Bragg was the archetypal local policeman. Well over six feet tall, he had a ruddy face which spoke volumes about his farming background. His accent was lyrically Somerset and although he fought to restrain it, with a few beers inside him it was broader than most. Both his brain and movements were plodding, systematic rather than incisive; he was a genuine asset to the backbone of the local force.

"Let's take each room individually and then compare notes," said Bragg as he set off for the living room.

Rogers decided to start upstairs. The cottage was not large – two bedrooms and a small den on the first floor, kitchen, living room and a small dining alcove on the ground floor – but it was tastefully furnished. The master bedroom, where Rogers began, showed signs of someone having slept in the bed. Opening drawers and cupboards he moved as little as possible in his search. At the side of the bed on the floor, he noticed a glass and an open bottle of gin. Lifting the edge of the quilt, he peered under the bed. Resting against the wall, where the headboard met the floor, was a rectangular brown box. Kneeling down he pulled the box closer. Finding no writing on the outside of the glossy cardboard he pushed out one end to reveal a white polystyrene package, nestled neatly in the middle of which was a large black vibrator – at least, Rogers assumed it was a vibrator as he had never seen one before. The image of the sleeping lady with the white thighs did not match his latest discovery, and he returned the box and continued his search.

Thirty minutes later Bragg and Rogers were back in the kitchen. Neither had anything of importance to report; both had reached the conclusion that the house was comfortable, displayed an occupancy of one, and that the former lady of the house had liked her tipple. Rogers mentioned the vibrator, his colleague, reluctantly, admitted that he not discovered it.

The remainder of the afternoon was spent talking to as many villagers as Rogers could find at home. Nobody had seen or heard anything but all were keen to tell their version of the events and, depending on their relationship with the deceased, castigate or praise her. By the end of the afternoon nothing further had been added to his pitifully small list of facts, but a general impression of Mrs Butterworth had emerged. He knew of her separation and ultimate divorce from Dr Butterworth. Tales of men friends abounded, although no one could say categorically if there had been a man in her life at the time of her death, and of course there was her drinking – everyone, including the vicar, knew of her passion for neat gin. Not a crime, but in a small village a definite sin.

Rogers had been told to meet Daniels at 5.30 that afternoon at Price's house to compare notes. The front door was open when he arrived and he found Price and Daniels in the living-room. Price was sipping a cup of tea while Daniels stared at a picture of two women enjoying a picnic which hung over the fireplace.

Daniels chose not to acknowledge Rogers' arrival but without averting his gaze he began to speak.

"We all know what we have: a murdered woman and little else, especially a suspect. I have the post-mortem report which confirms death by strangulation. A blue nylon rope was used, similar to that found on any garden clothes line; clean fingernails; no sexual assault; and no trace of foreign blood or semen. Also, no fingerprints were found in the immediate vicinity of the body. No one has reported seeing anything unusual around the time of death which is estimated to have been between 11.30 p.m. and 1.30 a.m. We do have a picture of the woman's life beginning to emerge. Hopefully, Rogers, you can fill in the missing pieces."

Rogers relayed with effective clarity the information he had gleaned from the villagers. It added little to their store of knowledge. Daniels let out a long sigh. He rose from the armchair in which he was sitting and walked towards the fireplace. He appeared as if he was going to look for the painter's signature but instead he turned sharply.

"Price, you know the village, the atmosphere, do you think it's someone local? Is it an ex-lover, a current lover, the milkman?"

Price looked flustered. He felt sure it was no one from the village but, that apart, he had no ideas. Daniels was about to fire a further question at Price but was precluded from finishing his sentence by the shrill ring of the telephone. Price moved quickly to answer it.

"Curry Rivel police, can I help you? . . . Yes, sir, it's Inspector Daniels and he's here. Hold on please." Turning to Daniels with his hand over the mouthpiece he said, "It's a Major Gambol, wants to speak to whoever is in charge of the murder investigation."

"Daniels here, good evening, sir . . . yes . . . yes . . . certainly. Can you give me directions? . . . Right, right . . . fine, we'll be there in about half an hour. Thank you, Major."

Passing the phone back to Price, Daniels grabbed his coat and he and Rogers walked out, leaving Price to watch the door close behind them.

Driving back towards Taunton, Daniels let one of his heavy silences hang in the air before informing Rogers that Major Gambol, from Trull, had some information for them that might be of use.

The major lived in some style in a commanding house on the outskirts of the village. The door was answered by the major himself who directed them into a large drawing room. A roaring log fire cast a cosy glow across one side of the room, but the image was dissipated by the opposite walls which were adorned by a lion's head and paintings of animals in various stages of slaughter. The major made straight for the drinks trolley and, without enquiring, poured three large scotches. He handed one each to Daniels and Rogers.

"Keeps out the night chills. Cheers."

Everything about the major was expansive. His voice boomed and every sentence was accompanied by a windmill of arms. Sinking into a tired leather chair by the fire, he indicated, with another windmill gesture, that his guests should also seat themselves.

"Rum business. Knew her well, you know. Well, since the lady wife went, you know, lonely, birds of a feather, eh what?"

Stopping as quickly as he had started the major stared mournfully into the flames. Daniels leaned forward slightly.

"You said on the phone, Major, that you might have some information for us."

"Eh? Oh, yes." The major pulled himself upright in the chair. "About a month ago, November 5th actually, a group of us, including Janice, went to the do in Taunton."

"What 'do' would that be, Major?" Daniels prodded gently.

"Lions, m'boy, Guy Fawkes, fireworks, jolly night. Something upset poor Janice though, she came back for a snorter afterwards – well, stayed the night, you know." The major stared sheepishly into his drink. "Couldn't tell you what it was about, only said someone had stared at her. She knew him but couldn't put a name to him. Scared her."

Daniels and Rogers waited expectantly but the major had finished.

"Did she mention it again or had she seen him since?" asked Daniels.

The major shook his head. "Damn rum do, probably wasting your time, but thought it might help. Nice gal, you know, pity."

Driving away from the house, Daniels hit the steering wheel in frustration. "Christ, someone has to have seen something."

Without further comment Daniels drove into the car park of the

Three Bells and walked inside. Rogers, compliant as ever, followed. Daniels consumed his first beer in silence, and it was only after a long pull at his second that he acknowledged Rogers by speaking.

"Somewhere in this nothingness we have missed something. The trail is always freshest immediately after the crime, ours was only lukewarm to begin with and is rapidly freezing over . . . "

The soliloquy needed no response and none was forthcoming. Draining his glass, Daniels stared at the foam slowly trickling down the inside of it.

"I've watched you with interest since you joined us. You're better than the rest, you have real potential. It's the spark. I had it once but my face didn't fit. An inspector in Somerset – a compromise for life in the big city. Don't let them get you, Rogers, rise above them. A spark extinguished is a grievous loss. Beat the bastards – for your sake and mine."

The silence returned and then, as if the last few minutes had not existed, Daniels said, "Half of Somerset must have had her."

"Sorry, sir?"

"Janice, the body. The major, our Sergeant Price, they both knew the inner delights of Mrs Butterworth. Who else did, and did one of them kill her?"

Daniels rose to leave. Rogers finished his beer and hurried after the retreating figure, remembering as he ran that he had forgotten to tell Daniels about the vibrator.

chapter 5

A large element of police work is drudgery: interviewing witnesses and suspects, searching through endless amounts of paper, trying to sort the wheat from the chaff, asking questions, typing reports, asking more questions, typing more reports. An endless round of painstaking minutia. The answer hidden in the maze, sometimes hidden forever; sometimes not even there to begin with. The elation of the success is what keeps all policemen going. They are not comic book heroes triumphing good over evil, they are ordinary people driven with a sense of moral justice. Rogers knew all of this but it still made it hard to drag himself out of bed at 6.30 the following morning. Never a morning person it was especially difficult as he had only climbed between the sheets at 1.30 a.m. Reports, the bane of his life, had to be completed. Discipline, his strong suit, had forced him back to the station after leaving Daniels and he knew that later in the day he would feel better for the effort. His small one-bedroom flat, just off the Crescent, was convenient for the station but little else. It was cheap and only loosely would it fit the description of home.

Arriving at the station shortly after 7.30 a.m. he found an air of excitement percolating through the dark corridors. The monotony of daily police life had been highlighted by the unknown. The talk was of suspects, theories and motives, just like every other office in the Taunton area that Tuesday morning. Rogers found Bragg hunched over the antiquated typewriter cursing his way through a misspelt report. Their conversation was cut short by the arrival of Daniels who, looking as if he had not slept either, demanded coffee and told Rogers to be ready to leave in ten minutes.

Rogers stared out of the windscreen at the all-encompassing grey which masked the countryside. For once he was grateful for the silence as they drove to Curry Rivel.

On arrival at Price's cottage, they found Price in a similar condition to themselves. He reported, over-anxiously they thought, that a farmer, Mr Coombe, from Deep Dean Farm had telephoned him early that morning to inform him that he had seen someone leaving the general area of the Butterworth house late on Monday night.

Daniels asked for directions to Deep Dean Farm and said that he would pay a visit to Mr Coombe later that morning. He also expressed a hope that they might be able to start putting a description of a suspect together. In addition, Daniels reported that the ex-husband had appeared, as well as a son who would he coming to the cottage today to see if anything had been stolen. Pausing, he looked around the room as if he was seeing it for the first time. His gaze stopped when it reached Price.

"It appears that our Mrs Butterworth was overly fond of the bottle and men." Price pointedly looked away from Daniels. "We have absolutely nothing to point towards a suspect yet, but in all likelihood we are looking for a jilted lover, a current lover or maybe someone local who knew she was an easy lay but had been rejected."

Rogers spoke up. "Excuse me, sir, but isn't that contradictory to the fact that no sexual assault took place?"

"A valid point, but as we know little about the actual murder I want you to bear this in mind when talking to the villagers and friends." There was nothing else of importance to report.

Price had been assigned to wait for the arrival of Jonathan Butterworth, the son, at Rose Cottage. Daniels and Rogers went back to Taunton to talk to Dr Butterworth. Pulling into the car park at Musgrove Hospital, Rogers asked what sort of doctor Butterworth was.

"A surgeon, I believe," replied Daniels. The receptionist directed them to the third floor where a harassed nurse pointed to a door at the far end of the corridor. Daniels knocked and walked in. He found himself nose to nose with a large florid figure coming in the opposite direction. The room behind the figure was some sort of rest area.

"Excuse me, where can we find Dr Butterworth?" enquired Daniels.

"You have found him. The police, I presume."

"Yes, Doctor, I am Inspector Daniels and this is Detective Constable Rogers. I believe you were expecting us?"

"Yes, yes, but this had better be quick. I am a very busy man."

To add weight to the statement he looked pointedly at his watch.

"Doctor, I appreciate your time is at a premium but your ex-wife is dead and we need to ask you a few questions."

Sighing heavily the doctor indicated they should follow him down the corridor. Rogers noticed that he moved with confidence, a man assured in his surroundings. Nurses moved deferentially to one side as he passed. Stopping in front of a wooden door he pushed it open and stood back to allow Daniels and Rogers in. As Butterworth moved to the chair behind his desk Rogers continued his mental observations. From the back the air had been of confidence, from the front it bordered on arrogance. His age was difficult to gauge but a good head of gray-streaked hair and a solid build suggested someone who took pride in his appearance. Extracting a pipe from his waistcoat pocket Rogers noticed the slimness of his hands, delicate and totally out of sync with the rest of his body.

Taking the initiative, Daniels asked when he had last seen his ex-wife. Dr Butterworth continued filling his pipe and ensured it was fully alight before looking up and giving Daniels an answer.

"Inspector Daniels, my wife and I parted a couple of years ago and were divorced last year. If you are not already aware of it, my wife was an unpaid prostitute and rapidly becoming a lush. I finally became sick of the whole charade and ended the marriage, a decision I should have made years ago."

"I appreciate your frankness, Dr Butterworth, but when was the last time you saw the late Mrs Butterworth?"

Butterworth turned sideways to look out of the window. "Last Friday. I visit her occasionally to check if she is alright."

Daniels seemed unmoved by the response. "According to several villagers you visited your ex-wife at least once a week, normally in the afternoons. Is that correct?" Before waiting for a reply Daniels went on, "It also appears to be fairly common knowledge in the village, that on the occasion of your visits you and your ex-wife engaged in sex." Butterworth swung round to face Daniels, his face impassive except for a pulse showing on the right side of his temple. "In addition, Dr Butterworth," Daniels continued, "your ex-wife has told several people that on more than one occasion she did not welcome your sexual advances and that what followed was probably rape."

Butterworth fought to control his emotions but the throbbing pulse failed to disguise his discomfort. Choosing a conciliatory response over an adversarial one Butterworth defended his actions. "It is true, Inspector, that Janice and I still had an active sexual relationship – but always with her consent. She was a complicated woman." He let the words hang in the air before adding, "I didn't kill her. I had no reason to."

Daniels ignored the last comment and asked if Dr Butterworth had attended the Lions' fireworks display in November. Looking non-plussed by the question he told them that he had not been there. His alibi for the evening of the murder, he maintained, was that he and his wife had been to the cinema and were home in bed by 11.30 p.m. In response to Daniels' question, did he know of anyone who wanted to see Mrs Butterworth dead, he replied negatively but assured Daniels he would let him know if he thought of anything.

Thanking Dr Butterworth for his time both Daniels and Rogers rose to leave. At the door a troubled Dr Butterworth asked, slightly too anxiously, if they would be visiting his wife. "If so," he added, "I would be exceedingly grateful if no mention of my visits to Janice were made." A small bead of sweat had formed on the doctor's upper lip and he looked significantly less assured than when they had arrived. Daniels said goodbye and left the question unanswered.

In the car heading back to Curry Rivel Rogers impatiently asked questions of Daniels: How did Daniels know about Butterworth's visits? Did Daniels believe he was involved? Could his new wife be the accomplice? Did he intend to play one off against the other and reveal the doctor's secret? Daniels was amused by his young companion's concern and naiveté. He calmly explained that Miss Tibbs had mentioned the good doctor's visits and that Janice Butterworth, in a drunken stupor, had one night told her about their afternoons together. The doctor, he surmised, was an egotistical womaniser and as such it was unlikely that he murdered the first Mrs Butterworth, far more likely that the new Mrs Butterworth had murdered her, but if the alibi checked out, as he was sure it would, she would also be in the clear. Feeling slightly more positive after the morning's jousting, Daniels suggested they walk across the fields to try and work out how the murderer had escaped.

By the time they reached the gate on the far side of the field it was raining. Daniels, like Rogers the day before, was unable to throw any light on the mystery unless, he suggested, someone had met the murderer at the gate with a car, which was unlikely but possible.

Returning to the cottage, they were in time to meet Jonathan Butterworth. He and Price had just concluded their search and the son felt confident that, to the best of his knowledge, nothing was missing. Daniels took over the questioning, and went through the established routine. When had he last seen his mother? Where was he on the night of the murder? Had he been at the fireworks night?

Had his mother mentioned anything out of the ordinary recently? And finally, taking the young man by surprise, he asked about his relationship with his father.

Jonathan Butterworth was a slight, effeminate man. His frame gave no indication that he had been sired by the doctor, nor for that matter that the deceased was his mother. His accent was a nasally tone of Queen's English that could only be obtained from a public school. He answered all the questions in apologetic haste but halted on the question of his father. An assertive note entered his voice as he told Daniels that he did not believe the question was relevant to the current situation but if the Inspector insisted upon an answer, he had not seen his father in over two years. He added that he found his father's views on life repugnant and their lifestyles had become incompatible. Jonathan Butterworth told them that he must return to his antiques shop and asked Daniels' permission to leave. At the end of this little speech Rogers observed that Master Butterworth's cheeks were glowing with colour and he was breathing heavily.

After he had gone, Daniels, speaking to no one in particular, commented that none of the members of the immediate Butterworth family seemed to be grieving their loss.

The euphoria of the morning was wearing off. With only the farmer left to talk to, the few leads they had were fast petering out. Price was dismissed and Daniels and Rogers set off in search of Deep Dean Farm.

The ramshackle buildings that comprised Deep Dean were about a quarter of a mile from the gate which they believed the murderer had left by. In the farmyard a dog of indeterminate breed barked furiously at Daniels' legs. A figure emerged from the barn and shouted at the dog to shut its noise.

"Mr Coombe?" enquired Daniels.

"Aye, and who be you?"

"Police, sir. We were told you saw someone the night of the murder."

"Be me son, you'm looking for, round t'other side of barn. Probably need to kick he to wake the bugger up." Spitting noisily on the cobbles of the yard Coombe senior returned to the barn.

The rain was still falling and both Daniels and Rogers had no choice but to walk through the puddles and mud to find the son. A small lean-to on the side of the barn housed a rusted tractor. A pair of legs poked from under the rear wheels. "Mr Coombe," Daniels called as he leaned forward, "Inspector Daniels from the Taunton police. Can we have a word?"

The legs moved and a dishevelled heap emerged from under

the tractor. While raising himself Coombe started, "Seen him I did, daft bugger nearly ran me down. I cursed at he but he didn't stop."

Coombe pulled a dirty rag from his rear pocket and started wiping his hands.

"Where did all this take place, Mr Coombe, and at what time?" Daniels waited patiently as Coombe wiped the rag across his forehead and replaced it in his pocket.

"'Bout midnight, bit later, I was coming home from the pub, bugger nearly ran right over me."

Daniels tried to hide his frustration, and asked again, "Where exactly did you meet him?"

"In t'middle of the road, no lights on, nutting, came straight at me. I mean, I come home every night along that there road . . . "

"Which road?" Daniels interrupted.

"This 'un," Coombe pointed over his shoulder.

"Would you come with us in the car and show us where?"

Coombe looked suspiciously from one to the other. "You ain't be going to arrest me, are you?"

"No, Mr Coombe," Daniels said reassuringly, "it's just that we need to know where you met this man."

"Okay, come wit me, then."

They trudged back through the mud and climbed into the car. Coombe sat in the front with the Inspector, and Rogers in the back. Directing them back past the gate leading into the field, they travelled roughly eight hundred yards before Coombe indicated that this was the place. Daniels stopped the car.

"How can you be sure this is the spot, Mr Coombe?"

"See yon oak tree?" He pointed to a tree twenty-five yards behind them. "I thought I saw someone coming but then I lost 'im in yon tree. Next thing I knew he were past me."

"Excuse me, Mr Coombe," asked Rogers from the back, "but if he was in a car without lights you must have heard him coming before you saw him."

"Car? Who said bugger all 'bout a car? He were on a push bike."

Daniels stared at Rogers, the implications of what he had just heard sinking in. Turning back to Coombe he asked him if he could describe the rider. The description that followed was of little use. Male – he thought – wearing a dark-coloured anorak, jeans and a balaclava-style helmet. The bike colour was also dark.

"Anything else you can remember, Mr Coombe?" Daniels put the car in gear and prepared to turn it around.

Coombe pulled at his ragged sleeve to look at his watch, "Um,

Inspector, as we be so close maybe you could drop me off at the pub." He pointed ahead. "No, can't rightly think of anything else. She were a nice lady, always kind." As soon as they stopped outside the pub Coombe hauled himself out. "Ta," he mumbled and disappeared inside.

Turning the car around Daniels drove back to the gate and pulled up. They both climbed out and stood looking at the road. Rogers broke the silence, "It doesn't make sense, sir. If he had a bike, where did he leave it? The ground was muddy so if he came off the road there had to be tyre tracks."

Daniels pushed the gate open and walked through. He walked over to a cow trough just inside the gate. Bending down he could just make out small deposits of mud similar to those that had been on the path of the house. Calling Rogers over he pointed, "There's your answer. He cycles down the road, opens the gate, carries his bike through and leaves it leaning against the trough, collects it on the way back, repeats the exercise, no mud, and off he goes."

"Tends to imply he was local, sir, if he was cycling."

"Either that or he had a car parked elsewhere."

A sense of desolation engulfed the scene. Daniels knew, and Rogers sensed, that they were getting nowhere. Their best hope of finding the killer lay in someone remembering something or the killer striking again. A depressing thought.

The days drifted slowly by and, as Christmas approached, they were still getting nowhere. Several possible suspects had arisen, all of whom had opportunity and reason, but there was no evidence to suggest they were murderers.

Rogers celebrated the New Year with a WPC from Taunton. Lying in bed she happened to remark to Rogers that one odd coincidence of the Butterworth murder was that eight or nine years ago there had been a similar murder in Yeovil. She remembered it because both murders had occurred around the same time of year and she had been a schoolgirl in Yeovil at the time. Rogers was immediately interested but his interest was cut short when she told him that there could not be a connection between the two – the killer had been caught and convicted for the first murder and was still in jail.

So much for coincidence.

Shortly afterwards Rogers returned to more mundane work and only Daniels remained on the case full-time. By the end of February the file was still open but all activity had ceased – an unsolved murder to collect dust on the shelf.

chapter 6

For almost a year I had been plagued by a gnawing sensation. It would appear without warning, beginning in the pit of my stomach and growing until my body felt bloated. The sensation would last a few minutes before an inner chemical restored the imbalance.

December had drifted to March, spring rolled through summer, and autumn arrived unannounced. The nagging sensation continued. I never attempted to reconcile it, instead I locked it deep away in the subconscious.

Like a cryptic clue in a crossword the answer was in the question, but I tried hard not to ask the question. Three times I had found myself passing Rose Cottage, mentally mapping the terrain, observing the norm. As December drew near I played mind games. If I see her in the street today it's meant to be. If I win at squash tonight the answer is yes. The bore tide was rising and a dam of matchstick doubts was unlikely to hold the surge.

For a year she had haunted me, abused me.

It had to happen. I knew we would meet, not contrived but naturally. The event was the Lions' Guy Fawkes fireworks party. Hundreds of people milled around the burning edifice, flickers of flame illuminated and died and there she was. An image held for a second that was minutes. Her head thrown back, laughing, snapped to attention as she felt the heat of my gaze.

I did not see her again but then I had no need; the message was clear, as if the post office had sent a card telling me my package was awaiting collection. I do not believe in luck, this was not chance or fate at work, this was destiny – the primeval consciousness asserting superiority, the troglodyte hunting not for need but for fulfilment. I pity my friends. They are all short-sighted; they move in a one-dimensional world of plastic images. Like an android I exist on this plane to conform; but, like the miser, when the world has departed, I have my gold to count: I know for sure that I could not survive the inanity of life without it.

Life at the expense of others is perhaps not a noble life, but reason has been surpassed, superseded by emotion and desire. For eight years I have lived a lie: it was never going to be a one off; the beast is insatiable and food is cheap.

The house was in darkness. The moon flirting with the clouds provided enough light to guide me across the fields. Moving cautiously to the back door I rapped on the window pane. Pure electricity ran through my body. The only element of doubt in the plan was the next few seconds. I had rehearsed the plan in my mind, covered all contingencies, drafted, revised and settled on a workable format. The only unusual aspect of my appearance was the thick socks covering my boots.

A light went on inside the house and then the porch light illuminated me and announced my presence. A voice from behind the door enquired who was there. I replied that my car had broken down and asked if I could use the phone to call for help. A moment's hesitancy. I added that the phone in the village was out of order. A key turned in the lock and the door opened slowly.

The glare of light silhouetted the form of Mrs Butterworth. Pushing forward she attempted to resist my intrusion but a solid shove with my shoulder against the door frame pushed her across the kitchen floor. I saw the mouth opening, drawing in breath to scream. The scream never materialised, truncated by the nylon rope that bit deep into her neck.

A demon had been exorcised, the gnawing pain was answered. It had been easier than anticipated. The sexual excitement was as intense and the desire to flee the scene was instinctive. The high was exotic, pulsatingly simple yet frighteningly graphic.

Sleep that night was impossible. An aurora of afterglow settled as I stared transfixed into the darkness.

chapter 7

"Peter, come on in, good of you to stop by, did you get the message?"

It was a trademark of George Douglas that he invariably ended sentences by stating the obvious. He seemed oblivious to the fact, although most of his colleagues were sure that it was a nervous impediment brought on by stress. As those same colleagues would also have said that Douglas was hopelessly out of his depth as manager of the Taunton branch of one of the country's largest insurance companies, the impediment was ever present.

"Sit down, sit down. Care for a sherry?" Douglas moved towards a glass cabinet and stooped to open one of the doors. Despite his best efforts the door would not budge. "Now where's that key?" He began a search through his pockets which produced numerous coins and pieces of paper but failed to produce any keys. "It's locked." He finally located the keys in his overcoat pocket and set about opening the cabinet.

He poured two schooners of sherry, setting one in front of Peter Wells.

"Cheers. Now where were we? Oh yes, I wanted to talk to you about Whittle. I've had an enquiry from Derby about him. It appears that they have an opening for an inspector and somehow they've heard about Whittle and want to know if we think he's ready for a promotion and if so will we send him up for an interview. Whittle that is. I wanted to let you know and then you can decide if you need to tell Whittle or not."

Peter Wells placed his glass back on the desk and waited patiently for Douglas to continue. Douglas however had a fixed grin on his face and was leaning back in his chair with his arms folded across his chest.

"I'm sorry, George, am I missing something here? If we want him to go for an interview surely we have to tell him."

"Interview? Of course we won't be sending him for an interview."

"Why not?" Peter Wells' voice had risen slightly higher than he intended.

"Well, for one thing he's too young and secondly, look at his appearance – hair below his collar, and a beard. Totally unsuited."

"George, I don't want to shatter any illusions but Simon has produced more new business for this office in the past year than any other inspector. He is popular with clients and agents and can hold his own with any of our senior staff. He has real potential. I've worked with him and trained him for two years. You can't hold his age against him. After all, in time he will probably get older." Douglas stared at Wells, whose head was twisting slightly to one side, trying to work out if a joke was being made at his expense. "At least he should be allowed to go for the interview."

Douglas was obviously flustered at this rebuttal of his authority. "Well, how do they know about him anyway? I'd assumed he would be here for at least another five years and then take over Robertson's patch when he retired."

Peter Wells knew full well that George Douglas believed in the principle of dead-men's-shoes – promotion based on longevity not ability. Personally he was happy with his lot: he enjoyed the life of a country inspector and had welcomed the opportunity to train Whittle when he had joined the company two years ago. He saw in Simon an ability and desire that had once existed in himself, but with a wife and family to support he had settled for domesticity over ambition. Simon and he had become good friends as well as colleagues and he knew that if a promotion was not forthcoming soon they would probably lose him to another company. He was not prepared to let Douglas's natural prejudices and petty concerns stand in the way of Simon's career path. The problem was achieving the objective without Douglas losing face.

"They obviously heard about him through head office. He's been up there on three courses in the past eighteen months and if you recall, his results were always first class. Still, the decision's yours, George. It's a shame for Whittle but I'm sure head office will understand."

Douglas shot forward in his chair. "What's head office got to do with this? They're not involved. I heard from the branch manager in Derby. He spoke to me about it. On the telephone."

"Sorry, I assumed that this sort of promotion would have to be cleared through head office. Doesn't that chap Fisher deal with all matters pertaining to inspectors?"

Douglas was looking decidedly nervous. "Perhaps I was a little hasty. I know, why don't we let him go for an interview – once they see him they'll turn him down anyway, and that should keep everyone happy."

Before Wells could reply he reached out his hand for the telephone and asked his secretary to get him the manager of the Derby branch. They both waited in silence while the call was connected. Douglas stared out of the window to avoid looking at Wells.

"Mr Lockton, Douglas here, Taunton office. I've thought further about our conversation and I don't see any harm in at least letting him come for an interview . . . Next Monday? . . . Fine. I'll ensure that he is with you by 12.00 . . . No, not at all. Thank you. Goodbye."

Peter Wells pushed his way through the crowd at the Griffin and found Whittle sitting on his own at the far end of the bar. He was making no attempt to engage anyone around him in conversation and Wells was struck, not for the first time, by the contradiction that Whittle represented. He knew full well that in front of a client or his peers Simon could perform at a level of maturity and competence well ahead of his years but put him in an everyday situation, a pub for instance, and he would withdraw into himself and present a countenance that bordered on brooding.

"What do you know about Derby?"

"They got knocked out of Europe mid-week and are second or third in the first division."

"Not the football team, the town."

"Nothing. Can I get you a drink?"

"Yes, please, a pint."

"Am I meant to know anything about it?" he asked, waving his glass at the barman.

"Depends, if you want to live there I suppose it would be helpful if at least you knew where it was."

"Live, as in move, as in promotion?" A wide grin spread across Whittle's face.

"There's a small matter of an interview, but I'm fairly certain that won't be a problem. I'm not in the habit of advising you but if you want this job, a hair cut might be in order."

"A hair cut? I might even shave!"

The interview, as predicted, was a breeze and less then one month later Simon Whittle severed his ties with Somerset and moved to the Midlands. All of this happened less than three months after the death of Mrs Janice Butterworth. The time frame was irrelevant as far as the police were concerned; they were no nearer to solving the mystery, and with each passing day the remaining threads of evidence moved further and further into the distance.

chapter 8

Derby would be home for Simon Whittle for almost four years and, if not for a series of unrelated events, he may well have stayed there longer.

Now a full inspector, he enjoyed the luxury of his first company car. The work was much the same as it had been in Somerset; some risks he now insured were bigger, more complex, but it was still insurance. He covered half of the town of Derby but also had an area that stretched north of Derby through the dales to the edge of Bakewell, a spectacular part of God's creation when the sun shone, but hell when it was snowing.

He moved into a small flat a few minutes from the office. Although offers were made for him to share a flat or house with other people he chose to live alone. He had grown used to fending for himself and in the main he preferred his own company in the evening to that of others. It was during his time in Derby that he perfected his lifestyle; by day he was the caring professional, the quick-witted amiable fellow, bright, articulate and forceful in his views. But most nights he withdrew to his solitude. He walked or read or would simply sit and reflect.

The Derby office was small: two full inspectors and five office staff. Simon fitted in well. He quickly established himself as a hard and dedicated worker. He would join his colleagues for lunch or the odd drink after work, and cultivated a host of acquaintances, but no real friends. During the four years that he lived in Derby he had two girlfriends. Both relationships fizzled out within a few weeks; Simon was not interested in making commitments to people. But, as with everything, he continued to learn and the relationships were as much a part of that learning process as was his job.

Simon excelled at the personal side of the business. He found he could successfully project sincerity, concern or humour with the minimum of effort. It was all the more satisfying as he never needed to commit himself, he merely had to project the correct image. To the casual observer he was the true professional.

Towards the end of 1979 a phone-call from Peter Wells, who had kept in contact since Simon had left Somerset, began a series of events that systematically carried him to the next phase of his development.

"Can you come down to Somerset for a night?" Peter asked.

"If the reason is compelling enough I could. What's up?"

"I'm leaving Somerset and was thinking of having a going-away party. Thought you might be interested."

"Sounds a good enough reason to me. So, are you leaving the old company or just doing the inter-company transfer bit?"

"Well, it definitely comes under the heading of an inter-company transfer. I'm . . . "

Simon interrupted. "Where are you moving to this time – still working your way south or going back up north?"

"Malaysia actually."

There was a silence from the other end.

"Are you still there, Simon?"

"Yes I'm still here, but this must be a bad line. It sounded like you said Malaysia."

"I did say Malaysia."

"Peter, I hate to be the one to break the news to you but Malaysia is not in the south or north. It's not even in England."

"I know that, you ass. I've decided I need a change so I applied for an overseas posting and they've offered me a job in the office in Kuala Lumpur. I leave in February."

"That's great. I'm really pleased for you. So when's the party? Give me a date and a time and I'll be there. What does Susan think about all this?"

There was a few moments' silence before Peter answered. "Susan won't be coming with me. She and I have split up. She left me for someone else."

"Peter, I'm sorry. I don't know what to say."

"There's no need to say anything, Simon. Perhaps in the long term it will all be for the best. So what about the second weekend in January?"

"Fine. Where are you going to hold it?"

"At the house. There won't be many people. It appears that Susan had the friends, not me."

"Hey, that's great news about the job. I'll have to go and look at an atlas to find out where Malaysia is exactly."

Peter laughed. "I had to do the same. Anyway, I have to dash. Look forward to seeing you in a few weeks' time."

"Okay. Bye for now."

"Bye."

Simon was surprised by Peter's news. Not so much by the fact that the marriage was breaking up but that someone whom he had believed to be so ordinary could change his life and life-style so dramatically in such a short time. He was still wondering about it when he arrived in Taunton for the party in January. A succession of friends and business acquaintances called in for a drink but by midnight Peter and Simon found themselves sitting alone, the debris of food and drink spread liberally around them.

"I hope I'm doing the right thing. I can't help worrying that this might be an over-reaction to Susan leaving." Peter's words were slightly slurred.

"So what if it is? It's probably just the therapy you need. They're not sending you there for the rest of your life. Do it for a couple of years, if you don't like it come home. Live a little, Peter."

Peter Wells laughed. "That's what I always liked about you Simon, you were never afraid to give someone advice. You have an uncanny knack for cutting through the crap and addressing the subject matter at hand. I suppose that's why you upset a lot of your contemporaries – you scare them."

"I assume coming from you there's a compliment in there somewhere. One more piece of sage advice, then I'm off to bed. Find yourself a local girl and enjoy yourself. Don't worry what those around you think, only worry about what you think."

Simon stood up and began collecting plates.

"Don't worry about that, I'll clean up in the morning." Peter Wells slowly pulled himself out of his chair. "While we are on the subject of sage advice, what the hell are you doing with your life? I assume your ambition has not been dented by the easy pickings in Derby? I wasted twenty years going nowhere. Don't make the same mistake, don't wait for them, it's up to you to make it happen."

Lunch with a local insurance broker on the first day of July forced Simon to further evaluate his current status.

"So, Philip, what's up?" he asked as the waiter handed them

menus. "It's unusual for a broker to buy a lunch so you must want something."

Philip Roberts was balding prematurely which made him look at least five years older than his actual thirty-six. He ran his own brokerage company, having started from scratch five years ago, and had built up a respectable clientele. The quality of his suits together with the gold Rolex watch and the Jaguar in the car park were testament to his success.

"It's really quite simple, Simon. I want you." Simon looked up in surprise. "Don't get me wrong, I'm not making sexual advances. I'm offering you a job."

Simon continued to stare at the figure sitting opposite him. Neither man acknowledged the two pints of beer that were placed in front of them.

"The business has really taken off over the last two years and I need someone to join me to help look after the existing clients and market to new ones. Whatever salary you are earning now I'll add fifty percent to and if things work out, one year after you join I'll guarantee you a partnership. By the way, if you're wondering why I'm offering you the job, it should be obvious. You are the brightest thing around this area and if you don't move on from what you're doing at the moment, you run the risk of atrophying and being overtaken by the next man coming through the ranks. When can you start?"

Simon had not been expecting a job offer and was unprepared to answer the question.

"I'm flattered. I thought you were buying me lunch to persuade me to insure some building that had already caught fire. I honestly wasn't expecting a job offer. I don't know what to say except that I would like some time to think about it."

"Of course, take all the time you want. I was only joking when I said 'when can you start,' but I am serious about wanting you on board."

Long after the office staff had gone home that evening, Simon remained at his desk, gazing out of the window. A colleague wandered in and dropped a pile of files on his desk. "Anything wrong?" he asked, crossing his arms and leaning against the wall.

"I was offered a job today, a possible partnership in a local insurance brokerage."

"Great news." Getting no response from Simon he added. "Isn't it?"

"Well, it confirms what I've always known: that I'm bloody

good at what I do – so good that I can sign my life away to Derby. At twenty-five I can't make commitments like that."

"I suppose I can see your predicament but, you know, at some stage we all have to make some sort of commitment, it's a recognised sign of maturity. It may not be what you want but if it pays well, it helps." There was a brief silence while they both sat and stared at each other.

Simon eventually broke the silence and rose to leave. "Thanks, I think."

"It's fairly easy to guess who made you the offer. Would it be unprofessional to ask you to put in a good word for me if you're going to turn it down?"

Simon resolved the problem in his own way. Systematically he pursued and evaluated his options, the first of which was to turn down the lucrative opportunity to wed himself to Derby for evermore.

Spurred by the example of Peter Wells, Simon applied for an overseas posting, only to be rejected on the basis that he was too young. Undeterred, he applied for positions with other companies and was gratified to find that his skills were appreciated elsewhere.

On January 20th 1981, Simon Whittle flew out of Heathrow Airport bound for Jeddah, Saudi Arabia, where he was to take up the post of assistant manager of an insurance company.

He left England with a hope for the future and the good wishes of acquaintances. He also left behind the grieving family of Samantha Strong.

chapter 9

The dreams, with their probing questions, had started at the end of the summer. They came frequently – twice, sometimes three times a month. Always the same format, different questions, similar content. Their effect was undeniable: like a battery on charge, they rejuvenated the spirit and fed the ego. I often wondered if I appeared different to the people around me. For some days after a dream I felt as if I glowed, that my body was radiating a halo of incandescence. Yet the mirror reflected nothing and nobody commented that anything seemed unusual.

I knew without question that I was different. For almost four years I had been lulled, duped, into believing that I was normal. But that bastard, life, had risen once again and laughed at the folly of my thoughts. I cannot deny this second life, this second existence.

And yet nothing about my second life was difficult. There was no negative side, no quid pro quo for the exotic high. Remorse was not considered and guilt was intangible. I had never had to lie or intentionally hurt those around me. Nobody ever excused me or hypothesised that I was a murderer. Lying in bed next to someone at night I did not break into a cold sweat, fighting the urge to grab them by the throat and force the life out of them. If anything troubled me it was the total normality of life. I could be Mr Average. The faceless man in the street.

By the end of November it was obvious that a third sacrifice was to be made. Research needed to be conducted. Sub-conscious files needed to be reviewed, ensuring that the lessons of experience had been learned.

Yet long before I recognised the obvious, I was planning. I was planning to move forward, onward. These friendships that mankind is meant to survive on are made of air and wind. Disposable and replaceable. If they were not what I wanted, what was it? The answer, like many things in my life, came from nowhere and everywhere.

We are led along life's path. Some of us are conscientious and study along the way, weighing the pros and cons, debating the alternatives; others are carried by the tide. Both groups end up in the same place – a grave. It's just the route for getting there is different. In matters of principle my views are built on solid foundations. In matters of intangibles I cherish, and enjoy the challenges which lie ahead. Thus, when a job as Assistant Manager in Jeddah was offered I had no hesitation in accepting.

My time in Derby had taught me a lot. I grew in mind and spirit, developed as a specimen of mankind, learned to manipulate those around me. I realised for the first time a fallacy of life that had been drummed into me as school: Respect your seniors. They have by natural course more experience, and as a consequence must be right and can be learned from.

Bullshit. People remain in positions because of incompetence. Incompetence breeds incompetence. Perpetuation of the mediocre. New thoughts, new ideas were anathema to the average British business. We won the war but are still losing the battle of life.

My position in the hierarchy was established. I was significantly younger than my colleagues and as such was the object of suspicion, not only from those below but also those on a par who had reached their own level of incompetence. I had my fair share of battles. I won a few but always felt better for the fighting.

Darker sides of business emerged. Talk of freemasons was common, hints that in time I would be asked to join the local lodge. And whilst it was explained that this would neither hinder nor help my career it was felt that it would complete the maturing of the person. Certain solicitors' offices were off limits as my provincial Somerset background did not gel with the minor public schools that these august partners had been schooled in.

More bullshit of the uncommon man.

Derby was a peaceful time. The topography of the dales mirrored my life: undulating, not severe; and it was only as the autumn of '80 became reality that the gnawing ache surfaced. The first time it had taken eight years for the desire to peak, this time it was only four.

The drug was becoming addictive.

The when I knew, the who and where had to be finalised. Deciding against Derby I settled on Nottingham. A large university city, with an active night-life, it overshadowed its less opulent neighbour. A plan was not formulated, just a vague notion. Someone had to be separated from the crowd, enticed away, quietly, unobtrusively, led by a curiosity that would prove fatal.

Setting out on the night of December 10th, I made for the Trip to Jerusalem, a well known local curio of a pub. The cave, which comprised the main bar, was always packed; even when the university was not in term the place did a brisk trade, and anonymity in the crowd was easy. I found a seat at the corner of the bar, ordered a beer and gazed around me. There was no immediate opening to single someone out. Every ten minutes or so I looked at my watch. If anyone remembered me they would only have noticed someone who appeared to be waiting for a friend.

At about 11.00 people started leaving. I tagged on behind a large crowd and followed as they headed for Adam & Eves', a popular disco. I disliked such places intensely but out of necessity established myself near the bar with a drink. A fair crowd was present and over the next forty-five minutes the room filled to capacity. A group of girls took my interest. One in particular had a vivacious smile. She was selective, but flirtatious, with her dance partners; anyone who was drunk was denied and those she accepted she quickly disengaged herself from when the dance was over. Her friends danced indiscriminately and several were obviously pairing off for the night. I finally caught her eye as she rested against the bar. She held my gaze and I knew I had found my kill.

I left a few minutes later. I waited patiently in the car for over an hour until she appeared with two of her friends. They walked to a bus stop a hundred yards away and waited. I could hear their laughter carrying on the still night air. For a moment I thought it had all been in vain but as a bus pulled abreast of them, she detached herself from the other two and waved goodnight. The bus left; she pulled the collar of her jacket up and began to walk away.

I stopped the car a few feet ahead of her and waited for her to catch up. I wound down the window and offered her a lift. She began to say no, I could see her mouth forming the word. Then she recognised me and smiled. I opened the door and she got in, shivering slightly from the cold. She told me her name was Samantha – Sam, and suggested we go to the coast. Laughing, I asked if she would settle for some lakes about an hour's drive from the city. Our conversation flowed smoothly. She was nineteen, she told me, and still lived at home, but her parents both worked at the local tobacco factory and wouldn't care what time she came home.

Reaching the lake we pulled off the country road. She wanted to walk. The air was crisp, the grass stiff with the coming frost. The desire for her was growing. This was a new experience and I had to remain in control if the objective was to be achieved.

Events overtook reason.

We were soon naked on the ground. The tips of the frosted grass rasped the skin and heightened the desire. Her blue eyes shone, concentrated, and the joy on her face rippled through her body. Running my hands across her face and lips, pausing only long enough for her to nip them hungrily, I let them idly fall to her throat. Squeezing gently, then firmer, I felt the heartbeat quicken and the raised Adam's apple felt fragile and exposed in the grasp. The eyes, which had been closed, shot open, worry and concern replacing pleasure. Her breathing ceased, held frozen in the night, until my hands broke free and continued their exploration of her supple flesh. Relaxing with an audible sigh, she allowed the gentle rocking motion of our two bodies to fool her emotions; her eyes resumed their sparkle and her body responded, on demand, to the chemical awakening. As the first wave of climax raced through her body her torso arched dramatically. At that moment I slid my hands swiftly and delicately back over her breasts and up to her neck, and reapplied the pressure, this time hard and unyielding. Her climax continued unabated as the last air was choked from her body. The arched back relaxed serenely onto the ground and I came inside her with a ferocity never before experienced.

I lay inside her for a few moments, not wanting to break the bond, not wanting to abandon the moment.

Once fully clothed again, I retrieved a flashlight from the car and surveyed the scene. Apart from the clothes randomly scattered, the scene was peaceful. The beam of light inadvertently caught her face, which was pallid, nondescript, the by-product of necessity. I turned away quickly, only wanting to remember the moment. My jacket over my hand, I carried her bag from the car, and placed it near her shoe.

The long drive back gave me plenty of time for thought. The emotions were not as high as before but the contentment was blissful, the mind crystal clear, the vision twenty-twenty.

part two

1981 – 1983

chapter 10

Simon Whittle was met at the airport by a tall, thin, jet-black Sudanese with a receding hairline and an infectious grin. He introduced himself as Omar, marketing assistant, and explained that they would be working together.

On the way to the hotel, Omar talked incessantly, pointing out places of interest and providing Simon with more facts than he knew what to do with. After checking in Whittle joined Omar in the coffee-shop and, while they ate and drank, Omar continued to educate him.

"Saudi Arabia is the enigma of the world. In 1979 when I arrived it was one of the wealthiest countries in the world, but the city and the country was chaos. It still is. Remember this country is not England with sun, this country is a bitch – and if you follow my advice you may just survive." Omar was warming to his task as educator. "Despite the fact that you are working for a British insurance company there are very few British nationals around. The majority of the jobs are held by either Indian staff with a few Pakistanis and the odd Bangladeshi. In general these people are poorly paid, but in general you'll find them to be trustworthy and hard-working. In addition, despite, or maybe because of their living conditions, they take pride in their appearance and a genuine interest in the job. The big joke is that they still respect you British, by an extension of colonial power it appears that you still run their lives.

"The locals, on the other hand, fit into the picture one way and one way only – they own a majority in everything. In order to transact business here you have to have a local partner. It's a good way of ensuring that the profits of the company are not siphoned out of the local economy. We are in league with Ahmed Bin Kaleef, one of the largest traders in the area. Ultimately you are responsible to them during your stay in the Kingdom."

Simon had been listening intently. "Where do you fit into all this?"

"That's easy, I speak the language. I'm not as well-paid as you but I'm higher on the ladder than the rest. The company needs me and although you don't realise it yet, you need me." Omar looked at his watch. "It's getting late. Unless you have any questions that can't wait until tomorrow I'll let you get some rest."

"Just one, how come your English is better than mine?"

A wide grin shot across Omar's features. "Two years at the LSE as part of my degree programme, plus English as a second language back in Khartoum." Despite his tiredness Whittle laughed. Omar rose to leave. "I'll pick you up at the front of the hotel at 7.30 in the morning."

The following morning he collected Whittle as promised and drove him to the office where he introduced him to his new colleagues, all of whom were either Sudanese, Indian or Pakistani, with the exception of Mark Hunt, the manager, who was English.

"I see you finally made it," Hunt remarked, not looking up from his desk in the large open-spaced office as Omar entered with Simon. There followed an embarrassed silence while Hunt continued working.

Omar coughed. "Mr Hunt, Simon Whittle. I believe you were expecting him?"

Hunt finally looked up. He dismissed Omar with a wave of his hand. No welcome was extended or handshake offered, nor was this an invitation to sit. Whittle nevertheless sat down in one of the two chairs in front of the desk.

Hunt removed his glasses and rubbed the bridge of his nose. He was a slight man with grey, greased hair slicked across the crown of his head. His complexion was sallow, the skin pulled tight across sunken cheeks. His yellow fingers and overflowing ashtray, combined with his generally untidy appearance, gave the overall impression of a very harassed individual.

"We can make this quite short. I did not request an assistant, I do not need an assistant. Those incompetents in Head Office, back in rainy England, who couldn't find the holes in their backsides, let alone find Saudi Arabia on a map, obviously feel differently about the subject. What you do here is your affair. You look young enough and naive enough to last about three months, six at the most. You upset the Arabs and I'll fire you on the spot. You'll work with Omar, he'll sort everything out for you." Hunt replaced the glasses on his nose and picked up a file from the pile on his desk. The formalities were obviously over.

"Nice to meet you too, Mr Hunt."

Whittle rose and left the room. Omar was waiting outside the door.

"I can guess how that went. He's been muttering about you ever since he heard of your appointment. Don't worry about him, we've got work to do. You need a car and somewhere to live but first I'll give you a tour of the city."

Jeddah was much larger than Simon had anticipated. There was construction going on everywhere and it appeared as if half the city was being erected, while the other half was being torn down. The only exception to this mass of building sites was in the downtown *souk* area which was set against the magnificent backdrop of the Red Sea.

Lunch was eaten at one of the local restaurants and comprised of heavily spiced goat meat, mixed with salad, in a pocket of freshly-baked unleavened bread, washed down with sweetened mint tea.

After lunch Omar drove Whittle around several residential areas, pointing out the advantages and disadvantages of the various locations. In the late afternoon he pulled up in front of a pair of unpainted metal gates not far from the *souk* area.

"This is where I live. Come and take a look inside, it will give you some idea of what's available."

In comparison to what Whittle had been used to back in England the flat was huge. The living-room alone was larger than the flat he had recently vacated in Derby. Omar busied himself in the kitchen while Simon looked around. There were three bedrooms, all with their own bathrooms. The house was simply, but brightly furnished; and numerous photographs of what appeared to be family and friends from the Sudan were liberally spread around.

Simon walked back into the living-room where Omar was opening a bottle of whisky. He had set up a tray on which stood two glasses, an ice bucket, a bowl containing a grey mixture and four or five pieces of bread.

"Neat or with ice?"

Simon regarded the bottle suspiciously.

"Isn't that stuff illegal?"

"Certainly, but we'll get to that later." He poured a large measure into each glass and passed one to Simon. "Help yourself to ice and the *hommus,*" he pointed to the dish, " – pâté of the Middle East, but better."

Simon dropped two ice cubes into the drink and sat down.

Omar stretched out in a chair opposite Whittle, his long legs reaching under the coffee table in front of him. A wide contented grin spread across his face, his perfect white teeth reflecting like jewels in a coal mine.

"Now we have finished the tourist bit, we get down to business. Firstly, the house rules. You learn them quickly, they're very simple: never drink if there is a Saudi in the house; never accept drink from a Saudi; never, ever sell drink to a Saudi, never drink and drive.

"You can sell alcohol to the locals at twice or three times the price that you paid for it. They'll gladly buy it from you for the first couple of times and then the blackmail will begin. You end up becoming their supplier of free drink secure in the knowledge that if you stop they will notify the police and simply find another gullible ex-pat to con. The same applies to offering or accepting a drink in their house. The price is too high."

Omar stopped his monologue long enough to scoop up some *hommus* on a piece of bread and put it in his mouth.

"Rule number two – everything here works by *baksheesh,* the bribe. If you don't pay, you don't get anywhere. This is so well recognised that our company, in keeping with most others, will reimburse us for all the bribes we have to pay. Your *Iggama,* the identity card you were given before you left England, has to be carried with you at all times. The police are entitled to stop you at any time and ask you to produce it. If you are unable to do so you will be fined on the spot, usually the amount of money equal to that which you have on your person. You are then taken to a special jail outside of the port area. You have three days to produce your *Iggama.* If you are unable to produce it you will be deported. You're not allowed to call anyone. Your only hope is that a friend or colleague will notice your absence and come and find you. It's standard procedure if someone is missing for a few hours. If they aren't there, then you check the morgue to see if they have become yet another traffic statistic.

"And finally – " It had grown dark while Omar had been talking. He leaned to his right and twisted the switch on a small table lamp. The pool of light cast by the lamp fell around Omar and his natural colour glistened with a fine sheen as if someone had sprayed him with a liquid. " – Whatever else you do, don't fuck, literally or metaphorically, with the local women. They are off limits. Drink is only prison, women are death."

They talked for several more hours, Omar teaching his pupil and master. The bottle of whisky slowly emptied and shortly after ten Simon's eyes closed and he fell into a deep sleep. Omar placed a thin gaily-coloured blanket around him and retired to bed.

He was pleased with his day's work. He had seen in Simon something special, something different. He knew instinctively that Simon was going to survive but more importantly he recognised that he had the potential to succeed and he was determined to stay around and watch the outcome.

chapter 11

Insurance is insurance wherever it is transacted. Buildings burn and accidents happen the same in the Middle East as they do in England. But culturally and physically Saudi Arabia was like nothing I had experienced before.

For a while my life began to resemble the chaos of the city around me. Try as I might I could not instil order into the maelstrom. The senselessness, the absurdity, the hypocrisy – Saudi Arabia was a waterfall of conflicts producing cloying clay that could be moulded into opportunity, or allowed to solidify and bring me down.

The pay was good but the work was demanding and time-consuming. The work day was from 8.00 a.m. to noon, and from 3.00 p.m. until 7.00 p.m. This alone took some getting used to. The business was there for the taking. I literally could not write insurance fast enough. Most nights I was lucky if I finished before eight and I rarely took the midday break. There were some immediate compensations to the new regime, the Red Sea being the major one. The company leased a beach house on the coast, about an hour's drive north of Jeddah. The coastline was spectacular. Totally unspoiled, simply desert meeting the sea. I soon found I was spending every Thursday afternoon and Friday, the Arabic weekend, there.

I needed to. The frustration, the absurdity and the bureaucracy reached monumental proportions at times. It became the norm to sleep at a colleague's house, or he to sleep at mine, rather than run the risk of being stopped by the police if we had been drinking. I always carried two or three hundred pounds in local currency with me in the car to bribe the police in the event that I was stopped. Fortunately I never had occasion to use it. I was however stopped several times for other non-existent offences. On these occasions I had to produce my driving licence and pay between twenty and fifty pounds to get it back. It was a lucrative income for the traffic police.

After four or five months I started to come to terms with my new environment. Life and perspective slowly rotated on its axis and began to refocus. What had at first seemed overwhelming I began to see as opportunity and although the road ahead was rutted and unpaved I knew with careful thought and planning I could navigate forward.

Hunt was totally uninterested in anything I did and I quickly realised that his apathy could be used to my advantage. I was in charge of marketing and had sole discretion over whether we wrote a piece of business or not. In the UK insurance market everything I produced had to be checked, rechecked and potentially declined, with me as the hapless producer having to inform the client. The same applied to claims. I dealt with the client while some clerk and his superior passed judgement. Here I was everything, and once the reality had sunk in I set about creating a name for myself. Hunt worked by the book, and achieved nothing worthwhile. His view of insurance, and life in general, was an atrophied extension of Victorian Britain. He was totally unsuited, and ill-prepared, for the dynamics of this expanding market. Ultimately I felt sorry for him. He was in his early fifties, a professional ex-patriot. He had worked for over twenty years in India, Kenya and the Yemen. He had lost touch with reality but was more at home in Saudi than he would have been in England.

I matured quickly and dramatically. Physically I was fit and healthy. A regimen of squash, swimming and windsurfing garnered the gangly youth and produced the hidden man. The wit, ever present, was harnessed in new directions. Dinner parties, the norm of the ex-pat circuit, flourished. I discovered an ability to entertain, to tell stories, exaggerated and modified for effect, and found myself in demand as a dinner guest. Money was more than plentiful, the only problem being that there was nothing to spend it on. A decent watch, a stereo, and bank the balance.

The whole experience was frightening, exhilarating, and emotionally demanding. I had taken a quantum leap forward and not only survived but thrived in this alien environment. Numerous people did not make it. Some lasted a year before departing, others months or weeks and in some cases only days. Saudi was trial by ordeal.

Nothing the world has thrown at me to date compared with some of the hardships that Saudi imposed, and I knew I was maturing in the process.

I realised in time that my two lives were beginning to run in parallel and an uneasy peace settled on my existence. The rules of education and planning applied equally to accomplishing a successful business career, or for that matter anything else I cared to turn my mind to.

Seasons ceased to exist, it was always hot. My internal clock was misled and by the beginning of December I was experiencing neither dreams nor pangs of hunger. As a deliberate ploy I tried to manifest the desire. There was nothing. A part of me was happy, a part was sad.

December 10th came and began as any other day. I was confused and for the first time I missed England. I had decided to celebrate by myself, a few drinks, some quiet reflections, and wait expectantly for the coming year.

After leaving the office I stopped at the supermarket for milk. The usual gaggle of Saudi men was everywhere. Local women in black abbahs moved silently, as if on wheels. Then I saw her – a European female shopping, self-consciously, pointedly trying to ignore the jostling of males around her. She was beginning to look distraught. The jostling and undisguised groping was becoming offensive. She searched the sea of faces for sanctuary and, as she spotted me, sighed with visible relief. As the supermarket prepared to close for prayers we were both propelled forward and out into the open air. She was lost in a sea of faces. I headed for the car and drove around to the front of the supermarket. She was easy to spot. She had withdrawn from the masses kneeling in prayer, and stood alone, partially hidden in the shadows of a palm tree. Her head was turning frantically in different directions searching for someone or something. I pulled alongside her, swung open the back door and told her to get in. As we drove away I explained that it was against the law for woman to travel in the front of a car with a man unless they were married. She nodded, still looking rather dazed by the events. Getting her to lie on the back seat was equally simple. The talk of police was enough to make her remain motionless. I drove to the house and got out to open the wrought-iron gates. Once the car was inside she followed me meekly into the house.

A glass of whisky revived her spirits, and within half an hour she was talking, and breathing normally. She told me she did not understand what had happened, and added that she had understood little of the last three weeks. She had not realised when she signed a three-year contract that she would not be allowed to drive and, in the three weeks since arriving in Jeddah, had not left the hospital compound. She had agreed with her friend Freda that they would go to the supermarket that night. It was simply an excuse for an outing as there was a shop on the compound that served all of the nurses' needs. When Freda told her that she couldn't go she had decided for the sake of her sanity that she would go on her own. She knew that taxis were out of the question, but several of the nurses had talked of the new bus service. Having found the bus number she needed, she had set off. Nothing had prepared her for what had followed, the men ogling and harassing her in the supermarket, despite her conservative dress.

She was grateful for my rescuing her and for the next couple of hours we talked, laughed and drank steadily. Like the seasoned professional of Arabia I regaled her with stories true and false. The whisky, and perhaps the contrast between her unpleasant experience and the comfort and security of my house, dulled her senses. She came willingly, if unsteadily, to bed. The sex was brief and unsatisfying and afterwards she slept.

It took several minutes to retrieve the length of nylon rope that had been one of my first purchases in Saudi. As I climbed back onto the bed she complained gently and rolled onto her side. Holding her hands behind her back with my knees I twisted the rope around her neck and began, slowly, to apply pressure. But where was the thrill? Where were the eyes with the look of abject terror? Apart from small shudders her body appeared to be asleep.

I released the pressure and pulled her onto her back. The coughing was instantaneous and racked her whole body. Dulled from sleep and alcohol it took several seconds for her mind to focus. Confusion, concern and doubt crossed her eyes before recognition set in and a faint smile spread across her pale features. Her relief was short lived as her hand moved slowly up to her neck and encountered the rope.

The smile hardened and froze.

Her reaction was epileptic but still too slow to stop the pressure being applied. Straddling her chest I could feel my erection growing as the look came briefly into focus, terror borne of comprehension.

Her body convulsed again and again before finally coming to rest.

The details were tedious, but essential. I dressed her, deposited her in the boot of the car and drove out of the city on the only main road going north. Once I was clear of the lights of Jeddah I dumped the body with her handbag by her side.

I dreamt that night of fame, of adulation bestowed by a concerned and loving public. I was growing – becoming omnipotent.

chapter 12

The shrill ringing finally permeated the depths of sleep. Sir George Armstrong extended an arm from under the bedclothes and pulled the phone towards him. He propped himself up on one elbow. "Yes . . . oh Christ!"

He juggled the receiver back into the cradle and dragged himself into a sitting position. The first rays of sun were fighting to grasp the day and although he could not see the numbers on his watch he knew it must be about 5.00 a.m. He pulled the covers back over his wife, noting, with satisfaction, that after all these years of Diplomatic Service she was immune to nocturnal and early morning calls.

Sir George was a career diplomat. The crowning achievement of his lifelong dedication to Queen and country had been the knighthood bestowed on him by Her Majesty, personally, on her recent state visit to Saudi Arabia. He was not a pompous man. In the overall scheme of things he was a very ordinary man, but this final recognition had gone a long way to soothe the disappointment of concluding his career in the Arabian desert as opposed to Washington. He knew his limitations and, despite all protestations to the contrary, he knew that he had been put out to grass.

His minor academic achievements at Eton and Oxford had left him ill-equipped. He forged a commendable, if not electrifying path through the Diplomatic Corps. Over the years he had risen systematically, methodically. His brand of diplomacy – placate at all costs – had earned him limited recognition. When he was finally elevated to the rank of Ambassador it had been in Indonesia and latterly Singapore. His dreams of Washington had evaporated, like the sleep from his mind. Pulling on his silk robe and carpet slippers, he moved silently out to the bathroom to wash and dress.

Arthur Brown, the night duty officer, was waiting for him at his office. Sir George, efficient as ever, asked for a full report. Brown looked down briefly at some notes in front of him. "At 4.42 this morning I received a call from the Jeddah police. The body of a female British passport holder, Elizabeth McFadden, had been found on the Medina road, about twenty-five miles north of Jeddah. It appears that she had been murdered." Brown stopped and then added, "That's all we know, except they will release the body to us later today or tomorrow."

The room was silent as the last flat syllables of Brown's voice faded. Sir George looked up as an Indian aide hurried in carrying a tray of tea which he placed on the table. Armstrong gestured him away, indicating that he, or more specifically Brown, would take care of it. Turning in his chair Sir George stared at the depressing brown colour of the compound outside the window. He grimaced inwardly and silently prayed that this was not going to be another diplomatic incident. His mind all too quickly recalled the "Death of a Princess" fiasco and the on-going Helen Smith affair; the last thing he wanted to face was yet another embarrassing showdown with the Saudis.

Pulling his attention back to Brown he felt helpless, knowing full well that events would overtake him and as usual he would be left to offer the appropriate platitudes and smooth any ruffled feathers.

"Right, Brown, let's kick the machine into motion. First find out if she was registered with us. Do we know if she was married?"

"No, sir."

"Right, get back to the police. Find out if she was single or married, check her *Iggama* . . . "

"Excuse me, sir," interrupted Brown, "but it will probably be quicker if we call the establishments that can employ women rather than wait for the police to confirm . . . " He let the words drift away.

"I suppose you're right. If there is a husband he will come forward quickly enough. Parents, next of kin, usual bumf, handle the details."

"Yes, sir." Brown rose to leave, taking his tea with him.

"Brown." Brown turned, his free hand resting on the door handle. "In the communiqué to the Foreign Office stress that we don't want any hysterical parents turning up at Jeddah airport. Let's try and keep this one clean."

Brown disappeared to the telex room where he sent a terse

message to the under-secretary at the Foreign Office responsible for Saudi Arabian affairs. The telex marked "Urgent" simply gave the bare facts and advised them to stand by for more information during the day.

More people were roused early but little could be accomplished until later in the morning when the administrators at the hospitals and Saudi Airlines started arriving at work. As was expected, no Elizabeth McFadden was registered with the Embassy. Despite requests for all British nationals to register upon arrival, very few did.

The airline was easy to dismiss. All of the female staff lived in a compound and were either flying or there in person. At around 10.00 a.m. the administrator of one of the hospitals, the King Fahad, called to inform them that Elizabeth McFadden had arrived at the hospital three weeks ago, and that she had not turned up for work that morning.

Meanwhile Sir George was left in little doubt as to what London thought about this latest Arabian escapade. The assistant Foreign Secretary had telephoned upon receipt of Brown's telex and spent ten minutes stating the obvious about containment and pacifying the natives.

Two female members of the Embassy staff, together with the deputy Ambassador, were dispatched to the hospital to retrieve the personal effects of Elizabeth McFadden. When they returned two hours later they were able to identify her next of kin as her mother, who lived in Perth. A second telex was dispatched and through the medium of the Scottish police force, Mrs Anne McFadden learned that her daughter had died in Saudi Arabia.

The Embassy staff waited patiently for the police to call to advise that the body was being released to them. It was 9.20 the following morning before the call was received and by then the Embassy had been inundated by the British press phoning and telexing for details of the latest Saudi scandal. It had somehow leaked that Miss McFadden had been murdered and the popular press was having a field day with innuendo attributed to "reliable sources".

The frustration of life in Saudi was not limited solely to the expatriate workers. It was also keenly felt by the Embassy personnel. The police would not provide any further information and when they finally released the body it was accompanied by a ten-page autopsy report in Arabic. In keeping with Arabic tradition the body had been gutted of all organs and embalmed. The coarse wooden coffin would suffice to fly the body back to England where it could be substituted for a more suitable one before it was flown north to Scotland.

The autopsy, after translation, revealed that the victim had been strangled, probably with a nylon rope. There were no signs of sexual assault although there were faint traces of something that could have been semen smeared across her breasts. There were no other marks on the body except for two faint bruises on the inside of her right arm. There was, however, a high level of alcohol in her system, and she had been dead for between four and six hours when the body was found.

The translated autopsy was telexed to the Foreign Office. The Embassy had no desire to prove the autopsy wrong. Their role in the affair was simply to get the body back to Britain and defuse any political fall-out.

At mid-morning the Ambassador received the phone call he had been dreading, but knew was inevitable. The Chief of the Jeddah police wished to see him in half an hour. This was not a request but an order. Armstrong duly attended thirty minutes later and was kept waiting for forty-five minutes in the corridor before finally being shown into the Chief's office. There was no pretence at friendliness and no apology for keeping the Ambassador waiting. Further, and more significantly, the traditional Arabic hospitality of mint tea was not offered. Armstrong fully understood the significance of these gestures, or lack of them, and was powerless to do anything.

There followed a twenty-minute diatribe against the western world, and the British in particular. There were veiled threats of severing diplomatic ties if the behaviour of British subjects did not improve. The translator at the police chief's side lost none of the point of what was being said. No mention was made of the murder. The Chief of Police was solely concerned with the alcohol level in the body. The lecture concluded and despite the futility of the question Armstrong had to ask how the murder investigation would be handled and tactfully offer the assistance of the British police in bringing the murderer to justice.

Yusuf Bin Alwhary had enjoyed these last few hours immensely. Despite his illiteracy he had risen to the lofty position of Chief of Police by "solving" every crime committed in Jeddah and the surrounding area. The fact that numerous innocent people had been put to death, had limbs amputated or were rotting in jail, was of no concern to him. His annual report to the King on law and order would always show a clean sheet, no open cases. The arrival of foreign workers to his country had increased the importance of his job but had not dampened his zealousness for an arrest and conviction for every crime. He watched as the Ambassador squirmed uncomfortably and took great delight in informing him that he would personally be in charge of the investigation. He contemptuously ignored the offer of help.

Armstrong returned to the Embassy and, before joining his wife for lunch, instructed his secretary to arrange a meeting at 2.30 p.m. with all of the Embassy staff concerned with the case.

His wife noted his sombreness at lunch and her attempts to discuss the children, one a solicitor in London and the other a marine biologist in Florida, fell on deaf ears. Sir George was a man of few words. He felt comfortable with his wife but rarely discussed his business at the Embassy with her. She knew of the murder and secretly hoped that this would be the catalyst which would convince him finally to take retirement, to leave the world of endless cocktail receptions and settle instead in her beloved Surrey countryside. She knew better than to express her view but still she hoped.

There were six people waiting in the meeting room adjoining Armstrong's office. Arthur Brown, the night duty officer, had become official liaison with British and world press; Simon Cheevey, Deputy Ambassador; Philip Marshall, head of chancery; Mrs Philip Marshall, officially secretary in charge of passports but whose role had developed to encompass the duties of unofficial contact between the Embassy and British workers, not just in Jeddah, but throughout Saudi Arabia; Timothy DeVeere, assistant to the Ambassador; and Helen Childs, Sir George's secretary.

They all rose deferentially as Armstrong walked in. He waved his hand indicating they should sit. As he walked to the head of the table he knew the meeting, like this morning's, would be futile but protocol demanded discussion, if not action.

To an outsider it could have been any meeting of a company, or charitable organisation, anywhere in England. The furniture was antique and matched the traditional oil paintings which hung at either end of the room. The only indication that this was not England was the regular background hum of the air-conditioning unit. The meeting, predictably, was a sequence of comments, questions answered by facts, and questions left unanswered.

"Where had she been?"

"According to her room-mate, they were both going to the supermarket after their shift. The room-mate had worked on and Elizabeth must have gone on her own. After that no one knows. In fact it was not even clear if she had made it to the supermarket at all."

"How did she get there?"

"Not certain, but highly likely that she used one of the new buses that have recently been introduced – double-length buses, with a concertina middle. They have a separate section at the rear for women, blocked off from the main section of the bus, with an honesty box for fares. Obviously she hadn't driven, nor had she had a lift from anyone in the hospital and taking a taxi was out of the question."

"Had anyone seen her at the supermarket?"

"No one, ex-pat or local, has come forward to say they had seen her anywhere."

At this point both the meeting and the leads on Elizabeth McFadden tailed off. All of the staff around the table knew that with typical Saudi enthusiasm, no one would be interviewed at the hospital or at the supermarket. What would happen, however, was that within a few days five or six Filipinos or Indians or Koreans would be selected at random and taken in for questioning. After the initial questioning one, the weakest or the most scared, would be detained, the rest released. The poor bastard would then be beaten and tortured until he confessed to the crime. Shortly after, his signed confession would appear on television and in the press. The following Friday morning he would be beheaded in the main square outside the mosque after prayers. Another case solved, another clean slate for Yusuf Bin Alwhary.

All present knew there was no point in protesting or stating the obvious. Beyond sending a dispatch to the Minister of the Interior, protesting the execution, they were powerless to intervene. The murderer would escape punishment, even if he struck again. This heathen country would guarantee him immunity by the very system that had been established to prosecute him.

It took the authorities only three days to come up with the murderer. A Filipino labourer from the port confessed to illegally obtaining a bottle of whisky and enticing the young woman to go into the desert with him. They drank the bottle together and then when she repelled his advances he strangled her in a fit of rage. He was duly put to death the following Friday.

As Sir George and Lady Armstrong dressed that night for their ritual attendance at a cocktail party at the American Embassy, Lady Armstrong noticed her husband smiling to himself in the mirror as he tied his bow tie. She knew, and despised the Saudi system, but also knew that the system had helped her husband avoid a major diplomatic incident and guessed that dreams of Washington had once more risen to the fore. Whatever the reasons she sensed they would now be allowed to continue with their job in Saudi Arabia – that of representing Queen and country.

chapter 13

Never could I have imagined that the very fabric of the country could have worked in my favour. Shackle the Saudi incompetence with the vulgarity of pomposity displayed by the Embassy and you can write Machiavellian magic. I listened and watched with incredulous disbelief the farce that was played out by the protagonists.

If the police were the stars, the Embassy were the perfect foil. In my naiveté I had believed that the British Embassy was present in part to protect the rights of British subjects who worked in the country. Like something from a satirist's pen I quickly realised that the Embassy fully believed they could do their job a lot better if they were not constantly bothered by these irresponsible expatriates, who had no right to be there in the first place.

It was two nights after Elizabeth that I was due to attend a reception at the Embassy. As a British company we would receive invitations roughly once a month, and on this occasion I could not resist the temptation to find out what was happening.

The pomposity, arrogance and in-breeding were a sight to behold. Every group I joined talked of one thing only. I heard the Embassy's view – disinterested, and the Embassy's view of the police view – undiluted hatred seeking vengeance. By the end of the evening I could hardly contain my laughter. Surely what I was listening to could not really happen, but indeed it did. The Embassy shunted the body, and responsibility, off to Britain and the police got their man.

Within a week the incident was over. Even the British press had moved on to more demeaning matters.

Saudi the enigma, like the desert chameleon, had changed its colour and repainted the horizon. Some months later I vowed not to repeat the exercise in Saudi as it was painfully wasted.

chapter 14

With an effortless grace the windsurfer cut through the crystal clear blue water. The multi-coloured sail bisected the horizon, providing the only contrast between the never-ending blue of sea and sky.

"And that's Simon." Two figures stood on the veranda of a beach house, one pointing in the direction of the windsurfer, the other focusing her eyes on where he was pointing. "You'll meet him later this afternoon when he finally gets tired. It's his beach house or more correctly it's his company's. Help yourself to whatever you need – there's snorkelling gear in the room at the back. I'd better help Wendy bring in the cooler from the car."

Bill Brooks left Angela Logan standing on the veranda. She continued to stare at the lone figure windsurfing. From this distance she could not make out any features but was immediately struck by the ease and grace with which he manoeuvred the board. Finally, to gain relief from the searing heat she changed into a bikini, equipped herself with mask and snorkel, and left Bill and Wendy sorting out the arrangements for a barbecue while she headed into the lukewarm waters. The sea went from ankle-depth to knee-depth in about a hundred yards where it met the natural wall of the coral reef. Once over the reef the bottom dropped away dramatically and it was here that the fish teemed in their thousands and the natural colours of the coral provided an underwater show that was unequalled anywhere in the world.

Angela floated with the current and marvelled at the serenity and beauty. Looking down was to discover a different world – a world that bore no relationship to the day to day life that continued a few short miles inland. A shadow passed quickly to her left and she turned, concerned that it might be a shark. Seeing nothing in the water she raised her head and saw the windsurfer heading away from her. The board turned with surprising speed and headed back towards her. As the rider came abreast of her a second time he looked down and spotted the head bobbing on the surface. By swinging the sail away from him the board stopped immediately. Angela removed the mask and snorkel and trod water.

"I don't believe it."

"What?"

"The rare and beautiful Red Sea angel-mermaid, long reputed to haunt these shores and lure innocent windsurfers to their death. Take me, I'm yours."

He fell forwards, jack-knifing at the last moment to enter the water gracefully. He surfaced a few moments later, a wide grin spread across his sun-tanned features.

"I'm Simon, Simon Whittle."

"I know that."

"Ah, beautiful and well-informed."

He swam with powerful, swift strokes after the sail-board which had drifted slightly with the current and hauled himself into a sitting position over it. He held out his hand and pulled her easily from the water to join him.

"Not a mermaid, I see, and by the feel of the skin not a mirage, so let me guess. You must be a nurse, or a stewardess, who at some stage in the past few weeks has seen me, on a flight or at a party, and has doggedly tracked me down with a view to making our meeting look accidental. You have visions of us marrying and raising two point three children, and having a country cottage, with a dog, Labrador perhaps, to sleep on the hearth. So, once you tell me your name all we have to do is fix the date."

She laughed nervously. "Considering we have never met your perceptions are surprisingly accurate. Angela Logan." She held out her hand. "There's only one small point that your rosy picture overlooked. I'm already married."

"So? I have a girlfriend, but as there's only room for two on this board, and one in my life, I have decided to give it all up for you."

"Wendy warned me about you on the drive down but she said nothing about your shy, reserved nature."

"Ah, yet more sense to the equation. You're with Bill and Wendy, and if I'm to believe this fictitious story of a husband, where is he? Lurking beneath the waters armed with a spear gun to defend your honour? Or is he, as I suspect, a mere figment of your imagination, designed to keep suitors away?"

"He's in the desert. He's working on the Trans-Saudi pipeline. I assure you he exists – not, admittedly, for long periods at a time, but he is real."

"Ever sailed one of these things?"

"No. I wouldn't have the strength to keep the sail up."

"It's not a question of strength, it's timing and balance, just like our meeting." Angela wasn't sure whether to feel angry or amused. She decided she was flattered. "If you swim back across the reef I'll bring the board over and teach you if you like."

"I like."

She slid off the board, swam back across the reef and floated on her back. She watched Simon manoeuvre the board onto the crest of a wave and slide nonchalantly over the top of the reef. For the next two hours he cajoled and coached until finally Angela was able to master the rudiments of windsurfing.

Bill swam out to join them. He watched Angela's efforts; her trim athletic body was silhouetted against the sail of the windsurfer gliding through the water and as she turned and sailed back into the wind, her mischievous eyes gave away her evident enjoyment.

"Wendy sent me out here to inform you that she's married, older than you, and to remind you that the penalty for adultery is stoning to death for the woman and a mere beheading for the male."

"Sorry, Bill, I can't hear you. The sun's too bright."

The day finished with a barbecue on the beach and a few drinks. The four sat around talking about nothing in particular. Angela and Simon exchanged glances, their eyes occasionally locking in the warm evening air. Wendy finally brought the proceedings to a halt at 9.30. The three of them busied themselves with packing up bags and coolers while Simon lounged in a chair on the beach.

"Are you not leaving?" Angela squatted on the sand beside Simon.

"No, this is my therapy. I spend the night here most weekends. See the jetty out there?" He pointed to a small wooden jetty that stretched out into the water. "I sleep out there. It rejuvenates the spirit and sets me up for another week of madness. Last time I checked it offered sleeping accommodation for two. Don't get me wrong, this is not a proposition, but I think you would find the whole experience therapeutic and immensely satisfying."

Her eyes glistened in the moonlight.

"Are you ready, Angela? We're off."

Angela hesitated for just a split second; then, smiling, she jumped up and ran to join the others in the car.

Angela Logan was just coming in from playing tennis when she heard the phone ringing. Dropping her racquet in the hallway she moved quickly into the living-room and flopped into a chair to answer it. "Angela Logan."

"I've been thinking. It was probably improper of me to invite you to spend the night with me without going through the formalities of at least a date first. I'm sitting here with a diary that shows every night this week free. So, starting with tonight, can I buy you dinner?"

She smiled to herself but did not answer.

"Okay, if you're going to play hard to get, how about tomorrow?" Still she didn't answer. "Monday?"

"Simon, you seem to be forgetting that I'm married."

"You know, that was the only thing I didn't like about you when we first met – you have this annoying habit of getting hung up on irrelevant detail. Look, I'll make it easy – tomorrow night, 7.30. I'll pick you up."

"No." The word was spoken more harshly than she had intended. "I mean I'm busy tomorrow night – but I'm free Monday."

"See you at 7.30."

They saw each other regularly for three weeks, a purely platonic relationship but with a strong undercurrent. It was as if they were both waiting for some unspoken signal. It materialised ultimately in the form of Sean Logan. His work in the desert necessitated him being away for six weeks at a time, after which he would return to Jeddah for two weeks.

His impending arrival was not a surprise. He met Simon and, together with Simon's Indian girlfriend, the four ate out twice during his visit. The atmosphere was congenial but laced with a certain degree of expectancy. As the days wore on Sean appeared keen to return to the desert and within hours of his departure the relationship between Simon Whittle and Angela Logan ceased to be platonic.

They met as often as four or five times a week, each drawing solace from the other in this otherwise barren environment. Angela lived in a compound which was run by the company that her husband worked for and although their attempts at discretion were well-intentioned, knowledge of the affair was soon commonplace.

The only one who appeared to be oblivious was Simon's girlfriend, Ajmira, an Indian air-stewardess who worked for Saudi Airlines. They had met at a party some months before and for Simon their infrequent meetings were a means of relieving sexual frustration and little else. For appearances' sake Angela felt it was important that Simon have a regular girlfriend and so his relationship with Ajmira continued.

A routine was established, something almost approaching domestic harmony. Then, in late October, the harmony was shattered. It came as a result of Simon's unprecedented success in Jeddah.

The company had three offices in Saudi, Al Khobar on the east coast, Riyadh in the centre of the country and Jeddah. The Head office was situated in Al Khobar. Paul Michaels, the general manager for Saudi, was based in Al Khobar and it was a call from him to Simon requesting him to come to Al Khobar that moved Simon's life inevitably into its next phase.

They met at the airport.

"Simon, good to see you again. Good flight?"

"As good as it can be on an airline without booze. How are you, Paul?"

Paul Michaels was the opposite of Mark Hunt. He was dynamic, keen to establish his own career and he saw the Middle East as a staging post. He had been impressed with Simon from the start. He knew that for the past eighteen months Simon had effectively run the Jeddah office and had been responsible for its rapid advancement. They walked out of the airport and fought through the lunch-time traffic.

"I thought we could have lunch in the new hotel on the coast road just north of the city."

They talked in generalities until they were seated in the restaurant which provided an uninterrupted view of the Gulf.

Paul was ill at ease, unsure how to broach his offer or how Simon would react to it. In the end it was Simon who made the first move. "Paul, I know you didn't fly me all the way across the country just to buy me lunch so tell me the news. If you're firing Hunt and I'm getting the job, you just made a friend for life."

Paul did not immediately answer.

"Okay, so the first guess was wrong. You're moving on and I've got your job?"

"You're half right. You obviously haven't heard but Smith from the Riyadh office has resigned – his wife's had enough and he's going home. I want you to take the job. I need you in Riyadh by the

1st November."

Simon looked crestfallen. "That's not quite what I was expecting."

"No, I agree, but it's the right move for you. Riyadh is growing even faster than Jeddah. This is your chance to demonstrate that you can run an office and manage people. You can't afford to turn it down."

They discussed details for the rest of the day and most of the night. By the time Simon left to return to Jeddah the following morning he had a substantial pay increase and a whole new world waiting for him in Riyadh. Paul dropped him at the airport.

"Good luck. I'll be out to see you in Riyadh early next year."

They shook hands and Simon climbed out of the car.

Arriving in Jeddah Simon took a taxi to Angela's house. The door was opened by Sean who was back unexpectedly for two days. He hid his surprise well at seeing Simon and congratulated him enthusiastically on his news. Angela was non-committal. They stood in embarrassed silence, each deep in their own thoughts, sensing the beginning of the end or simply a new beginning.

In a flurry of action, farewells and doubts, Simon severed his ties with the coastal area that he had come to love and three weeks later strapped himself into yet another aircraft seat that would carry him again into the unknown.

chapter 15

I never came to terms with Riyadh. It was an unattractive city, nestled in the hills of nowhere. It lacked the activity and vibrancy of Jeddah, yet if anything it was developing faster than Jeddah. Home was a magnificent villa situated in splendid isolation on the western edge of the city, where the desert and the buildings met. It came complete with swimming pool and servants' quarters and was one of the few compensations in this outpost of humanity. When I arrived, our office in Riyadh was the smallest of the three and I set out with a determination to ensure that before I left it would be larger than Jeddah and Al Khobar.

Riyadh was my cancer. A malignant growth of dissatisfaction that enveloped and destroyed. My personal growth still continued apace but my soul, the life blood of my past, was tested beyond endurance. In darker moments I questioned everything except existence itself.

I spoke to Angela daily and twice during November I contrived to spend weekends back in Jeddah. The passion of the affair was constant but I detected a change – minuscule as it was I perceived that I could become an unwelcome intruder. Doubts nurtured and grew. Angela denied their existence but I felt their presence.

Her invitation to meet was typical of her own inimitable style. I was intending to go back to England for Christmas, stopping off in Cairo on the way out and having a few days in Morocco on the way back. Dates and final detail were still to be arranged. I told Angela of my plans one night over the phone. There was a silence at the other end and then she said she would ring me back, and hung up. She rang back about an hour later and informed me that she was intending to go to the UK on her own for the first two weeks in December. She was going to visit her parents in Worcester. She suggested that if I could make it to London at the end of her stay she would stay on for a couple of days and we could have some time together in London. The impact of her words stirred the lethargy. A gift. She readily agreed that we should meet in London on the 10th.

Angela took care of the details. She booked herself into the Bristol Suites Hotel off Park Lane, and left for England at the end of November. I left for Cairo on the morning of December 9th.

Arriving in Cairo shortly after noon I took a taxi to the Hilton Hotel, overlooking the Nile and with a view of the pyramids in the background. I checked in, and filled out all of the voluminous documentation that invades all of life in the Middle East. Once in my room I called Egypt Air to confirm my reservation on their overnight flight to London. I had a late lunch in the excellent coffee shop before taking in the immediate sights.

At about 9.30 that evening, I transferred a few small items into an overnight bag, hung the "Do Not Disturb" sign on the door and took a taxi to the airport. A twenty-pound bribe, together with a story about visiting Israel in the near future, ensured that my passport was not stamped when I left the country.

The flight was on time and by midnight I was bound for London. I dozed fitfully, unable to sleep, savouring the delicious feeling of anticipation.

London was cold and miserable. I had just enough time after clearing immigration and customs to make it to the hotel for our prearranged meeting. Arriving at the hotel I asked to be connected to Angela's room from one of the courtesy phones. She was in room 421 and in no time at all we were naked in bed enjoying the delights of each other's passion. With her foresight and attention to detail, a chilled bottle of Moet & Chandon champagne was also waiting.

Since entering the room my senses had divorced from my body. They floated tantalisingly out of reach but by implication directed all movements.

We made love twice. Satiated, we rested, sipping champagne. Angela had led a cloistered sexual existence: she was passionate but reserved. I had often joked with her about tying her to a bed and exploring her body without consent. She was mellow from the wine and warily receptive of the idea, but interested enough to agree. Using a pillow case and the sheet, I bound her naked body to the bed. Lying face up her body writhed, silently, senses heightened by the unknown. I poured the remainder of the champagne over her breasts and between her spread-eagled legs before proceeding to lick away the tiny droplets. The sexual effect was electrifying. Her nipples glistened crimson, the tanned skin glowed, small murmurs of pleasure escaped her lips, her eyes gratifyingly awaited the climax. As her tongue moved excitedly across her lips I reached up and pushed her jaw open. The eyes questioned but the muscles responded. I began to force the corner of the sheet firmly into her mouth. The eyes became concerned. Then, slowly, I gripped my hands around her neck and watched as pure undiluted fear replaced pleasure.

A short sharp knock on the door and the muffled call of "Housekeeping" broke the spell. Vaulting from the bed I ran for the bathroom and waited as a key was fitted into the lock and the door pushed open. The maid stood framed in the open doorway staring at the bed in disbelief. I threw myself at her, kicking the door shut with my foot. I grabbed the back of her head and propelled her forward and downward, smashing her skull into the corner of the rose wood dresser. There was an explosion of blood and bone as she rolled grotesquely across the carpet. At first I thought she was still alive but quickly realised that it was only the forward momentum that was moving her. She finally came to rest, her face to one side, blood gushing from the dark hole where her left eye had been.

My senses, stunned by the turn of events, reacted sluggishly. It was several minutes before I was able to pull myself up off the floor and it was only then that I remembered the trussed figure on the bed. Her head was raised a few inches from the mattress, eyes, pupils expanded, staring at the inert form in a vacant petrified manner. Her body glistened with sweat despite the coolness of the room.

I mounted her easily and drove into her as if my very existence depended on it. The look never left her eyes but the methodical hammering of my body finally produced the desired effect. Her body shuddered and convulsed and a single tear rolled from the corner of her eye.

I continued to drive forcefully into her as I regained my grip around her neck and watched as the last breath escaped her lungs. Finally spent, I lay atop her, smelling the fear but also the love that had once been mine.

Opening the door I surveyed the deserted corridor. Apart from the maid's cleaning trolley there was nothing in sight. I wrapped a towel over my hand, and moved the trolley slightly, to imply that it was outside the adjacent room. The bodily emotions were not coping with events and the urge to vomit welled up inside, I grabbed a laundry bag and heaved for several minutes.

The vomiting was like a cleansing and once the mist had lifted I could see clearly again. Quickly washing and dressing I readied myself for departure. I cleaned the glasses and bottle, then smashed the glasses hard onto the bathroom floor and placed the bottle in the laundry bag. I tied the bag tight at the neck and dropped it into the holdall. Making a final inspection, I wiped the door handle of prints. I hurried down four flights of stairs and headed towards Victoria Station to catch the Tube back to Heathrow, depositing the nameless laundry bag in a rubbish bin along the way.

By 9.15 that night I was in Amsterdam boarding a KLM flight to

Egypt, and by early morning I was back in the Hilton enjoying the view of the pyramids spectacularly ominous against the morning sky. A repeat of the bribe and the Israel story produced a stamped piece of paper, inserted in the passport, in lieu of an entry stamp.

Later that morning I took a taxi to the pyramids. The walk through the great pyramid was painful; the chamber containing the empty sarcophagus was hauntingly still. The presence of spirits from centuries past warmed the chill air. I stood transfixed in the wonderment of Man's creation; the colossal monuments which dwarf the accomplishments of the uncommon man.

I heard nothing during my remaining stay in Cairo and, although I didn't try too hard, I was unable to locate a British newspaper. My passport was duly stamped as I left Cairo airport. My parents met me at Heathrow and for the first time in several years, we seemed glad to see each other. We talked non-stop on the way back to Somerset but it was only when we were close to home that Mother mentioned the dreadful murders in London. She produced two days' of papers and while I stared into the familiar eyes on the front page she asked me if I knew her.

The visions were contradictory, the emotions sad. The picture did not do her justice. I looked up with genuine tears in my eyes and replied that, yes, I knew her well. The reading of the articles prevented any immediate questioning but when I finished I had to tell them something.

Safety in half-truths was better than lies and if they read anything into what I didn't say they never showed it. She was a good friend from Jeddah. I knew her and her husband. We played tennis together and I taught her to windsurf. The silence was emotional, the comforting words of no help.

The emotionally charged atmosphere was punctuated by the arrival home from school of Karen. For most of the time it was easy to forget that I had a sister. We had never been close, never had time for each other. I was not there for much of her growing up and yet of course she was the root of all the troubles. Without her I might have been an ordinary person, mundane and plastic. I knew that I should be grateful, not resentful, but nowhere within me could I find any compassion or understanding.

She stood framed in the doorway unaware of the impact that her presence had on me. As usual the focus shifted, she became the centre of attention. The day was spoiled and I was glad to be able to retreat to the solitude of my bedroom.

A look of disapproval crossed my father's face as I poured a glass of whisky to take to bed with me. He looked as if he would say something but chose to remain silent.

I read the newspaper reports over and over. In typical sensational journalistic style the murders were described as bizarre and gruesome. The first day's reports were sketchy. Two bodies, one that of a hotel employee, the other of a British woman visiting from Saudi Arabia, had been discovered in the Bristol Suites hotel in London. Identities were withheld until the husband of one of the victims who was still in Saudi Arabia could be notified. The police indicated that further investigation would be required before a statement could be issued. The second day's paper contained the photograph, together with a police report that was surprisingly accurate in all its assertions. The police went on, however, to admit that they had little to go on at this stage and were appealing for witnesses to come forward.

Sleep was muddled that night. The hotel employee was easily dismissed from my mind, but Angela had been a possession, cherished. A conscious thought wailed that I was wrong. An inner voice argued, disdainfully, but emotion could not rule reason. The past was negative, the future positive.

I had little time to reflect the following morning on what would happen as events overtook circumstances. I slept late and was awoken by my mother who said someone called Sean was on the phone and he insisted on speaking to me. The conversation was rambling and one sided.

"I can't believe she's gone. Why would someone . . . ? It's incomprehensible. The bastard. She never meant anyone any harm. She was peaceful, fun loving. Why?"

The ramblings continued for some time. There was no cohesion or comprehension. Sean was devastated, but like the maid, his was a bit part – inconsequential. I let him talk. I felt neither sorrow nor compassion and when he finally indicated that he was going to have to go I felt only relief. As he was about to hang up he mumbled, "I had to tell them, Simon, I'm sorry, I had to tell them. You were good for her, a passing concern, she was a good wife . . . I had to tell them. I'm sorry."

The news was not the hammer blow that it should have been.

It was later that afternoon that the police called. A Chief Inspector Mann of Scotland Yard introduced himself over the phone and, after treading delicately for a few seconds, explained the purpose of his call and asked, politely, if Detective Inspector Rogers and he could come and ask me some questions in connection with the murder of Angela Logan. As they would be coming from London we fixed an appointment for ten-thirty the following morning.

The parental concern was touching, but difficult to cope with. It was easy to dismiss the police interest as superficial and my mother agreed to make herself scarce the following morning. This was not quite the homecoming they had planned but their understanding of life outside of Somerset was so limited that they could not conceive that I was connected to the murder other than as an innocent bystander.

Niggling doubts arose and were dismissed. Ponderous concentration was not my style. I had a tried and trusted formula for business meetings and I could see no reason why it should not work with the police. The strategy was simple: other than essential background information I never prepared for meetings. I felt confident in my own ability to answer questions as they were asked and my knowledge of the product being sold was solid enough to get me through. Obviously it was not always a successful presentation but the success ratio was very high.

My only concern about the forthcoming meeting was that I knew far more than they did and I had to ensure that over-confidence did not cause me to slip.

I slept well, looking forward to the coming test of skills.

chapter 16

As the Singapore Airlines 747 taxied to the walkway at John F. Kennedy Airport in New York, Detective Inspector Alan Rogers felt the familiar tightening in his chest. The next few minutes could be decisive. If any mistakes were made now, two years of surveillance and dedication would be wasted.

He knew that his involvement was purely that of spectator but he had confidence in his counterparts at the FBI. He carried an overnight bag and mingled casually with the other passengers awaiting the arrival of the flight. Won Chi was easy to spot. He was tall for an oriental and a withered left hand made him quite distinctive. A young couple emerged from the plane behind him and tracked his progress through immigration and into the baggage hall. As was expected he collected one small suitcase and proceeded through customs. A few minutes later he was swallowed inconspicuously by a limousine illegally parked outside the terminal. The tail was taken up by a fleet of fifteen vehicles whose job it was to stay with him until he took delivery of the four tartan suitcases that had been loaded in Singapore but had not materialised on the baggage carousel.

Rogers' job was over. He was booked on the overnight flight to London and despite the frustration of not knowing if the arrests would be made he realised there was little else he could do. It could be several days before the handover was made and Chi received the packages.

Rogers had followed Chi and his cohorts for what seemed like a lifetime. His usual routes of shipping and dummy companies had, to date, made him untouchable. So when the tip came that Chi himself would be handling a shipment that was destined for a senior US Government official, the whole slick operation had been put together in a very short time.

Rogers was content that the London end of the surveillance had allowed them to get this far and hopefully the net result would be the closing of one more route for heroin coming into the United States and Europe. It should also put an end to a portion of the murder and mayhem that was such an integral cog of the subterranean world of drug trafficking. The depressing thought was that as quickly as this route was closed a new one would be established and there were hundreds of Mr Chis waiting to take his place.

Sam Duffield from the FBI drove Rogers drove down to the British Airways terminal.

"Still flying the Bloody Awful Airways?" joked Duffield. "The world's worst airline."

Rogers had become used to Duffield's acerbic humour. Basically if it wasn't American, it couldn't be any good. The two had developed a grudging respect for each other during the course of the investigation. Rogers kept insisting that one day he would get Duffield over to Scotland Yard so he could see how a real police force operated. Duffield's response was that he would look forward to meeting Sherlock Holmes. The two parted amicably, Duffield assuring Rogers that he would let him know the outcome and that he looked forward to teaching Rogers some more basic police work in the future.

On the flight home Rogers, as usual, toasted his good fortune and offered a silent prayer and toast to his mentor Andrew Daniels. He knew he had come a long way since his Somerset days and though his hard work and dedication would, he felt sure, have earned him the respect he deserved eventually, it had been Daniels pushing from behind that had opened doors long closed to Daniels himself. His first move, into the London Metropolitan force, had given him the exposure and taste for the big city that he yearned for. Three years later his request to join Interpol had been accepted at the first time of asking, and he knew he could make a name for himself.

It was two days after the news of his move to Interpol that he learned of Daniels' suicide. Few people outside the force knew of the debilitating cancer that was slowly wasting his body and, in order to avoid the final indignity, he chose to take his own life. Rogers was sad, and frustrated, that Daniels had not been able to turn to him in his hour of need. Since their first murder investigation together in Somerset they had grown close.

Rogers had slowly learned of Daniels' trials with the establishment. He was not, and never would have been, a yes man. The consequences of his actions were that, although he reached the rank of Chief Inspector, it had been in Somerset and not the Met or Interpol that he had longed for.

It was after Rogers had been with Interpol for a year and was promoted to inspector, that he finally understood the true debt of gratitude that he owed to Daniels and which, with hindsight, explained the timing of his death.

Over a celebratory drink in one of the numerous bars frequented by the Yard in the Victoria area he had heard a drunken colleague refer to him as Daniels' favourite bum boy. Rogers was a pacifist by nature but it was obvious that the remark had been deliberately loud enough for him to hear. He confronted his aggressor and in keeping with his style informed him that if he heard him mention Chief Inspector Daniels' name in a derogatory way again, he would personally ensure that he would spend the rest of his days cleaning his teeth by pushing his toothbrush up his backside. An embarrassed silence followed but the drunken oaf, muttering profanities, slouched away.

The incident annoyed Rogers and the following morning he asked to see his commander. In response to his questions Rogers discovered that Daniels had personally intervened when his application had been rejected. Daniels had argued forcibly, and the board had seen fit to reverse its decision. The Commander stressed that Rogers had already been earmarked for acceptance at his second attempt. Rogers felt compelled to offer his resignation on the grounds that he did not feel it was correct that a fellow officer had influenced the board's decision. Commander Philip Travers, in a rare show of anger, told him that no one influenced the board and that Rogers should have been flattered by the attention Daniels had shown in his career, and, further, he could already hear Daniels' disgust if Rogers resigned.

It was during the course of this meeting that the Commander first mentioned the formation of an elite force, which was to be based within Interpol, but would report directly to the Home Office. The purpose of the force was to establish liaisons between British and foreign police forces and their governments. It would operate not through official channels but instead would be involved in selected cases.

When an offer to join the newly-formed force was made just

over one year later Rogers had no hesitation in accepting. He left the Commander's office not necessarily a happier person but certainly a more determined one.

In retrospect, at 35,000 feet, it appeared to Rogers that Daniels' knowledge of his success had left him free to depart this life a more contented man. He drank another silent toast to a good friend.

Rogers' only regret was that he and Daniels had not been able to solve their first murder investigation together. He had been a young university recruit, raw and malleable. Daniels, in his own inimitable style, had brought him into the investigation from the beginning and, although it was true to say that it was not a textbook case, the experience had been invaluable. He could still recall the name: Janice Butterworth. An odd lady, divorced, with a colourful liking for men and gin. The murder had all the classic ingredients – numerous lovers, a bombastic ex-husband who, when the fancy took him, still frequented his ex-wife's bed, an estranged son, and a village idiot the nearest thing to a witness. If there were clues to be had they disappeared with the body as no murderer was ever found and no motive was ever established.

It was eventually dismissed as the work of a local lover spurned who had the good fortune or ability to get away with it. An event that entered the annals of village folklore, but frustrated Daniels by its sheer simplicity.

They had worked together on several murder cases since that time, and always produced a satisfactory result, but Mrs Butterworth always evaded them. Even after he moved to London Rogers had kept in touch. He and Daniels spent many hours reviewing cases by phone and on occasions Rogers would drive down to Somerset to enlist Daniels' help in fathoming out the contortions of the criminal mind. He would often stay overnight and without fail, at least once during every visit, Daniels would mention the riddle that was Janice Butterworth.

Rogers felt the loss deeply over the years but he also knew that his personal standards had been orchestrated by Daniels and he worked tirelessly to see that he did not drop below the demands and expectations of his friend.

As the plane prepared for landing, Rogers contemplated his three days off. He had been tempted to stay in New York but the biting cold wind and sub-zero temperatures made him decide against it.

As it turned out he need not have concerned himself. The problem was solved for him. Waiting in the arrival lounge was Commander Mann of the Yard.

"Good flight, lad? I hope you're well rested. We're off to Somerset."

"Bloody hell, sir. I haven't slept in a bed for two days and . . . "

"You're young, lad, it's a simple day out. You'll be home in bed before dark."

Rogers had worked under Mann during his time with the Metropolitan force and he had immense respect for the man's talent and integrity. However, at 7.15 in the morning he was less than enamoured with the prospect of a drive to Somerset.

As they drove out of London on the M4 Rogers' spirits lifted. The morning was delightful, the sun highlighted the barren countryside and, as he sipped his black coffee, Mann filled him in on the details.

"I requested you on this one personally. Thought it would make a nice change from playing cops and robbers with the Yanks. It's possible there will be no involvement for you at all but I thought it would be better if you got in on the ground floor rather than having to flounder later.

"We have a double murder at the Bristol Suites hotel in London. One death is easy to explain, the other could be a problem. Angela Logan was visiting her parents in Worcester from Jeddah in Saudi Arabia where she lives with her husband Sean. She was staying in London for three days purportedly to do some shopping and see friends before she went back to Jeddah for Christmas. The photographs will tell you the rest."

Mann indicated a file on the rear seat. Rogers scanned the photographs.

"It appears that the maid disturbed the murderer. Before, after or during the murder of Angela Logan, we don't know. All we do know is that she was grabbed by the neck from behind and propelled forward. Our best guess is that the murderer was in the bathroom at the time the maid entered as this is the only place he could have come from to be behind her. She died of a fractured skull, caused by her head being forcibly slammed into the dresser. She died instantly. We have interviewed the other guests but no one heard any screams or noticed anything unusual connected with the room. In fact very few people were around. We know the maid finished her lunch break at 1.15 and mentioned that she had a couple of rooms to finish on the fourth floor. Her supervisor went looking for her just after three and discovered the bodies in room 421.

"As you can see from the photographs of Mrs Logan, her death was not as simple. In execution, yes, she was strangled, but we have no satisfactory explanation for the bondage. Her husband insists that she would not have submitted to, as he put it, any such perverted acts and yet all the indications are that intercourse had taken place with her consent, at least once, possibly more than once, and parts of her body were covered with champagne and semen."

Rogers had listened intently to the discourse.

"Why the Somerset connection?"

"Her husband, Sean, who is now in England, told us that he thinks his wife was having an affair with a Simon Whittle over the past few months in Saudi. Simon Whittle comes from Somerset and he's home on leave."

"Pardon my ignorance, sir, but it sounds fairly straightforward."

"It would be, lad, except that Whittle was in Cairo at the time of the murder and her husband was in the Saudi desert."

Rogers spent the remainder of the trip acquainting himself with the file. For a murder so horrific there was a disturbing lack of evidence. The only trace of anyone, other than the deceased, being in any way connected to the room, was a phone call from a house phone. The operator, who handled hundreds of such calls a day, could remember nothing unusual about the voice. She described it as male, polite, friendly, probably British but it could have been European or American.

In addition they knew that Angela Logan had taken an early train from Worcester on the morning of the 10th and arrived at the hotel shortly after 11.00 a.m. The receptionist remembered her vividly, firstly because of her suntan and secondly because she was there an hour before the hotel's regular check-in time. As the hotel was not busy and room 421 was ready, she had given her the room keys. She was sure that no one was with her and the room had been booked in her name only. However, she had asked for a room with a double bed as opposed to two singles.

The porter who had taken her luggage up to her room confirmed that there was no one with her, nor had he or any of his colleagues seen anyone loitering in the lobby or corridors during the time prior to the murder.

Rogers looked for a mention of room service, and found none. He remarked that Logan must have purchased the champagne outside of the hotel or her visitor must have brought it.

The autopsy report confirmed what Mann had already told him, death by strangulation and evidence of sexual intercourse. There were no cuts or abrasions on the body. Looking at the photographs again, Rogers had to admit that she had a well-proportioned body, too thin for his taste but worth a second glance.

The semen had revealed an A-blood type, no help there, and two hair fibres found in the bed, if they came from the murderer, implied he had dark brown hair. The forensic report showed that there were fingerprints galore but as certain surfaces, namely the door handle and taps, showed signs of having been wiped clean, they were fairly certain that none of the remaining fingerprints belonged to the killer.

The remainder of the file consisted of interviews with all of the sundry people who might have in any way come in contact with the deceased. They varied from a helpful old lady whom Angela Logan had spoken to on the train that morning, to an abusive hotel manager who was only concerned with the damage the adverse publicity would have on his Christmas trade. Interviews with family, friends and a couple of old boyfriends produced nothing concrete. The only discrepancy between what Angela Logan had told her husband and what had actually happened was that she had made no arrangements to see any friends while she was in London. The conclusion was that she had made arrangements to meet her lover, and murderer, in London.

Rogers, absorbed in reading the case file, was surprised when he looked up to find that they were passing through Ilchester. He knew the area vaguely, its largest claim to fame being that the Fleet Air Arm of the Navy was based there, and it was here that Prince Charles had learned to fly helicopters.

Fifteen minutes later they were on the outskirts of Yeovil and had to stop and ask directions to the Avalon Estate. They pulled up outside the Whittle house ten minutes late for their appointment.

The door was opened by a sun-tanned athletic-looking young man in his mid-twenties. Before introductions were made it was obvious that he was Simon Whittle. The house was small and provincial but comfortable. An older woman appeared and was introduced as his mother. After tea and coffee were declined she left them alone in the living room.

Mann's approach to anyone he was questioning was the same whether the interviewee was suspect, witness or known criminal. The approach was constant, deferential but firm.

Once they were seated Mann slipped into his routine.

"Thank you for taking the trouble to meet us, Mr Whittle . . . "

"Simon," interrupted Whittle, "please call me Simon."

Mann nodded his head in compliance and continued, "We understand that you are on leave from the Middle East, Saudi Arabia?"

"Yes, I work for an insurance company out there. I lived in Jeddah until November 1st of this year. Now I live in Riyadh."

Rogers looked up from the small black notebook he had been writing in. "I thought insurance was against their religion."

"It is, Inspector. Primarily we are insuring the numerous building projects which are going on out there. These are managed by European and American companies who fortunately recognise the business sense of insurance, although all the projects are backed by Saudi money."

Rogers nodded and returned his gaze to the notebook.

Mann coughed gently. "Simon, I'm sure you know why we are here. You knew Angela Logan well, I believe."

Rogers' eyes were now fixed firmly on Whittle and he noticed the beginning of a smile as Whittle answered.

"Intimately, I believe is the word you are looking for. I met Angela in Jeddah in July this year. She was lonely. Her husband is required to spend significant time at his company's various work sites throughout the kingdom."

"So you have been lovers for five months?" asked Mann.

"No, the affair didn't begin until November and we have – had – only seen each other twice since then."

Rogers raised his head from his writings and asked when was the last time he had seen Mrs Logan.

"It would have been the third weekend in November."

Rogers flicked to the calendar at the front of his notebook. "That would have been the 22nd and 23rd November?"

Whittle nodded agreement.

Commander Mann started to speak. "Did she . . . ?" Before he got any further Whittle interrupted.

"I'm sorry, Inspector, the dates you just gave me are probably wrong. I assume the 22nd and 23rd are the Saturday and Sunday?"

"Yes."

"The Arabic weekend is the Thursday and Friday so in fact the dates would have been the 20th and 21st. I stayed at her house on the Thursday and Friday nights and caught a 6.00 a.m. flight to Riyadh on the Saturday morning." As an afterthought he added, "Her husband was away."

"Thank you for clearing that up, Mr Whittle. Did Mrs Logan tell you of her planned trip to London?"

"Yes. She wanted me to meet her in London at the end of her trip."

Both Mann and Rogers waited for an explanation but none was forthcoming.

"Excuse me, but why would you turn down the opportunity to extend the relationship, especially if you were intending to be here sometime in December anyway?" Mann leaned forward to add emphasis while asking the question and now relaxed to await the answer.

If the effect was designed to unnerve Whittle it did not appear to work, although he did appear to think quite some time before answering.

"Commander, I am sure it has not escaped your notice that Angela Logan was older than myself, seven years in fact. Within the confines of this room I will admit that I am not overly experienced with women, nor for that matter with life itself. Two years ago I left England to see some of the world. I cannot adequately describe to you what has happened to me during that time. The best description I can offer is a roller-coaster ride of the proverbial peaks and troughs. In the middle of the confusion arrives an attractive, lonely, woman seeking attention. I am not going to say that I was duped. We both used each other. But when I left for Riyadh it was the beginning of the end. A feeling of remoteness had entered the relationship and I was rapidly coming to the conclusion that it could become bothersome. We argued about it that last Friday and despite her denials I knew that when I left on the Saturday morning it was over. The famous final scene. She had pleaded with me to meet her in London, but my mind was made up."

The room fell silent, the rhythmic movement of an electric clock the only background noise. Whittle had coloured slightly during the speech and Commander Mann once more adjusted his attitude to a conciliatory one, thanking Whittle for being so frank and apologising for the intrusion into his personal life.

Rogers, sensing an opportune moment to attack while defences were low, shattered the melancholy mood by asking if he and Mrs Logan had engaged in any unusual sexual practices. Whittle's head snapped up, all signs of embarrassment erased.

"No . . . I mean . . . I'm not sure what you mean."

In reply Rogers passed over one of the black and white photographs.

"Jesus Christ, you mean they found her like this?" The voice wavered with emotion and a slight mist, over both eyes, was visible as Whittle looked pleadingly towards Mann.

"I'm sorry, this must come as a great shock if you didn't already know but Mrs Logan was found bound and gagged and all the indications are that she submitted to these humiliations voluntarily."

Rogers rose and took the photograph from Whittle. Whittle released it without looking at it again. His face was firmly set and he appeared to be in deep thought.

Mann again coughed apologetically and said, "Two last questions, if we may, and then we will leave you in peace." Whittle sighed heavily but did not say anything. "We understand that you were in Egypt between the 9th and the 12th. Were you there on your own?

Whittle appeared non-plussed by the question.

Mann in an attempt to clarify his intent added, "Did you have a travelling companion, male or female?"

"No, I was alone. I did some sight-seeing and relaxed by the pool."

"Do you have anything to confirm your stay, sir? A hotel bill or something similar?"

Whittle turned his attention from Mann to Rogers but without replying he pulled himself upright and walked out of the room. He returned less than a minute later, carrying a small brown leather bag, which he opened on the coffee table. Amongst the contents were his passport, an airline ticket and a receipt from the Cairo Hilton. He handed the receipt to Mann who passed it to Rogers without comment. Having noted the hotel address and telephone number he passed it back to Whittle. Whittle placed it on top of the other papers on the table.

Rogers reached out for the passport and air ticket. He asked Simon for his assistance in deducing which of the stamps in the passport were Saudi and which were Egyptian. He made some more notes as Mann asked the final question.

"Can you think of anyone who may have done this? Did she ever mention an old boyfriend or lover?"

Whittle shook his head. The sun-tanned face was pallid and any assuredness which may have been present when they arrived had disappeared.

Mann and Rogers rose to leave. Mann pulled a business card from his pocket and laid it on the table. "If you think of anything, please get in touch."

Attempting to improve the atmosphere Rogers asked when Whittle was going back to the Middle East. He appeared not to have heard the question and, instead, started talking in a flat monotone voice.

"It's odd, I always thought he knew but if he did why didn't he say something? There must have been others. God, how could I have been so blind?"

Whittle looked at them both directly, inclining his head slightly. Rogers was going to answer when Whittle said, "January 3rd. I was intending to go to Morocco for a couple of days on the way back, but now I'm not sure."

They drove away from the house in silence. Approaching Ilchester they stopped at a transport cafe and during a veritable feast of greasy food, they dissected the morning's events.

Mann was interested in his younger colleague's views and listened patiently as Rogers spoke between bites of a monumental bacon, egg and sausage sandwich.

"I wasn't sure about him until I gave him the photograph. I didn't think much of his poor misused little boy speech but he did seem genuinely affected by the photo. I have the phone number of the hotel in Cairo but it looks as if his alibi will hold up. If he was screwing someone else in Cairo he isn't going to tell us. I can't see him doing it somehow but then I have difficulty seeing anyone as a murderer."

Taking a hearty drink from his mug of tea Rogers waited for the opposing view.

"I agree. I can't see how he could have murdered her, but I think he knows more than he is saying. Notice he didn't volunteer any information, except in his speech distancing himself from the relationship? He interacted with everything we said. He has to have read the newspapers and talked with the husband and yet he passed no observations. Almost as if he knew more than we did and was afraid to lead in case he let anything slip." Mann wiped the paper napkin across his lips and tossed it onto the table. "Still, I agree, lad, he did seem genuinely upset by the photograph."

Outside in the car, Rogers looked at his watch. It was just after midday and despite his extreme tiredness he asked Mann if they could detour through Taunton and take the M5 back to the M4 and across to London. Mann had no objections and twenty-five minutes later they pulled into the Taunton crematorium. The Commander waited in the car while Rogers stood silently in front of the wall where Daniels' ashes were interred.

As they joined the motorway heading north Mann commented, "I never knew Daniels but his reputation and stubbornness were well known." He held the car steady at 70 mph, then added, "I think I would have liked him."

On the drive back they discussed other cases until Rogers fell asleep. The traffic, as usual, started to build up around the Chiswick flyover and it was another fifty minutes before they pulled up at the entrance to the Yard. Commander Mann sat drumming his fingertips on the steering wheel. From past experience Rogers recognised the careful deliberation process and sat quietly awaiting the outcome.

"I still can't decide on your involvement. I'm going to suggest to the chief that we work on this together and that we equip you with bucket and spade, lad, and send you off to the desert. We need to talk to a few people in Jeddah and I would like you to pay a surprise visit on young Whittle in Riyadh, once he's back."

The arrangement suited Rogers fine. He was of the mould of policemen which fully believed that all departments should work for each other's benefit and not act as mutually exclusive units. He was constantly amazed at the number of times egos obscured the objective of police work.

He finally left for home three hours later, having typed up his report. A gin and tonic to calm the nerves was called for before sleep.

He had only been asleep a matter of minutes or so it seemed, when the telephone rudely awakened him. He grunted into the mouthpiece and over the static heard an American voice announce that Mr Chi and thirty accomplices, plus a deputy secretary at the State Department, had been arrested. Rogers told the distant voice to fuck of and call at a decent hour. The voice chuckled and told him that where he was, it was a decent hour.

chapter 17

Oh, this was easy; the actions, the mannerisms, the emotions. Like slides in a projector they were held for a prescribed time and replaced by the next one.

The younger man, Rogers, was completely taken in. The element of revulsion and shock at the photograph was perfectly gauged. The numbing after-effect produced pity, and the distracted monologue sealed the commitment.

Mann was harder.

He was more objective, balanced, but the sheer weight of the alibi was bound to sway the hardened mind.

The constant badgering from my mother was becoming oppressive. Seizing the opportunity to discuss the situation with my father and, despite the effect that I knew my words would have on him, I told him about the affair. He nodded understandingly and agreed to steer future conversations away from probing questions.

As it turned out I was only just ahead of the press. They had hinted at an affair or a boyfriend from the beginning and, although I was never named, I knew that my mother worked it out when two days later the press confirmed that Angela Logan had been having an affair with someone in Saudi Arabia. I'm not sure what my father told her but the rest of the holiday passed in peace.

It did not occur to me to attend the funeral or even send flowers. I was not proud of my actions, but the essential had been accomplished. Fortunately Sean did not telephone again. I immersed myself with friends who enquired for two minutes about life in Saudi and then proceeded to bore me for hours with mundane chatter that represented their trivial lives. I was intolerant of the absurdity of it all but it had a soothing effect, a penance, and by the time I left for Morocco, I was at peace with myself.

Morocco was Saudi with a French accent. I left a day early. A sense of foreboding approached, like storm clouds, as we descended into Riyadh.

If life before was bad, it was soon to get much worse.

During my absence I had given little thought to Ajmira. I had only been back in the house one day when she called. She sounded excited and informed me that she would be in Riyadh the following day. I dutifully noted her flight details and arranged to collect her from the Sheraton Hotel once the crew bus had dropped her off.

I realised, as I put the phone down, that I had lost interest. This meeting would be the last. I found I was missing Angela, and Ajmira, through no fault of her own, was no substitute.

Ajmira was placid by nature, reserved, almost serious, so I was surprised when I collected her the following day to find her so vibrant. She insisted we went to bed as soon as we reached the house. Her body glowed and moved with a passion that had not been previously present. As we lay in each other's arms afterwards I knew there was no easy way to tell her.

Before I could speak my thoughts she rolled on top of me, a half smile spreading across the corners of her mouth, and proudly announced that she was pregnant.

chapter 18

Alan Rogers always knew that the police force had a perverse sense of humour. As he stared at his Saudi Airlines ticket to Jeddah on January lst, 1983, he wondered about the minds of clerks who concocted such wonderful New Year's delights. He did not object so much to the New Year's day travel as to the choice of airline. If he was going to nurse a hangover all the way to Jeddah he wanted to do it over at least one Bloody Mary. His protestation brought no relief.

Three weeks ago he knew very little about Saudi Arabia other than its strategic importance in Middle Eastern politics, but a crash course on local customs, and a familiarisation of the senior staff at the British Embassy had left him considerably wiser. In between his education he had closely followed the developments of the Angela Logan case. One of the odder facets of murders that always intrigued him was the way the press could sensationalise a murder, elevating it from the morbid to the fascinating. This was achieved by the details of the murder itself. The bondage aspect coupled with an affair, throw in the Middle Eastern connection and you have all the right ingredients. The press almost completely ignored the murder of the maid, reference was only made to Angela Logan. The Yard was just as guilty – the case was always referred to as the Logan case and, as a consequence, very little attention was given to the maid. Find the murderer of Angela Logan and, *ipso facto*, the whole file can be closed.

Rogers had personally interviewed the parents, the husband, friends and hotel staff but had been unable to throw any further light on the case. The husband was a contradiction. He knew of his wife's infidelity with Whittle, and yet was the first to proclaim Whittle's innocence of any involvement with the murder. In a perverse way he seemed to be grateful to Whittle for keeping his wife entertained while he was away. At one point he even claimed that Whittle had helped preserve his marriage. If his alibi had not been one hundred percent Rogers would have been convinced that Logan was the guilty party. So concerned with Logan's attitude was Rogers, that he pursued a line of inquiry, with Mann's blessing, of the possibility of a hired killer.

He knew before it began that it would lead nowhere but he had to satisfy himself completely that Logan was in the clear. It was an easy theory to dismiss due to the length of time that Logan spent out of communication with the rest of the world. How do you hire a killer when you are in the middle of the desert with a field-link telephone that has to have calls patched through if you want to speak to anyone further afield than the Jeddah base? The evidence of the murder also seemed to discredit the notion. Why would a hired killer go to great lengths to get his victim into bed? Surely the whole point of a paid assassination was that it was quick and effective and usually accomplished at arm's length. The only aspect of a hired killer that fitted was that Logan had the money to be able to afford one.

Rogers had not spoken to Whittle since their meeting in Somerset. He had, however, checked the Cairo hotel which had confirmed that Simon Whittle was indeed a guest during the dates indicated. In addition he had requested copies of the passenger lists for British Airways flights that Whittle had taken from Jeddah to Cairo and three days later from Cairo to London. Both showed Whittle as a passenger.

There was of course always the possibility that Whittle had paid someone to murder Angela Logan, but for most of the same reasons that the case against Sean Logan fell down, it also failed in respect of Whittle.

The oddity of the case was that so far no one had come forward to tell them who Angela Logan was meeting in London. Rogers knew full well that people loved to talk. In his experience, there was no such thing as a secret, yet during her two weeks in England it did not appear that she had confided in anyone that she was planning an illicit few days in London and yet the hotel reservation had been made some days before her arrival. Rogers hoped that this was one mystery that would be cleared up when he started talking to people in Jeddah, although he doubted if it would produce a name as no one had come forward and volunteered the information to the Embassy staff.

By the time Rogers reached Jeddah his hangover was all but gone and he had to admit that the flight had been very congenial. The service was impeccable with hostesses who seemed genuinely interested in their jobs. He would have loved a drink but you couldn't have everything. The original intention had been to send Rogers out on a diplomatic passport and pass him off as one of the many visiting Embassy personnel. The Embassy in Jeddah quashed this suggestion and as such special permission for Rogers to enter the kingdom and carry out a police investigation had been sought. It had taken personal intervention by the Ambassador to ensure that the visa was granted and that it was also granted within days rather than the weeks that it normally took.

The airport was a revelation. He had expected a few tin shacks and the odd camel; he was confronted instead with a marble edifice crammed with every hi-tech aid to efficiency. This was in reality, as he was soon to find out, a facade. The airport was new. It had only been open a couple of months and while it was a monument to the burgeoning economy it was staffed almost entirely by Saudi nationals and as such did not work.

Immigration took his passport and asked him to wait. The Bedouin behind the desk ambled off. He returned twenty-five minutes later and explained, in halting English, that Rogers had been denied entry. The Saudi dismissed him and called the next frustrated passenger forward. Rogers, who could feel his self-control slipping, asked what he should do or with whom he could talk. The immigration clerk took great delight in ignoring him. He had been warned by the department before he left that he might experience some hostility towards his presence, from both the locals and the Embassy, but, it had been stressed, he was not to challenge the locals in any way or he would probably be thrown in jail or deported. Rogers looked around for help. Apart from the armed security guards, who were everywhere, there did not appear to be anyone in charge. A harassed British businessman had just cleared immigration. Before he disappeared through the smoked-glass doors Rogers called out to him. Despite protests from the immigration officer that he should go through to customs the businessman stopped to listen to Rogers. He explained his predicament as quickly as he could as he was due to be met by Arthur Brown, from the British Embassy, in the arrivals hall. The businessman was sympathetic and, muttering something about unhelpful bastards, promised to find Brown for him. It was another hour and a half before he heard his name being called by an officious-looking Arab in a dark green military uniform. Without apology or explanation, Rogers was ushered through immigration and shepherded into the customs hall. He was greeted by the sight of his open suitcase on a table with the contents liberally strewn around. The desire to hurl abuse at someone was mounting by the second. There were no customs officers in sight, only the silent official. Rogers decided to take charge of the situation and calmly began repacking the suitcase. Snapping the catches shut he walked through into the arrivals area without arousing any comment.

A sickly-looking, white-faced man stepped forward and introduced himself as Arthur Brown. Even in his general state of agitation Rogers wondered how anyone could live in this climate and yet be so white. Brown dismissed the whole immigration episode and laughingly said, "It could have been worse – they could have strip-searched you."

The city was twenty-five miles south of the new airport and the drive in was yet another revelation. Rogers had expected some sleepy backwater with a few modern buildings. Instead he found himself on an eight-lane highway speeding towards a conglomerate of high-rise buildings in various stages of completion. They passed donkey carts and Rolls Royces, mud huts and splendid dwellings. The traffic came to a grinding halt at what Brown called a "donkey roundabout". A general cacophony of noise filled the air as the Arab drivers sat with their hands pressed firmly on the horns of their cars. Brown smiled and again dismissed it all as par for the course.

When Rogers finally climbed out of the car inside the Embassy grounds he was struck by the ferocity of the midday sun. The sky was not the clear blue that he had anticipated, although it was cloudless; instead it was more of a blue-brown. He had noticed on the drive in that everything was brown, the plants by the side of the road, the cars, the buildings – they all carried a fine film of brown dust. Wherever the city was not paved or concreted the desert was to be found.

Brown showed him into a small cottage, advised him that there was little he would be able to do until Saturday, handed him a note of his extension number in order that Rogers could contact him through the switchboard if he needed anything, and left.

Rogers was not overly concerned: a day relaxing around the pool in the sun quite appealed when you had just emerged from a cold miserable British winter. The accommodation was comfortable, typically British, with only the noise of the air-conditioner differentiating it from a small suburban dwelling. There was a well-stocked fridge which included six bottles of chilled beer. Rogers smiled gratefully as he took one and retired to the sofa to savour the contents.

The Embassy staff were reserved but accommodating. They placed Arthur Brown and a car with a driver at Rogers' disposal. He politely declined the services of Brown, but the Deputy Ambassador pointed out, frostily, that it was not an offer, it was a necessity. Rogers, not wishing to upset his hosts, explained that he was involved in a murder investigation and that certain information was likely to come to light which was for the eyes and ears of the police only. Simon Cheevey, in his most diplomatic voice, assured Rogers that Brown in his capacity at the Embassy dealt with matters of state and as a member of Her Majesty's Foreign Office, he was sworn to the Official Secrets Act. Rogers in turn knew from experience that this fact was not worth the paper it was written on, but he deemed it unwise to argue further.

Cheevey extended an invitation for Rogers to dine with himself and the Ambassador the following evening at the Embassy; an invitation, which, even if he had felt so inclined, could not have been turned down. Rogers spent part of Friday at the pool and the rest closeted from the heat in his cottage. After two hours in the sun he looked healthier than the anaemic-coloured Brown.

The dinner that evening was a tedious affair. The Ambassador spent the greater part of the evening regaling the company with stories about his overseas travel. The meal itself was predictable: roast beef, Yorkshire pudding, apple pie and custard.

"Must keep up the traditions, old boy," voiced Sir George Armstrong as he poured yet more gravy over his over-cooked beef.

On the Saturday morning Rogers asked to be driven to the Logans' house. It was in a compound on the east side of Jeddah and in the slow-moving traffic it took some thirty-five minutes to cross the city. Once they had been signed in at the gate they followed the one-way system until they arrived outside number seventeen. Rogers noticed as they drove along that the compound was elliptical in shape. The thirty or so houses formed a perimeter surrounding a swimming pool and two tennis courts.

At the far end was a large wooden gate which appeared to give access to a two-storey concrete office block beyond. This he assumed was the offices of the engineering company. Rogers toyed with the idea of making himself known to the relevant people in the office, but decided against it. He had obtained a key to the house, from Sean Logan, and let himself in through the front door. Wishing to eliminate the after-dinner kudos that Brown could derive from his duties, Rogers requested that he remain in the car while he carried out his initial search.

The house was spacious, tastefully furnished and invitingly cool. Brown had pointed out on the drive over that it was necessary to keep the air conditioners on all day even when no one was living there. The house revealed nothing out of the ordinary and Rogers was preparing to leave when the front door opened and a middle-aged man, perspiring heavily, walked in with Brown trailing behind.

"Excuse me, this is private property. You've no right to be here."

Rogers had left his jacket in the car but carried his identification in his pocket with him.

"Oh I'm sorry, sir, we did get a telex a few days ago saying someone from the Yard would be visiting. Terrible business, nice couple. No harm in a girl like Angela, great shame." The accent was Cockney and Rogers waited for the man to introduce himself but no introduction was forthcoming.

"Sorry, you said your name was?"

"I'm sorry, Mullins, Bert Mullins. I'm in charge of admin here."

"Glad to meet you, Mr Mullins. I've finished here for now. Can we go somewhere and talk?"

Mullins looked as if he was going to indicate the living room and then thought better of it.

"Of course, come on up to my office."

Arthur Brown had been hovering in the background during these discussions and made to follow Rogers and Mullins to the office. Rogers intercepted Brown's intentions.

"Mr Mullins, is there a front entrance to the office?"

"Yes, out the main gate, turn right, then right again."

Rogers turned to Brown. "Have the driver take the car round the front will you, Brown. I'll see you back in the car in about fifteen minutes."

Brown, realising that he was going to be excluded from the interview, trudged around the passenger side of the car and instructed the driver to move the car. He climbed in and slammed the door forcibly.

Settled in the cubby hole that served as Mullins' office Rogers accepted the offer of iced water. He was amazed at how quickly his throat became parched. Saliva did not form quickly enough to accommodate the fierce heat and after only a short period outside you needed liquid to satiate the dryness.

There was no need for Rogers to ask any questions. Mullins was wound up like a gramophone and began talking as soon as they sat down.

"So sad about Mrs Logan. We all feel so helpless. We're all stuck here in one way or another. The ladies are bored without their fellas and us bachelors with our wives back home are just as lonely. Now don't you get me wrong, sir, we're just like a little family here – very close. Angela was one of the best – always having dinner parties, inviting men from the mess down, heart of gold, and her husband Sean the life and soul of the party, when he was in from the desert.

"We all play tennis and Angela was always ready for a game. I knew she was bored and unhappy but she never said nothing. Of course, things changed a few months back: she got a young fella, Simon something or other. I saw him around a few times, nice enough bloke, but it wasn't right, she was married. Everyone knew it was going on, except Sean, but we all ignored it – none of our business."

"His name was Whittle, Simon Whittle," Rogers interjected. "Apart from Mr Whittle was there anyone else Angela saw regularly, especially during the last couple of weeks before she went home on leave?"

"No, sir. We were all close. Angela was a bit depressed those last couple of weeks, but then it gets to all of us after a time. Could have been to do with that Whittle fellow. Someone said that he had moved to Riyadh. Of course, she knew a lot of people outside of the compound. She used to go out to a beach-house at weekends. Could have met someone there, I s'pose."

"Thanks, Mr Mullins, you've been a great help. I'm going to need to come back a couple of times over the next few days, I'd like to talk to all the people here and go through the house once more. Do you have a list of who lives in which house?"

"Certainly do." Mullins reached round and pulled open the second drawer of an over-stuffed filing cabinet. Extracting a file from the rear he pulled out two sheets of paper and handed them to Rogers. "I'll tell you what, to make it easier I'll send round a memo tonight telling everyone to expect a visit from you sometime during the next couple of days. Suggest you avoid Tuesday morning, though, that's the morning the company bus takes the wives to the supermarket. Apart from that you should find them all at home or at the pool. The menfolk could be anywhere but the wives can fill you in. The list of the single blokes in the mess are at the bottom of the second sheet."

"Thank you, that would be most helpful."

As Mullins walked Rogers to the front door he called out to a figure that was just about to disappear into an office.

"Mr Grant, this is Inspector Rogers, Scotland Yard – about Mrs Logan."

Grant looked up from the papers he was reading.

"Inspector, welcome to our humble abode. Michael Grant." He extended his hand towards Rogers. "I'm the general manager of the whole show. Damn shame about Angela, I heard from Sean this morning. Said he would be rejoining us next week. If there's anything I can do, don't hesitate to ask. Mullins taking care of you all right?"

"Yes, thank you, Mr Grant. If I could see you for ten minutes sometime tomorrow that would be helpful."

"Afraid I'm going out to one of the camps tonight for a couple of days." Looking at his watch and back at Rogers he said, "Do you have time now?"

Rogers nodded and Grant led him into the office. Mullins walked off in the other direction, calling over his shoulder that he would make sure the memo went out that night.

"Mullins is one of the old breed, ex-army, lot of them out here, wife and four kids at home. He's been so used to seeing them for a couple of weeks at a time all his life that he couldn't adapt to life outside the army. He, like many others, sign up for jobs out here, mainly administrative. The money's good and they love the work."

"What about Sean Logan? What's his background?"

"New breed. Degree in mechanical engineering. Excellent site-worker, knows this pipeline better than anyone else working on it."

"And his wife?"

"Angela? Vibrant, attractive, adapted well to life out here. They have – had – been here for two years. I'm sure you've heard the rumours of her affair? I suppose it's obvious that he did it or you wouldn't be here."

"No one has been eliminated from the investigation, sir, but we have accounted for the husband's and Mr Whittle's, the lover's, movements at the time of the murder. Mrs Logan, we believe, knew her murderer well. It is possible that it is someone from her past life or someone from her life in Saudi Arabia. If it is someone from Saudi then someone out here must know something."

"You're probably talking to the wrong man, Inspector. I'm not big on gossip, but if there was someone else in her life you can guarantee that somebody in the compound will know something about it. Linda Slattery was her closest friend. The husbands work together. She may be able to help you."

"With your permission, Mr Grant, I would like to talk to all of the residents in the compound over the next couple of days."

"Of course, help yourself. Some of them will be away on leave, but Mullins can give you all the details."

"Thank you, Mr Grant. In case you do hear anything, I can be reached at the British Embassy while I am here and through Scotland Yard when I'm back in London." He handed Grant his business card and left.

A quietly sulking Brown awaited him when he returned to the car. Ignoring him Rogers asked the driver to take them back to the Embassy.

The next two days were an endless round of repetitive questions. Gossip and innuendo were rife but nothing of substance was learned.

Everyone knew of the affair but no one could confirm that anyone new had entered Angela's life since Whittle had left for Riyadh. Her friend, Linda Slattery, threw two new pieces of information into the ring. Linda knew of the affair from day one and, while she did not condone it, she could understand it. Angela had told her that she would be spending a few days in London shopping and visiting friends, but she had a feeling that Angela was intending to meet someone special in London and she had assumed that it was Simon. She admitted that she was surprised that Angela had not told her about it, as they had often talked about him. In addition, she believed that if Angela was intending to meet anyone then it had to have been Simon as there was no one else in her life, except Sean, and Angela was just not that sort of girl.

The other piece of information she passed on was that Simon, before leaving for Riyadh, had asked Angela to leave Sean and go away with him. Angela said that she might have seriously considered it, except that she did not believe that Simon would be serious enough in the long run, and she was worried about the age difference.

Rogers wanted to visit the beach house but in order to do that he would have to visit the office where Whittle had worked in Jeddah. If he did, it could lose him the element of surprise of his turning up, unexpectedly, in Riyadh. He decided to fly to Riyadh, meet Whittle, and then return to Jeddah. Whittle had said he was returning on the 3rd, so by now he would have had a couple of days to settle in.

For two days Rogers had left Brown in the car while he conducted his interviews. If Brown had been sullen after the first day, by now he was downright hostile. It was imperative that Rogers make the trip to Riyadh unaccompanied and he was not prepared to argue with Cheevey over the matter. He simply asked the travel co-ordinator at the Embassy to book him on the early morning flight to Riyadh the following day, returning on the Wednesday morning.

He summoned the driver to his room, gave him the flight details and asked him to run him to the airport early the following morning and meet him from the flight the day after. He slipped the driver one hundred riyals and asked him not to tell Brown. The driver was only too happy to comply: he had enjoyed the last two days watching the way Rogers had dealt with Brown and would gladly have done the job for nothing, but every little helped towards the cost of his new house back in Bombay.

Rogers spent the evening watching an old James Bond movie that was shown by the Embassy for the benefit of its staff on the outside wall of the squash court. The staff sat around sipping their gin and tonic or whatever, oblivious to the world that existed outside their walled garden. Rogers enjoyed the climate; the night air lost the humidity of the day as the desert cooled, but the absurdity of what he was witnessing was not lost on him.

He arrived in Riyadh in the middle of the morning. His first impressions were of a much older city that lacked the sophistication of Jeddah. He had been warned by the Embassy driver about taxis, but to get to the offices of Yusuf Bin Alwhary he had no option but to take one. He had to ask three taxi drivers before he found one that knew where the office was and, although they seemed to take a roundabout route to get there, the cab finally pulled up in front of a four-storey concrete and glass building. He did not argue about the fare: there were no meters, and despite the obviously inflated amount, he paid the driver the money he asked for.

Walking through the reception, he was ignored by three disinterested Arabs who were laughing and drinking tea. The insurance division was on the second floor and rather than wait for the lift he took the stairs.

Over the secretary's protests that he didn't have an appointment and that Mr Whittle was on the phone, Rogers walked in. Whittle looked up from the notes he was writing. A puzzled frown appeared on his brow, a look that said "I know you from somewhere". The eyes opened slightly as recognition dawned. Whittle indicated a chair in front of his desk and Rogers sat down. Whittle made no attempt to cut his telephone conversation short – it was regarding a motor accident – and it was some ten minutes later that he finally hung up. Rising from his chair, Whittle extended his hand across the desk.

"Inspector Rogers, isn't it? Sorry about that," he apologised, indicating the phone. "I can guess what brings you to this part of the world. You should have let me know that you were coming."

"Sorry, it was a bit of a rush trip. We wanted to talk to some people in Jeddah. The visa came through surprisingly quickly so I jumped on the first flight out here. I'm only in Riyadh for a day. I thought as I was this close that I might as well come and see you again."

Whittle appeared calm and in control. He called to his secretary to bring them in some tea.

"Your timing isn't too good I'm afraid, Inspector. We have just been advised of a rather serious accident on the Al Khobar road and I need to go and take some photographs before the local police destroy everything."

"That's alright. I wouldn't mind seeing the city, so I can wander off and amuse myself for a few hours. Perhaps we could meet later this afternoon?"

Whittle thought for a few seconds. "I'll tell you what, Inspector, you could come with me if you like. I'm not sure how long this is going to take, at least two or three hours and we could talk on the way."

The tea was delivered and Rogers tasted the sweet, mint-flavoured brew before answering.

"That would be fine, if you're sure I won't be in the way."

Whittle laughed. "If the only inconvenience to everyday life here was a visit from a London bobby, we would be laughing."

chapter 19

I had finished with Ajmira swiftly and cleanly. The cultural difference that had at first seemed charming was the poisoned chalice of ignorance. To me she was a diversion, to her I was a passport. Blinded by the lifestyle I had been leading, I had ignored the signals. Worse, I had ignored the warnings from friends.

But I was still in control. After her revelation I had dropped her off at the hotel and she walked away from me, head-bowed, her previous animation subdued into painful disappointment.

The end of a chapter.

The abortion, I learned, was performed the following day.

Despite my escape, clouds of depression descended upon me. I was not in control. Outside agencies were controlling my emotions and actions. I was confused. There was no one to turn to, I was isolated and, for a time, almost afraid.

Life and all its complexities needed to be examined, re-evaluated. Only two months ago all the pieces fitted, jigsaw-like. Now edges were missing and nothing fitted.

I had come to hate Riyadh. I did not fit within its confines. It did not want me in its bosom. The city would exact its toll but I was determined to survive. Life would march on. I had come this far and the horizon still beckoned. This was not the end, not even the middle; it was a hiatus, a temporary resting place in my personal sojourn.

Work had been my past saviour. Results were my ticket out. Fail now and life failed with me. Picking up the pieces I assessed the damage. The peripheral was dented and bruised, the resolve needed attention but the core and fibre were sound.

I started the morning positive, assertive; the past was through.

When he walked through the door I realised the past was present.

chapter 20

Heading west from the city, they talked easily. Whittle pointed out the sights and cursed other drivers. Rogers could not believe the standard of driving and he relaxed visibly once they reached the open road, even though the car they were in was dwarfed by the gaily painted trucks that thundered by on the adjacent carriageway. The roadside was liberally strewn with wrecks which were testament to the folly of driving in Saudi. Rogers knew he was the bait in the trap and he waited patiently for Whittle's opening move. They drove in silence for a few minutes as Whittle adjusted to the speed of the open road traffic.

"So, do you tell where the investigation stands or do I have to guess?"

"Sorry, I was more concerned with our self-preservation. How the hell do you drive in this?"

"It's not easy. If you remember constantly that all of these drivers have a lower IQ than the camels, you stand a chance of surviving. I don't leave the city very often, there's nowhere to go. The death toll on the roads is horrific. They lose one British person a week in road accidents." He paused and waited for Rogers to speak. After a few moments of silence Whittle asked, "So, come on, have you found Angela's killer?"

"No, but we seem to be making progress."

"Progress? Can you talk about it or is it sub-judice?"

"If we took a vote from her friends in Jeddah you would lose hands down. That's not to say that anyone dislikes you but everyone knows that it can't be Sean, his alibi is better than yours, so in their eyes that only leaves you. Why didn't you tell us about Ajmira?"

"She was, and is, irrelevant to what happened."

"Did she know of your involvement with Angela?"

"No, at least I don't believe so. They met on several occasions. Once I started seeing Angela I wanted to drop her. It's not my style to see more than one woman at a time, but Angela thought it was good cover for me." Explaining further he added, "Having a regular girlfriend made our relationship seem more platonic."

"Would you have gone away with her?" Rogers would have preferred to have been facing Whittle in order to gauge his response to the question. Turning to look at his face sideways, Whittle appeared relaxed: his eyes concentrating on the road; one hand resting lightly on the gear lever, the other jiggled the steering wheel holding the car on its correct path.

"Difficult one. When I asked her, yes, but now who knows? We had something special but it was held in a vacuum. I suspect we really didn't know each other. It wasn't important. We clung to each other to survive. No, I probably wouldn't have gone."

A filling station appeared from the shimmering heat haze and Whittle pulled in for petrol. He disappeared inside to pay and returned with two soda waters. The Riyadh climate was substantially drier then Jeddah and at this time of day the temperature was a pleasant seventy degrees. At night it could drop to freezing and although no snow had ever been recorded Riyadh did occasionally get violent hail storms. Rogers was thankful for the soda as he was still finding that his throat was always dry.

They had been descending from the mountain top on which Riyadh rested, and the huge plain that opened up before them was barren and arid.

"Having dismissed Sean and me – " Whittle turned to face Rogers, " – I assume I have been dismissed – who is the mystery killer?"

"No one is ever dismissed from an investigation, Simon, but let us say that you are about as far from the centre as you can get. The hotel in Cairo confirmed your presence as did the airline that you arrived and departed on."

"That's because I didn't do it. I may have regretted losing her, but she was too vital to snuff out like a candle. Sean and I were friends. We were not in competition for her affections, the affair was an aberration. Saudi is not England and its omnipresence pervades all life and affects judgement. We all come here with ideals, prejudices and commitments, we leave with the same ideals, prejudices and commitments but they are modified, hardened or relaxed. No one lives here for any length of time without being affected by the abnormality of the situation. Somewhere in this mess Angela, Ajmira, Sean, and a whole host of others, are tossed uncontrollably. We had our moment, it passed. I'm sorry she's dead." Whittle paused. He drank the remainder of his soda. "You know what I miss most? The companionship. The sex was great but transient. After I moved to Riyadh I used to phone her almost every evening. We talked for hours, saying nothing but meaning everything. I miss that – I suppose life is like the plain." He gestured with his hand at the all-encompassing emptiness.

Rogers sensed that he had pursued the line far enough. "How will we know we have reached the accident site?"

Whittle shifted in his seat, pulling himself more upright. His voice, which had been soft, reverted to a deeper, firmer tone. "In about fifteen miles we should see an adobe house with a television aerial sticking out of the roof. The crash was another five miles after that."

They returned to chatting casually. Rogers explained about his troubles with immigration, complained about the Embassy attitude and asked how they dealt with the heat. Whittle simply laughed and told him that you learned to cope with all three.

They found the house. The burnt-out wreck was easy to spot. A workers' bus, which fortunately had been empty, had collided head on with a mini-bus which had been full. Eight Pakistani workers, plus the bus driver, had died in the accident. The minibus which had been over twenty feet in length was compressed to a length of less than six feet. The unmistakable stench of warm flesh and blood filled the air. Rogers stared in morbid fascination as Whittle took Polaroid photographs. They climbed back into the car and Whittle wrote a few notes before swinging the car round in the middle of the road and heading back to Riyadh.

"What will happen? I mean, how do they extract bodies to send home?"

"My guess is they won't. They will probably send back sealed coffins, with some bits in them and a marble slab to make up the weight, with specific instructions that the coffins are not to be opened. We insure the contractor that the men were working for. We will pay for the minibus and one hundred dollars each for the loss of life. The money will be paid to the next of kin back in Pakistan and next week there will be a mile-long queue of fellow Pakistanis waiting to come and work in squalor for a pittance. It's not quite slavery but it's the next worst thing."

On the outskirts of Riyadh Whittle turned off the main road and drove along a small dirt track. "Show you some history while you are here."

They pulled up at what appeared to be the remains of a walled city. "The ancient capital of Saudi – Dirayh," Whittle informed Rogers as they climbed the earth steps cut into the slope. There were a few children and goats running about but, that apart, they were alone as they wandered along the narrow streets. The majority of the buildings were in a poor state of repair but the layout of the city was easy to see. It had not been a large place and as they turned a corner they faced what appeared to be a meeting-hall of sorts. All of the buildings were constructed of mud mixed with straw supported by wooden stays and beams. The mixture had baked in the sun and, although it was crumbling in places due to lack of upkeep, it had stood the test of time well. Whittle walked to the rear of the building and pointed to the large wooden doors.

"This is one of the few remaining tributes to Saudi craftsmanship."

Rogers had to examine the door carefully to pick out the different coloured woods that had been bonded together to form the solid door. The sun had bleached away most of the effect but it was still possible to make out the intricate patterns that represented a bygone era. Moving from the door they walked on a downward slope for some fifty feet. A solid earth wall faced them, forming a small courtyard in the middle of which was a well. Whittle dropped the bucket over the side and pulled it up full. He cupped the water in his hands and drank. Rogers did the same. He was surprised to find that the water was clean and refreshingly cool.

After washing the desert sand from their faces, they walked back the way they had come, but instead of passing the meeting-hall, Whittle started to climb a small rise in front of him. When they reached the top Rogers discovered that they overlooked a dry river bed. It was perfectly carved into the sand some five or six feet deep and about sixty feet across.

"I come out here sometimes during the day. It's so peaceful. Nothing moves. The tranquillity of the place is a pleasant change from the rest of the country. In Jeddah it was the Red Sea, here I have to settle for the desert."

Rogers was impressed with the desolation and was also touched by the inactivity. He found it difficult to relate to the scene of carnage that they had recently left.

It was late afternoon by the time they reached Riyadh and Whittle suggested a swim. As they pulled into the drive of the house, Waji, the Ethiopian maid, materialised from her quarters at the rear of the house. Whittle waved her away and, after smiling profusely at Rogers for several seconds, she disappeared as silently as she had arrived. Rogers had not come equipped for swimming but he and Whittle were roughly the same build so borrowing trunks was not a problem, although, Rogers noted in discomfort, Whittle did not have the paunch over his belt that he had started to carry.

As the sun began to dip into the west, Whittle and Rogers shared the delights of gin and tonic and spent a pleasant hour relaxing. Darkness arrived suddenly and the temperature dropped considerably. Changing back into his clothes, Rogers explained that he had better find a hotel for the night. Whittle suggested that he stay the night at the house. There were three bedrooms and he would be a lot more comfortable here than he would be in one of the hotels.

Rogers thought about the offer. He admitted that it sounded attractive to spend the evening with company rather than isolated in a hotel without a bar. He was, however, cognisant of the fact that however remote the possibility, if it ever materialised that Whittle was implicated in the murder, it would not look good if he had spent a night at the house. He decided that Saudi was a good enough excuse for anything and optied for the line of least resistance: he accepted the offer.

Waji was raised from her lethargy to make up one of the spare beds. She seemed to have taken a liking to Rogers and fixed him with a large white-toothed grin every time she walked through the room.

"Ever eaten Korean food?" Whittle enquired as he poured a refill of drinks.

"No, can't say I have, but I would be game if that's what you are suggesting."

"One of the few redeeming features of Riyadh is the quality of its restaurants. The European ones are so-so but the Far Eastern, Indian and Pakistani are excellent. Only slight difference to eating out here is that you have your cocktails before you leave and you come home for your after-dinner drinks. Cheers."

Rogers had to admit that the meal was one of the best that he had eaten in a long time. He left Whittle to do the ordering.

The soup which they had started with was a clear broth spiced with scallions. It was followed by the largest, juiciest prawns that Rogers had ever seen or tasted. They were served lightly battered and accompanied with three different sauces. The main dish was heralded by the arrival of what Rogers could only describe as a small metallic Mexican hat. The conical object was placed over a gas burner. Large platters of raw chicken and beef were placed on the table. The meat was sliced wafer-thin. The waiter poured a brown pungent liquid into the brim of the container and finished by placing another platter of raw vegetables next to the meat. Faced with a spread of uncooked food Rogers looked to Whittle for help. Whittle dextrously used the chopsticks to place some of the vegetables in the brown bubbling liquid and then dipped a piece of meat in the liquid and threw it on the cone. The meat hissed violently and the table was enveloped in the steam and smell of aromatic spices. After only a few seconds Whittle removed the meat and placed it, together with some of the vegetables, onto Rogers' plate. Rogers fought manfully with the chopsticks and was soon accomplished at cooking the food. The chilli-based sauce and the heat from the small stove guaranteed that they both perspired heavily. Rogers prayed silently for a cold beer to wash it all down. His prayers went unanswered and they had to settle for Saudi champagne – a mixture of apple juice and Perrier water.

Rogers was surprised at how quickly a meal went when you were not drinking and despite the do-it-yourself element, they were in and out of the restaurant within an hour.

As they stepped outside, the cool night air was pierced by a high-pitched wailing from the minarets. They were slightly off-sync and the effect was a reverberating echo. Rogers watched in fascination as the cars on the highway pulled to one side. The drivers climbed out with their prayer mats in hand and supplicated themselves to Mecca. An unnatural quietness fell over the city as the last wail drifted into the desert. A few cars still moved but the constant blaring of horns had died in deference to the rite of prayer. Whittle appeared unmoved by the spectacle but Rogers found himself captivated by what he could only describe as part of a pagan ritual.

"Would you like to see the downtown area? The *souk*?"

Rogers was pulled back from the spectacle. "What? Yes, that would be great."

They returned to the car and drove onto the almost empty road.

"*Souk*, isn't that Arabic for market?"

"Very good. Your crash course must have taught you something."

They managed to make it into the heart of the city before the prayers finished and by the time they had parked the car, the shops had all re-opened for the night's business.

The centre of Riyadh is built around a large decaying fort. The construction was identical to that which they had seen in Dirayh that afternoon. Rogers would have liked to have seen inside the fort but was told by Whittle that it was closed to visitors. He went on to explain that despite Saudis' fascination with things new, the government had in fact recently allocated funds for both the restoration of Dirayh and the fort. After years of neglect they were slowly waking up to the need to preserve their heritage. Rogers followed Whittle around the side of the fort to a door that was similar in design and build to the one they had seen that afternoon. Pointing to the top right hand corner, Whittle indicated a metal object that was almost completely buried in the wood.

"That's supposed to be the head of a spear that Lawrence of Arabia threw at the door in frustration."

"Is it genuine?"

"Who knows? If it is I for one could understand his reasons."

The shops were full of cheap glitzy trash. Brightly painted objects attracted Arabs like moths to a flame. Rogers was appalled at some of the purchases that he saw the locals walking around with. Whittle, seeing the look on Rogers' face, just shrugged his shoulders. They fought their way through the crowds of the *souk* into an area where the shops had been carved from the cliff face at the back of the fort. The walls of the shops were deep red sandstone. The aromatic smell from the spice stores gave way to the deep musk of leather and finally the musty dampness of antiques. Rogers was captivated, and for the first time since he had arrived in Saudi, he felt he was seeing something of the country, not just a confused people.

Rogers purchased an Arab dagger, a process that took over half an hour. Having been offered a huge selection to choose from he finally settled on one with an ornate wooden handle and plain beaten blade. The store owner, seeing he had a potential buyer, called for tea. Rogers was invited to sit on one of the many rugs festooning the floor and partake of the sweet mint tea. In keeping with the lessons he had learned in London he knew that he must keep the soles of his feet pointing downwards while sitting cross-legged, a position that for most westerners becomes excruciatingly painful after a few minutes. Whittle was also offered the tea but he chose to stand while drinking it. In true Arabic tradition they took three cups before declining the fourth. The stage was now set, the bartering for the dagger could begin. The transaction took place by each party writing down in Arabic numbers the amount that they wanted to pay or were willing to sell for. Whittle ascertained from Rogers how much he was willing to pay. Rogers thought around fifty pounds seemed reasonable. Whittle wrote the riyal equivalent of twenty pounds on a piece of paper.

The amateur dramatics began.

The protestations were great and lengthy. Eventually the trader responded with a price that was three times the original offer, and so it went on. Twenty-five minutes later Whittle made a final offer equivalent to thirty-five pounds. The trader threw his hands in the air and walked away to the rear of the shop. Whittle indicated to Rogers that they should leave. Rogers was somewhat miffed at the turn of events. He had enjoyed the bartering scene but he also wanted the dagger. Outside the entrance to the antique *souk* he was about to protest to Whittle when the owner of the shop appeared and indicated, in dramatic fashion, that the dagger was theirs.

"Christ almighty, do they do that for everything they buy?" Rogers enquired as they walked away with purchase in hand.

"Anything that you buy down here, yes. The modern shops have fixed prices but you have to remember that the dagger you just bought does not have a price. The owner probably acquired it through a trade or was simply given it. Depending on the first offer you could have paid anywhere between the price you paid and five hundred pounds. He would have gone through the same performance irrespective of the price. It's the way they do business. If you had wanted to buy one of the rugs on the floor we could have been there all night."

While they had been talking they had left the *souk* and were now in a large open area with a mosque on one side and a range of official-looking buildings on the other; it was pleasantly quiet after the hubbub of the traders.

"The next time you hear that someone has been flogged or executed in Riyadh you will know where it takes place." Whittle pointed to the front of the mosque. "Outside the mosque on Friday morning after prayers."

Rogers stared at the peaceful symmetry of the mosque and had trouble reconciling this with the barbaric acts that were performed there.

"Do the executions happen frequently?"

"Usually two or three times a month. They have a lot more here in Riyadh then elsewhere. Riyadh is stricter than the other areas and they also try crimes that occur in outlying towns. Thousands of people turn up here every Friday in the hope of some spectacle."

"Have you ever witnessed one yourself?"

"No, but I know a few people who have. If the crowd spot you, you are pushed to the front, the best seat in the house. It's supposed to be a reminder that you are a guest in their country and you will abide by their rules. The executions, I am told, are swift. The most barbaric act is the stoning to death of women for adultery – the woman is placed in a sack on the ground, a pile of rocks is provided, and the other women are invited to throw the stones repeatedly at the form until it no longer moves. Twentieth century man in the guise of Philistine."

The mosque was brilliantly lit and stood out against the jet black sky. Rogers felt a shiver run down his spine and found himself unable to answer the question of whether or not he would choose to watch if he were given the opportunity. He was no stranger to death, but this was different: this was calculated punishment, the ultimate deterrent. A part of his mind told him that he would rebel against such behaviour. Another part knew that the fascination would probably be too great.

By the time they had driven back to Whittle's house, Rogers was more than ready to accept the offer of a drink. The contradictions and ironies of Arabia engulfed his mind and, as he sat savouring the amber liquid, he realised that on top of everything else he was no further forward with the Logan case. He was rapidly coming to the conclusion that her murderer had not come from the Middle East and therefore had to be someone that she met during her stay in Britain or someone from her past life. To accept this he had to discount Linda Slattery's intuition.

Whittle leaned forward to top up Rogers' glass and dropped in two more ice cubes.

"You look pensive."

"I suppose I'm confused. I came here on a murder investigation and end up getting a lesson in life. The Embassy exists as if this place was somewhere in England. You have a home and a lifestyle which the average person of your age would envy and yet in order to qualify you have to survive in an alien environment. Angela's husband told me at one stage that he thought you saved his marriage. I thought he was joking but now I realise that he was serious and I think I can understand what he meant. I know the money has to be good, or you and thousands like you, wouldn't be here, but how the hell do you survive in this zoo?"

Whittle relaxed with his feet on the coffee table. "The answer is more complex than the question. Each of us has our own reasons: divorce, unhappy marriage, financial problems at home or just simply, like myself, an inquisitive nature and a pathological hatred of the Old Boy network that pervades the English landscape.

"At twenty-five I was going nowhere. I was good at my job, it was held against me. Initiative was frowned upon. Toe the line, respect your elders and a pension will await you at sixty-five. This and other bullshit was the order of the day. I did not have the right accent or attend the right schools or have parents with the right connections. Doors were not just closed, they were nailed shut. The answer was simple – join the Masons. Not, I stress, for personal gain – perish the thought – but for mutual protection, to give a common purpose to the common man. The club for those excluded from other clubs. Join or be damned. I chose to be damned."

Whittle looked up from his drink and detected an embarrassed silence from Rogers.

"Of course, how tactless of me – we have one in our midst. The force, the Yard, propagators of the faith. Excuse my insensitivity, to each his own. I ask for nothing from life or my fellow man. I take what I want and eat when I'm hungry. Saudi is a means to an end. When I reach the end, I shall let you know."

Whittle refilled his glass and slid the bottle towards Rogers.

"The joke of this place is that it is classless. We ex-pats are as one. The plummier accents carry no weight, the education counts for nought. In fact, the ones who fare worse are the public-school types. Faced with adversity and a genuine need to work they flounder and are supported by us heathens. For this, and this only, I give thanks to this wretched hell." Whittle raised his glass in a mock toast and drained the contents.

To Rogers' ordered way of thinking, the lifestyle was anathema. He could not envisage a life without order, an existence of contradictions. He wanted to know more about the place, not only because it might help his investigation, but also because he was genuinely fascinated. His mind worked slowly trying to piece together a question that he hoped would produce the answers that he was looking for. He need not have bothered as Whittle was obviously happy to talk without prompting.

"The contradictions, the peaks and troughs, are what holds me here – and the money. The country functions around one doctrine, '*Bukrah Inshallah*' – 'tomorrow, God willing'. Everything is governed by the will of Allah. If tomorrow you sleep late and miss your flight it is the will of Allah. If you walk in front of a speeding car Allah will save you. If not, it is the will of Allah that you die. I have seen men, women and children tossed to their deaths on this faith. It is naive and ill-founded but it is their belief.

"The wealth is unevenly distributed – ninety percent of the money held by two percent of the population. The two percent visit the West frequently; they drink and whore, gamble and blaspheme. Upon their return they don pious robes and lecture the ignorant masses on the folly of the Western world. The rules of Allah are munificent in their blessings and tolerable within liberalism, but you, of limited wealth, intelligence and foresight, shall pay the price for my sins for I am your protector. I shall return to the West next week, next month, to ensure that the vices of mankind are held in check and prevent their influx into our inner sanctuary.

"And the masses nod and pray for the souls of their protectors. Hypocrisy as wide as the land, as deep as the seas, as dark as the crude. Hypocrisy in all its splendour, swallowed by the ignorant, perpetuated by the few.

"The scotch you drink is imported with the blessings of those on high. *Baksheesh* paid in the ports and airports to ensure that shipments get through. The mullahs, the zealots of the faith, fight the corruption. They claim small victories but have already lost the war. You know," Whittle paused to take a drink. In his haste to continue his sermon, he dribbled a small quantity down the front of his shirt. "You know, when I lived in Jeddah the mullahs had enough power to have the port searched. Every container that entered the port was searched; they stood guard and monitored the proceedings. They found drink, pornography, even a roulette table. It was all smashed or burned in a frenzy of destruction. For two weeks it was difficult to get drink, then the supply started up again. The bottles arrived salt encrusted. Ships were dropping fishing nets of cases, outside the port, with marker buoys. At night small boats went out, retrieved the bounty off the sea bed and landed it a few miles up the coast. The mullahs have lost but still they persevere.

"When the Sunni Muslims from Iran attempted to take over the grand mosque in Mecca last year we were isolated from the rest of the world for thirty-six hours. The Saudi authorities cut all telephone and telex links out of the country. There were soldiers in the streets and we were all shit-scared. No one knew what was happening. It was a day and a half before we found out what had happened. The Embassy were as helpful as usual. Ignorance is bliss."

Whittle slumped in his chair, his head resting on his chest, his drink lolled from one hand. The cool night air drifted through the open window. Rogers thought Whittle had passed out. With a galvanising movement Whittle pulled himself upright and headed for the bathroom.

"For this I get paid and can elect to ignore everything. I do not agree with any of it but for now I can tolerate it."

Rogers stretched his legs. Walking to the floor-length window he looked out onto the city lights in the distance. From here it could be London, Paris, New York. He heard Whittle re-enter the room and turned to face him.

"Why do you stay?"

"Why not?"

The mood was sombre, almost morose, and Rogers perceived that a drunken Whittle, in his present frame of mind, could be a depressing sight. He decided on one more tack about Angela Logan before calling it a night.

"If you had been going to kill her, how would you have done it?"

Whittle's laughter split the darkness. "Fucked her to death in hedonistic splendour."

The light from the table lamp did not reveal Whittle's face but the abrupt end to the statement told Rogers that he had hit a raw nerve. Tentatively he continued.

"Did you ever see her outside of Saudi? Bahrain or Egypt perhaps?

"Officer, I confess. In a moment of jealousy I killed her in a Cairo hotel, stuffed the body in a suitcase and dispatched it to London. You have winkled out my secret. Handcuff me and lead me to my fate." Whittle held out his hands.

Rogers punctured the tension. "If you sent the case on BA it probably went to Australia."

"No, I never saw her outside of Saudi. Only in my dreams. I still wonder what it would have been like to take her arm and lead her into a restaurant; to order wine with a meal or to have stayed in a hotel with her; to order room service. To have been decadent, not deceitful; to have been free, not oppressed. But turn the page, Inspector, would I have fallen for her in another time, in another place? You pass hundreds of Angela Logans everyday on your way to work, as I used to, and while you may look at some with interest you don't try to ingratiate yourself with each of them. In London she may have been a friend, more likely a face in the crowd. Here she was an angel of mercy."

Rogers poured the remnants of the bottle into his glass. The two sat in silence. Rogers had exhausted his questions and did not want to pursue the conversation further. He sought a concluding statement and exit.

"Murder is the ultimate enigma. Years ago I worked on my first case, in Somerset in fact. I can recall all of the facts with graphic detail. The motive was always elusive. Angela Logan and Janice Butterworth have one thing in common . . . " The sound of breaking glass stopped Rogers short.

Whittle jumped from the chair slightly unsteady on his feet. He held the back of the chair for support.

"Sorry, I must have dozed off and dropped the glass."

Rogers knelt down to pick up the pieces.

"Leave it, the maid will clear it up in the morning. I'm off to bed."

Rogers stood in the dim light and watched the receding form of Simon Whittle weave its way across the lounge. He could not explain why but he felt sorry for Whittle, perhaps even pity. He drained his glass and made his way to bed.

Whittle was seated at the breakfast table the following morning, a steaming mug of black coffee in one hand, his head resting in the other. Rogers knew how he felt and declined the eggs which were proffered by Waji.

Whittle dropped him off at the airport on his way to the office. The conversation en route was mundane, pedestrian. They parted if not as friends then at least as acquaintances who might one day look each other up for a beer. Rogers still pitied Whittle and although he could not know it, Whittle pitied Rogers; a pity bordering on contempt.

chapter 21

Coincidence, nothing more than coincidence. Fucking alcohol dimmed the perspective.

Why wasn't I looking at him when he said it? Easy – I had no idea he was going to say it. Janice Butterworth was the past. He admitted it himself. The case was closed.

I needed time to think. The hangover was making reasoned thought difficult.

He was good, very good, but not good enough. He had guessed that I might have travelled from Cairo to London and back – a good guess, but he lacked the imagination to work out how it had been done. He thought he understood the relationship and the desire to run away with Angela – academic; whether he understood or not was immaterial.

With each passing minute I felt better. A weight around my shoulders lifted as once more I realised that I had fooled the fools.

But hark. Heed the lessons. The web was complex, fragile and strong: the weaving was intricate but random. Look for holes and repair the damage. Distance myself from the weak points, perhaps even discard the whole and start again, or why not stop, quit while ahead?

The inner call of yesteryear was glimpsed in those moments. The body, fluid and functional, was at peace with the mind. An inner voice dictated control. Like the limitless sky above, it pushed beyond the known boundaries and I was carried on the flotsam of its seductive tones. I knew from where it spoke and from where it came: I was merely the vessel of its doing.

Peace.

It was coincidence, pure coincidence.

chapter 22

Rogers was getting used to being met from aircraft and the sight of Commander Mann waiting to whisk him away from the Saudi flight into the cold, damp January morning brought home the reality of the time difference, actual and imagined, that he had experienced.

They talked of Saudi, the place, leaving the case details until they were ensconced in a secluded booth at the Commander's club. Breakfast here was a tradition – the best bacon, sausages, fried eggs and bread in London. Kidneys, mushrooms and black pudding were also available but Mann dismissed the trimmings and settled on his usual for both Rogers and himself.

"I suppose, lad, officially I should start by reprimanding you. The chief was not amused by the terse communication from His Excellency." Rogers lifted his head to speak but Mann continued, "In view of the country and the circumstances we don't need an explanation or a justification; however, perhaps a suitably-worded letter from yourself to the Ambassador thanking him and his staff for their co-operation and time may go some way towards smoothing ruffled feathers."

Rogers smiled. "I have to be fair, you did warn me. If I learned nothing else on this trip except how insufferable our embassy people abroad can be, it was worth the airfare."

There was a pause as the piping-hot food was served.

"So, apart from antagonising the khaki-clad Corps Diplomatique, did you learn anything?" Mann asked, dipping a piece of fried bread in the yolk of his egg.

In between mouthfuls Rogers filled him in on all of the details, including the overnight stay at Whittle's house. He concluded by stating that, in his opinion, the murderer did not come from Saudi Arabia. And, more specifically, he did not believe that the murderer was Simon Whittle.

Mann raised his eyebrows at the last comment. "I know what you are thinking, sir, perhaps I did become a bit too close to the suspect, but in very unusual circumstances. I saw him in a different light, a different environment and the mantle of murderer does not fit well on him. And that's apart from the pure logistics."

Mann leaned back for a moment to digest all of the information together with his breakfast, then began to quantify what he had just heard.

"My own conclusions are that from overseas it's Whittle or no one. We have a rough, very rough, description that we have been able to piece together: blood type, probable hair colour and approximate height; but as the maid was short, the last of these factors could vary by up to six inches. If you take our plastercast with its rough edges it can be made to fit Whittle; however, it can also be made to fit a fair percentage of the population."

The silence filled the air, thoughts disturbed only by the clink of cutlery as the staff prepared the dining-room for its luncheon guests. Rogers was tired from the flight and the food had dulled his senses. He stared at Mann, his eyes drifted out of focus and he pictured Andrew Daniels sitting opposite him, the master of the pregnant pause.

Mann guessed his thoughts. "How would he have approached this?"

Rogers pulled himself back to the present. "My guess would be the same way with the same negative results."

A waiter glided silently by and offered more tea. Mann held out his cup, Rogers placed a hand over his – the Arabic gesture would, he thought, probably stay with him for the remainder of his days.

"I take it from the general discussion that nothing has been uncovered in the real world?"

"No," Mann replied, stirring two sugars into his tea. "In fact I think it's time to call it a day on your participation. I'm being badgered to give you back and my only hope of retaining your interest was that you had something concrete to report. We're getting nowhere, lad, so after a few days rest they tell me you are off to Malaysia debriefing a British subject who has given himself up to the authorities over there and is prepared to trade valuable drug-trafficking information in return for immunity from prosecution. A doddle for you, lad, all you have to do is stop the natives hanging him."

Rogers stared at the receding back of Commander Mann as he rose and walked away from the table. Another day, same old shit.

chapter 23

Life marched on, not with a swagger or confident step, but with a plodding persistence. The cool of winter was rudely blasted into the hills by the onslaught of summer. No gentle change of symmetry, just an explosion of heat.

Two months had passed since I had left Alan Rogers at the airport. No word was forthcoming and none was expected. Like Ajmira and Angela, Rogers had disappeared from view.

I was alone.

The brilliant daylight could not heat or touch my inner self, which was cold, isolated and weary. I was a living paradox of myself, ill at ease and ill content with my surroundings. I knew that I had to get out before the brooding presence destroyed not only the spirit but the flesh also.

Relief, of sorts, appeared without warning; and, in keeping with the perverse nature of this place, it came at the expense of others. Joe Fagan, my alcohol supplier, was arrested. I had inherited him from the previous manager, and in the easy-going, forced, environment of Saudi, we had become friends. His wife Mary was distraught. She was abandoned and ostracised by the local community; the American authorities were sympathetic but reserved; Joe's employers were ambivalent. Mary had become an embarrassment. The world had withdrawn its support and she was left to fend for herself.

We came together not so much by accident as by necessity. I rang her when I heard about Joe and suddenly, for the first time in my life, I found myself cast in the role of protector. To my surprise, I did not resent the intrusion. I found it a comfort. It helped to detract from the daily trial of life in Riyadh.

She was devastated, unsure of every move. For two months after the arrest I stayed with her. At night she would cry herself to sleep, or I would lay holding her until she fell asleep and then remove myself to the spare bedroom.

And so, for a while, I found that my life was fully occupied. The office was growing dramatically in size and in early July an assistant manager, John Ambrose, was recruited to provide me with support. Ambrose was a gruff but likeable Australian with an incredible talent for procuring anything and everything; he was constantly trading favours. From blue-movies to brandy or passes to the local hospital, John saw everything as a challenge. He joined the routine that rotated around Mary and took over from me for a few days while I had a short holiday in Greece. Stripped of the constant activity of the past few months, I found I did not enjoy the solitude. Conversely I did not look forward to returning to Riyadh. I felt trapped but knew that the only way forward was to fight from the inside.

As December drew near I found myself increasingly at odds with my surroundings. The dreams returned. They were demanding and perverse. Ominous shapes spoke of personal failings, mocked me for my human inadequacies. They gnawed constantly. Tentacles reached and prodded, sweeping me into their vortex, tossing and turning me over and over. Always I awoke in a cold sweat unable to pinpoint my surroundings.

I argued with myself, awake and asleep. This year there would be no sacrifice. Riyadh was dangerous.

Abject frustration left me testy and ill-tempered. A pressure was growing inside. I attempted to release it in various ways: sport, sex, bullying of staff, all failed. I was chided and ridiculed from within; my skin felt tight, stretched like a canvas on a frame. John and Mary both saw it but were powerless to help because they did not understand.

On the 10th John organised a barbecue at the edge of the dried-out river bed near Dirayh. In the sweltering heat of the afternoon we gathered as mad dogs and Englishmen. Mary and others toasted my good health. The few locals that passed laughed and pointed at the eccentricities of Western man and left us in peace.

I was restless, uneasy. The afternoon clouded over and the brilliant sun was momentarily obliterated as a large grey cloud floated across it. I turned and there, on a slight rise, was the black-clad shape of a Saudi girl. The all-encompassing abbah hid her form and features except the eyes. The grey irises, highlighted by the black kohl, stared transfixed at a point above my head. The cloud released the sun and a flash of brilliance illuminated the plateau. I moved my head slightly to adjust my vision and she was gone.

The party returned to John's house and rolled sedately into the evening. Around 11.00 p.m. people started to drift away. I excused myself to run Mary home. She was quiet on the drive back and asked me to stay with her when we arrived at the house. The answer was beyond my control and for the first time I refused, though I felt guilty about leaving her.

The drive back to Dirayh was easy. I parked away from the few houses and walked to the dried-out river bed. The moon was full and illuminated the baked mud with a greyish tinge. I heard the movement of stones as someone descended the small rise to my right. She was there, just as I knew she would be.

She walked towards me. The black abbah, translucent in the pale light, clung to her body. My mind was split, one side fooled by her beauty, the other warning me of the dangers and trying to protect me from myself.

chapter 24

The two bodies stood just inches apart. Whittle lifted the thin veil that covered her lips, moved his head forward and kissed her tentatively. She responded and the two sank slowly onto the parched earth. She was naked beneath her *abbah* and she moaned softly as his hands parted the fabric. He bent his head to kiss, and suckle her firm, rounded breast.

A cry of pain, from her lips, shattered the calm. Simon's head drew level with hers and he saw the blood gushing from a cut above her left eye. He raised himself to his knees just in time to see three bodies hurtling down the slope casting stones. As they saw him fully for the first time their Arabic voices filled the air with screams of pure hatred.

Simon ran for his life. A sharp rock caught him between the shoulder blades and knocked him forward. He regained his balance and charged for the car. The engine caught first time and he swung hard on the wheel. At that moment a rock came smashing through the rear window and sent a shower of glass into the car. One of the Arabs appeared at the side window and fought manfully to open the door. As the car picked up speed, he lost his grip and fell away. The door flew open and smashed against a rock at the side of the track. Simon reached over, pulled the door closed and headed for the main road.

John had finally ushered out the last guest and was relaxing with a night-cap when Simon burst through the front door. John was aware immediately that something was wrong but it took a few seconds for him to work out exactly what. Simon stood in front of him, his face a contorted grimace of pain, but it was his eyes that scared John most: they were manic, pleading in their intensity. His clothes were covered with a fine brown dust and his hair was flattened to his scalp.

"What the hell happened to you?"

"It doesn't matter. I need your help with the car."

"What do you mean?" John looked over his shoulder through the open door and let out a low, soft whistle. Ambrose moved back into the room, took a glass from the table and filled it half full of whisky from the bottle that was standing there. He gave the glass to Simon. He walked around him to go outside and take a closer look at the car but stopped when he saw the blood-soaked back of the shirt.

"Jesus H. Christ, have you been shot?"

Simon shook his head slowly.

John placed the drink on the table and tried to take off Simon's shirt; the blood had congealed and he had to settle for ripping it off. The fabric being torn from the flesh caused the wound to start bleeding again. Simon did not move or flinch. John left the room; he returned seconds later with a bowl of water and some cotton wool. Whittle had still not moved but the glass in his hand was empty.

John got him to sit while he bathed the wound. "Simon, this is deep. We need to get to the hospital, get it stitched."

Whittle leapt from the chair. He spun to face Ambrose, his face a ball of flame, his eyes black slits piercing through his enraged countenance.

"Have you lost your fucking mind? Don't you understand? Can't you see that heap of mangled shit out there?" White spittle had formed at the corners of his mouth. "I fucked a local." His head slumped forward and rested on his chest. An unnatural silence hung between the two of them, John unsure of what to say. Whittle's head shot up suddenly. "You're the fixer – fix it."

John was grateful for an excuse to leave the house.

He turned to leave the room but stopped at the door. "Are you going to be okay?" Whittle was either asleep or chose not to answer.

It cost a considerable sum of money but Ambrose was able to persuade a Lebanese garage owner, who owed him a favour, to repair the car while he waited. He thought several times of phoning the house but decided that it was better to let Whittle either sleep or get drunk.

The sun was just beginning to creep over the horizon as he drove the repaired car back home. Having had time to reflect on Whittle's revelation the previous night he reasoned that it was no big deal and that if he hadn't been caught at the time he would probably get away with it. He stopped to collect the morning paper and stared at the headline:

LOCAL GIRL RAPED BY INFIDEL

Only then did he realise the enormity of the situation.

Whittle was sat in the same chair as when he had left him, but he had showered and changed and now looked relatively normal. He opened his mouth to speak as John walked in but got no further.

John threw the paper at Simon. "Congratulations, you're famous. You're also a fucking idiot. Ever since I arrived here you've preached the rules: alcohol's only prison but women are death. Have you lost your fucking mind? If you really hate this place and yourself so much, get out. Don't sit there and look for sympathy. Just pack your bags and go."

John slumped heavily into a chair. The room became unnaturally quiet after his outburst.

"If those guys had caught up with you last night they would have fed you your balls. What you did was dumb and irresponsible. How the hell did you find a local anyway?"

"She was at Dirayh, during the barbecue. I saw it in her eyes, I knew if I went back she would be there, and be willing. I did and she was."

Ambrose fell silent.

"Look, John, I know it was dumb, but it's over. What happened with the car?"

"It's outside and you owe me a ton of money."

Simon pulled himself from the chair and looked out of the window.

"Good as new. I'm not sure how you did it, but thanks – I owe you a big one. Why don't you take a shower and then it's time to head off for the office."

"That's it? You just get up and life goes on as if nothing has happened?"

"What do you want me to do? Hide in the attic for a month? Get on the next plane out? Okay, I screwed up, but I got away with it." Ambrose went to interrupt him, but Whittle continued, "So I made the local paper – big deal. Read it again." He tossed the paper to Ambrose. "There's no description of me and all they know is that the car was white. It all happened out at Dirayh, not in the gold *souk*. The locals are going to be morally outraged but who gives a fuck about them. If I stay off work I'll attract attention. If I go about life as usual nobody, with the exception of you, is any the wiser."

"Well, you've either got balls or no brains, and I guess the next few days will tell us which."

"I do need one final favour. Can you bandage up this shoulder? It hurts like hell this morning."

They took John's car to the office and were stopped three times on the way but, after a cursory glance inside, they were waved on. As they walked into the office and were greeted by the usual pile of messages and problems, Ambrose realised that the lucky bastard had probably got away with it. Begrudgingly he admired Whittle's nerve.

It took just over a week for the city to return to normal. The police waited for the car to appear in one of the local body repair shops and when this did not happen they announced in the local press that the family concerned, in order to maintain good relationships with Western countries, did not wish to press charges. This ploy was equally unfruitful. The Bedouins couldn't read so they hadn't been able to give a registration number and the only description of "about six foot tall with dark hair" fitted half the ex-pats in Saudi Arabia.

Simon never told Mary about the incident but admitted to John one night it was almost as if she knew. "Something's changed with her. Perhaps she guessed because of my shoulder." John looked at him questioningly. "We slept together a couple of nights ago, for the first time. I don't know, it seemed to me as if she wanted to try and make up for everything. It may have worked for her, but for me it's somehow cheapened all that has gone before, almost as if Saudi by its very existence can reduce everything to basics and by doing so remove any of the pleasure from the act."

John was still concerned about Simon. He seemed to withdraw further into himself after the incident and he seemed angrier at himself and the world in general. John knew that Whittle would not leave of his own accord; it was as if the country and he were locked in a war of attrition, but he more than anybody was relieved when in early February Simon was promoted to Branch Manager in Bahrain.

John, as well as Mary, was sorry to see him go, but they both knew in their own way that it was probably for the best.

Simon was not sorry to go. He knew that deep down he owed Saudi Arabia a debt of gratitude, but true appreciation of what the country had done for him would not become fully apparent until he had time away from its confines to pause and reflect. He also left Saudi with one permanent reminder – a crescent shaped scar above his left shoulder blade.

part three

1983 – 1987

chapter 25

The final drumbeat of the last Samba bands echoed through the cavernous mountains of Rio de Janeiro. The last group dispersed to dance and party and greet the dawn. Manquilla di Gamba wandered unobserved through the dancers. The brilliance of the costumes made her keenly aware of her drab, torn tee-shirt. Like many who were too young to dance in the carnival she revelled in the heady experience of just being part of the atmosphere. The dazzling costumes were, in many cases, mere threads or single strips of cloth that hung provocatively over the bodies of the lithe dancers. The colours, offset by the coffee-coloured skin, added a lustre to the parade which was little short of breathtaking. Manquilla smiled. Next year, she thought, next year I will dance in Carnival.

The early morning sun saw the dancers and party-goers drift off for rest. Carnival, with all its inherent greed, mayhem and splendour, was over for another year. Manquilla joined the masses trooping along Ipanema. The luxury hotels and apartments meant nothing to her. Just a few hundred yards back from the dramatic promenade the steps that led into the rabbit warren squalor of the flavella greeted her tired feet.

The flavella was still humming with the electricity created by Carnival. It would last a day, maybe two, before the monotony of day to day existence returned. Manquilla grimaced as she entered the one-room shack that served as home for her mother, her two younger brothers and herself. The shack was built of timber, the windows merely openings cut into the wood. The floor was covered with dirt and, apart from an armchair without legs, the only facilities of the room were a single gas ring and a gas cylinder. A naked lightbulb hung from the roof and a dirty sheet served as a room divider at one side; a second sheet hanging at right angles made two small sleeping areas. One side, where Manquilla and her brothers slept, had a threadbare blanket on the floor and the other side, where her mother slept, contained a mattress.

It was from her mother's side of the divided chamber that Manquilla could hear the grunting and moaning that told her her mother had company. She crept silently into the adjacent area and lay down to sleep. She was glad to have the area to herself. Her brothers were either not yet home or were out scavenging for food. She tried to block out the animal noises from behind the sheet and quickly fell asleep.

Life in the flavella was never easy. There was no running water in the house: a single open-air tap serviced some fifty homes. The toilet facilities were an open pit at the rear of the house; rats, disease and pestilence were everywhere. There were shortages of everything, except people.

Manquilla had never met her father, and her two brothers were in fact half-brothers. At one time she was contemptuous of her mother and the steady stream of male callers but as she matured she realised that her mother's body was their only means of survival. Very few of the nocturnal visitors paid, but most would bring some food or clothes to help the family. In her youth her mother must have been attractive; now at thirty-one she was haggard, with missing teeth and a body that was more suited to a fifty-year-old; but still the male occupants of the flavella came and she performed three or four times a night to provide food for the following day.

Her brothers were adept at stealing from the tourists but it was rare that they managed more than a few dollars a day. The tourists had become wary of Rio's reputation, and more and more the mugging of a tourist would result in an empty wallet. Manquilla did what she could. She walked the bars and restaurants of Ipanema and Copacabana at night selling roses or chewing-gum to the tourists who gathered to watch the sunset or simply watch the city go by. She knew from the admiring stares she received that she had a commodity of greater value to sell. Her mother implored her not to sell herself for fear that she would end up like her. Manquilla was still a virgin, but to the men at the table she was an enigma; she was not one of the numerous prostitutes who openly flaunted their business in the same way that she sold flowers, and yet beyond the childishly blue eyes they could see the supple body of a young woman. She endured the taunts and innuendo, the constant attention of straying hands as they reached out to take a flower. She endured it all because it helped her sell more flowers and, ironically, retain her dignity. She knew that by the morning the flower would have lost its heady scent of the previous night and be discarded by the purchaser. She had no desire to be treated the same way.

Manquilla awoke around noon. She tried to pull herself back into the world of dreams but the warmth and comfort was gone, replaced by the steamy humidity of Rio.

The silence told her that she was alone. She was hungry but knew full well that there would be nothing to eat in the house until the evening. Rising, she pulled a tee-shirt down over her body and walked into the midday sun. She headed for the beach and, avoiding the multitude of scantily-clad girls, made straight for the surf and dived in. She was an expert swimmer and a few powerful strokes took her past the lines of bathers playing in the surf. She dived beneath the water and pulled the tee-shirt over her head, tying it tightly around her waist to ensure that she didn't lose it, and set about washing in the cool salty water. She ran her hands through her short spiky hair, and over her body, silently admitting that her strong firm breasts and long legs were an asset that had to be used cleverly to maximise their advantage.

Manquilla was only fourteen but she had no illusions of her place in the scheme of things; in this macho society finding a good man was her only escape from the flavella. Her assets were her body and a quick mind, her liabilities were her lack of education and her lack of understanding about life.

She pulled the tee-shirt back over her head and set off in search of a midday meal. As she crossed the promenade to reach the restaurants, her wet shirt hugging and amplifying her form, she ignored the comments and stares. Moving to the rear of one of the numerous restaurants she waited patiently, leaning against the wooden fence. She was in luck. After about ten minutes a young chef's assistant kicked open the back door and hurled two boxes of vegetable leaves onto the pile already rotting there. He turned to re-enter the restaurant but stopped as a movement caught his eye. His mouth opened to shout abuse at the intruder but was replaced immediately by a smile when he spotted Manquilla. He disappeared and returned seconds later clutching a brown bag. He reached out to give her the bag with one hand, and with his free hand pulled her to him. She did not resist the attentions – his rough kissing and fondling of her body were a cheap price for a meal. He attempted to slide his hand under the shirt but to that she objected and pushed him away. He backed off, laughing, and returned to the kitchen. Lunch consisted of three pieces of chicken and a bread roll. It went some way towards replacing the fetid smell of stale breath that hung on her lips from her amorous admirer.

One month after Carnival, the samba school of Ipanema met to review this year's carnival and to begin the planning process for next year's event. Two or three hundred listeners turned up on the beach to be addressed by the head of the school committee. Manquilla and her mother sat on the warm sand and listened to the speakers. Manquilla understood little of what was going on but she knew that she wanted to be there. The talk was of the success of having come second in the overall parade but the speakers called for renewed efforts that would once again win them the coveted trophy for first prize. The meeting broke up with the group dancing and chanting rhythmically to the samba beat.

Over the next few months Manquilla attended numerous meetings. The numbers in attendance grew until by late September it was not uncommon to see a group of fifteen hundred people dancing on the beach at sunset. There was always an air of excitement about the meetings. For most of the participants it was something to look forward to, something to break the stupefying monotony. Material for the costumes was garnered from benevolent sources; trinkets, beads and sequins were hoarded to await the commencement of the costume-making.

The theme of the carnival for the coming year was to be rebirth and the Ipanema school had chosen the rising phoenix as its particular theme. Manquilla was to be one of the five hundred dancers that would be in attendance with the float, following behind and in front of the eight hundred-strong drum band. She practised the dance steps religiously, painfully conscious that in her first carnival she wanted everything to be just right. Her mother sat on the sidelines and watched her daughter develop under the skilled tutelage of the dance master. She knew her own dancing days were over but she could still recall the feeling of excitement that came with a first carnival dance. The dancemaster's assistants moved among the twirling figures, directing here, pointing there, aiming to achieve the ultimate in group dancing. Manquilla's mother noticed with interest that one young assistant in particular kept close to Manquilla and was always on hand to coax her along. Manquilla herself was not unaware of his attentions and she looked forward to his few words of praise after the sessions.

In early January Manquilla turned fifteen. Marco, the dance

assistant, presented her with a single rose that night as the rehearsal ended. They sat and talked as people dispersed. Marco was shy. He explained haltingly that he could express himself through the medium of dance and music but found words difficult. Manquilla tried to put him at ease, but it was some little while before he felt comfortable in her presence and was able to talk to her normally. She discovered that he had a job in a record store that also sold musical instruments. The pay was reasonable and he hoped to move into a small apartment at the far end of Leblon before Carnival. He currently shared a large run-down house with friends near the base of Corcovado.

They walked slowly along the beach and just before they parted he pulled her to him and kissed her quickly, but affectionately, on the lips.

Manquilla knew that she had found her passage out of the flavella and her desire to tell her mother was tempered only slightly by having to wait patiently while another unknown male misused her mother's body.

Carnival was an exceptional time in Rio. For two weeks in February or March, depending on the date for Easter, the city became the scene for impromptu parties and dances. The dances began in the parks and beaches and spilled onto the roads where cheering, laughing throngs would wend their way happily through the streets, disintegrating as quickly as they had started. Traffic was halted but no one seemed to mind; cars were left in the middle of the road as drivers abandoned them to join in the festive atmosphere; the cariocas displayed at their most impetuous. The first week was only the appetiser to the main event that would follow. Tourists poured in from all corners of the world. Prices in the cafes and bars rose dramatically and the practice of charging tourists for drink and food that they had not ordered flourished. Everybody pretended to speak only Portuguese which made disputing the bill even harder. The crowds were good-natured. By day they took in the sights; they rode the cablecar to Sugar-Loaf or took the little train to the feet of the mighty Christ that daily blessed the city from its perch on Corcovado; they headed into the hills and marvelled at the natural beauty that led to historic Belo Horizonte; they sunbathed and watched the macho men working out on the beach, or admired the bronzed female bodies seemingly held together with pieces of string. But by night they came in their thousands to Copacabana, Ipanema and Leblon, the couples to enjoy the splendid food and ambience, the single men to watch and perhaps enjoy the ladies of the night.

The city preened itself for the big event, fingers worked anxiously in the homes and in the flavellas sewing the costumes, so fragile and yet so exotic, that would ignite Carnival from a mere festival into a magical event.

Manquilla could not contain her excitement as her mother banished her sons and all male visitors from the shack to ensure that the ornate costume would be perfect for her daughter. Each costume for the dancers was hand-sewn but identical. The costume consisted of five multi-coloured, sequinned straps which were draped across each shoulder. Two of the straps formed a spiral which wound around each breast, the sequinned centre of the spiral just large enough to cover the nipple. The three remaining strands extended down across the navel, then joined to form a small v-shape over the pubic mound before spreading in a fan across the buttocks and ending in a plume of purple feathers which sprang from the base of the back. Six strands of silver beads hung from the waist and three snaked their way down the hips to encircle each thigh.

Manquilla had tried the costume on at various stages but even she was not prepared for the full effect when she finally donned the intricate garment that had the look of gossamer and the tensile of steel. The room did not contain a mirror but Manquilla could tell by the reflection in her mother's moist eyes that the effect was spectacular.

The night before Carnival was traditionally transvestite night on the main promenade. Nobody knew where the tradition came from but the streets would be teeming with men dressed as women. Some were gross masquerades parodying the female form; others were intricately made up, dressed exquisitely, with only the odd mannerism or exaggerated Adam's apple revealing the truth.

Manquilla had arranged to meet Marco to view the spectacle. They had seen each other regularly over the last month and Marco had provided some clothes and food to help the family. Manquilla carefully removed the costume and slipped into a clean white shirt and denim mini-skirt that Marco had given her. She pulled a comb through her hair which had recently been trimmed and turned to kiss her mother goodbye. Her mother pulled her gently into her arms and held her tightly, realising that very shortly she would have one less mouth to feed.

Manquilla hurried down the steps. As usual she had to fight her way through the throng of males who habitually hung around at the foot of the steps leading into the flavella. They called and whistled but few reached out to grab her. Marco was on the promenade waiting for her. He could still not believe his luck that Manquilla had fallen for him and he fully intended to ask her to come and share his apartment once Carnival was over. The four-year age difference was nothing. She was old enough to have children and that was what they wanted once they were established.

They followed the winding brisk path that dominated the promenade of Copacabana. They were passed by obscenely-dressed males and beautiful visions with plunging necklines. The festive air was contagious. They laughed and danced until the early hours of the morning, revelling in the absurdity of the night and waiting expectantly for the following night when the culmination of almost one year's work would be put to the ultimate test of the most discerning audience, their fellow Brazilians.

Marco saw Manquilla safely back to her home in the flavella. He still found it difficult to reconcile her beauty with the surroundings but the pain it brought was eased by the knowledge that it was now only temporary. Despite a few inept fondlings on the beach, by mutual agreement they had not slept together. Manquilla was secretly waiting for the night, or morning, after Carnival, convinced that this would be the perfect climax to the perfect night.

She slept late the next day but once awake there was only one thought, one talking point. Her buoyancy was infectious and it seemed to take years from her mother's face: the lines that were permanently scored under her eyes were softer and the worry lines around her mouth were closer to the laughter lines they had once been.

Despite the fact that they did not have to report until late afternoon, Manquilla dragged her mother out of the flavella shortly after noon. They headed towards the area at the back of the city where the floats were undergoing their final preparations. The scene was one of organised chaos. The float itself was a masterpiece of colour. Workers, like ants, crawled across the huge stage to perfect every last detail. Under the skirt of the float, mechanics worked in suffocating heat to ensure that the engine was running smoothly and could be relied upon to pull the float along the two-mile course.

Manquilla and her mother walked arm in arm drinking in the atmosphere. As the sun set and darkness descended, a new heightened level of static ran through the area. Small knots of people sang quietly and danced slowly. No one was untouched by the event: small children stared in wide-eyed wonder at the glorious splendour; grandmothers crossed themselves, recalling no doubt their own youth and what this evening had meant for them.

Systematically, everything started to come together; drab clothes were discarded where people stood and the costumes of fantasy were donned. Manquilla moved to her place near the front of the float with the rest of the purple colours. Behind her the brilliant reds and blacks led onto the stage and in front of her the subtler colours formed, leading to the front of the parade where the pastel yellows and pinks set the whole concept in motion. The float itself was a reflection of the colours surrounding it; huge bolts of chiffon and silk had been draped ever upwards to a volcanic-type summit where the reincarnated queen was standing. Her costume was fanciful, recalling the legends of the phoenix; translucent wings of a multitude of colours spread twenty feet either side of her and her feather crown rose to the same height into the black evening sky.

There were no speeches, no last minute changes. An all-embracing silence fell over the group. Slowly, the sound of drums was picked up; row by row, the dancers followed, moving sedately, almost shuffling their feet; the growing wave moved past Manquilla, engulfed the float and reached the final row of drummers. The sound increased, the motion accelerated. They danced on the spot for fifteen minutes or so. Any initial doubts or concerns were dispelled as the swell grew to a crescendo and the mass of swirling brilliance edged slowly out to begin its parade.

From the first tentative steps Manquilla knew that the next few hours would change her life forever. She had spoken to Marco just before they had started the parade. He was animated and could only repeat over and over how lovely she looked. He promised to meet her at the finish line and spend the rest of his life with her. She moved in unison with women around her and only after they had progressed some two hundred yards along the carnival route did she begin to relax and take in her surroundings. The stands on either side of the street were full to overflowing; the people stood and cheered, flashlights popped continuously; the noise, colour and atmosphere carried her to new heights and she danced with a vigour and passion that many around her could only describe as sexual. The male dancers danced in a zig-zag pattern through the women, their dark costumes off-setting perfectly the brilliance that rotated around them.

For over an hour the float moved slowly along the course. When the private boxes came into sight Manquilla felt a sense of desolation, knowing that shortly it would all end. The drummers reached for new levels and the dancers windmilled hypnotically. Their hips seemed to bisect their bodies and the two halves danced in harmonious isolation.

Ten minutes later it was over. The beat died away and the eyes and ears of spectators turned to welcome the next spectacle.

An electric sensuality seemed to fill the air and Manquilla noticed that several men and women were drifting behind convenient structures to relieve their pent-up emotions. Manquilla searched in the crowd for Marco and her mother. The teeming mass was difficult to dislodge, and she was propelled forward. Bodies crushed her and strangers reached out to kiss and embrace her. She became frightened. The crush was tremendous, but the jostling, singing crowd did not seem to notice. Her feet were swept off the ground and just as she felt she would fall, the human log-jam spewed out into a large open area and there in front of her was Marco. Forgetting her sudden fear she ran and jumped into his arms. Her mother was behind Marco and the three embraced, happy in the delight of the moment.

The rest of the night was a succession of parties, impromptu street dances and good-natured revelry. At some point Manquilla saw her mother pair off with one of the men from the flavella and, although she felt a small pang of guilt as her mother left, she reconciled her guilt with the thought that life must go on.

Marco had tickets for a private party that was being held on Sugar-Loaf and in the early morning hours they headed for the cable car that would carry them to the pinnacle above the city. The car was full; the party-goers were singing and they persuaded Manquilla to dance for their enjoyment. Some of her insecurity returned but with the prompting of Marco she once again lost herself to dance and was transported back to the carnival atmosphere.

They were greeted enthusiastically at the party and, as was the custom for anyone who had taken part in Carnival, a large round of applause and cheering greeted Manquilla and Marco as they walked onto the dance floor. There were several other women in costume but everyone stood and watched in awe as the couple danced to the haunting beat. The intensity of the rhythm amplified the foot-stamping and hand-clapping as Manquilla whirled as one with the music. Marco dropped to one side as a single spotlight depicted the lone gyrating figure. He felt a wave of passion sweep through him. The dance finished. Manquilla, suddenly self-conscious, looked around her. Bemused by her loneliness, the spontaneous applause relieved the feelings as Marco stepped forward to reclaim his prize.

The view from Sugar-Loaf was spectacular. The jet black water crashed incessantly against the rock, disturbing the reflection of lights that emanated from the city. The noise from the city carried faintly on the still night air. It was said that if you looked closely on nights such as this even the Christ statue could be seen to be moving his hips in time to the music. Just before dawn a firework display illuminated the sky. Manquilla hugged Marco tightly, imagining the delights of the morning that were yet to come. As the last explosion lit the sky people started to drift away.

Marco agreed that it was time to go. They separated to find the rest rooms and arranged to meet back at the entrance to the cable car. Manquilla, singing silently to herself, was momentarily distracted as she walked out of the harsh glare of the lights into the darkness of the path which led to the ladies' room. She felt a small shiver run down her spine as her body began to cool from the passion of the night.

She never saw the hands that reached out and pulled her into the bushes but she saw the eyes, she felt their anger. She died within minutes of losing her virginity.

chapter 26

In preparation for landing at London's Gatwick Airport Theresa Evans politely requested over the intercom that all passengers ensure their seat belts were fastened, that tray tables be stowed in the locked position, that their seat backs be upright and that all smoking materials be extinguished. The announcement produced a buzz of activity around the cabin as the passengers complied in a distracted way. Somewhere in the back of the plane a baby was crying.

The 6.30 a.m. flight from Glasgow to London was always a chore. The passengers, mainly businessmen, were normally half asleep, although you could guarantee that at least one randy bastard would slip you his business card and wink. Theresa had been flying this, and similar routes for two years and she was becoming heartily sick of it. She had left school unqualified and after attempting hairdressing and waitressing she applied for a job with British Caledonian as a stewardess. Having never flown before she had no idea what the job entailed but it appeared glamorous and as such fitted her notion of what life should be.

To her surprise she had been accepted and after a twelve-week training course, which she only narrowly passed, she found herself serving tepid coffee and inedible food at 30,000 feet. The work was easy, if not as glamorous as she would have liked. She had no aspirations or abilities to rise higher in the ranks and for two years she had turned in a routine performance. She liked the attention that the male passengers and the cockpit crew gave her, always following their innuendoes with her hollow, throaty laughter. It was not that

Theresa was incapable of thinking, it was just that no one had ever asked her to do so. She was a decoration and a good lay. Even Theresa did not object to this description as long as she was wined and dined first. After all, girls have to have their standards.

Somewhere in the last few months the lustre had gone. The pallid faces smiling back had begun to offend her. The jokes, at her expense, were more often greeted with a withering stare as opposed to the former laugh. She put it down to the weather. The winter had been miserable, cold and wet. Although spring had now given way to summer, it was still cold and wet.

She fixed a smile to her face and muttered goodbye to the departing passengers. They had an hour on the ground before they took off again bound for Amsterdam; then they were back to London, finishing with an early afternoon flight to Paris, or was it Dublin? Who cared? Theresa certainly didn't.

Walking through the maze of corridors that is the inner sanctum of Gatwick, a poster displaying sunshine and beaches caught her attention. As she was considering a holiday in the sun she stopped to read it. She was surprised to find that it was a recruiting poster, for staff for Bahrain Air. She had not the slightest idea where Bahrain was but the sunny disposition of the poster was enough to attract her. She noted the number and resolved to telephone them upon her return from Paris.

The following two days were uneventful. Her one attempt to find out where Bahrain was, failed, as her colleagues could only tell her that it was in the Middle East, and although she had a vague idea that the Middle East meant Arabs she could not have found the region on a map. She completed the application that had followed as a result of her phone call and sat back to await the outcome.

She finally received a reply asking her to attend an interview at 2.30 on the afternoon of September 22nd, at the Mansion Hotel in London. She was overjoyed at the news and, although the interview was two weeks away, she set about planning what she would wear and whether she should have her hair up or down. A minor obstacle was that she was supposed to be flying to Madrid on the morning of the 22nd. This could easily be resolved by calling in sick the day before. The only inconvenience of the white lie was that she would not be able to fly down to London the following morning. She solved the problem by travelling the day before and calling in sick from London.

The morning of the interview was warm and sunny which Theresa took to be a good sign. She spent the morning at the hairdressers and, having decided that she looked more mature with her hair up, she opted for a manicure as well. The bill was expensive but surveying herself in the hotel mirror she decided that the effect was worth it. In a conservative royal blue suit and cream blouse Theresa thought that she looked distinctly business-like and despite her initial butterflies she felt confident to take on the world.

The first rude shock was when she was ushered into suite 820 to find that there were some twenty other girls waiting, all in similar style and colour suits. She slid into a chair and spent the next hour evaluating the competition. Personality and intelligence never entered the equation. It was purely a matter of looks and dress. It was easy to dismiss a few of the applicants just by size: short and dumpy in two instances and in one case excessively overweight. She had satisfactorily boiled the competition down to about eight when her name was called.

The interview was not taxing. She smiled a lot, particularly at the two male interviewers, and answered all of the questions to the best of her limited ability. She reddened slightly when the sole woman interviewer asked her if she had any children and answered politely, but firmly, no. On the walls behind the three of them was a map of an area of the world that did not include Britain. She assumed therefore it must be the Middle East and presumably included Bahrain. She was concerned that they might ask her to identify Bahrain and was relieved when one of the men pointed in the general direction of the map and indicated where it was. He made a joke of it, stating that it was only the pilots who needed to know the exact location. She laughed. She did not understand the point of one of the questions; they asked if she had any dealings with foreign nationals, specifically Arabs. She was confused -- surely dealing with any nationality was the same? You simply gave them food and drink and if you liked them patted their arm.

The interviewers talked about Bahrain, the airline, accommodation and salary. It all went over her head, except the salary which she quickly calculated was three times what she was earning now and she had missed the point about it being tax free. They asked her if she had any questions; she shook her head and the interview was over. She was asked to wait in an adjoining room and took a seat with the others who had been interviewed.

Another hour passed slowly. The room filled until Theresa was sure that all of the girls who had been in the first room were now in the second. The door opened and the younger of the two male interviewers, Theresa thought his name was Dean, thanked them for their patience and asked them to bear with them for a few minutes longer while they sorted out the final details, after which they would return to announce who had been successful. The minutes ticked slowly by. No one spoke. The only noise was the sound of a nail being filed or the rustle of a magazine page being turned.

The waiting was finally over and twelve names were called. Theresa at first missed hers as she was not used to being called Evans. The eight unsuccessful applicants were shepherded politely, but decisively, from the room.

The remaining twelve girls suddenly became animated. No longer competitors they struck up conversations, mere expressions of relief, before they were called back to the present by their prospective new employers. They were each given a contract. They were asked to take it away with them and return it signed within one week. If the signed contract was not received within one week the job offer would be withdrawn. Allowing them one month to give notice to their current employers and sufficient time to put their affairs in order, they were informed that they would be flying from London to Bahrain on November 30th and that their training would commence in Bahrain on December 2nd.

Theresa was in a dream. She, like several others, signed the contract there and then. She made sure that she handed it back to Dean and for her troubles received a grateful smile. He assured her that she was going to enjoy working for the company and, although he personally was based in London, he felt sure that she would enjoy the Middle East and Bahrain especially. The little knots of girls started to disperse. Some had been eyeing the map in the main room but Theresa was only interested in eyeing Dean. She engaged him in conversation for a few minutes longer and this time it was rewarded with an invitation for dinner. She told him that she was due back in Glasgow that night as she was flying the following day. He in turn pointed out that she would only be working for them for another month.

She dined well that night and afterwards performed to the best of her God-given abilities.

Boarding the DC10 on the morning of November 30th, Theresa saw for the first time the uniform that she would be wearing. The stewardess who greeted her was Asian, and the green jacket and trousers that she wore appeared to be designed to specifically hide the figure and in no way accentuate it. The pale yellow piping around the jacket and the seams of the trousers added some much needed colour but the pill box hat, of the same green and yellow, perched on her head made her look positively gawky.

All of the twelve girls were present and from their adjoining seats they spent most of the flight observing, with detached interest, what was going on. Theresa was surprised to find that most of the girls did not come from an airline background. In fact only three of them had previously worked for an airline. She immediately felt superior and when the film started she feigned boredom and slept.

Her complacency was blown apart when they stepped into Bahrain airport. There were people everywhere; objects covered in black from head to toe moved across the marble floor; different nationalities, people of all races and colours, moved frantically in the confined space. The twelve girls were collectively herded through immigration and customs and forty-five dizzying minutes later they were in a Bahrain Air bus heading for some buildings in the distance which Theresa took to be the city.

They crossed a long bridge and were held up as a donkey cart trotted sedately in front of them. Theresa observed to no one in particular that if this place was going to be as hot as this, at least it was nice to be near the sea. They drove through a small built-up area and their co-ordinator who had met them at the airport informed them that it was Manama, the capital. Theresa could not immediately recall what she had been expecting but she knew that it wasn't this. There were men dressed in long white robes everywhere and most of them were holding hands. The streets looked dirty and despite the air-conditioning in the bus it was very hot and there was a pervading smell of rotting cheese that she found offensive.

By the time they were established in their apartments, three girls to each, Theresa was having second thoughts about the whole venture. She was tired, hot and hungry and had not been at all pleased that their rooms were pre-assigned and they did not get to choose with whom they wished to share. They had a day of acclimatisation before the training started in earnest. Theresa clung to her two room-mates; wherever they went she went. A trip to the supermarket and a brief visit to Manama were the extent of their excursions and neither did anything to brighten her flagging spirits. Her two companions seemed unfazed by their surroundings and each new event to them was an adventure. To Theresa it was a trial.

A bus collected them the following morning and drove them back to the airport where the training centre was located. They were measured and fitted for their uniforms and then it was straight into four weeks of training. For Theresa this was viewed merely as a refresher course. The group was divided into two for training purposes and their numbers were supplemented by the arrival of two local males. Theresa immediately dismissed both as being of no consequence as, apart from being Arabic, which she admitted was not a drawback in her book, they were both short with pock-marked faces, which definitely was. In the first few days of training Theresa felt superior to her colleagues as she had covered most of the ground before. However, as the week went on she remembered all too well that she had only just scraped through a similar course once before and was soon left trailing in the wake of the rest of the class. The monotony was unremitting. In the first week it was off to the training centre every day, followed by an evening of study to ensure that they were ready for the tests and exams that were scheduled for the week's end.

Life was full of surprises for Theresa, most of them unpleasant. She screamed unmercifully the first night a cockroach ran across her foot as she was getting ready for bed and was not at all pleased to find that lizards, or geckos as the locals called them, were permanent house guests. She tolerated their presence when she was told that they ate the cockroaches and ants but never totally accepted them.

Her two room-mates spent hours explaining things: the local religion, the weekends, the money, and a whole host of never-ending questions that arose daily. When they were not answering questions about Bahrain and their new home they were trying desperately to stuff enough knowledge into her head to get her through the course.

At the beginning of the second week they had a swimming test. The training centre had a small indoor pool and they were required to swim four lengths. Theresa's spirits lifted somewhat when they all stepped out in bathing suits. She was the only one in a bikini and she noted with satisfaction that hers was definitely the best figure. The fact that she finished last in the swim and was hopelessly out of breath did not concern her.

At the end of the day's session, after the two locals had departed, an announcement was made that their group had been invited to dinner the following evening at the home of one of Bahrain's prominent local families. The purpose of the evening, it was explained, was to give the girls some insight into the local way of life. It was pointed out that they would be there as representatives of the airline and as such should conduct themselves accordingly.

The taxis that collected them the following night drove them away from the city. They crossed the barren centre of the island and arrived at a superb mansion nestled against the rocks which prevented the sea from eroding the small beach on which it stood. They were greeted at the door by a liveried butler who led them through a cavernous hallway into a book-lined library. There were six locals present, all male. The eldest of the six stepped forward and introduced himself. Of the remaining five two were introduced as his sons and the other three as friends. The names meant nothing to the girls and most of them appeared acutely embarrassed by the situation. The exception was Theresa.

Since arriving at the front of the house her internal radar for detecting opportunity had been at work. She had spotted the Rolls Royce parked at the side of the house and was not disappointed by the garish opulence of the interior. Within minutes of the introductions she had the situation worked out and had selected which of the six men was going to be hers.

Her companions hung back and had to be coaxed into conversation by the group. Theresa, using her finely-tuned hunting skills, homed in on the elder of the two sons. He was immaculately dressed in a Saville Row suit and his cultured English accent left no doubt that he had not been educated in Bahrain.

The uneasy atmosphere slowly evaporated although it was obvious that at least two of the girls would rather not have been there. The others were prepared to enjoy the dinner but would be equally happy to leave when it was all over. Dinner was a splendid meal, the service impeccable, the wines only the best, and the men attentive and amusing. Theresa knew that she had snared her man. They sat next to each other at dinner and everyone else was excluded from their conversation. She knew that she was getting slightly drunk from the wine but in the grandiose surroundings she did not care. This was the most fun she had had since arriving in Bahrain. Her suitor's attentions were becoming amorous; sliding his hand beneath the table, he located the split in her skirt and gently caressed her thigh.

The dinner finally ended and, although Theresa was finding the pomposity of her colleagues amusing, out of gratitude they accepted the offers of the men to dance. They were led from the dining room back into the library and through a concealed door to the right of an ornamental fireplace. Theresa let out a squeal of delight when she saw the room. It was fitted out as a complete disco. A few switches were thrown, music filled the room and a sophisticated light show set the tone. Theresa noticed with satisfaction that even her colleagues were impressed and were partaking with some vigour in the dancing.

None of the other men, however, were making headway with any of the girls and half an hour later, at their request, they prepared to leave. Their congenial host was the perfect gentleman to the end and he saw them safely to the taxi. He presented each of them with a small box. Waving off their protestations he informed them that it was a small memento of the evening and a welcoming gift to the island. The boxes each contained a set of gold and pearl earrings and once the taxi was out of earshot of the house the five fell about laughing at the effrontery of the whole evening. No one commented upon the fact that Theresa was not with them.

They danced alone in the disco for another thirty minutes or so. The music changed to a slow beat. Theresa felt her body being caressed and knew that mentally she was already his. She was vaguely aware of a wall panel sliding back across one side of the room. A circular bed appeared from a wall cavity and her lover pushed her gently backwards. She fell into the silk sheets and watched as he disrobed. Lowering himself onto the bed he began to move his hands and lips with practised ease over her body. Her skirt was moved slowly up her thighs and the probing fingers dug deep into her warm moisture. His lips slid from her neck and nibbled at her breasts through the silky fabric of her blouse. Her nipples hardened as he rolled them slowly in his teeth. Theresa was lost in a sea of emotions and when he finally removed her clothes she abandoned herself completely to his desires.

Slowly, gently, she was manoeuvred around until her back was to him. She was facing the opposite wall where flickering images of herself were reflected back at her. Her mind registered surprise but before she could react she was forcibly pushed face down into the bed and, despite her muffled screams and fighting, was brutally sodomized.

Theresa felt that she must have passed out for when she lifted her head from the bedclothes a few minutes later she was alone. Her clothes were on the floor and despite the pain and nausea she gingerly pulled herself upright and dressed. She had no idea how she was going to get back to the apartment but she knew that she had to get out in case he came back. She caught her reflection in a mirror as she prepared to leave. Her face was a mess where her make-up had run as a result of her tears, but her desire to get away was greater than her desire to look presentable.

She fought back more tears as she limped painfully down the stairs. She pulled open the front door and was greeted by a liveried flunky who held open the rear door of the Rolls Royce for her and indicated that she should climb in. She looked at him the way she would have looked at a leper. He quietly assured her that his instructions were to take her to her apartment. Seeing that she was greatly distressed he added that she had nothing to fear from him.

She sat rigidly in the rear of the car but gratefully accepted the snifter of brandy he handed her. She had no idea where they were and as a consequence did not know if they were heading in the right direction. She was therefore quite relieved some minutes later when she saw the lights of Manama in the distance. She had lost all track of time and was surprised to find as she looked down at her wrist watch, that it was only just after midnight. The action of looking down caused her to notice a box on the seat next to her. She reached out and opened it; inside was a gold and diamond encrusted ladies' watch. She stared at the watch as once more tears coursed down her cheeks.

The car was stopping at the side of the road and the panic that she had felt earlier returned. She rudely demanded to know what the hell was going on. The driver turned and told her as sympathetically as he could that something was wrong with the car. To illustrate the point he gestured towards the bonnet where a steady stream of vapour was escaping into the night air. He asked her to wait in the car while he went to investigate.

Theresa was nervous and agitated. She wanted nothing more than this nightmare to be over and to be safely back in her bed. She kept looking around to ensure that no one was waiting to approach the car. The moon was full and the desert was well illuminated. The driver reappeared and told her that he was going to walk over to a house, he pointed off to the right, to get some water for the car. Her panic grew and she began to cry again. He comforted her and assured her he would only be gone a few minutes. She pleaded with him to lock the car and when she heard the central locking click into place she breathed a little easier. She watched him walk away and finally lost him in the darkness.

Theresa began to look around her. The desert stretched endlessly to her right but for the first time she noticed the sea off to the left. The evening was still and the moon reflected off the calm, dark waters. A couple came into view. They were too far away to see clearly but as they turned and kissed she again felt the pain of her own encounter. About fifty feet away from the car a lone tree stood between the sea and the road. The couple moved towards it and Theresa was able to distinguish that they were male and female. The male unfolded a blanket that he had been carrying under his arm, and spread it on the ground. The couple seemed oblivious to her presence and Theresa wondered if the dark colour of the car merged against the desert, or perhaps they were just too absorbed in each other to notice. She watched, curiosity and fascination getting the better of her, as they began making love.

Then, in an instant, the scene turned from serene to terror. The man grabbed his partner around the neck and violently shook her head up and down; the woman's legs began to thrash wildly but were contained by the weight of his body.

Theresa felt a tightening in her chest and tried to scream but there was no air. She grabbed the door handle, desperate to get out, to get away, but the handle would not budge. She was trapped.

The woman's thrashing stopped; the man released his grip on her neck and her head lolled lifelessly back against the ground. The man continued to thrust deep within her and it was several minutes before he finally pulled away. He dressed, rolled the body off of the rug, folded it, and walked back along the beach.

A few minutes later the driver returned. He unlocked the car door and leaned in to tell Theresa that he had the water. Only the first words left his lips as he found her slumped form lying on the back seat, her eyes open and staring straight ahead in terror. He grabbed the car phone and in desperation screamed for help.

The following morning the stunned classmates of Bahrain Air training course 124 were told the sad news that Theresa had suffered a massive stroke while being driven back from the dinner. Theresa was paralysed and had lost her ability to speak. She was being flown back to London later that day for treatment.

chapter 27

If you travel roughly one hundred and eighty miles due west of Little Rock, Arkansas, you will arrive in the small hamlet of Republic, population one hundred and sixty-three. The single bar-cum-diner and hardware store are a fitting testament to rural America. The town has never been prosperous. It is of no historical significance and its single unabashed aim is to serve the local farming community. The farms are sparse acres of poor soil, neither healthy enough to grow good crops nor to sustain healthy livestock. The work is hard and the rewards by no means justify the physical effort, but like much of rural America, tradition runs deep and the small-holdings are religiously passed from one generation to the next.

Rarely if ever is new blood introduced to the small community and years of in-breeding have diluted the quality of the human stock. The result is an area populated by generations of simple folk with vacant, mystified expressions on their faces. The males are generally hard-working and hard-drinking, the women mere work horses who produce children.

Mike Haig was born into this community just prior to Christmas 1965. His father pointedly ignored him, as he had his other three children, and merely berated his wife for her stupidity in producing another whining mouth to feed. His complaints fell on deaf ears for over the next five years another four offspring would be added to the house.

The Haig family owned eighty acres of land that had been hacked from the forest by their German ancestors two generations earlier. The land begrudgingly yielded a small annual harvest of corn or wheat while the penned livestock provided milk, eggs and pork or beef off the hoof. The house was a spacious wood dwelling, the furniture sparse and ancient. The only two creature comforts of the twentieth century were a generator that provided electricity, and a television set. There was never any spare money and the basic principle of life was that if you didn't grow it or couldn't make it you went without it.

The children supplemented the inadequate farm machinery and most of the planting and harvesting was done by hand. Education was sporadic and it was rare that any of the children found themselves on the local school bus more than two days in any week. Mike Haig, like his brothers and sisters, accepted life for what it was. He knew no different and so could not make comparisons. Mike was an unspectacular child; he did his share of the chores and worked hard at keeping his father away from him. His father had a violent temper and his tendency to lash out at the children with only the slightest provocation did not endear him to them.

In the first twelve years of Mike's existence on the farm, life changed little. Every waking moment was governed by the changing seasons, every thought restricted by his environment. He had no friends outside of his family and his family was a mere bloodline of familiarity. His education was both limited and limiting, but somewhere in the dark recesses of his mind something was stirring. His contempt for his father was growing, as was his dissatisfaction with his lot, and, although he did not recognise the symptoms, a new sexual maturity was arising. This, and this fact alone, would lead Mike on a path which was destined to take him far from the home he had come to despise.

His elevation to manhood opened new thoughts and it was not until he had fought through two painful years of conflict that he finally accepted, although he still did not understand the reasons, that he much preferred men to women and more so that he was convinced his body was that of a woman trapped inside the physical shell of a man. He joined in the juvenile tittering at the Health & Efficiency magazines that found their way in to the school yard but, while his classmates boasted of erections at the sight of large-breasted female naturists throwing beachballs, he found himself unaroused, yet vaguely interested in the male forms that were shown catching them. His thoughts troubled him and with no one to turn to he became insular and reserved.

In a house of so many people it was difficult to be alone. The features that he observed in the cracked bathroom mirror were undeniably softer than his contemporaries. He had no facial hair, his face was well-proportioned, the cheekbones high, giving it an oval-shape. He was of average height; his hands and feet were small and his skin, although tanned by the sun, was smooth. He discovered the sexual satisfaction of caressing his skin and soon found that he could watch himself masturbate by standing on the edge of the bath tub. He was fascinated and disturbed by these new sensations. He knew that several of the girls in his class were keen to take him into the fields after school and he relied on his ignorance in an attempt to hide his discomfort but he knew that the tactic was only delaying the inevitable. Alone in the bathroom Mike experimented with wearing some of his mother's undergarments. The fabric was rough and worn but he still felt a surge of excitement run through his body.

This state of flux lasted for two years and during that time Mike became increasingly aware that he had to get away from the house. He had no plans and no money but he knew that for the sake of his sanity he had to break away from the family tradition. His father no longer beat him for fear of being hit in return but would still take out his frustration on his sisters. Two of his sisters already had children and a third was pregnant. Although no one asked it was obvious who the father was.

As is often the case, events overtook circumstances and by January 1981 Mike found himself banished from the family home. After fighting off the advances of Paula Smeet at school for several months, Mike had found himself trapped at her home one night when they were supposed to be working on a history project together. Paula's parents were absent for a couple of hours and despite Mike's protests Paula had dragged Mike upstairs and onto her parents' bed. Mike had lain there feeling slightly sick as she had taken her clothes off. He was repulsed by her body. Like most of the country girls she was fat all over. She leaned forward and pushed her large fleshy breasts into his face. Taking his lack of response as encouragement she slid down to his hips and unbuckled his trousers. Dipping her hand inside his shorts she pulled out his flaccid penis and stared in disbelief at its unaroused state. Sinking him deep into her mouth she worked her jaws frantically for several minutes with no response. Rolling on top of him she sat astride his thighs; her immense breasts jiggled unco-ordinatedly as she pumped furiously first with one hand and then the other to get life into his useless organ. After a few minutes of fruitless pumping she grabbed her clothes and ran crying from the room. Mike was relieved at the opportunity to flee the scene. He felt no urges towards Paula Smeet but as he walked slowly home he felt the need to relieve other sexual desires.

The house was in darkness by the time he slipped in through the front door. He crept silently up to the bathroom. His mother's discarded clothes were on the floor. He stripped naked and donned the clothes, caressing the fabric across himself as he did so. He felt his penis stirring and held it tight against the cotton fabric. When his father walked in and found him a few minutes later it was the end of life as he knew it. He collected his few items of clothing, put them in his school bag, and left.

For the first week after leaving Republic he slept rough and ate little. He was carried along like a leaf in a stream, meandering with no pre-defined course.

He made it to Little Rock and quickly found that you could be invisible in a large city. He spent two months working in a car-wash earning just enough to keep himself alive. In his naiveté he mistook most of the passes that were made to him by the female drivers of the cars and for that matter some of the men as well. He was well-built for a fifteen-year-old. The years of working in the fields had given him a lean physical frame and he easily passed for eighteen. He had no driving licence but had driven a tractor enough times to know the rudiments. He was filled with trepidation, however, when the owner threw him the keys of a car one morning and told him to deliver it to the address on the chain. It took him some minutes to get used to the controls but after a few close calls he was off driving through the mid-morning traffic.

The address was in an area of town that he was not familiar with and it took him a little while to find the right street. The area looked prosperous in comparison to where he lived. The gardens were neat and tidy and the houses showed no signs of paint peeling off. Parking in the tarmac drive, he rang the bell and waited. A head leaned out of an upstairs window and asked him to hold on. He waited patiently. Eventually the door was opened by a tall red-headed woman pulling the folds of a silk dressing gown across her body. She told him to come in while she searched frantically for her purse to give him a tip. As she came back clutching a five-dollar bill she seemed to notice him for the first time and was immediately interested. A cold soda led to conversation in the comfort of her deep armchairs. She wriggled occasionally to ensure that the robe slowly parted. The less he seemed to notice the more interested she became. Deciding she could not wait all day for him to make a move, she stood up and leaned over him to take the empty can; the robe fell open to reveal her nakedness. Mike instinctively turned his head away and in doing so nudged his face against the silky fabric. An electric charge raced through his body. Seeing the reaction on his face she sat down in his lap and pulled his lips to hers. Mike was oblivious to what was happening; his hands roamed over the robe as he felt himself becoming erect. She slipped to the floor and relieved him orally while he sat absently caressing the fabric. When she stood up he noticed her body for the first time as she pulled the robe around her. She was thin, her breasts little more than hardened nipples, her stomach was flat, her legs long and elegant.

Mary Lou, as she was called, drove Mike back to the car-wash, explaining along the way that her husband was a bank inspector who spent most weeks away travelling. Thus began a satisfying and educational relationship for both of them. Mary Lou would pick Mike up from the car wash on nights when her husband was away and he would spend the evenings with her. The sex at first was difficult but as he grew comfortable with her he talked about his problems. He had expected her to laugh but instead she was sympathetic and curious. She readily agreed to the wearing of underwear and over a period of time got used to the idea of him wearing her underwear in bed. She took out books from the library and bought magazines about gays and transvestites; they read together and tried to fathom out the complicated predicament that Mike found himself in.

Mike made it clear that he had no desire to change. He did not want to be a man chasing women. He was happy with his current lifestyle. Mary Lou had no experience of this type of sexual activity and, after her initial reservations, she became excited about her new secret life; she bought Mike presents of lacy underwear and found to her surprise that she could be contented with their relationship. Mike found himself loved for the first time in his life and more importantly had someone to talk to. He knew that Mary Lou was of limited intelligence and experience but at least she accepted him and tried to understand him.

As the weeks drifted by he sensed an unease. He was role-playing when he was with Mary Lou and, although it felt good, it did not change the fact that he knew deep down that he did not just want to act out being a woman in bed. He wanted and needed to dress and act as a woman all of the time. Some of the magazines they read talked of transvestite clubs in New York and he knew that he had to go there and experience them for himself if he was to develop. Mary Lou needed gentle, persistent persuasion but eventually she agreed to teach him how to apply make-up, how to wear women's clothes with style and, most importantly, how to walk in high-heeled shoes without falling over. This development changed their relationship. Mary Lou was still a good friend but she was less inclined to sleep with someone who considered himself a woman. Mike did not mind as the transitional development was everything to him.

They visited back-street restaurants and cinemas with Mike in full dress and even Mary Lou admitted that he looked the part. Whenever males turned to eye them up she wondered what their response would be if they ever got Mike into bed. Apart from the clothes, a wig and chest-padding was all that Mike needed to make the adjustment from one sex to the other. He felt comfortable when they were out together but it was the simple things like remembering which bathroom to use that confused him most.

Mike felt he had gone as far as he could with Mary Lou's help. It was time to bite the bullet and make his own way into the world. He had managed to save fifty dollars and with Mary Lou buying his one-way ticket to New York he pulled out on the Greyhound bus one morning, hoping that this would be the final stage of his journey to finding the real Mike Haig. Mary Lou watched the receding bus with a heavy heart. At times she had loved and pitied him but now she felt only sadness as she realised that she had not really known the person. Indeed, she surmised, he did not know himself.

The bus pulled into the 34th street terminal in the early morning hours of the following day. The stark reality of his fifteen and a half years struck Mike as he looked around the abject poverty that met his eyes: people were sleeping at random on benches, piles of rubbish were everywhere and the early morning smell was of stale urine. He recalled the sweet-smelling countryside of Republic and for the first time was homesick. He was approached by three males all offering him accommodation. He declined and headed for the terminal exit, his bag of clothes slung across one shoulder. Unaware of the perils of city life he started up 7th Avenue in the early morning gloom. He never saw his attackers but he was left with a bleeding lip, a cut above his right eye, no clothes and no money.

Dazed by the experience and disgusted by his lack of awareness, Mike sat with his head in his hands and cried. Eventually, steeling himself to succeed, he returned to the bus terminal and accepted the first offer of accommodation that came along.

The man, who introduced himself as Sly, drove him a short way along 10th Avenue before pulling up in front of a dirty brownstone just off 45th Street. For the next two days he nursed Mike, showing him the city, teaching him how to be street-wise and generally taking care of him.

His cuts healed quickly and it was on his third afternoon in New York that Sly asked him if he felt strong enough to work. Before he could answer Sly was walking him over to 42nd Street. Mike had seen the area on his travels and had been astounded by the sexually explicit posters advertising live sex shows and pornographic films. He was led through the door of one of the numerous sex shops and up some stairs where several women were hanging around in various stages of undress. Sly pointed to a door in the back of a round cubicle on the side of the room. He told Mike to go in and take his clothes off. Before he could protest he was pushed through the door and was faced with the sight of a young girl lying naked on a bed with her hands pushed deep inside her open thighs. As his eyes became adjusted to the dim light, he noticed shafts of light coming from the walls in front of her. The light would go on and off as some sort of shutter was raised and lowered. In the gloom he could just make out the gleaming pairs of eyes watching the scene in front of them.

The girl roused herself enough to acknowledge his presence and told him to get on with it. His reaction was to turn and head out of the door. As he pulled open the door he was faced with the huge, muscular form of a black man who made it clear to Mike that he could perform as instructed or have both his legs broken. Mike spent fifteen minutes lying between the legs of the girl, moving spasmodically. He was aware of the shutters sliding up and down but could not fathom what enjoyment or satisfaction any of those watching could have derived.

After his first performance he was led away to a small office. The hulk who had threatened to break his legs stood deferentially behind a seated man. Mike had never seen anyone dressed in such an odd manner; the room was dark and stuffy and yet he was wearing sunglasses, a green fedora with a large yellow feather rising out of the side, and his floral patterned shirt was open to the navel revealing a collection of gold chains. Around his shoulders was a fur coat. Mike was not invited to sit down but was informed by the apparition behind the desk, in no uncertain terms, that he now worked for him. He would be paid ten dollars a show for performing and by night he would be hired out as an escort to either males or females that wished to hire him. The fee would be one hundred dollars, which was to be paid over to his employer. Any money that he earned for services he performed would be split fifty-fifty between the two of them.

Mike performed on stage three more times during the course of the day and afterwards he was taken by the black man to a run-down apartment building on the far west side of Manhattan. He was unceremoniously shown into a room that had three beds, peeling paint, bare floorboards and several cockroaches. He stood in bewildered amazement for a few moments, unaware that his protector had left him and been replaced by an ancient crone with facial hair and rank breath. When he had recovered sufficiently to take in his surroundings, he found the woman civil and, in an odd way, friendly. She laid down the house rules, gave him a key and a dog-eared schedule with his name scrawled across the bottom in pencil. The schedule told him when he was to be available and that he could have Sundays off. On leaving the room the woman announced he owed fifty dollars for the first week's rent.

Mike met his two room-mates later that evening. They both looked a lot older than him although he found out later that in fact they were only a couple of years older. They welcomed him unenthusiastically to the hell hole before dividing two snorts of cocaine between them and becoming oblivious to their surroundings.

Mike knew from his roster that he was on call that night so he lay down on the bed to wait. By ten o'clock nothing had happened and he was just thinking of turning in for the night when he heard his name being called in the corridor. The old crone suited him out from a rack of clothes near her desk and told him to report to room 2125 at the Grand Hotel.

Mike considered heading straight for the bus terminal but he had no money and no idea where he should go so, despite his reservations, twenty minutes later he found himself in bed with an overweight middle-aged executive from Ohio. She was attending a conference in town and was much the worse for drink. By thinking of Mary Lou he was able to perform and was rewarded with a one-hundred dollar tip in addition to the agency fee. On his walk back through the city he felt a little more confident about life. This was quickly dashed when he had to pay over one hundred and fifty dollars when he got back and the remainder had to be paid as rent.

Thus began a routine that would last for the next five months. Mike quickly realised that he was a prisoner. The drug pushers were the leeches of his existence. He rebelled against them not because he did not wish to sink into the mindless oblivion that they were offering but because if he was going to escape from this hell he would need the money. Business was good. He became a great favourite with two or three special customers on the Upper East side; women with idle afternoons and money to burn. They treated him well and thought it cute or risqué to go along with some of his suggestions of cross-dressing. He disliked intensely some of the evening clients that he had to deal with but, as long as the tip was there, he found he could suffer it.

The block of apartments was full of young people similar to himself. He avoided personal contacts, and learned to ignore the terrifying night-time screams and the odd body that was carried out in the early morning hours to be left elsewhere in the city. A suicide or murder – he did not care as long as they left him alone. He quickly realised that he could not leave his money in the room. He had no knowledge of banking and so finally settled on a left luggage locker at Grand Central station. It cost him fifty cents a day but gave him the security that he wanted.

At first he only knew that he had to escape from the stranglehold; the problem was how. He came to know the city well and, by reading the various magazines in the sex shop, he discovered that the Village was the accepted area for gays and transvestites. He spent his free time in the area locating the clubs where reviews and drag acts took place. He discovered bars in the meat-packing district where men dressed as women could congregate and not be hassled. He bought new clothes and began to mix a couple of times of week with the people he felt most comfortable with.

Some of his clients, the men especially, enjoyed cruising the bars and clubs with him. He became known in the area as Mike or Michelle depending on how he was dressed. Like any society, the world of transvestites was divided: there were those men who simply wanted to dress as women; and there were those, the transsexuals, who wanted to become women.

The first stage of the process to change sex was easy and readily available; hormone treatment reduced hair growth, toned down the masculine features and over a period of months produced breasts. Some men decided that this was not enough for them and had breast implants to produce the desired size. Thus, a completely new breed of men had appeared in the Village described variously as he/shes, chicks with disks or TVs.

In addition to these, there were some who would settle for nothing less than a complete sex change. This not only necessitated the removal of the male sexual organs and the implantation of a surgically-made vagina but also required, in most cases, the shaving of the Adam's apple to reduce its size and, frequently, plastic surgery to reduce the size of hands and feet. The few who took the latter route did so in the knowledge that they wanted to re-enter mainstream life and be accepted not merely as a man who desired to be a woman but as a woman.

Mike was unsure that he would ever go that far, not because he feared rejection as a woman, but because of the horror stories he heard of the operations themselves, and because the ageing process in those who underwent surgery seemed to accelerate dramatically; as such they were ostracised from a society that constantly strove for eternal youth.

All of this came as no real surprise to Mike but it was nonetheless educational. For the first time in his life he knew what he wanted and, more importantly, how to achieve it. The only problem was getting away from his present employer who did not accept letters of resignation and would never agree to him joining someone else's stable in the Village.

In early 1982 Mike got the break he was looking for when one of the club managers asked him if he would do a one-night drag act to help him out. As he would not have to perform until after midnight, he saw no problems in meeting his obligations elsewhere first. He asked one of his afternoon lady friends to help him and they spent a pleasant time shopping before selecting a deep blue sequinned dress that displayed his legs and body to good effect.

The evening itself was a disaster.

Mike had never thought about what he would do on stage and ended up moving disjointedly to the music and disrobing in extreme haste, which left the audience whistling and jeering in mock anguish. He had seen this as his big chance and knew that he had blown it. The owner came to see him in the dressing room and they talked for some time. Despite the debacle he was convinced that Mike had real talent, and the figure to match, for a female impersonator. He was prepared to pay for lessons in ballet and dancing to improve his posture and movements if Mike would join the club. He knew of Mike's current employment and left it for him to make the decision.

Mike had to get out of his current arrangement. The squalor and mind-numbing boredom was slowly getting to him and he knew that sooner or later he would succumb to drugs as the only way to tolerate them. Once that happened he was finished. Having made the decision, he left one night for an engagement and headed straight for Grand Central station. The client called the agency an hour later to say that he was still waiting. The agency quickly dispatched someone else, and spent fruitless hours searching the city for Mike. They eventually gave up, concluding that he had either left town or become another John Doe statistic. Mike meanwhile had walked out of the men's room at Grand Central dressed in his smartest women's suit and headed for a new life in the Village.

He worked hard at his training. He learned poise and balance and within a month was one of the main attractions on the stage of the Black Hole Club. Mike now dressed exclusively as a woman. Even when he slouched around in a jumper and jeans he tried to be feminine, he kept his make-up expertly applied at all times. He began a course of hormone injections and was pleasantly surprised after two months to notice a definite change. His features, which had always been feminine, were now even softer; the contours of his legs lost any manliness; and, with his short blonde hair, he knew that he definitely passed for female. He could just detect the outline of breasts forming across his chest and his nipples which he had always dismissed as useless, were now sensitive to the touch. He did not consider how far he wanted the change to go; for now he was happy for nature, or more correctly science, to take its course.

The changes were slow but inexorable. He sold himself by day and early evening and performed his drag act into the early morning hours. He was constantly amazed at the number of men and women who were prepared to pay to sleep with him and by the summer of '82 he had reached a crossroads. His breasts had developed into small round globes and although he was not unhappy with the effect he felt that he would like them to be fuller. He enjoyed wearing evening dresses and would have loved to wear ones with a plunging neckline that gave him a cleavage and another weapon in his arsenal to satisfy his clients. On the recommendation of friends he made an appointment at a clinic on Fifth Avenue. The procedure as described to him was simple: a small incision beneath each breast would allow for the insertion of a small plastic sack which was filled with silicone gel. The doctor examined Mike thoroughly and saw no problems with the surgery. They discussed size and shape, as if Mike was intending to buy a car, and an appointment was fixed for the following week.

One week later Michelle Haig emerged into the sunshine of Fifth Avenue, her 36C breasts mounted prominently before her as she sauntered through the park accepting the many appreciative stares that came her way.

The job in the club had to go. Michelle obtained her clientele from advertising and the numerous bars that she frequented. She was happy with her lot but kept reminding herself that she was still only sixteen and could not see herself remaining in New York for the rest of her life. She quickly learned that if she did leave it would have to be for Los Angeles or San Francisco on the west coast or further afield to other countries. Other places where she knew that she would be accepted were Australia or some of the countries of the

Far East. She had heard Singapore mentioned a few times and set about finding out more about that area of the world.

As the heat of the summer drifted through to fall, Michelle decided that she wanted to see the Far East with a view to settling in Singapore for a few years. Paying for a ticket was no problem and applying for a passport Michelle Haig reverted to Michael Haig in order to have his photograph taken. Leaving New York in early November she spent a few days in London and then headed on for what she hoped was to be a great adventure. In London and Singapore she walked through immigration wearing baggy clothes and no make-up, an effect that must have worked as no one questioned her appearance.

Michelle had several contact names in Singapore and in no time at all she found herself immersed in the night life of Singapore that revolved around Boogis Street. By day, Boogis Street was a typical Far Eastern street market full of traders and local hustle. By late evening the scene changed. The market stalls were removed and a new crowd entered. Tables were set up through the narrow street, stalls reopened to sell fried shrimp, spiced chicken and numerous other Chinese delicacies. Wizened coolies and young boys ran between the tables taking drink and food orders and would disappear to return seconds later with platters of steaming food and bottles of ice cold beer. As the area filled during the early morning hours the scene would become more chaotic. Most nights it was friendly; the odd fight would break out but Boogis Street with its internal policing quickly restored order.

Once a good crowd was in attendance, the ladies would appear in gleaming evening dresses or sheer figure-hugging blouses and mini skirts. They moved through the ranks of the tables, their exquisite figures attracting the eyes of all who they passed. They would sit and talk, joining in the festive atmosphere and a revered hush would always proceed the arrival of the Queen of the street. During the course of the evening the women would pair off with males and disappear to the rooms above the market.

Michelle fitted gracefully into this world; this was what she had always wanted. In New York she had been considered beautiful; here, her beauty was transformed into pure glamour and she was much sought after. Like New York this under-life attracted numerous undesirables. The street had an unsavoury reputation and the odd triste would turn into a mugging. Michelle resolved from the outset that she would have nothing to do with these less wholesome aspects and, although she had to pay a fee of twenty-five percent of her earnings in order to operate in the street, she was her own boss and could come and go as she pleased.

Her fee covered the use of the rooms in the market, which were fine for a quick visit but Michelle preferred to try and attract one person who would take her to his hotel room, apartment or house.

There seemed to be no rules or restrictions on Boogis Street. As the drink flowed, the inhibitions receded. It was not uncommon for sex to take place on one of the tables in front of a baying crowd, and fellatio or masturbation of any client was commonplace while they sat at the table. Again Michelle was disdainful of these activities but she knew that the girls who took part made substantially more money than she did in a night. To Michelle the money was of secondary importance to the overall ambience and style of life that she was now leading. In the electricity of the night she had found herself and was happy in the sanctuary of her desirability.

In the early morning of December 10th, 1985, she left Boogis Street in the company of a tall, handsome, sun-tanned man who drove her to her house on the outskirts of the city.

chapter 28

Saudi was a long time ago, a reptile skin that was outgrown and discarded. The pain of Riyadh eased slowly and the dark, threatening clouds of despair gave way to a bright new dawn.

It began in Rio, a magical holiday to a magical city. Carnival – an indescribable riot of colour and action, the panorama of the city bathed in the quixotic beauty of its coast. Rio had pumped oxygen into flagging lungs, it had exorcised the demons, the remnants, that continued to exist long after those around me had forgiven and forgotten the events of the previous December, and, where Rio had left off, Bahrain took over.

Bahrain was no paradise but it was heaven in comparison to its neighbour. I was free of the petty constraints of Saudi feudalism and yet still qualified for all of the financial benefits of living in the Middle East. I was in charge of the flagship office, and although the dynamics of the economy were not in the Saudi league, they were enough to challenge the mind and ensure that my quest for growth continued. Bahrain was also able to offer me a sacrifice. The nerve ends that had been eroded by the sandblasting of the desert began to heal. The dreams no longer rose as cobras to spit contempt. I was in control again.

But then there was Singapore. The memories still rise to haunt me and I shudder in revulsion.

Walking back to the hotel in the early hours of the morning I stumbled across a street of vivid activity and life. I viewed it from a distance, mesmerised by the selection of beauty in front of me. I was approached by a woman and we talked for a while. She invited her own death.

We went to her house and she led me to a small room at the back. The room, dimly lit by two small, marble-based table lamps, contained a double bed and little else. She lay on the bed, her long evening dress, split to thigh length on one side, fell open to reveal a perfectly sculptured leg. She pulled me down beside her, climbed on top of me and sat astride my chest. She slowly pulled down the straps of her gown and her breasts spilled out; she held them, gently caressing the nipples and then moved forward to offer them to me. She took my arms and lifted them above my head; my hands touched cold steel and jerked away. I looked behind and saw a pair of handcuffs hanging from the brass headboard; a similar pair were at the base of the bed.

She laughed and rolled onto her back. She did not resist as I manacled her hand and foot. Instead she playfully pulled against the constraints accentuating the curves of her body. I left her tied to the bed and, although I could hear her calling for my return, I searched the house for signs of other inhabitants. Concluding that she lived alone, I returned to her and stripped naked. I then removed her dress and it was as I peeled off her panties that the contradiction of her body was revealed.

She laughed, no doubt at the stunned expression on my face, but the laugh was the final sound that ever came from her mouth. I stuffed the panties into it and in an instant wiped the smile from that face. My hand shot out, driven by some internal force beyond my control, and grabbed one of the table lamps, yanking it from its socket. I swung it above my head and brought it down with full force between her legs. The force of the blow caused the skin at the base of the penis to rupture and the flaccid organ fell to one side. Blood seeped pulsatingly from the open wound. Five, six times I pounded the heavy base into her groin until there was only a mass of pulp and blood.

Enraged at the duplicity of her body, and how it had deceived me, I attacked her breasts, smashing bone and tearing flesh. Finally, with a dying strength, I brought the lamp down on her face to destroy the last vestige of her human form.

I sank to my knees unable to move, but the over-powering smell of blood and fear finally forced me from the room. I showered, scrubbing my body endlessly to cleanse it of the filth. My mind was clearer, but I felt no better for my actions. I had to return to the room to collect my clothes. The sheets were crimson red and droplets of blood hung suspended from the ceiling.

I drove away in her car, abandoned it near a taxi rank, and took a taxi to the hotel. I spent the day at the hotel unable and unwilling to lose the picture from my mind, but all the time formulating a plan. I had known from the moment I left her house what had to be done.

Selecting a victim was easy – I chose a girl from behind the check-in desk at one of the major hotel. As she left that evening I followed her to her car. The rest was tedious details, and yet long after she lay dead I continued to make love to her, climaxing over and over until the mistake was replaced by the contentment I was seeking.

Early the next morning I left for Bahrain, back to a life of normality.

Too much normality. I was restless. Life was becoming repetitive, boring. I had to move on to the next stage, even if I didn't know what that stage entailed or how to get there. During a recent board meeting I upset a few of the older establishment by simply asking where I was going next. The answer was nowhere, at least not for a couple of years. Once the true implications of their reply had sunk in I felt compelled to resign. I needed more, I needed a greater challenge.

The glorious pomposity and arrogance of youth. I was thirty – a mere five years ago I was grateful to accept any job that would carry me to foreign shores; now I had mastered the environment, climbed the personal mountain of growth and, although I could not have specified what I wanted, it had to be more.

"Been there, done that," was a popular expression of the day. It epitomised our thinking and ruled our emotions. My annual employment reviews had been good, and suckered by the frailty of yesterday's results, I basked in personal glory. In June of 1986 I resigned, not because I had to, not because I had any plan in mind but simply because it felt the right thing to do.

With no map to follow I drifted for a few weeks. Tying up loose ends I eventually headed back to England. I suppose we all make mistakes in life and in an attempt to save a few dollars, I bought a ticket out of Bahrain to England on one of the local airlines that flew to London. What I had not realised at the time of purchase was that the plane would stop in Lebanon en route to London. The approach over the beaches was a contradiction: the sparkling Mediterranean on one side of the aircraft, the bombed-out structures of a destroyed city on the other. A two-hour stopover became five when the shelling started. Spending three hours on the floor of the terminal with shells and rockets flying overhead is not my idea of fun. When the noise finally abated we were led by armed soldiers back onto the aircraft and took off as the fires of religious revolution burned around us. I suppose it was fitting that my final flight out of the Middle East should be traumatic – it summed up precisely the whole absurd conflict of their religious differences.

A friend from Bahrain loaned me his flat in the south of England for a few weeks. It was good to have a base aside from my family, but the novelty of England soon wore off. I had had a desire for some time to travel, to see the world. I had no desire to start work again immediately and so, with the minimum of preparation, I set off from Heathrow with the intention of making my way from America to Australia. If my parents thought I was mad they kept it to themselves.

Carrying a small bag which contained a spare shirt and shorts I set off,

New York bound. I had resolved that the trip would be done on the cheap, not because I could not afford to do it any other way but because I wanted the experience, I wanted time to think and decide about my future. I did however cheat on the first leg. I had always wanted to travel on Concorde and as a reward for surviving the Middle East I flew from London to New York in three hours and fifteen minutes, arriving before I had left. Memories of Concorde: the food and champagne were excellent, the crew chosen for their competence, not their looks, and the curvature of the earth from that height an unforgettable sight.

The ticket included a three-night stay in a mid-town hotel. The city had an atmosphere all of its own, an air of regenerative birth that seemed to keep it going despite its notorious problems. I had a vague notion that I wanted to drive across the vast continent that is North America, but having made some enquiries about hiring a vehicle for three or four months I quickly realised that the cost would be prohibitive. I ended up purchasing an RV, a small recreational vehicle, which came complete with sleeping accommodation, a shower and a toilet, a gas stove and fridge. It was ideal for my purposes and, at the price of $4,500 with the potential of resale value, it suited my budget.

During the next three months I covered fourteen thousand miles, driving from New York to San Francisco along the Pacific coast highway and into Vancouver, from Vancouver to Ottawa and back into the States at Detroit. Heading south to Texas I crossed the border into Mexico and spent two weeks battling the highways and dirt tracks. The memory easily recalls the splendid isolation of the Grand Canyon at dawn, the ritzy opulence of Las Vegas and the sheer majesty of Niagara Falls; but it was the thunderstorm in Wyoming, the desolation of the Saskatchewan plains and the natural havoc that had been reeked by Mount St Helens that bound the fragments into a permanent mural.

By the time I returned to Texas the RV was complaining; the milometer was on its second circuit and it was time to part company. I sold it in Brownsville for $1,800 and took a Greyhound bus from Texas to Miami.

From Miami I travelled through the Islands; the Bahamas, pleasant; Jamaica, hell; Haiti, an open sewer; Puerto Rico, America in the Caribbean; St Martin, friendly; Antigua, poor; Martinique, France in the sun; Barbados, splendid in its beauty; Trinidad, Jamaica in the south.

The West Indies constitute one of the world's greatest vacation dreams if you go there with money and hide behind the luxury of a hotel wall but do it on the cheap and you see the true plight of misguided policies. Dreams of coasting between the islands on banana boats or tramp steamers were rudely shattered by the knowledge that very few boats still operated within the islands and, in order to get into a country, you had to have a valid ticket out. Much to my disgust the only practical way to do it was to buy an air ticket that took me as far as British Guyana but allowed me to stop at as many islands as I wished.

British Guyana, considered by most to be part of the West Indies but in fact located on the mainland of South America, is a beautiful country of Dutch colonial architecture, financially bankrupt and gloriously ignored by everyone. I spent a night sleeping at the airport as the only flight out to Boa Vista in Brazil left early the next morning. As I settled down to sleep on the chairs I became aware of some activity in the closed restaurant that I was facing. Closer inspection revealed the place to be infested with rats; not just a few but hundreds had taken over the restaurant, scavenging for food. The macabre scene lasted all night: as the first rays of sun broke the horizon they left and the staff arrived to serve breakfast.

From Boa Vista I took a bus and headed south to Manaus. The bus drove on a dirt track through the rain forest, and every few hours we would stop at a clearing in the forest where the locals were operating refreshment stalls powered by a generator. They served fried chicken, cake and ice cold beer; the setting was incongruous but I can still recall the smell of the chicken and the taste of the warm moist cake. I was the only non-Brazilian on the bus and locals would frequently request a stop in the middle of nowhere, disembark with their families and disappear into the forest. We did not pass any dwellings and the absence of wildlife was disappointing. The only memorable highlight of the eighteen-hour journey was the ferry ride across the River Negro. The early evening mist which hung over the water heightened the peaceful isolation but, that apart, it was unspectacular.

From Brazil I flew to Chile. I had wanted to see Argentina but in 1986 they were not keen on giving visas to British subjects. Chile was a disappointment but it was a useful starting point in getting across the Pacific. I hopped from Chile to Easter Island, on to Tahiti, Fiji and into New Zealand. New Zealand was like Scotland in summer, cold and damp. By the time I reached Sydney to spend Christmas with John Ambrose. I was physically exhausted. I had in no way appreciated that the trip would be so hard.

I spent two weeks with John. We travelled around the east coast of Australia together and I had to admit that it was a pleasant change to have a companion. For the majority of the journey I had travelled alone. I met other people doing the same thing as myself and we exchanged stories of our travels, but in the main I preferred my own company. John was on home leave from Saudi and I saw him off from Sydney airport as he returned to Saudi for his final six months.

I headed in the opposite direction, taking in Melbourne, Adelaide and the Nullarbor plain on my way by bus to Perth. By the time I reached Perth I had had enough; the travelling had been fun, but it was over. The thought of trekking through Asia, India, Pakistan and the Middle East to get back to Europe did not overly excite me and so in early March I boarded a Qantas flight, and headed for London. We refuelled in Bahrain but I chose to stay on the aircraft. During my time away I had deliberately avoided reading newspapers and had seen hardly any television news. It had been self-indulgent to be ignorant of the world for so long but it did not take long to slip back into old habits.

I'm not sure the trip answered any questions but it did re-instate the appetite for work and so once I was back in London I set about finding a job. Seven months of idleness was enough and I was keen to resume my overseas career. Along the way I had considered the idea of changing careers; two things prevented me from doing so: firstly I wasn't trained or skilled to do anything else, and secondly I was not prepared to forgo the money that I knew I could command within the insurance industry.

It was surprisingly easy to become employed. Confidence is everything and just six weeks later I was flying out of Britain again, this time to the colonies, Bermuda, where I was to take up the post of Vice President for an offshore insurance company.

During the course of my travels I had passed my thirty-second birthday. I happened to be in Wellington, New Zealand. It was a Wednesday and the city appeared to close down shortly after 9.00 p.m. I had booked a passage on the late-night ferry to the South Island and was killing time until it left at 11.30. The weather was as unappealing as the deserted streets; a cold damp mist hung over everything, the few bars that were open near the port provided little comfort and little opportunity. There was not the pressing desire or need that there had been in previous years but still I had been on the look-out throughout the day to see if opportunity, for continuity sake, would raise its head. I searched the area for signs of the ever-present prostitutes but there were none in evidence.

The ferry became my last hope. Watching the disembarking passengers, there seemed to be few possibilities. Most of the foot passengers were couples or single males, and the cars which came off the ferry quickly drove off into the night. After I had been watching the scene for several minutes I became aware that the steady stream of cars which went down the one-way street were halted periodically as cars coming from a side road joined the line. The cars were all driven by women who were, without doubt, cruising, on the look-out for male passengers off the ferry: hookers on wheels – a new slant on an old job. I was on an elevated promenade above the ferry and looking down. I watched the vehicles do a complete circuit around the buildings before rejoining the line. Some would not appear a second time having secured a client. The cars were well-spaced. With good timing on my part I realised that I could meet one of the cars as they came round for a second or third pass.

The red Ford pulled up suddenly. The passenger door was opened and in seconds we were off. While she concentrated on driving I rubbed my sleeve along the arm rest, obliterating any finger prints I may have left when I closed the door.

Instead of heading back to the ferry she turned right. We followed a deserted road alongside some warehouses, the headlights picking out scurrying rats. Turning the wheel sharply, she pulled the car up between two large buildings. I had already seen enough to know that I was not dealing with Miss New Zealand. Thick pancake make-up and bright red lips only highlighted the advancing years. The breath hinted of alcohol and the fleshy figure squeezed into a tight jumper and leather miniskirt did nothing to arouse the desire. She was all business – one hundred dollars for a blow job with her topless, cash in advance. As I paid over the money she pulled her jumper under her chin and disposed of her chewing gum before dropping her head into my lap. The whole sordid episode lasted only a few minutes. The desire to grab her neck while she was performing was immense but the thought of the permanent damage her teeth could do me gave me the strength to wait.

As she raised her head and smiled a sickly smile I realised that a car was not the easiest of places to murder someone. She turned away modestly and pulled her sweater down. I reached behind her and pinned her arms while attempting to put my other arm around her throat. She may not have been young but she could fight. Her first instinct was to throw back her head. I managed to move my head sideways and she merely caught me a glancing blow on the forehead. I buried my face in her hair and fought to retain the grip around her neck. I felt her left arm slip from my grasp only a split second before a bolt of white hot pain shot through my groin as her elbow punched wildly at my abdomen. Fighting to regain control I gripped the flailing arm but only at the expense of having the elbow forcibly lodged into my groin. The combined pain was frightening in its intensity and in a cry of anguish I let her go, recoiling into my seat. I waited for a further assault, none came. As my vision slowly cleared I made out the outline of her slumped form. She was alive, a slow rasping breath emitted from her open mouth. Her eyes opened but only in time to see two hands grab her around the neck and force her head, repeatedly, against the steering wheel.

The distant sound of the ferry horn brought me to my senses. I discarded the lifeless form and climbed out of the car. As my feet hit the tarmac I collapsed in pain. Squatting beside the open door I had to fight the urge to vomit and it seemed like hours before I was able to stand. The damp evening drizzle had formed beads of moisture on the car and using both hands I scooped up the moisture to wash my hands and face. I ran in the shadow of the buildings back to the port and boarded the ferry. The pain in my groin was receding but a large, purple and yellow bruise was my reminder of her desire to live. Retiring to one of the reclining seats I slept, despite the pain, and in the early morning woke to a gloriously refreshed dawn. It was only after I left the ferry that I remembered that I had forgotten to retrieve my one hundred dollars.

It was later that day that the reality of the hollow victory struck. The thrill was absent, the warm glow just a shadow of earlier victories. No self-congratulatory applause, no sense of achievement. When the unthinkable becomes the norm, when the absurd becomes commonplace then the reason for life is questioned. I knew then that I had to expand the unthinkable, embellish the absurd, for what good is appetite when the food is mere fodder?

chapter 29

In September, 1987, Judith Childs met Simon Whittle at a cocktail reception in the Sun Beach Hotel on one of Bermuda's south shore beaches. She was far too immersed in ensuring that the small company gathering was going well to take much notice of him but when they met again three weeks later at a dinner party she recalled enough of their first meeting to be interested.

She found him a witty, if slightly arrogant, dinner companion and was not surprised when he telephoned a few days later and asked her out to dinner. She readily admitted to herself, while waiting for him to collect her, that her work schedule did not allow for serious romance and as such this date would probably go the way of many others in the past. On his own she found the arrogance eroded and the pushiness to impress replaced by a personable individual who did most of the right things and made her feel comfortable and relaxed for the first time in a long while.

In the next few weeks everything happened so fast it just seemed to be orchestrated around her. Sexually experienced at twenty-eight, she had learnt the hard way that you should sleep with someone only when you were sure of their feelings towards you and of course that you felt the same towards them. Thus, when she reviewed why she was living with Simon Whittle after only three weeks, it defied rational explanation.

She had doubts, not about Simon, but about the speed of events. She kept them to herself and decided that she had always been cautious, meticulous in her movements and choices and that perhaps it was time to throw caution to the wind, ride the currents and see where they led. To date it was fun, exciting and exhilarating. The novelty of finding someone at home waiting for you when you finished a late-night banquet, or spending a day just relaxing in someone's company, was so new it was frightening.

She knew that she had to tell her parents at some stage; for now they were a mere inconvenience on the horizon. Judith always felt that she had been a disappointment to her parents. She had a successful career in the hotel industry and yet somehow she seemed to fall short of their expectations of her.

She had been nine when her sixteen-year-old brother, Max, died; and it was another four years before she learned the truth that he had died of a drug overdose. At the time, everyone had muttered darkly about the accident. His name disappeared from conversation over the years but Judith knew that she was now expected to perform for both of them. The September following his death she was sent away to boarding school in Hampshire, an abrupt severing of the friendships and comforts of her parents' London house. She suffered the indignities and rigors of the antiquated school system, returning to her parents home only for holidays. She found her father remote, removed; as if by the death of one sibling he wanted rid of both. Her mother compensated for him by constantly arranging Judith's life for her; there were subtle introductions to other families with eligible sons as she grew older, and plenty of hints about her not needing a career for she was bound to be snapped up. She came to dread the holidays, preferring the lonely sanctuary of school.

Her first major battle with her parents came over the question of university. Her father dismissed the notion of her wanting further education and would hear nothing further on the subject. Her mother, acting as peace-maker, tried in vain to talk her out of it. Judith duly attended Bristol University but it wasn't until she had been there for almost a year and a half that her parents finally accepted it; they rationalised that it was better to let her run for a few years before she settled down, married and had children, than it was to apply the firm hand.

Apart from losing her virginity to an economics lecturer, Judith enjoyed the experience of university and graduated with an honours degree in sociology. From university she further disappointed her parents by joining a hotel management training program for graduates. In the next three years she moved from Cardiff to Liverpool to Chester, each time learning another facet of the hotel trade that had come to fascinate her.

Her contact with her parents was limited to the odd phone call and a visit at Christmas and Easter. During those holidays she had to tolerate the almost constant complaining of her father about the lack of consideration and understanding of the youth of today. The visits were soulless affairs, a charade to conceal indifference, and yet her parents still controlled her. Like strings on a puppet they would pull occasionally and she would respond with a knee-jerk reaction of guilt. She tried as hard as was possible to make them proud of her and yet the more successful she became the greater became their resentment; they could not understand why she was not running a small country house with a Labrador trotting at her side.

Her work became her passion. She was always the one who would volunteer for the late shifts which in turn led her to choose catering management as her specialist field. The hours suited her and were a great excuse to fend off invitations from well-meaning suitors. It was not that she didn't want to be married and have children one day but at the moment it seemed an unnecessary complication. She found it hard enough to fight the chauvinists at work without having to defend her principles in her spare time.

In early 1984, she was appointed Assistant Catering Manager at one of the group's hotels in London and, in her usual style, threw herself wholeheartedly into her work. She liked the excitement and intensity that organising banquets, receptions and cocktail parties produced; the uncertainty of success was always offset by the satisfaction of a job well done.

In 1986 she was promoted to head of the conference department at the Heathrow Airport Hotel and she finally began to believe that she had arrived. The satisfaction in her work now over-rode everything else. Her reputation for providing first-class service preceded her and the hotel had soon built an established clientele for conferences, training seminars and unobtrusive meetings. In her previous positions she had been exposed to a smattering of non-British businessmen but now about forty percent of her time was spent dealing with overseas clients, mainly American. This greater exposure to the worldwide implications of her business was stored away, like most information that she collected, for future reference.

At times, sitting alone in her flat in Staines, she reflected on her absence of friends: she had many colleagues but no true friends. Her relationships with men were entirely unsatisfactory and although she blamed herself she felt no inclination to try and resolve the situation. Her relationship with her parents showed no signs of improving and in an attempt to over-ride these personal failings she immersed herself even more completely in her job.

In August, two weeks before her 28th birthday, her world fell apart. Looking back on it, it was a memorably painful experience and yet she could offer no explanation as to how or why it had happened other then it was convenient, easy and he was there. Earlier that summer a new Assistant Manager had joined the hotel, transferred from one of the resort hotels in Scotland. In his early thirties, he was keen, ambitious and destined for higher things. His home life was what it should be: a wife, two children.

They saw a lot of each other around the hotel, even though his areas of responsibility were quite different to Judith's, and when they met he would always smile and occasionally stop her to discuss certain aspects of the running of her department. His invitation to join him for a drink in his office one night, after a particularly long and tiring day, seemed innocent enough and she accepted without hesitation. She relaxed in his company, forgetting for just a few minutes the exhausting schedule that she was committed to. She enjoyed his conversation and when he moved towards her and kissed her it seemed only natural to respond.

After that they met often, but always in secret: in his office, her apartment and, on the odd occasion, in one of the spare rooms in the hotel. The whole concept of an affair with a married man was anathema to her moral views but for once she quashed her prejudices in favour of a little excitement and romance.

The affair ended as quickly as it had begun and with it went her job. The phone call summoning her to the General Manger's office did not on the surface appear to be threatening. They met regularly to discuss future events and Judith merely assumed that there had been a change of plans with a function or she was to be given the details of a new event.

Her reception was frosty but still she did not pick up the signals. However, within a few minutes she was fully aware of the purpose of the meeting and could feel herself colouring under the accusations of the affair. Denial was out of the question and the threat of resign or else . . . was left hanging in the air. In a fog she returned to her office, drew up her resignation and walked out of the front door of the hotel for the last time.

Her calls to her lover went unanswered. She even risked calling him at home on the assumption that by now he would also have time on his hands. She received a letter from the hotel enclosing a glowing reference and her severance pay, and one call from a colleague expressing his sympathy on the way that she had been treated. She learned then what she had already begun to suspect – that she had been the fall guy and her comrade in arms, after a slap on the wrist, was still in harries.

The injustice of the situation left her quietly fuming. Having considered and dismissed all avenues of revenge, she eventually decided that a holiday was what was needed. She opted not to tell her parents and set off for ten days' relaxation in the Greek Islands. The sun and peace suited her and when she returned to London, greeted by the onset of autumn, she felt much more positive about life. She knew that she wanted to get back into the hotel business, the only question was where. The problem of location was solved for her on the evening of her return.

Phil Covetski had been a guest at the Heathrow Hotel on numerous of his trips from the States and had always made his reservations through Judith. She handled all his arrangements and assisted in setting up meetings for him. Earlier that year she had arranged a training seminar for him and he had been effusive in his praise when it all ran like clockwork. He had been calling her each day since he found out about her resignation and was anxious to talk to her about her future plans before she made any alternative arrangements. They made an appointment to meet for dinner the following week when he would be in London. He asked her to make the reservations and call his secretary with details and she would arrange for a car to pick her up. Hanging up the phone she smiled thinking it was just like the old days, and although she knew little about the American Corporation that Phil Covetski worked for, other than it was called Amtra, she felt that something positive would come from the meeting.

Phil was a large boisterous character with a southern twang to his voice, although for the past eleven years he had called Boston home. They were seated in a small Italian restaurant on the outskirts of Staines. Phil had asked her only once why she had resigned and, seeing that she was reluctant to answer, he dismissed the question as irrelevant. Attacking his calamari with gusto he outlined what he had in mind. The Amtra group of companies was a diversified collection of manufacturing and service industries. As Vice President of its European operations he was responsible for the co-ordination of transport systems, paper manufacturing and a whole host of smaller companies throughout Europe. He went on to explain that in the last two years the company had expanded into the world of travel, had bought three hotels and were looking to expand this new division of the company. Two of the hotels were in Europe – France and Germany; the third was in Bermuda.

Not wanting to appear over-eager Judith waited patiently while the entrées were served and had to endure a further couple of minutes of suspense as the wine was tasted and Phil savoured the first mouthful of his Tournedos Rossini. At last, he explained to her what he was proposing. The Bermuda hotel had a sensational location overlooking the sea, it had easy access to golf courses and provided all the other amenities that vacationing Americans would want; as yet, however, it had no convention trade. He talked at length, right through to coffee, about how the American offshore insurance business worked and how he could see a future for conventions and business meetings that combined business with pleasure. He was quick to point out that other resort destinations such as Mexico and the Cayman Islands were already well-established in this field but, he assured her, there was enough of the cake to go around; and, more importantly, due to its size restrictions, Bermuda was ideal for the small- to medium-sized company, an area that their market research had led them to believe was relatively untapped.

Depositing his napkin on the table, he asked her what she thought. She had to admit an ignorance of the geographical area he was discussing and a total lack of knowledge about the offshore business that he kept referring to but, she hastily added, she knew her business better than most and she was definitely in the market for a job that would challenge her. Phil told her that he had three days of business in London before returning to Boston and he wanted her to accompany him on the trip back. Before she could reply he put his hand in an inside jacket pocket and pulled out an air ticket which he placed in front of her. He laughed as he told her that he had already taken certain liberties and that he hoped that she was not offended. Judith was too stunned to be offended and they parted after agreeing to meet in the departure terminal in three days' time. He told her to bring enough clothes for about a week and that the trip would include a visit to the hotel in Bermuda.

Judith was not easily impressed by the actions of others but, when she finally came down from her cloud of fantasy, even she admitted that Phil Covetski was a master at painting pictures in the imagination. The meetings and interviews in Boston went well and Bermuda was perfect. The image of the pastel-coloured houses offset by the azure-blue water was like a fairy tale. The hotel location on the beach was nothing short of spectacular with every one of the two hundred rooms having a sea view.

Phil was proud to show off his latest acquisition and wanted to ensure that she was correctly sold to the management of the hotel.

Once back in Boston a formal offer of employment was made – an offer that she had no hesitation in accepting. She could now sit back and wait for what Phil called the bullshit formalities in Bermuda to be taken care of. She needed a work permit for Bermuda and was told that it would probably take between six and eight weeks to process. Her new employers suggested that she spend a month putting her affairs in order and then travel to Boston where she could learn more about the group and its activities. She would then be transferred to Bermuda once the permit was approved.

Back in London she paid an unscheduled visit to her parents and told them of her plans. As usual they were less than enthusiastic but Judith was not prepared to let their visions of doom ruin her happiness. She finally took up her position in December 1986 and set about her job with a flair and panache that earned her the nickname of "the White Devil" from her subordinates.

Her lifestyle was not that dissimilar to London. She found herself invited out to more dinner parties and barbecues but still distanced herself from male companionship. Her days off were spent relaxing at the beach and learning more about the history of the isolated paradise in which she now lived. After six months she concluded that life could not have been more idyllic, and then along came Simon Whittle – and added a dimension that she had never known existed.

chapter 30

The island had a soothing effect. I felt my outlook changing. The irritations of the Middle East were to a great extent removed and those that remained were better coped with in this balmy environment. Without consciously realising it, I had somewhere along the line given up marketing and was now into the management and public relations side of the business. I took up golf and traded squash for tennis. I liked the reflection that I saw in the mirror; it looked happier, softer, it laughed more and, ultimately becoming more welcome in its appearance, it was better accepted.

The demons of the past, if not removed, were held in abeyance. Occasionally they rose and spoke their mind. They were not happy with developments. They called, in reasoned voices, for the carnage to continue – not in the wimpish, unfulfilled style of New Zealand but in the strongest traditions of its former glory. Accept the challenge and scale new heights, increase the risk and stoke the fires. They argued singly and collectively, imploring that the end, which I thought I glimpsed, was only the beginning. I was a responsive listener and an accomplished debater. They sensed they were losing me and they were not prepared to give up without a fight.

I saw her first at a cocktail party she had organised. She moved with a grace and assurance that was both striking and off-putting. It was as if she operated within a wall that did not permit trespassers. She harried her subordinates in a way that told them who was in charge but underlined to the guests the simplicity of a well-managed event. Bored by the evening I found myself watching her; she would drift in and out of the room absorbed in dedication. She either failed to observe my attention or very deliberately ignored it. I toyed with the idea of asking her out but decided that the approach was unlikely to work and would probably offend.

I found out her name and a few phone calls to friends managed to unearth a couple who knew her or at least had met her on one occasion. Gentle persuasion was required but they eventually agreed to host a dinner party to which we would both be invited. She appeared not to remember me from the cocktail party but that, in the grand scheme of things, was immaterial. She was attractive in a simple way. Her eyes and mouth were ordinary until she smiled. The effect was like someone turning on a light in a darkened room: it transformed her face into a delightful bubbling countenance. Just as quickly the smile would disappear and I would patiently await its return. She was not overly tall and I was conscious while talking to her that I towered over her.

The dinner conversation was lofty, interspersed with awkward humour. She was quick to argue her point and, although I had to admit that I did not concur with all her views, I found her mind to be as animated as the rest of her personality. She drank little and left before I did.

The inner bodies were ecstatic, drooling with anticipation, chuckling with glee: the victim was ideal; the scenario, though still to be mapped out, would be undeniably intricate.

We dated and within weeks, much to my surprise and I'm sure hers, we were living together. Her work hours made for little flexibility in our planning but despite a few frustrations the arrangement worked. We had very little in common. My interests leaned towards the sporting, hers towards the arts. I took great pleasure in simple things, the flowers, the tress and nature around me, and, while she also delighted in them, she never looked beyond the beauty to see the inner delicacy of the creation. She glossed quickly over her former life which was for weeks taboo. But somehow we grew closer. I realised one night, while waiting for her return, that in previous relationships I had started with a solid block and carved it down to a shape that was comfortable for me. With Judith we were going the other way, starting with nothing and building the pillar. I had no idea if the end result would be any different but it was fascinating to experiment.

I would be lying if I said that all the growth was natural. I was aware, sometimes acutely aware, that the voices were suggesting ideas, writing episodes for my life which I found, despite my reservations, I was following; I argued all the while that I was in control and only taking their advice because it served my purpose. They only spoke when I was alone. When I was with Judith they withdrew, cowed by the formidable presence of emotion over reason. It was their suggestion to ask her to move in. It was their suggestion to buy her a small gift or send flowers. They were in their element. In the past the voices had been fragmented, contradictory, but now they were as one and when one spoke the others would sagely murmur their approval. I was on an escalator to the unknown, being moved slowly but perceptively upwards; the top was shrouded in mist, the open sides were vast chasms of emptiness; and the only way off was to jump.

December arrived. We made plans for Christmas and tentative arrangements for a trip away together in the New Year. I heard a voice snigger and a loud sshhh from somewhere deep inside. The inner turmoil itself produced a satisfying contentment. In the past it threatened, cajoled, even resorted to guilt but this time it was all different. It was a game of skills, educated discussion; anger replaced by persuasion, contempt replaced by challenge.

Judith was different, special. She seemed to have some of the qualities of all of the others, as if an unseen hand had extracted a small part of each of the victims and moulded them within a single form to produce her; but then, perhaps I was mistaken, perhaps I was looking too hard for symmetry where there was only pattern.

Judith was away in Boston the week prior to my birthday. It give me time to think and the contest began in earnest. The voices played "what if" and, drugged by their soporific intensity, I went along. The voices dealt in concepts, not specifics. They made it clear that I was their vessel and I was up to the task. It was only a matter of application. Despite my hesitancy I knew they were right. I spent hours trying to reconcile how and why but no firm plans came to mind. It was only by pushing out doubts and fears that it became clear. What had appeared to be lack of opportunity due to complexity was revealed as the simplest of answers.

I was sitting in my office staring absently across the harbour when the plan in the form of liquid gel eked into my consciousness. Gradually it began to solidify and then to freeze. And there it was, the answer, simplistic and brilliant.

The voices were stilled, respectful. They did not gloat; in fact they left in orderly fashion.

Leaving the office early I hurried from the building determined to test the limits of guaranteed success.

Bermuda had once been served by a railway that ran from one end of the island to the other, primarily along the coastline. The advent of the motor car and escalating costs had brought about the premature closure of the line; however, the route the train had followed was still very much in evidence, and the Bermuda Government and the National Trust had cleaned up the trails and reopened them as picturesque walks that highlighted the splendour of the coastal areas. One such trail ran behind an area known as Ferry Reach. The route stretched from the oil storage terminal on North Shore to Whale Bone bay. If you push on past the bay you reach the water's edge and the remains of the pylons that supported the bridge between Coney Island and Whale Bone Bay. The area was secluded, with only one house nestled in the trees that formed the boundary of the overgrown public park.

It was to this area that I headed upon leaving the office. The skeleton plan was to murder Judith at my house, put the body in her car and transport it under cover of darkness to Ferry Reach. I would deposit the body in the water, by the old pylons, to coincide with an outgoing tide, then swim the short distance to Coney Island. Using the foliage as cover, I would make my way back to the house which was only a half mile from the far end of Coney Island.

Taking an early evening stroll along the railway trail I added flesh to the bones.

The whole charade was designed to imply suicide. With the fickle nature of the sea the body might be discovered within hours, days or not at all. If the death was supposed to be from drowning there should be salt water in the lungs. Collecting sea water in a bottle and keeping it at the house would not be a problem; getting it into a dead body might prove difficult but I had no way of testing it. The swim would have to be done naked with clothes and a small towel secured in a rubbish bag tied around the wrist. A swimming cap would be needed to ensure that my hair didn't get wet. The rubbish bag and hat could be disposed of in the hedgerow on Coney Island and the towel would be wrapped around my waist and hidden under my clothes. Once I made it to the end of the road where the house was, my defence was that I was out looking for Judith. The scenario was simple – Judith had stormed out of the house after an argument and taken her car. The car would be found, probably early the following morning, with the keys in the ignition, where I had left it at Ferry Reach.

Not foolproof but not bad.

I returned home. The house itself was ideal for the purpose. It was set back from the road and provided perfect shelter for getting the body into the boot without being seen. I settled into a favourite chair to savour the plan and a twenty-year-old malt, and gradually drifted into sleep.

Around midnight I awoke in terror, with cold, clammy sweat on my forehead and neck. I could not immediately recall where I was or what had awakened me. From nowhere the question, "why?" escaped my lips; the answer from somewhere in the dark echoed back, "because." The terror eased and my breathing returned to something approaching normal.

On the Friday afternoon I met Judith at the airport. A spur-of-the-moment decision to buy some flowers on the way was greatly appreciated by her and we talked easily in the car. I could not fathom out my feelings: one side argued that it was great to have her back and that I had missed her, the other side said, "Crap." I was ultimately glad that indiscretion had not robbed me of opportunity.

We dined out on the Monday night as Judith would be working late on Tuesday. Her birthday gift the following morning was two water-colour prints of the Maine coast. The colours matched my mood: subtle, but ominously dark in the distance. A bottle of champagne and relaxation in bed was the order of the night once Judith returned, and by eleven-thirty she was asleep. I moved slightly to disengage my arms and rolled her onto her back. She murmured softly but her steady breathing returned within seconds. I gently placed two pillows over her wrists and, picking up a third, delicately straddled her. Looking down I was struck, not for the first time, by the ordinariness of her features. The voices, silent for so long, began to urge, setting up a rhythmic, hypnotic beat in the front of my mind. I moved the pillow from my chest to within a few inches of her mouth. I adjusted my weight to bring my knees on top of her wrists, which were protected from bruising by the pillows, and sank forward to extinguish her life.

At the last second her eyes opened and a suppressed smile from a dream ignited her face and reflected into her eyes. In the same split second a shutter slammed down, trapping the voices in mid-syllable, silencing them.

I rolled to one side of her.

She sat up, the smile replaced by a puzzled countenance of concern. I reached out, took her hand in mine and asked her to marry me.

part four

1992 – 1993

chapter 31

"For Christ's sake, Cynthia, what the hell do you expect me to do? I have to go . . . "

Alan Rogers sat with his head bowed over the telephone as he listened to his wife's tirade. She rolled out the usual litany of complaints, including the final one of, "why don't you get a proper job?" before slamming the phone down.

He sat holding the silent instrument conscious of the guilt which it exuded. Finally placing it back in its holder, he swivelled sideways in his chair and stared distractedly at the small triangular courtyard two storeys below. The swirling wind, trapped within the confines of the buildings, threw splashes of rain against the window and the one sad excuse for a tree in the concrete mass bent its limbs as if to apologise for its mere presence.

Rogers' thoughts followed a familiar pattern: how the hell had he got into this mess? In the early days there had been time for everything. He travelled constantly but still there seemed to be time for the odd fling on home turf. He had run, worked out and watched his diet. The future had looked rosy. Then, without warning, it had all started to fall apart.

He had met Cynthia at a Christmas party in 1982 and had dated her for almost two years. She seemed to appreciate his absences and welcome his returns. Marriage had followed as a matter of course and for two years everything had been fine. Now, six years later, they had two children and his absences were construed as intentional; the arguments and painful silences had become monotonous.

When Chief Inspector Mann had been pensioned off, there had been other changes: he was given the permanent position of police liaison between the United States and the Home Office; not that he objected, but it appeared to him that it had just happened and not been by his choice. He still worked diligently and thoroughly at his job but was constantly aware of the bright new stars of tomorrow that were matching his footsteps today. He waited patiently for his next promotion but somehow it never seemed to come.

"Shit!" he exclaimed to no one in particular. The door opened and a WPC walked in carrying a plain blue folder.

"She didn't take it too well?"

"Agghh." Rogers collapsed face down on his desk. He tilted his head and looked sideways at the WPC. "No, she didn't take it well." The WPC placed the folder on the desk and turned to leave. "Come on, Brenda, what am I doing wrong? How do I juggle all this in the air at once and prevent my hair falling out?"

Brenda looked at him sympathetically and sighed. "You don't, or more specifically you can't. I'm sure she still loves you and when she married you she knew that she was marrying the job and that the job would always come first. Now when the going gets tough she wants you within reach, not constantly in your playground across the Atlantic. She doesn't blame you but that doesn't stop her resenting you for it."

"Thank you, oh Wise One, but what do I do?"

"Easy, put your life in rewind, go back eight years. Tell her it's all over instead of proposing, stay single, and that paunch and receding hairline will all be history. Now be a good boy and get home in time for Christmas." Brenda turned on her heels and left the room.

"If I'm not, my balls will be a late holiday decoration hung in our house," Rogers shouted to the closing doors. He heard laughter from the far side of the door as he picked up the file. He already knew the contents but, not trusting other people's abilities, he checked the reservation on the ticket BA 101 to New York: the following morning, December 6th, 1100 hours. Drug traffickers had no respect for holidays, wedding anniversaries or birthdays and the call from Sam Duffield, although expected, had annoyed him when it came.

Surveillance of a farm in upstate New York had been going on for over a year now. So far they had managed to track the incoming sources of drugs mainly from Colombia via Miami and a few deserted airfields in South Carolina, but it was the distribution network that had held the FBI's attention for so long. Six months ago

Rogers had been able to confirm that a large drug haul in London had come from the farm in New York but the exact route was not known.

Now, following a joint operation, they had been able to establish that the drugs were being shipped in crates of machinery and repacked at the premises they were now surveying. The work involved in monitoring just one of a hundred such different operations was both painstaking and tedious. It was only when the pay-off came in the form of arrests that the months of tedium paid dividends, and even then the case had to be watertight or the low life involved were likely to walk free on a technicality.

The call from Duffield told him that a new consignment was ready for dispatch and that this time, as agreed, they would be moving in to make the arrests once the shipment was on the way. The intent was to substitute undercover agents as the arrests were made in the hope that by the time the consignment arrived in London for unloading, the British end of the operation would be none the wiser and Rogers' team could step in and clear up their end. Duffield wanted Rogers in New York with him and then they would fly back to England together to form part of the welcoming party in London. Rogers also guessed that Duffield was keen on another trip to England to look up the merry widow he had befriended in Hampstead on his last visit there seven months ago. Rogers went along with it because it was all part of the job and if it went according to plan some fifty or sixty people were going to be arrested on either side of the Atlantic; if, as a bonus, Duffield got to pursue his extracurricular activities at the American taxpayers' expense, so be it.

Rogers tidied his desk into some sort of order and walked out into the unwelcoming winter's day. As he boarded the underground he felt confident that he would be home for Christmas but he also had an uneasy feeling that the consignment of drugs could well arrive at the same time: Christmas was a good time for the importers to try and clear customs.

The flight into JFK was uneventful. The night before, Cynthia had for once been contrite, almost apologetic, and after the children had been put to bed they had a couple of drinks, relaxed and talked. It was at times like this that he knew why he had married her; she offered the security and stability that his day to day life lacked and ultimately she represented good in contrast to the evil that he fought constantly.

Duffield met him from the plane and, flashing his badge for all to see, whisked Rogers through all the formalities; only stopping long enough at immigration for Rogers to have his passport stamped by an official who, in deference to Duffield's authority, completely ignored him. Duffield was full of his usual good cheer. He treated his younger colleague from London as his pet, always keen to display the brittle efficiency of the FBI and show him off to his colleagues while feigning indifference. Rogers and Duffield had worked together for many years and Rogers had a healthy respect for the streetwise American. He knew that Duffield would have been kicked out of the British force years ago but within the FBI he was an enigma, respected for his phenomenal success in closing down drug factories not just in the States but also in the Far East as well. He was also a loner, working outside of the auspices of the Unites States Drug Enforcement Agency. Duffield appeared unperturbed that as soon as you closed down one route another one opened and he merely viewed the South American connection as yet another challenge.

Talking all the while he led Rogers back through the departures lounge and opened a door marked "No Admittance". The ensuing alarm brought two security officers running with guns drawn; Duffield merely kept walking, flashing a smile along with his badge, and politely told the security guards to "fuck off" in response to their derogatory remarks about cops. At the bottom of two flights of stairs he ushered Rogers through a swing door and they emerged into the cold air of the December morning. A driver reading a newspaper in the front seat of a waiting car quickly threw it to one side and jumped out to open the rear door. Never one to pass on free attention, Duffield waited for his door to be opened. Rogers climbed in unaided.

Rogers realised they were on the tarmac and watched in dreaded fascination as the car set off at high speed, coasting between huge jets before coming to a halt in front of two large hangers which showed the tail fin of a plane trapped snugly between the giant closed doors. Rogers climbed out while Duffield again waited for his door to be opened. "Your chariot awaits." Duffield bowed politely to the right where a blue and gold helicopter was waiting and in no time at all, much to Rogers' amazement, they were airborne and flying over the borough of Queens.

The noise was deafening. Duffield indicated earphones which Rogers slipped on and began adjusting the controls on the right ear-piece. He saw Duffield switch the knob on his headset and, although he saw his lips move, he heard no words. The pilot's head nodded and Duffield's New York twang was back telling him they were going on a tourist ride before heading up to Rochester.

As the helicopter swept over Staten Island, Rogers could see the whole of Manhattan laid out like some jewelled carpet ahead. It was one of those crisp clear mornings in New York when the sun shone brilliantly which, combined with the sub-zero temperatures, made for excellent visibility. They swung over the top of the famous Staten Island ferries and then did a circle of the Statue of Liberty. This was the closest that Rogers had ever been to the statue and he was impressed by the intricate detail. He could clearly see the stains where the cleaning process used in her recent face lift had left her with marks that resembled tears.

"Look at the nose," shouted Duffield. "Definitely Jewish."

They followed the course of the Hudson River. The financial district was dwarfed by the twin towers of the World Trade Centre, with the Woolworth building adding a touch of class to the glass and concrete structures that surrounded it. The teeming traffic appeared to be blocked everywhere and the numerous buildings being constructed in mid-town reached up like severed fingers. In the midst of this disorder was the triangular beauty of the Flat Iron building and the solid majesty of the Empire State building. Other buildings stood out and although Rogers knew some of them Duffield was not to be denied his running commentary and pointed out the Chrysler building, Madison Square Garden, Trump Tower and the Gulf & Western building standing guard on the southern edge of Central Park. Stating the obvious Duffield also indicated Central Park and Harlem in the distance as they flew over the George Washington Bridge. Pointing to the left into New Jersey Duffield indicated Giant's Stadium, obviously forgetting that on a previous trip he had taken Rogers there to watch the Giants play. Swinging in his seat the other way Duffield shouted, "Yankee Stadium." He offered no further explanation but Rogers was fully aware that it was the home of what many Americans considered to be one of the greatest American institutions – the New York Yankees.

As they left the city and headed north Duffield reverted to type and started discussing the case. He interrupted his own dialogue only once to point out West Point military academy nestled against the banks of the Hudson River. The pilot interjected at one stage to tell them they were passing over the state capital of Albany and that their route would now take them directly into Rochester.

Rogers was relieved when they finally landed. He did not like flying in anything so small as a helicopter, particularly over such a long distance. A car was waiting for them at the airport but it was obvious that whatever influence Duffield had in New York City it did not extend to Rochester as they had to drive themselves. In keeping with his normal approach to life Duffield drove straight to a diner and was half-way through the door when he thought to enquire if Rogers was hungry.

"I recommend the steak and eggs here; some of the best I've ever had."

"Fine with me," Rogers indicated to the waitress as she poured them both coffee.

"Medium rare, eggs over easy." Duffield gave her one of his winning smiles. She turned to Rogers who nodded his concurrence.

"So, any news?" Duffield asked, taking a huge pull at his steaming coffee.

"Not much. No promotion, same old grind and it was still raining when I left."

"I don't mean the frigging weather report, Sherlock, any news of Heather?"

"Heather, ummph . . . ?"

Duffield threw a screwed-up paper napkin at Rogers who finally pulled a letter from his inside pocket and laid it next to Duffield's knife and fork. Duffield tried hard not to grab it instantly, but lost, and was absorbed for the next few minutes reading, and occasionally chuckling. Rogers was amused to note that he mouthed the words as he read.

The food was as good as Duffield had promised although Rogers could never get over the mammoth portions that American restaurants, and diners in particular, served. The twelve-ounce sirloin steak was served with three eggs, french fries, a side salad and three slices of buttered toast. The coffee was constantly topped up and, although Rogers declined desert, Duffield consumed a hearty slab of key lime pie, washed down with yet more coffee.

Pulling out of the car park they headed east from Rochester and were soon into thinly populated farming country. The plan as outlined by Duffield was fairly simple: just before nightfall the house would be surrounded and the occupants would be arrested. This assumed that the consignment of drugs left as scheduled that afternoon. The other key players in the drugs ring would be picked up systematically from then on, including the dockers on both sides of the Atlantic who were pivotal in getting the goods through customs. All that was left after that was to pass the case to Rogers to wrap up the finer details of the British end of the operation.

Duffield slowed the car as they rounded a bend. "There on the left, that's the property. The goods are packed in the large barn on the right."

They were past before Rogers could make any observations but he had enough time to note that the buildings were wide open which would make surrounding them easy but also meant that if the occupants wanted to shoot it out they would be very exposed. Guessing his thoughts Duffield reassured him that by the time they moved in later there would only be a few people in the building and they would only be there to clean up; the major players he stressed would be arrested elsewhere. He swung the car off the road, up a paved drive and brought it to a stop at the rear of a barn. They climbed out and entered the barn via a stable door. Climbing into the loft Rogers noticed all the signs of surveillance including cots for members of the team to sleep on.

The next four hours were an agonising wait. The barn in which they were housed was about half a mile from the drug-packing operation and was well hidden from the main road by a row of Douglas firs. However, from the loft they had a straight line of vision into the barn and farmhouse that had come under so much scrutiny. Half-way through the long afternoon a flat-bed truck arrived and was promptly concealed inside the barn. About an hour later it pulled back out of the barn with three crates strapped to its back and thereafter six people left the premises in two vehicles fifteen minutes apart. In the bone-chilling cold of the late afternoon a peaceful quiet settled over the seemingly deserted countryside.

The arrests went like clockwork. Rogers always felt self-conscious participating in the commando-style raids that the US police adopted; charging at doors with guns drawn. In this instance they met no resistance but on other occasions he had seen men shot and had himself been shot at twice. Satisfied that the plan was running smoothly Duffield and Rogers left to arrest Saul Stein, president of one of the local banks. He had been one of the men leaving the farm that afternoon.

Simultaneously, four deputies arrested two of Stein's colleagues at their homes. The second car, with its three occupants, was pulled over on the interstate to Boston and two men and one woman were arrested at around the same time as Saul Stein. Twenty people were arrested in New York City and the records of a law firm in California and one in Florida were seized.

On the way to a hotel for the night, Duffield remarked that the easy bit was over – the hard part was keeping all of the arrested people in jail long enough for the whole operation to succeed.

The next couple of days were uneventful. Arriving back in New York from Rochester on a scheduled flight they were met by copious quantities of paperwork. Working from his downtown office

Duffield tried to clear everything as quickly as possible but it was still late on the afternoon of the 10th before they were finally free. The good news was that for once, in a rare show of inter-state co-operation, three sympathetic judges had listened to their case and agreed to hold all defendants, denying them bail, for a period of three weeks, by which time the results of the rest of the operation would be known. The consignment was safely aboard a Panamanian-registered freighter bound from Boston to London and the port of Tilbury. Duffield felt pleased with himself and he knew what he wanted as a reward. It was a very willing Rogers that followed him to a mid-town Irish bar and restaurant to eat, drink and make merry.

Rogers noticed that Duffield was beginning to show the signs of age common to the job – the large bags under his eyes hanging only just above the jowly features that made the face look so lived in; the rotund frame, testament to too much booze and hamburgers or hot dogs on the run. Rogers was struck by the similarity of policemen all over the world. He easily recalled Somerset pubs of years gone by when Andrew Daniels would adopt the same thoughtful pose, a vulture brooding, before emptying his drink and luxuriating in the calm it brought.

They had been drinking for a couple of hours and both were subdued after the mental pressures of the past few days.

"They should make the fucking stuff legal." Duffield had pulled his head up from his drink and it struck Rogers that he was addressing someone sitting behind him. "The economic cost to this country alone of attempting to keep pace with the tidal wave of shit is staggering. At least if you make it legal the government can make the profits and you can eliminate the pushers, the traffickers, and take it out of the schoolyards." Without shifting his gaze he tossed down the remainder of his drink and signalled for a refill. "Regulate the shit out of it and let guys like you and me retire peacefully."

"You can't believe that. What . . . "

"You wanna bet I can't? I didn't use to. I had dreams and aspirations that we could win. But now . . . " Duffield gestured emptily with his hands, "you see enough kids die and you become immune. It happened in Vietnam. The liberals adopt it as a cause and soon the conservatives see the political mileage. The band wagon is rolling, the groundswell is growing and hell, we're outta 'Nam. We couldn't win then and we can't win now. Surrender to the bastards and then blow them out of the water legally. I shoulda been a politician. I'd show the fuckers the right way."

Rogers smiled at the thought. "You might make a good dictator but I don't see you as the democratically elected leader of the free world. Not yet anyway."

The food arrived – more steak, more calories. The conversation ebbed and flowed, Duffield regained his good humour and by late evening neither he nor Roger was feeling much pain.

Leaving the bar shortly after midnight they were discussing their plans for the flight to London when Duffield's eyes caught the flashing lights of a New York squad car parked in front of a brownstone half a block away. A small crowd was congregated outside and although all he wanted to do was go home and sleep he felt compelled to wander over and find out what was up. Rogers followed in his wake.

"What happened, son?" Duffield flashed his badge at the young rookie at the front door.

"Female body found in the second floor apartment." He added, "sir," as an afterthought.

Duffield pushed past indicating over his shoulder that Rogers was with him. Climbing the single flight of stairs Duffield again flashed his badge and walked straight past the cop at the door.

"C'mon, Duffield, fuck off. This isn't your jurisdiction." A short, overweight figure in a battered fedora and raincoat was staring aggressively at the two of them, his short, meaty fingers hooked into the loops of his trousers.

"Just passing, Kelly. Thought you might need a hand."

Ignoring Kelly's attempt to stop him Duffield walked through a small passageway and into the bedroom. A table lamp provided the only illumination and the thin stream of light that it cast displayed the naked form of a young girl lying across the bed. Rogers stood silently behind Duffield. The girl gave the impression of being asleep with her hands thrown above her head. As his eyes adjusted to the light and his thought process struggled to function through a haze of alcohol Rogers realised that she was tied hand and foot to the bed frame. A flood of memory engulfed him as he stared in his mind at the lifeless form of Angela Logan.

Pulling his thoughts into some sort of order he knew that it wasn't her, but the slight form and the bondage had thrown him. As Duffield walked over to the bed, Rogers muttered quietly, "Strangulation."

"Whadaya say?" Duffield's guttural tones seemed to fill the room.

"Strangulation. She was strangled, wasn't she?"

Duffield gave him a quizzical look. Kelly had also moved into the room and although Rogers had not seen it, Duffield had noted the glint in his eye. Duffield leaned over the body and, without disturbing anything, noted the bruising on either side of the throat. He looked up to say something but was stopped by Rogers' fixed stare. Following the line of his eyes Duffield's gaze came to rest on an empty champagne bottle that was lying on its side on the small table next to the bed.

Over Kelly's protestations Duffield led Rogers out of the building and back to the bar they had recently vacated. When they had two scotches in front of them Duffield spoke, "How'd you know?"

Rogers was still stunned by the events and his voice was flat, devoid of emotion. "It was an educated guess. Seven or eight years ago I saw an identical murder scene, photographs of it anyway, in a London hotel; the bondage, the champagne and the strangulation. In addition, the body is almost identical; slim, young, and it was around this time of year, just before Christmas . . . Duffield waited for him to continue but Rogers had lapsed into silence.

"So who did it?"

"That's the odd part – we never got anyone for it."

Over the next twenty minutes Rogers recalled all he could about the murder. While he was talking his mind relived his visit to Saudi Arabia, and the name of Simon Whittle, which he had not heard for almost a decade, came to him with such vivid clarity that it surprised him. He became aware of Duffield waving a hand in front of his face.

"Wakey wakey, Sherlock. C'mon, it's almost certainly a coincidence. There are only . . . "

Rogers interrupted almost as if he had not heard. "Check the local area and see if you have a resident called Whittle, Simon Whittle. He's British, age about late-thirties." Duffield was looking at him with growing concern. "If he doesn't live here, see if he travelled through New York in the last few days." He saw the expression in Duffield's eyes. "Hey, come on, indulge me. Call it my Christmas present."

The pounding in his temples would not go away and pulling the bed covers over his head did nothing to stop the dull thud.

"C'mon, asshole, open the door."

Rogers pulled himself upright and realised that the pounding was both internal and external. He swayed to his feet and lurched awkwardly towards the door. He knew the voice was Duffield's but was having difficulty in placing the rest of his surroundings or accounting for why his head felt like it had been used as a punch bag. The shaft of light that followed Duffield into the room temporarily blinded him and he was only vaguely conscious of Duffield talking at a rate of knots, breezing past him and depositing a brown paper bag on the table.

Duffield hauled back the curtains to reveal the dawn of another splendid New York morning. Rogers was having difficulty with the light and he collapsed into the nearest chair. Duffield placed the brown bag in his hand and Rogers had to fight the urge to throw up as his eyes encountered a chilli dog with the works when he looked inside. Duffield was behind him closing the door and as he slowly came into focus Rogers saw that he was in the process of taking a large bite from a similar breakfast. He dashed for the sanctuary of the bathroom. Emerging two minutes later he felt better but only just. He was aware that Duffield had commenced talking again.

"Well, whadaya think? Do we arrest him? C'mon, Sherlock, get your act in gear. Hey, you don't want breakfast? Then allow me." Duffield took Rogers' bag and consumed half of the congealed mess in one bite. Rogers turned his head away in order to fight down the nausea that consumed him. He had no idea what was going on but the word "arrest" had registered a spark somewhere deep down. Holding up his hands to form a "T" he called time out. Duffield, in mid bite, paused.

"What the hell is going on? You wake me in the middle of the night with rancid hog flesh and talk in sodding riddles. Arrest who?"

Duffield looked hurt. "Rancid hog flesh? These are Jewish dogs. No hog has been within a mile of these and it's almost 6.30. Arrest Whittle. Whadaya think?"

Arrest Whittle, arrest Whittle . . . Slowly the door in his mind opened and the light went on. "Whittle – you've found him?"

"Sure have. Moved into a house in New Jersey two and a half years ago, works for an insurance company in the city."

Rogers sat and stared at Duffield. The implications of what he had just been told sent fresh bolts of pain through his brain. When he asked, demanded, of Duffield the previous night to check the notion out for him, it had been the result of an unreasoned reaction, the ramblings of a mind befuddled by drink. In the cold light of morning the truth was frighteningly real. He reached across the bed to pick up his watch and stared at it as if to confirm what Duffield had said about the time.

"How would he get into the city from New Jersey?"

"Depends. He lives with his wife in a town called Edison in the middle of the state. Works downtown. He could drive or take a bus but more than likely he takes a local train, meets the PATH and comes into the World Trade Centre."

"Path, what path?"

"Port Authority Trans Hudson, it's a train system, a subway, that connects from Penn station in Newark, New Jersey, to midtown and downtown Manhattan."

"Give me five minutes and we're off."

By the time they arrived at the World Trade Centre, just after 7.15, there was already a steady stream of people emerging from the cavernous exit that led into the bowels of the subway to the main concourse. Despite Duffield's protests that the chances of spotting him were remote, Rogers was determined to see the exercise through. By leaning against the brick surround that guarded the exit he could look down onto the escalators and see the arriving commuters. By 7.30 the steady stream had become a flood and for the next hour thousands of bodies spewed onto the concourse where they scurried, like ants to their various destinations. They both stood and waited and watched. Duffield ferried large plastic cups of coffee from a nearby vendor and by 8.30 Rogers was beginning to believe that the idea had been foolish, but having waited this long he was not going to give up now. And then he was there, Simon Whittle, riding the escalator oblivious to his surroundings. He appeared wearing a grey overcoat, with a red scarf around his neck, and carried a book under his arm. He dismounted from the escalator and, driven by the masses, turned left and made for the exit that would take him into the morning air. Rogers pointed him out to Duffield who nodded and watched the retreating figure.

Sitting in a corner booth away from the rapidly receding commuter frenzy Duffield ordered a second prodigious breakfast. Rogers settled for a toasted English muffin and a large orange juice.

"So, Sherlock, what did that prove?"

"It proved that it was him. I had to be sure that it was the same Simon Whittle."

"What the . . . Why didn't you ask me? Goddamn Brits, no brains." With that he pulled a photograph from his jacket pocket and flicked it across the table. The upside-down, smiling visage of Simon Whittle stared up at him.

chapter 32

The flight back to London was enlivened by the presence of Duffield. In the years that Rogers had known him Duffield had not let much in the way of work get to him, but it had taken a lengthy, argumentative explanation to convince him that they were not letting a murderer walk the streets of Manhattan.

"Come on, Sam, it was a hunch. You can't arrest someone on the strength of a hunch. If – and it's a big if – there is a case against Whittle, then Angela Logan and the dead woman in the Manhattan apartment might not be the only two. Barging in and alerting him at this stage will only make the job harder in the long run."

"So whadaya gonna do? What's the plan?"

"I don't know. Let's get this drugs deal out of the way and then review some files in London, okay?"

Duffield was not okay but he knew that Rogers held the cards and at least for now he was going to have to go along with him. The information that had been given by Rogers at the murder scene in the presence of Kelly had led to an unsatisfactory meeting with his superior before departing for London. Duffield tried to pass off Rogers' diagnosis of death as an educated guess, similar to a scenario that he had witnessed before. It cut no ice but, like all good things in life, it bought him time.

Rogers had spent his last free hours in New York shopping furiously at FAO Schwartz, the famous toy store. This meant that their passage through British customs was slow and resulted in Rogers paying a hefty duty bill. However, he reasoned, his

Christmas shopping was now over and Cynthia would be pleased that he had remembered the children while he had been away.

Dropping Duffield off at his hotel, Rogers arranged to meet him at his office the following morning to review the Logan case. The plans were subject to change pending any developments in the drug case.

Cynthia was relieved to see Alan back in one piece and greeted him with a peck on the cheek, while in a flat in Hampstead a lonely widow welcomed her American lover back with significantly greater enthusiasm.

Rogers had called central records the previous evening to request hard copies of the files pertaining to the Logan case, and when he reached his office the following morning his desk was covered with open files. Duffield, with Danish and coffee in hand, was reading avidly. Rogers had had little time to think since he walked into the darkened Manhattan apartment but what little there had been was spent dredging his memory to try and bring all the facts of long ago events into focus. He was struck by the horrifying thought that Whittle could have been killing for ten years. He thought of Duffield's concerns but dismissed them, together with his own notional fancies, as highly unlikely. It was sometime during the flight back to London that he recalled the hotel maid; he had been so preoccupied with the memory of Angela Logan that he had forgotten about the second murder. He kept pulling up scenes of Jeddah and Riyadh and Whittle in his alien environment.

"Morning. Sleep late? December 10th 1982, December 10th 1992, what else was December 10th?"

Duffield paused to drink his coffee but his eyes held those of Rogers as Rogers discarded his overcoat and threw it over a chair in the corner.

"Christ, how do I know? Hitler's birthday?"

"Close, but no cigar – Whittle's birthday." Rogers reacted as if he had been struck by an electric cattle prod. His arm shot out as he demanded the file.

"Woo, testy this morning, Sherlock." Duffield moved the file out of Rogers' reach and began to read. "Date of birth. December 10th, 1968." The expression on Rogers' face told Duffield the answer but he asked the question anyway. "You didn't know that?"

He handed the file to Rogers who sank into a chair. A secretary walked in unannounced and placed a mug of tea in front of Rogers. Duffield winked at her and asked for more coffee. She left without any acknowledgement from Rogers.

"How on earth did I miss it?"

Duffield longed to reply but sensed that this was not the time to be flippant and held his peace. Rogers answered his own question. Addressing the papers in front of him he simply shook his head and muttered that he had never actually asked to see the whole file, nor had it been offered for his perusal. He had followed one lead for Interpol before the Yard had taken the case over. Whittle had certainly not volunteered the information and he had never thought to ask but there it was on the inside cover of the file, typed by some clerk who had dug the information up from Somerset House or the passport office. He threw the file on the table in disgust, not because this now proved that Whittle was the murderer, it didn't, but out of anger at himself for having had a piece of information at his disposal and missing it.

The secretary returned with Duffield's coffee. "Tea, please," requested Rogers.

Duffield pushed the mug in front of Rogers closer, bringing the contents to his attention, and remarked to the secretary that it was the jet lag that was addling his brain. Seeing Rogers' dejected countenance he attempted to repair the shattered ego. "C'mon, Sherlock, it may be irrelevant, coincidence, the proverbial red herring. After all . . . " he was prevented from saying anything further by a knock on the door.

The secretary's head reappeared and informed Rogers that his ship had come in and he was required at Tilbury.

The drive to the docks was painfully slow in the early morning traffic. The UK end of the operation had been handled by the Yard in Rogers' absence and reading the file at home the previous night he had been pleasantly surprised to find that things were running very much to the plan that he had advocated.

In a windowless office in Tilbury he introduced Duffield to the others present and presided over a quick briefing to ensure that everyone was aware of the importance of what was going on. The three crates would be unloaded last as they were in the hold and they would be cleared through customs in the normal way. The tractor trailer that was to collect them for their journey to their final destination, a warehouse about eighty miles west of London, was already outside the docks. As in the States, people would be arrested one by one as they handled the cargo. There would then be a final swoop at the warehouse once the key figures had arrived to check the consignment.

Having seen the crates unloaded and secured to the flat-bed, Rogers and Duffield set off for the drive to Wiltshire. A hurried call to Cynthia informing her that he would be away for two days brought anger as opposed to the animated longing that Duffield received when he telephoned Heather.

The drive was tedious, the traffic heavy, the roadworks endless and the weather foul. Rogers was quiet, brooding. Duffield attempted to lighten the atmosphere but gave up when all he got for his troubles were grunts and nods. He finally settled back in his seat, closed his eyes and fantasised about his future with Heather.

They booked into a small provincial hotel in Swindon and within an hour were meeting again with most of the people that had been at Tilbury that morning, plus some of the local police force. The plan was gone over once more; the details were simple but precise. The operation was now ninety percent successful but to get a perfect score they were well aware that they could not afford any mistakes at this stage.

When Rogers had finished his briefing the Detective Chief Inspector for Swindon stepped forward to give a few words of encouragement and asked if anyone had any questions.

Duffield spoke up. "When do we get issued with firearms?" He knew the answer but just felt like bugging the locals.

"Duffield, you are fully aware that this is England, not America. We have no reason to believe that the recipients of this cargo will be armed and, as such, neither will you be."

Before Duffield could reply, he had turned and walked out of the room. Duffield looked across the room at Rogers who, for the first time that day, smiled.

As usual the waiting was the hardest part. Rogers did not bring up the Whittle case, so Duffield didn't either. The following afternoon, December 18th, two cars pulled up at the warehouse. It was quickly assessed that all the players, bar one, were now present and the order was given by Rogers for the operation to proceed. The building was surrounded and in keeping with British police policy Rogers stood outside the main doors with a megaphone and announced who he was, told the occupants that they were surrounded and that they should give themselves up peaceably.

Duffield stood at Rogers' side, marvelling at the stupidity of their exposure but trusting in the innate decency of the British criminal.

The silence after the noise of the megaphone hung in the air. The cold damp drizzle of the afternoon matched the grey of the deserted area. A rook screeched as it took flight from the branches of a nearby tree; the noise punctuating the silence caused most of the men around the building to stir. Duffield himself was taken by surprise. He turned his body to look towards the bird. He was half hidden behind Rogers when the large sliding door of the warehouse was pushed open. A figure ran out with a pump-action rifle in his arms and fired indiscriminately as he veered to his left. Rogers and Duffield both threw themselves to the ground, Rogers with a cry of pain. A further single shot rang out and the gunman fell. It had only been a few seconds but the returning silence seemed to take minutes to permeate the scene.

A voice called from inside the building that everyone was coming out with their hands in the air. Duffield was aware of a figure standing over him, holding a rifle trained on the open doorway as a steady stream of figures emerged. The police moved quickly to intercept and handcuff them. As Duffield rolled onto his side to assist Rogers, a stabbing pain shot through his right leg and, looking down, he discovered blood oozing from a hole in his trousers. Rogers was unconscious and a stream of blood was flowing from his side.

The story that was pieced together for them over the next twenty-four hours was that the operation had been a complete success: some forty people had been arrested, the drugs had been impounded and a lone madman with a rifle had been shot and killed by a police marksmen from a van that had been parked behind Rogers.

Rogers himself had been shot in the side just above his hip and the bullet had passed through him and lodged in Duffield's right leg. Duffield was recovering after surgery to remove the bullet and Rogers, despite losing a lot of blood, was expected to make a fairly speedy recovery.

"So, Sherlock how you feeling?" Duffield, in an ill-fitting bathrobe, flopped down on the side of Rogers' bed, his right leg extended in front of him. He chose to ignore the look of pain that passed across Rogers' face as he landed on the bed. "Just stopped by to say thanks for taking the speed off of the bullet. Could have rendered me a serious injury if you hadn't been there."

Rogers smiled. "If I'd known I was going to deflect it I would have aimed it at your head where it couldn't have done any damage."

"The nurse warned me you might be delirious. Hey, I gather we are heroes, true blue ones at that. You seen the papers?" Duffield pulled the local paper from his dressing-gown pocket. "I love the quote from the esteemed ass down here." Duffield coughed and then began to read. "We considered the necessity for arming our officers but in our estimation we felt it was unlikely that the suspects would be armed and as such, a decision was taken to have just one back-up marksman who in the event proved to be sufficient." Duffield threw the paper on the bed. "Sufficient, my ass. Someday you guys will learn that standing in the open and asking a bunch of criminals to give themselves up is not the safest way of earning a living, but what the hell, this is England, criminals aren't armed over here. Have you seen Cynthia?"

"Yes, she was in earlier, all tears and forgiveness."

"I asked them for a double bed as Heather was visiting but I'm still waiting."

The door opened and a young nurse walked in carrying a tray with some tablets on it. "Mr Duffield, what are you doing here? Mr Rogers needs his rest. Come on, out."

"Just going, nurse. I'll go back, strip off and wait for you to come and give me a bed bath, or if you have time you can sit on my lap and we'll talk about the first thing that comes up." He left the room, leaving a smiling nurse to administer to Rogers.

Rogers was home before Christmas, and invited Sam and Heather for the traditional Christmas lunch with him and his family. Duffield walked with a pronounced limp and Rogers had to try and avoid laughing, but that apart they were both well on their way to recovery. Deep down they both knew that they were lucky to be there and a toast to their good fortune was only one of many that day. Duffield presented Rogers with a framed copy of the picture of the two of them lying in a dishevelled heap on the tarmac outside the warehouse. The print was signed with the legend: "How the mighty are fallen".

The forced atmosphere between Rogers and his wife did not escape Duffield's notice. He observed Cynthia and could see the traces of the figure and beauty that had once attracted Rogers. She was a tall, dark-haired woman, with long legs and large hips, but her weight appeared to have shifted downwards over the years. Comparing her with Heather, Duffield was struck by their physical similarities; they even looked the same age, although Cynthia was twenty years younger. Her excess weight seemed to have accumulated by neglect, while Heather's was attractive and appeared as a natural progression of age.

Rogers had been put on sick leave for the next month, a prospect that he was not looking forward to, especially as the whole problem of Simon Whittle had yet to be resolved. Before leaving that night Duffield offered a solution. "New York have told me to take my time and they don't expect me back for at least a couple of weeks, so how about we set up an office here? I can do the legwork, no pun intended, you can do the brainwork and let's see if we can build a case or not."

Rogers knew that beneath the rough and gruff exterior there beat a true policeman's heart and he openly welcomed the opportunity of having a partner on an investigation that had the potential to turn into a major case, but, as he secretly hoped, would lead up a blind alley. "Yes, I'd welcome it. Give me a ring after Boxing Day and we'll get everything set up." Seeing the puzzled look on Duffield's face he added, "The day after tomorrow."

Cynthia silently accepted the arrival of boxes of files into the house and Rogers' small office was put off limits to the children. The two men sat down to review all of the facts they had. Duffield produced a photograph of the New York murder which was chillingly similar to the ten-year-old photograph of Angela Logan. The only noticeable differences that they concluded from the murders was that in New York rope and not bed sheets had been used to tie the victim, and there were no traces of semen or champagne on the body. However, the autopsy of the body in New York revealed a high level of alcohol in the bloodstream. Rogers also pointed out that in the London murder the champagne bottle had been removed from the hotel room.

Reviewing all the information mid-way through the second morning, they concluded that they had sufficient circumstantial evidence to link the two murders which in turn might or might not link it to Simon Whittle. Both knew that coincidences were not proof and more importantly that lightning did strike twice, and sometimes more.

Rogers threw down the notes he was reading. "I don't know, it's exactly the same as last time. This report I wrote on my meetings with Whittle is as true today as it was then. I concluded ten years ago that he was not involved and I see nothing ten years later to change my opinion."

"Okay, Sherlock, the only way we can prove anything here is to establish a pattern. We have two murders almost identical in execution, on the same day, ten years apart, which just happens to be the only suspect's birthday. What about the intervening ten years or the period before? If he's guilty, my guess would be that there are more than two. So, in our super-sleuth style we find the others and we have him cold. We find no more, we put the file back on the shelf and Kelly in New York has another open case to solve. Whadaya think?"

"Certainly I agree the strategy, but how do we go about it?"

Rogers had risen and walked to the window in the cramped room. He winced as he attempted to stretch. "What do we start with? His early life and work forward, or start from '92 and go back?"

"Both. You must have a central passport office here somewhere, right?"

"Yes, you trip over it every time you visit the yard – it's next door in a building called Petit France."

"Okay, you could do with some fresh air and a hero's welcome. Go pay your friends a visit and call in at the passport office. Find out when his passport was issued. If you have the same as us you have to turn in your old passport when you get a new one. If that's the case, get a copy of his old one so we can find out where he's been since. In the meantime, we know where he was born and where he was before he went globe trotting. I'll find Somerset somewhere in this country and start asking questions."

"Great. One fatal flaw though, how will you drive?"

"I'll drive him, where are we going?" The door had opened and Heather walked in carrying a tray of coffee and biscuits. Cynthia was behind her, framed in the doorway.

"Somerset, hon, do you know where it is?"

"Of course I do. When are we off?"

"No time like the present, unless you have any objections or thoughts." Duffield turned his attention to Rogers who was resting against the window sill.

"No, none at all."

Duffield collected some papers and stood up to leave.

"I know I'm wasting my time but please don't upset the locals."

"Don't worry, Alan, I'll keep an eye on him."

Patting Heather on the rear as she walked out, Duffield whispered loud enough for them all to hear, "I just love it when you assume the dominant role."

Cynthia followed them out of the room, leaving Rogers alone with his thoughts. Despite the potential time bomb that he could be looking at in Whittle, all he could currently feel was envy for the satisfaction that Heather and Duffield seemed to find in each other's company. Duffield had told him his life story in a New York bar one night. It was nothing special and common enough amongst policemen: a wife, kids, no time, divorce and acrimony. Rogers knew the route and felt himself sliding, slowly but relentlessly, down it. He pulled himself out of his lethargy and made an appointment with a Miss Samson at the passport office for 9.30 the following morning, and devoted the rest of the day to playing with the children, while Cynthia did some shopping and had her hair done.

"Miss Samson will see you now, sir." A young leggy secretary with cascades of chestnut hair held the door open for him.

"Inspector Rogers, come in please. A pleasure to meet you. It's not everyday that one gets to meet a real live hero." The voice and body of Miss Samson lived up to her name; a strapping, horsy lady in her mid-fifties wearing woollen tweeds.

"Thank you for taking the time to see me at such short notice."

"It's no trouble, the pleasure is all mine. Tea?" She handed Rogers a bone china cup with a delicacy which belied her size.

Rogers adjusted himself in his seat trying to get comfortable, but the nagging pain and constant itching in his side were a major irritant. "Miss Samson, I need to try and trace the movements of a certain individual over the last ten or eleven years. As I understand the procedure, anyone applying for a new passport or a replacement passport would have to have their details processed through this office if they were stationed overseas at the time."

"That is correct. We keep all old passports which are returned to us from the various embassies and consulates overseas. The problem you will encounter is the one of when your individual last obtained a new passport. If it was a ten-year passport the individual could well be nine years into it and as such we will not have any records of their movements during that period."

Rogers attempted to speak but Miss Samson was in full flow. "In addition, as you will appreciate, not all countries now stamp passports when people pass through immigration control, the EEC being the prime example. Now, if you can give me details of the individual." She stared at Rogers, waiting for a name.

"Simon Whittle, middle initial P, born in 1954."

"No more?"

"It's possible that the original application came from an address in Somerset and, if there has been a renewal, it may have come from the Middle East – Saudi Arabia." Rogers found himself intimidated by the woman behind the desk; her manner was friendly and helpful but like most bureaucrats she managed to give the impression that he should have been able to provide all of the information that he was requesting himself, which would have made her job substantially easier.

"Well, I am sure our computer will find something for you. I will telephone you in a couple of days." Miss Samson stood and extended her hand.

"Err, I'm afraid this matter is rather urgent." Rogers hesitated, hoping that Miss Samson would offer some help but none was forthcoming. "Perhaps I could come back at about two o'clock this afternoon?" He reached out to take her outstretched hand. She seemed to be considering either breaking all the bones in it or complying with his request. He smiled as an afterthought and she released her grip.

"Two o'clock then."

Rogers entered the yard building, where he had his office, for the first time in two weeks. He was greeted everywhere with friendly and hearty congratulations. It felt odd, and perverse, to receive so much attention for getting shot. He spent the rest of the morning talking to his colleagues and he dined out on the story of his heroics.

At two o'clock he was back at the entrance to the lion's den and, in the absence of a secretary, he knocked and walked through the open door. The room was empty. Four brown manila folders were in the middle of the desk. The typed tab on the top one read "Simon P. Whittle". Rogers moved the top folder slightly to see the ones underneath but was stopped by the booming voice of Miss Samson asking him to kindly leave the papers on her desk alone. Rogers felt himself blush. Daniels had taught him a long time ago never to apologise for his actions as a police officer but, cowed by this formidable woman, he muttered "Sorry," and waited for her to hand him the folders.

"We apparently have four Simon P. Whittles. Two are either too young or too old. The other two were born in 1954 and 1958 . . . "

"It has to be . . . " Rogers interrupted and immediately wished that he hadn't.

"Neither," continued Miss Samson, "applied for their passports from Somerset although one," she reached out to pick up the top folder of papers, "did apply for his first passport, a one-year affair, at a post office in Derby and listed his place of birth as Wellington, Somerset."

There was a silence as she finished talking. Rogers wanted to be sure that she had finished before he spoke. "May I see the details of the Whittle born in Somerset which should also be the one born in '54?"

"Your assumption is correct. If this is the Whittle that you are looking for then you are in luck as he applied for a ten-year passport in 1983 from the British Embassy in Jeddah in Saudi Arabia."

Miss Samson passed the folder over. The details were not a lot of help. The folder contained the original application from Derby, dated 1975, a second application in 1980 for a three-year passport which listed an address in Yeovil, which he was sure he recognised as Whittle's parents', and a copy of the renewal application from Jeddah. Stapled to the inside of the folder were three photographs of the face that he was becoming familiar with. The first of the three showed Whittle with a beard and long hair, the other two showed him clean-shaven and smartly groomed. In addition, the accusing date of birth was liberally sprinkled throughout the file.

"There appears to be something missing." Rogers looked up expectantly.

"I think not, young man," came the frosty reply.

"Excuse me, but what about his three-year passport that he would have surrendered in Jeddah when obtaining his new ten-year one?"

"VSC, Inspector Rogers, VSC."

"Pardon, I'm sorry?"

Tutting as if addressing an imbecile she continued, "Visa still current. His original passport must have contained a valid visa, probably for Saudi Arabia, so rather than have the visa re-issued, the Embassy simply attach the two passports with an official seal and notes it in the new passport accordingly."

Already knowing the answer he felt compelled to ask the question anyway: "There is presumably no way of finding out the details in his current passport?"

A simple but terse "No" terminated the interview and Rogers left little wiser than when he had entered. He hoped that Duffield was having more success in Somerset than he was in London.

Duffield and Heather had arrived late the previous afternoon in Yeovil. The town struck Duffield as unimaginative but quaint in that peculiar British way. Under Heather's guidance they made it to the local police station, a modern red brick structure on the outskirts of the town. The young sergeant behind the desk was impressed at meeting someone from the United States.

"We don't get many American policemen in this part of the world, sir. Come to think of it we don't get many Americans at all." A quizzical frown passed across the young man's features. "Are you the one that were shot, up in Wiltshire?"

Duffield looked embarrassed. "Uh, yeah, actually I am, but," he continued quickly before he could be interrupted, "I am here on official business. Can I see the Inspector or whoever is in charge, please?"

"Of course, sir, let me just see if he's free."

Duffield waited patiently while the young man dialled a number. He could not hear the conversation but at the end he was asked to go up a flight of stairs at the end of the corridor; the last door on the left was Inspector Weekes.

Inspector Weekes was a man of impressive stature. His ruddy complexion gave away his country-upbringing and, like the young sergeant below, he appeared to be in awe of a visiting FBI agent. Having exchanged pleasantries Duffield got straight down to business. Before he began asking for help he produced a letter from his inside pocket and handed it over to the Inspector. "As you can see," he indicated the letter, "I am currently assisting Scotland Yard, or more specifically the Home Office with an investigation that could link a murder in London with a murder in New York. The two murders happened ten years apart but they have some of the same characteristics, including a suspect who lived for most of his youth in Yeovil. We're not sure when he left Yeovil but it was prior to 1981. We do know that he was born here in 1954. We're interested in knowing if there have been any murders in the local vicinity, unsolved murders, from, say, the early sixties to the late seventies, and more specifically, murders that may have occurred around December of any given year."

The Inspector handed back the letter which he had been holding and set about filling a briar pipe but he made no attempt to light it. "You talk of murders as if they happen every day. We have had three murders in the Yeovil area in the period that you have mentioned."

Duffield looked at the Inspector hard as he assumed he had to he kidding, but from his expression he realised that he was serious. Without reference to any papers the Inspector continued, "One was a fight between two sailors in early 1965 where a knife was pulled and one of the sailors was stabbed to death. The last one was a domestic dispute in the summer of 1977 where a jealous husband murdered his wife and gave himself up to the police, and in between we had a girl strangled in some local woods – that would have been around December of 1968."

Duffield sat up, his inner senses telling him that he was on to something.

"But her boyfriend was convicted of that murder." Duffield slumped back, deflated. "That's it? No hidden skeletons? What about missing girls whose bodies could be buried in the countryside out there?"

"It's possible, but unlikely. Most teenagers who go missing from these parts head for the city and eventually turn up. I could check for you, if you like. Our records are kept in Taunton but we could phone through and get a listing for you."

Duffield appeared deep in thought. "Yeah, yeah that would be great." He rose to leave and extended his hand. Pausing, he withdrew it. "Could I see the files on those three cases? Having come this far I guess I should check out that our guy wasn't in any way involved."

"Certainly. Everything's in the dungeon."

As they passed through the ground floor Duffield asked the Inspector to wait for a moment. He went outside to where Heather was waiting patiently in the car. "Be a good girl and find us a Sheraton to stay in and pick me up in about an hour." She laughed, blew him a kiss and drove off.

In the basement storage area the three files were easily located. They held pride of place, each on its own shelf, against the far wall. There was a small desk with a telephone on it. "I'll leave you to it. If you need me I'm on extension 1. You'll find paper and something to write with in the drawer."

"Great. Thanks for your help. I'll holler if I need you."

Despite the cold Duffield removed his jacket and sat down to start checking the three files. He pulled down the file on the fighting sailors and found he could quickly dismiss it. The same was true of the file relating to the husband and wife. There was nothing in either of them to indicate that Whittle had been involved. The third file was bulkier, with two smaller files lying beside it. Checking them first he discovered they were merely overspills from the larger file. He sat down and began reading the Tracey Gates story. Within minutes he was focused on the body having been discovered in the early morning hours of December 11th and the estimated time of death up to eight, possibly nine hours earlier.

chapter 33

It had taken most of the following day but eventually, with the combined help of the various police forces and Exeter jail, Duffield was able to ascertain that Andy Simms had been released from jail after serving twelve years of his sentence. He had been a model prisoner and had learned a new trade as a motor mechanic whilst in jail. He now lived in Dorchester and according to the information provided to Duffield he was married with three children.

It was dark by the time they completed the short drive from Yeovil to Dorchester. Duffield concluded that he preferred Dorchester in the dark to Yeovil in daylight.

Heather, determined to improve Duffield's knowledge of all things English, pointed out the statue of Thomas Hardy.

"Dorchester, ancient town of Casterbridge in the county of Wessex, the Mayor thereof, Jude the Obscure and the ill-fated Tess."

Heather stared at Duffield in disbelief. "When did you study Hardy?"

"Oh, sometime in my past." He waved his hand dismissively. "Come on, we have to find Arnott House."

"Abbotts House," she corrected. "Wind down your window and ask that policeman."

In his politest tones Duffield asked for directions. And, having been pointed in the right direction, Heather pulled the car out again into the late afternoon traffic. Duffield could guess the scene that was going to unfold and drummed his fingers on the dashboard.

Abbotts House was situated halfway along Monks Lane just

outside the town on the main road to Weymouth. There were lights on in the house but, as there was no car outside, they drove past. Duffield instructed Heather to turn the car around and then pull into the side of the road.

Conversation between the two of them had never been hard but as the engine idled he found he had nothing to say. Looking across at Heather he noticed, not for the first time, the lines that ran from the edge of her eyes to the corner of her mouth. Her figure hidden beneath the bulky sweater was still accommodating although he knew full well that, like himself, she had seen younger days.

"Penny for them." She had turned and caught him staring at her.

"What?" he replied a touch guiltily.

"Penny for them, a penny for your thoughts. It's a British expression."

"They were about you, but they're for mature audiences only."

She laughed and leaned across to kiss him on the cheek. "Do you enjoy this, all the hanging around, snooping on people?"

"After a while enjoyment doesn't come into it. I do it because I'm good at it." He put his arm around her shoulder and pulled her to him. "The future is about enjoyment," he kissed her, "the present is work. Okay, kiddies, time for action." He pulled himself upright as the headlights of an on-coming car swung into the driveway of Abbotts House. He struggled out of the car, pushed his head back in and said, "So you sit here and plan out the enjoyment while I do the work, oh fair wench of Wessex."

She watched his retreating back. She had enjoyed the last few weeks with him and was not looking forward to his departure back to America, whenever that might be; but, believing that you should live life for the moment, she relaxed in the warmth and awaited her hero's return.

Duffield's loud knock on the door was answered by a scruffily-dressed woman in her early thirties. A baby with a dummy in its mouth was attached to her left hip.

"Hi. Is Andy Simms home?"

She viewed him suspiciously. "Who wants to know?"

A second youngster, aged about three, emerged from a room where a television set was blaring, and clung to her right leg.

"It's a personal matter."

She deliberated but finally held the door open and ushered him into a room opposite the one with the television. The room was cold and she turned on the light as they entered. "I'll call him, he's washing." She left without further explanation.

A couple of minutes later a small thin man with a bald head walked in. He was dressed in blue grease-streaked overalls and did not offer his hand.

"Mr Simms, my name is Duffield. I'm . . . "

"I know who you are. I spent twelve years with you and your kind. What's happened? They trumped up some new charges against me for some other crime I didn't commit?" The contempt and anger in his voice was impossible to miss.

Duffield tried again. "Mr Simms, you may not care any longer but I believe that you may not have killed Tracey Gates." Simms looked up. He was about to interrupt but instead he just let his shoulders sag and Duffield continued, "I don't know what happened that night, but I have some unsubstantiated evidence that you may have been a victim of circumstances. To prove your innocence is gonna take a lot of hard work on my part and I can't do it without your co-operation." Duffield watched as his breath evaporated. His feet were cold but he resisted the temptation to stamp them up and down.

"Trust him, Andy, you have nothing to lose." The door had opened and Simms' wife stood framed against the hall light. The child, now asleep, was still clamped to her left hip. Simms turned and glared at her. She stared him down and he dismissed her with a flick of his head. As she closed the door behind her Simms indicated a chair. Duffield sat down, glad of the opportunity to move.

"I'll tell you the story. It's the same one I've been telling for twenty years now. Whether you believe it or not means nothing to me, but it's the truth."

Duffield left the house about half an hour later. When he climbed back in the car his mood was sombre and it was not until they were seated for dinner in the Castle Hotel a couple of hours later that he finally spoke about the meeting with Simms.

"The worst possible thing in this job is finding out you were wrong. We deal with the scum of the earth all day and our unwritten motto is, 'So what if the bastards didn't commit the crime you have arrested them for, they've committed others so you've got them for that one instead'. You develop a thick skin over the years – it's necessary for survival; but the downside is you miss the obvious." He paused to drain his glass of scotch. "And then the obvious stands up and you realise that one, just one, is innocent and if he is innocent what about the rest?"

Heather looked at Duffield, her wine glass halfway to her lips. "But is he innocent?"

"I'm ninety percent sure of it and I intend to prove it." Looking at her pensive expression he added, "Starting tomorrow."

Their desserts were served and Heather sat facing a mound of ice-cream crowned with a single red cherry. Glancing at the bowl Duffield smiled. "That reminds me, what enjoyment did you plan?" He reached across with his hand and, scooping the cherry onto his finger, pushed it firmly between her lips. She never discovered what flavour the ice-cream was.

The following morning, while Heather was in the shower, Duffield phoned Alan Rogers. They had talked before Duffield visited Simms and Rogers was keen to hear the outcome. Rogers listened intently to Duffield's edited version and was silent when he finished. Duffield thought the line had gone dead when Rogers asked, "Do you believe him?"

"Who knows, I think so, but maybe I just want a case against your friend. I have to be honest and say Simms didn't strike me as the murdering type . . . "

Rogers laughed at the other end of the line. "That's what I thought about Whittle. Anyway, emotion aside for a minute, I know that in 1973 he started work in Taunton and in 1977 he moved to Derby before going to Saudi in early '81."

"Taunton, that's down this way, isn't it? But where the hell is Derby?" He pronounced it Derrby.

"In the middle of the country about one hundred and fifty miles north of where you are." There was a pause while Rogers collected his thoughts. "What if he has been killing one a year since 1968? That would make the tally around twenty-four and Christ, he was only, what, fourteen in '68."

Duffield could sense that Rogers was about to start a guilt trip. "Look, Sherlock, unless he went further afield to murder there are no other murders in the Yeovil area from '68 through '73. He was then in Taunton until '77. Maybe we should check . . . "

The sentence was never finished as an anguished choke came down the phone-line. "My God, Janice Butterworth. He murdered Janice Butterworth." The line was silent.

"Sherlock, Sherlock, are you there? Goddamnit, don't hang up on me." Heather emerged from the bathroom to find Duffield shaking the phone in his hand. She looked at him quizzically. "I'm here. I'm thinking. Can you get to Taunton? I'll get a train. Meet me at the police station in the Crescent at three this afternoon." Before Duffield could reply the line went dead.

"The manners of the English," Duffield remarked as he hung up the receiver. "We, it appears, are off to Taunton. How far is it?"

"An hour and a half, maybe two."

"Good," he replied. "Time for breakfast." He reached over and pulled her down on to the bed with him.

The drive for once was pleasant; the day was beautifully clear. They had to cover much the same route as the previous day and skirted around Yeovil to reach Taunton. After an excellent pub lunch Duffield left Heather to do some shopping and arrange accommodation for them for the night while he strolled leisurely in the direction of the Crescent.

The sun was still shining but the air was cold. The walk refreshed him after the cramped ride and the smoky atmosphere of the pub. His mind was mulling over what Rogers had said on the phone and although he could not draw any conclusions from it he was sure that all would be revealed shortly. His major concern was that if Rogers knew of another murder that could be attributed to Whittle they could well have a one hundred percent certifiable basket case on their hands.

Pushing open the swing door to the station the middle-aged policeman behind the desk looked up from his paperwork.

"Inspector Duffield, would it be, sir?"

"Yeah, um, I'm here to meet Inspector Rogers."

"He's already here, sir, down in the basement reading some files. Asked me to send you down."

Duffield found Rogers with his head bent over an open manila file similar to the ones he had been reading in Yeovil. The light was bad but it looked as if Rogers was close to tears. Duffield pulled out the chair from the far side of the table and, turning it around, straddled himself across it. Without a word, Rogers swung the file to face him. Duffield read for just over five minutes. The salient facts were easy to digest and the conclusion that Rogers had reached was as clear as the name that was liberally documented on reports and statements. Trying to sound positive Duffield said, "There is no conclusive evidence that this murder is linked in any way to the others . . . " He got no further.

"Rubbish!. Are you blind or just feeling sorry for incompetents today?" Rogers exploded. He pushed his chair back and started pacing the room. "How the hell did I miss it all? It was there, all of it, right under my fucking nose and I missed it. Jesus Christ, what an idiot." Duffield was getting tired of the self-pity. "Look, asshole, you missed nothing. There was nothing to see. There was nothing to link a murder in Yeovil that you knew nothing about with a murder in Taunton and another one in London six years later. If, and it still is a big if, Whittle committed any or all of these crimes then, because you spotted something in New York, we'll nail the bastard. The time for recrimination is over so get your ass in gear, knock off the 'I'm no good' crap and let's go build us a case."

While Duffield had been talking he had moved from the desk and was now standing by the door. He held it open and waited while Rogers collected the file and followed Duffield back up to the reception area.

"Inspector Duffield, a message from your wife." Duffield looked hard at the sergeant before he realised that he must be talking about Heather. "She has booked you in at the St George Tavern and she's asked you and the Inspector to meet her there."

Rogers deposited the file of papers on the desk. "Could you get that file copied for me?" It was an order not a request. "And have it delivered to the St George within an hour."

Not waiting for a reply he grabbed Duffield's arm and led him out of the station. "Christ, I don't know, we leave you yanks alone for two days and you get married."

Duffield stopped as Rogers walked on. "Feeling better, are we?"

Things always looked better after a good meal, especially as Duffield banned all conversation about the case, but after dinner the two men adjourned to the comfort of a secluded corner in the residents' lounge while Heather took the hint and retired early.

In the comfort of a well-worn leather wing chair, and savouring the twenty-year-old scotch that he had ordered, Duffield basked in the combined glow of his well-being, the meal and the fire roaring in the hearth.

Rogers had alternated between brooding and sullenness all evening, although for Heather's sake he had tried hard to join in the conversation at dinner. The lecture given to him earlier by Duffield had not really lifted his spirits although he had to admit that most of what he had said did make sense. The files that he had requested had arrived within the hour, together with another file on the only other murder in the area between '74 and '77. That one had been solved and the timing did not fit the pattern that they were looking for.

"So we have a pattern," said Duffield, "random killings. The first we believe was Tracey Gates in 1968; then an eight-year gap until Janice Butterworth; and then possibly two more in 1982, which is a further six-year gap; then we have New York in 1992, which may or may not be connected. The one common link that we have been able to establish is the presence of Simon Whittle in the vicinity of each of the murders.

"If we assume Gates was his first, and his age would tend to support that assumption, and that Butterworth was the second, were there any more before Logan or between Logan and Staples?" Rogers looked up from his drink. "Martha Staples was the name of the deceased in New York. The problem as I see it," continued Duffield "is how do we proceed? We have nothing but circumstantial evidence to tie Whittle to any of the murders. In fact in one case he has already been checked thoroughly and he was cleared of any involvement." He hurried on before Rogers could speak. "However, it is also fairly safe to surmise that if he murdered Angela Logan he knew that he would be a prime suspect and as such would have worked out all the details beforehand to ensure that the finger of blame could not be pointed in his direction. Therefore I feel our options are limited and we should continue with our current line of investigation. Let's follow his life and see if we uncover more bodies. In addition, while we are here, we should trace some people who knew him and see if we can't tie him directly to your infamous Mrs Butterworth. Work colleagues or friends should be helpful. Your report said she was fairly free with her favours. Maybe she put out for Whittle or maybe she didn't and that was the problem. We have here the beginnings of what could turn out to be a major crime; a serial killer who gets his weird kicks on his birthday. We have time on our side – if we're right he isn't going to strike again in a hurry, next December at the earliest, by which time we will have his balls nailed to the wall if he is guilty and if he's not we'll be back on the street kicking the shit out of the drug barons of this world."

Duffield signalled for a refill and then, remembering which country he was in, picked up the two glasses and went over to the bar.

Rogers reached for the glass as Duffield placed it in front of him. Staring at the amber liquid he swirled it slowly around. "Two things concern me. First we're going to need some sort of permission from at least my boss and probably yours to follow this up, and secondly, how did Whittle murder Angela Logan when he was in Egypt?"

Duffield stared hard at his friend and colleague and watched him drain his glass. He decided they should call it a night after this drink as he did not feel inclined to deal with a drunken Rogers. "The solution to the first shouldn't be a problem. If we finish up here and then head off to Derby we can report back to your chief within a week by which time we should have a good case and my guy will go along with your guy because of the political mileage he'll get out of it if we're right. As to how he killed Angela Logan I don't know for sure but I could have a good guess." Rogers leaned forward but Duffield kept him waiting while he finished his drink. "He wasn't in Cairo at the time the murder took place; he was there before and after but not in between. If you check the flight times, barring major disasters, you will find that he somehow could have made it across and back giving the impression that all the time he was somewhere he wasn't."

"No good," Rogers replied. "I checked that plan. I don't remember the details but, yes, it was possible, through one of various routes, but we checked all the passenger lists. He was not listed on any flight into or out of London or any other British airport."

"He travelled under a different name . . . "

"No way. Whittle was not sophisticated, or knowledgeable enough, to have a false passport in another name." Rogers' words were slightly slurred.

"He bought the ticket in a different name but used his real passport. Remember we are talking mid-seventies here, and the Middle East. There was a good chance no one would check his ticket against his passport and if they did he could blame it on a computer mistake, a clerical error. Airports were not as security-conscious as they are now . . . "

Rogers interrupted again. "How about the entry visa into Egypt? He only had one and that was for the correct date?"

"Best guess would be that he told them he was visiting Israel and asked them not to stamp his passport on his second entry. Instead, they stamp a piece of paper which you throw away when you leave the country. The request coupled with the traditional bribe would work wonders."

Rogers slumped back in his chair looking thoroughly dejected.

"C'mon, Sherlock, time for some shut-eye. That was all guesswork. Tomorrow we need to hit the beaches running and we need clear heads." Duffield got up to leave and was relieved to find that Rogers was following, muttering something about yanks being too smart for their own good.

They climbed the two flights of stairs and made their way down the corridor. Rogers spoke as they reached his door. The frustration and anger in his voice could not be missed.

"It's just so confusing, there's so much here and yet nothing at all. The dates, his movements, it's all a fucking jigsaw with pieces missing. He appears to flit from country to country murdering at will."

"C'mon, Sherlock, sleep on it. It'll all seem clearer in the morning."

"I suppose so." Rogers' whole body was slumped forward. He looked as if someone had taken all the air out of him.

Duffield walked to the adjoining door, inserted his key, and looked up. Rogers still hadn't moved.

"Sherlock, bed," he ordered. "We'll attack it again in the morning, starting with when he left Saudi and what he's doing in America."

chapter 34

Flying has to be the ultimate relaxation – literally, lost in the clouds. The thick bank of texture nestles seductively below the silver-hulled frame of the aircraft; protection from the dark gray ominous presence of the brooding Atlantic Ocean which accurately forecasts the season of the year. Up here the sunshine is eternal. Here you could be lost forever, suspended not in time but in meditative motion. The vast reaches of emptiness that stretch in all directions remind me of the desert, but here is friendly whereas there was hostile.

The decision to marry had been spontaneous. The words were the catalyst that caused the tightly-wound internal mainspring to unwind, permitting openings where there had formerly been only ignorance. Life and light were looked at anew. No longer alone, the encrusted shell had opened enough to allow someone in. The warmth generated by the sharing surprised and frightened me. Fortified by the sustenance, I moved forward – not tentatively but bullishly, as if I were subconsciously afraid that the warmth would disperse and the malevolence of old would return as a cruel joke. It didn't happen. Instead, the warmth of the moment was enervating, sapping the very life-blood from the unseen hand which for a lifetime had controlled and dictated movement, thought and rationale.

The voices had become fainter, weaker until finally they ceased. Permanently stilled or merely biding their time for an encore I could not say. I prayed for the former and could not contemplate the latter.

We were married in May 1988 and quickly settled into a routine. We were not the life and soul of our environment; instead we settled for the quieter life of dinner parties and carpet slippers. We had no desire to emulate those around us. Our life was simple but fulfilling. We both pursued our separate career paths – I travelled occasionally, Judith worked irregular hours. I taught her golf and tennis and the beauty of an afternoon walk. She fed me contentment, harmony and love.

The offer of a position in New York, with my current employer, had been in the air for a few months. Judith was keen to move. Her own company was prepared to offer her a job at the hotel they had recently acquired at Newark Airport in New Jersey. The future looked as bright as the sun on the wing.

The captain announced the beginning of our descent into Kennedy Airport. I knew that decision-time was approaching, although secretly I knew that I had already decided to accept the position. The discussions would hopefully be a formality. If all went well Judith would fly to New York for the weekend and we would set about finding a home in New Jersey. The world of commuting was beckoning, its siren call a plaintive note on the north wind.

I moved with a confident step into the cold snowy morning. Icicles of despair and frustration, which once would have demanded attention and satisfaction like some petulant child, were easily held at bay. The secret of longevity was the future and the future was only a thought away.

chapter 35

The following morning they went to the insurance offices where Whittle used to work. The local manager was accommodating but reserved; he wanted more information than Rogers and Duffield were prepared to give him. Realising that he was not going to be given anything in the way of concrete information he became obstructive, pointing out that he had not been the manager when Whittle was with them and he had no idea where he had gone from the Taunton office. Reluctantly he telephoned his secretary and asked her to dig out Whittle's file. He hung up the phone and smiled smugly. "It will take some time; perhaps you could call back tomorrow."

"We'll wait." Duffield settled back comfortably and placed his hands behind his head. Peterson, the manager, tried to stare him down, but lost. "Excuse me." He stood up and walked out.

"Pompous twit," Rogers remarked, "the living epitome of what is wrong with this country. I think I'll put in for a transfer and work with you in the concrete jungle. "

"Funny, I was thinking of requesting a transfer to come and walk the beat in Somerset. I think I could enjoy this sort of life." Duffield leaned forward and picked a golf ball off a stand on the desk and started throwing it gently into the air and catching it.

The door opened and Peterson strode back into the room. He was carrying a green file with a name tab in the left hand corner. Peterson resumed his seat, opened the file and without looking at either of the men in his office simply stated that Simon Whittle had been transferred to the Derby office in 1977. He closed the file and laid it on the desk.

Duffield leaned forward, replaced the golf ball and reached out for the file. Peterson grabbed it and held it to his chest. "Mr Peterson, we are carrying out a police investigation. If you insist, we will go away, obtain a court order and be back in approximately one hour to read the file." Duffield added for emphasis, "Any information we see on this file will go no further than this room, you have my word on that, so how about it?" Duffield reached again for the file and this time Peterson reluctantly handed it over.

Rogers moved behind Duffield so that he could read over his shoulder. Both read silently for a few minutes before Rogers looked up and asked, "Peter Wells, the chap he trained with, is he still here?"

"No. He's still with the company, he was in Malaysia for a few years, but I think he's somewhere up north now, Manchester or Liverpool." Leaning forward Peterson picked up the telephone and asked his secretary to find out which office Peter Wells was currently working in.

"What about the other inspectors that were working here at the time. Any of them still around?"

"Only one, Mike Smith, been here all his life. The others have either moved on or in one case retired."

Peterson's attitude seemed to have swung one hundred and eighty degrees and he asked if they would like to talk to Smith. Rogers looked at Duffield who nodded. Another call on the internal telephone followed and the three sat back to wait the arrival of Mike Smith.

There was a gentle tap at the door as it swung open in the same motion.

"Come in, Mike, come in." A small shrew of a man in his sixties shuffled into the room at Peterson's beckoning. Rogers quickly calculated that Smith would have been in his late forties at the time of the murder.

Before Peterson could say anything further, Rogers spoke up. "Mr Smith, I'm Inspector Alan Rogers and this is Sam Duffield. We are trying to trace the whereabouts of someone who used to work here: Simon Whittle. Do you remember him?"

Smith chuckled. "Certainly I remember him." The voice was raspy, indicating a lifetime of smoking and as if to confirm Rogers' thoughts he pulled out a packet of cigarettes and set about lighting one as he continued talking. "Smart bugger, but a nice lad. Worked with Wells mainly but helped us all out if we needed him. What's he done, murdered someone?" Rogers ignored the comment.

"Anything unusual you can recall about him or any idea where he went after Derby?"

"Nothing unusual. He chased women and drank as much as anyone. He was a decent fellow, cocky but friendly." He dragged thoughtfully on his cigarette. "He went to the Middle East somewhere, I think. Never heard from him since. Wells might know; they were very close."

"Thank you, Mr Smith. You've been most helpful."

Peterson nodded his head and indicated that he could go.

As he reached the door Rogers asked as an afterthought, "Did he ever know a woman called Janice Butterworth, lived in Curry Rivel?"

Smith stopped, his features giving nothing away. He looked at his fingers and his cigarette and walked slowly back to the desk to stub out the cigarette in the ashtray. Turning to look at Rogers he then answered, "Name means nothing to me. Doesn't mean that he did or didn't know her. We were friends in the office but outside it was different."

As Smith left, the secretary pushed her head around the door and informed them that Peter Wells was now Assistant Manager at the Manchester branch office. Thanking her the two men rose to leave.

On the street outside they turned up their collars against the rain and walked back to the St George. Over coffee in the bar Duffield asked thoughtfully, "Why did he lie about knowing Janice Butterworth?"

"You noticed that too? If you want time to think of an answer, do something – light a cigarette, stub out a cigarette – and then when you do answer, distance yourself from the events. I don't know, but for now I suggest we store it and head north."

They found Heather, settled the bill and set off up the M5. The conversation on the drive was light and little reference was made to the case. The weather was diabolical and as only Heather could drive the two men spent the trip joking and talking over old cases to keep her awake.

In Derby they booked into a hotel in the centre of the city and over dinner formulated the next stage of the plan. They agreed that it made sense for Duffield to travel on to Manchester the following morning and interview Wells, while Rogers stayed in Derby to talk to the local police and visit the office where Whittle had worked.

The following morning it was still raining as Heather and Duffield dropped Rogers off at the city police station. They made their way back to the motorway to continue the drive north with

Duffield hopeful that they would be back that night or at worst early the next day.

The local police were both cheerful and helpful. Their computerised records quickly showed Rogers that for the period in question, 1977 to 1980, they had no unsolved murders around December 10th and further examination revealed that of the solved cases only one came close to the date and that was in January 1977. Rogers was sure that the date was the significant factor and as such did not pursue the case.

The young PC that was assisting him informed him that as they were in the Midlands there might well be outstanding cases in some of the other major cities or county areas. He offered to ask the other stations and told Rogers that he should have all the information by late morning. Rogers thanked him for his efforts and set off for the insurance company's office, saying he would come back later to see if any had turned up.

It was only a five-minute walk across the city centre but Rogers was fairly wet by the time he arrived. The Derby office where Whittle had worked was small, only six staff, and the woman at reception informed him that the manager was out and was not expected back until after lunch. Rogers left his name and said he would call back at 2.30.

Trying to shelter from the rain he stood under the cavernous opening of the cathedral doors. On impulse he decided to go in. He felt self-conscious as he had not been inside a church since his son's christening. The cathedral was virtually deserted, his shoes on the flagstones the only echoing noise. All outside noise, including the hiss of the rain, was blotted out.

He walked slowly around the cathedral, not really sure why he was there. He felt lonely, and despite Duffield's constant reassurances he felt guilty. The horrifying thought that people had died due to his incompetence kept surfacing and his own assertion that he had done his best was not enough to satisfy the nagging doubts. The unnatural quiet coupled with the sheer majesty of the building began to have an impact on Rogers. He could feel his anger rising. For once it was not anger at himself but instead was directed at the embodiment of evil that Whittle had come to represent. He stopped in front of the alter and looked up at the imposing stained glass window that cast a comforting glow on the brass and marble. The imagery of Christianity was lost; all he could see before him was blood and pain.

He shuddered violently in the cold, and moved quickly, very quickly, to the door. The cathedral had not provided the answers he was looking for, only more questions, and twenty minutes later he was back with the PC drinking coffee.

Over the next hour seven replies came in from around the region. They were all dismissed except one; a murder that had taken place in Birmingham on December 9th, 1978. It was a stabbing. The victim was male, a visiting football fan. Several youths were charged in connection with the death but they were found not guilty. The pattern did not fit the mould but the date was significant enough to promote Rogers' interest. He was still mulling the information when the phone rang.

"PC Withers, hello Scotty . . . No problem, it happens with ours all the time . . . certainly, carry on." Rogers watched as Withers began making notes. "Yes, hang on, can you? I think this is what we are looking for." Withers pressed a button to put the call on hold. "Sir, we may be onto something." Looking down at his notes he read, "December 10th, 1980, a female body was found near a lake north of Nottingham. The victim had been strangled. The case is still open." Withers finished and stared at Rogers.

Rogers felt as if someone had pushed a needle under his nail. A feeling of nausea flooded his body and the desire to run from the room was intense. He closed his eyes trying to think rationally. Opening them he found Withers staring at him. "I need a copy of that file. Which force is on the line, Nottingham?" Receiving a nod in reply he continued, "Can they get a copy to us within the next hour, or better still, how can I get over there?"

Withers was perturbed at how white the Inspector looked but the urgent, almost manic tone that had entered his voice told him this was not a time to enquire about Rogers' health "I can drive you, sir, it's only about forty-five minutes away."

"Great, make sure they have the file ready for us."

"Scotty, you still there? . . . good, we need a copy of the file or at least the Home Office does . . . No, no need, we'll pick it up, say, in about an hour . . . Great, see you soon."

A little under an hour later they were walking through the doors of Nottingham police station. Scotty, an amiable red-headed fellow, had had the file neatly copied and waiting in a folder. Rogers signed the necessary releases and they were off once more back to Derby.

The temptation to read the papers in the car was immense but, unsure what his reaction would be, Rogers forced himself to wait until he had been dropped back at the hotel. Thanking Withers perfunctorily for his help he went to the sanctuary of his room and immersed himself for the next hour in an all too familiar case that bore the trademark of Simon Whittle.

He found when he had finished that he was surprisingly calm. The contents had acted as a leech to drain much of the anger and frustration from his system; his main thought now was that Whittle had made a fool out of him and he was going to make him pay. The possibility that it could have been someone other than Whittle never entered his thoughts.

Within half an hour he had proof positive that he was on the right trail. He started to read parts of the file again. A photograph of the young girl, before the murder, was stapled to the right hand side of the file. Inside the file were copies of photographs of the body after death. She looked like a child sleeping, the face at peace with the world; only the vivid bruising around her neck gave away her secret.

Rogers was jolted from his thoughts by the shrill ringing of the telephone. He leaned across the bed to answer it. "Hello."

"Sherlock, we have the bastard. Peter Wells remembers Whittle visiting Janice Butterworth exactly one year before the date of her murder. It appears that his colleagues set him up; sent him to sell her some insurance in the hope that she would seduce him, a 21st birthday present. One year later she's dead . . . Sherlock, you there?"

"Yes. We've got another one: December 10th, 1980."

"Jesus. We'll head back tonight. See you in a few hours."

As Rogers replaced the receiver he remembered that he hadn't kept his appointment at the insurance office but with the news that Duffield had given him it now seemed unimportant.

chapter 36

"There was one other incident that always struck me as odd. We, that is, some of the other inspectors and myself, set him up on his 21st birthday. We sent him out to see a Mrs Butterworth to arrange some insurances. Mrs Butterworth liked men and if the fancy took her she was capable of showing a young man a good time. I never found out the whole story. Simon was a good sport, always saw the funny side of anything. I don't know for sure, it was just a feeling, but I don't think he enjoyed our little prank. Anyway, a year later, to the day, she was murdered. I never drew any conclusions from it and no one ever mentioned the coincidence but Simon remarked, very unkindly I thought, that she deserved it."

The click of the tape-recorder button being depressed by Duffield stopped the voice of Peter Wells. Duffield was with Rogers in his hotel room in Derby. The almost continuous travelling of the day had left him drained and he felt disinclined to get into a philosophical discussion with Rogers on the merits of his incompetence and Whittle's abilities as a murderer. He rose to leave.

"C'mon, Sherlock, we have the facts, the beams to build the scaffold. Let's jack it in for today and start afresh tomorrow."

Rogers failed to acknowledge his departure. He finally fell asleep in the chair lulled by the melodic tones of Peter Wells who had been duped as easily as he had been; the difference was that Peter Wells was not a policeman.

At breakfast the following morning Rogers looked like hell.

"Christ, Alan, you look like you spent the night on the floor."

Heather's concern was touching.

"A chair, actually."

Duffield chose to ignore his colleague's ill-humour and set about demolishing his usual mammoth breakfast while laying out a strategy for the next two days. Rogers mumbled agreement without enthusiasm and the two of them spent the next forty-eight hours interviewing people connected with Samantha Strong. They discovered that Samantha's parents were divorced, but little else. The outcome was inconclusive; no one had heard of Simon Whittle. Despite this temporary set-back both men were convinced that they were on the right track.

Whilst Heather drove them down the Ml back to London, Rogers and Duffield worked out the case they would present to the Chief Inspector the following day. The next logical step was to visit the Middle East but they were both keenly aware that their case was based on speculation and assumption. Like much of their policework they had the links of the chain but no shackles to join the links and provide the strength.

Rogers' mood had improved considerably over the two days. His personal quest to avenge the injustice was the beacon that kept him going. The one who was tired and irritable was Heather. The non-stop driving had finally got to her and she was unusually quiet as the late night traffic hindered their progress around London.

Rogers and Duffield both spent the following morning at the hospital having their respective injuries treated. Duffield was given a clean bill of health but Rogers emerged with his bandages intact and the prospect of another few weeks' discomfort ahead. They adjourned for a pub lunch before their 2.30 meeting with the Chief.

The Chief Inspector was a giant of a man well over six feet tall. He must have weighed over two hundred and fifty pounds although his carefully tailored uniform hid the real extent of his girth. He was known for his short temper, intolerance of sloppy work and his fair-mindedness. Rogers presented the case to him in succinct but accurate terms, omitting any reference to his part in prior investigations except for the Logan case.

At the conclusion of Rogers' summation the Chief turned to Duffield. "I take it you concur with the Inspector's report?" The voice matched the body: it was voluminous, reaching into every corner of the room.

"Yes, sir. In my opinion we have an A1 certifiable serial killer on our hands. As usual we only need the proof to nail him but that should only be a matter of time. He's good but not that good."

"I agree, but with reservations. I think you may be on the right track and that the key is in the Middle East. Another two weeks' sick leave should see you both clear. Let me know what happens when you get back."

The Chief Inspector opened a file in front of him, extracted a pen from the leather holder attached to his blotter and started signing letters. "Shame about your leg still incapacitating you, Duffield. Who do you report to in New York – Goodson?" The Chief looked up as Duffield nodded. "I'll speak to him and explain about your continued ill-health.

Outside, Duffield nudged Rogers, inadvertently pushing him into the wall and jarring his side. "Not bad for a Limey, now how the hell do we get to Saudi Arabia?"

It took only two days for the visas to Saudi to be issued utilising the services of the American Embassy. While they waited for the wheels of officialdom to go round they visited the Foreign Office in an attempt to find any reports of murders coming from the Middle East which may have involved an English expatriate.

They had phoned earlier to explain what they wanted and were ushered into the office of Jane Madison upon their arrival. The plaque on the door stated that she was an under-secretary of Middle Eastern affairs.

Jane Madison was a petite, attractive woman in her late thirties. Resuming her seat as Rogers and Duffield sat opposite her, she picked up a pair of large-framed glasses and held them in her hand.

"Gentlemen, as you requested I have checked our files for deeds most foul and unfortunately, or possibly fortunately, have come up blank. We concentrated around the dates you gave us and there were only two incidents . . . " Her voice, full of public school inflection drifted as she placed the glasses on her nose and picked up a file to her left.

The glasses dwarfed her face, indeed seemed to dwarf her whole body. Duffield was coming to the conclusion that they made her look unattractive when she began speaking again.

"Here it is, December 11th, 1981." Rogers stiffened noticeably in his chair. "Elizabeth McFadden, a nurse from Scotland, was found murdered in the desert outside Jeddah, in Saudi Arabia. The accompanying reports are vague, only really says that she had been drinking and that she was strangled." Rogers could not sit still and rose to walk around the small office. "Despite her British connections it appears that a Filipino labourer killed her. He was caught two days after the crime, signed a confession and was executed."

Jane Madison looked up expecting some response but none was

forthcoming. Rogers was examining a Turner print on the wall and Duffield was staring at a spot above her head. Disconcerted by the silence she coughed gently and picked up a second file.

"The second incident is totally different except for the cause of death. A Sri-Lankan maid was murdered in Bahrain on December 10th, 1984. An Indian driver was arrested at the scene of the crime and was convicted of the murder of the maid plus the raping of an English girl. We were only advised of the incident because it involved a British subject."

"Could we have copies of both files, please?" Duffield requested politely.

"I anticipated your request." She pulled two manila folders from under the originals and handed them to Duffield. He signed the release forms on the inside cover of each file and rose to leave.

Rogers had not moved from in front of the painting but hearing Duffield rise he walked to the door and went out to the reception area. Duffield extended his hand to Jane Madison and thanked her for her time. He thought of apologising for Rogers but decided against it. Intrigued as ever by the female form he stopped at the door and turned for a last look. Madison had returned to her seat and was sliding the offensive glasses back onto her nose.

"Smaller glasses would accentuate the positive." He departed and she stared after him, blushing slightly.

Duffield caught up with Rogers at the lift. They rode down in silence and went to a coffee shop that Rogers knew. It was only after they had two mugs of coffee in front of them that Duffield spoke.

"So, Sherlock, how d'he do it?"

Rogers stirred sugar into his coffee. "The first one is easy, Whittle himself told me how it works. Saudi has no crime, or more accurately, Saudi has no unsolved crime. A murder happens, there are no immediate clues to the identity of the killer, so the police round up a few labourers, choose one and torture him until he signs a confession.

"Could the Bahrain murder be the same?"

"Could be. I don't know much about Bahrain. She said the Indian was arrested at the scene, which strikes me as odd, and the rape is definitely unusual. Who knows? Basically it's academic – it's Whittle. All we have to do is prove it."

That night two different scenes were acted out in separate London boroughs. Sam Duffield and Heather had a candlelight dinner and made love on the rug in front of the fire. Alan Rogers and Cynthia had a furious argument, followed by a chilly night in separate bedrooms.

chapter 37

Jeddah was much as Rogers remembered. It was bigger, noisier, dirtier, but essentially the same. The embassies were no longer in Jeddah having been moved to Riyadh in the middle of the '80s but all still had staff based in consulates in Jeddah.

The American Consulate turned out to be far more efficient than the British Embassy had been and the two of them were whisked through immigration and customs formalities in minutes. They were met by Bud Hayne who shuttled them downtown into the comparative sanctuary of the American Embassy.

Bud was an effusive, amiable American in his late twenties with CIA written all over him. He was placed at their disposal for the duration of their stay and was happy to be involved in something other than reading the local paper to report to Riyadh on what was happening politically in the city.

The local police were as unhelpful as ever. Hayne arranged a meeting with the Deputy Chief of Police for Jeddah, who was cordial but obstructive, pointing out through his interpreter that the McFadden case was closed and that he was not prepared under any circumstances to reopen it, nor was he prepared to release a copy of the police file on the case.

Hayne had not attended the meetings, opting instead to wait in the car. Seeing Rogers' expression as they emerged from the building he could guess what had happened.

"Fucking Arabs." Rogers slammed the door as he threw his jacket on the back seat next to him. When are they going to realise that we are in the twentieth century, not still stuck in feudal times."

"Guess old Mohammed wasn't too helpful, heh?"

"That's an understatement. 'Drink your mint tea and piss off' should be the motto of this place."

"I take it you would like a copy of their file on this case?" Hayne turned his head to address Rogers and nearly lost the front of the car to a truck that decided to veer across the highway.

"Look out! Christ, you drive as badly as they do." Hayne swung the wheel hard left and pulled the Buick into another lane, causing a loud blast on the horn from the car behind.

"Of course we'd like to see their file. What do you suggest, we break in tonight and steal it?"

"No, it's far simpler than that. We buy it."

Twenty-four hours later the three men were sitting in the coffee shop of the Meridien Hotel and Rogers was reading an English translation of the file. It was obvious that the old practice of *baksheesh* was alive and thriving.

The good news was getting the file, the bad news was that it told them nothing. According to the file the police had done very little between the discovery of the body and the arrest of the suspect. His signed confession was the one prominent document and the time of death had established that she was murdered on December 10th. Using the back of the menu Duffield drew up a chart:

1968 Tracey Gates – Yeovil, England.
1976 Janice Butterworth – Curry Rivel, England.
1980 Samantha – Strong Nottingham, England.
1981 Elizabeth McFadden – Jeddah, Saudi Arabia.
1982 Angela Logan + 1 – London, England.
1983 ?
1984 Unknown – Bahrain.
1985/9 ?
1992 Martha Staples – New York, USA.

Bud Hayne let out a low whistle as Duffield placed the menu on the table for them all to read.

"The plot worsens. We're fairly certain about eight murders and we have numerous other years unaccounted for. Not taking into account an executed Filipino." Duffield retrieved the menu as their club sandwiches were placed in front of them. He took a bite before he continued speaking. "My biggest concern at this stage is that we can't tie any one of these murders to Whittle."

Hayne interrupted. "You mean you know the fruitcake who's doing this?"

Rogers looked at Hayne as if he had just arrived from another planet. "Certainly we know who's doing it. It's the birthday boy. Seems he gets his jollies on his birthday by knocking someone off. He's not fussy either, some he knows, others are unlucky enough to meet him for the first time that day."

"So what's the problem? Run the piece of shit in, face him with what you have . . . "

It was Duffield's turn to interrupt. "What we have, or more specifically don't have, is a case. Sure we have a growing mountain of circumstantial evidence that a first-year law student could drive a truck through and have him released within hours. Somewhere along the line this guy is going to have screwed up; we're going to find out where and nail him." Duffield threw the remainder of his sandwich onto his plate. "How the fuck can you make a decent club sandwich without bacon?"

Another day of fruitless searching in Jeddah convinced them that they should move on to Riyadh. Bud Hayne was keen to stay on as their guide and it was he who finally convinced them that they should drive to Riyadh. Rogers had serious reservations about the mode of transport but was eventually swayed by Duffield's enthusiasm to see some of the desert. The new highway between the cities was spectacular but the scenery was flat and monotonous. The last couple of hours, climbing the escarpment into Riyadh was scenic, but even Duffield, upon arrival, said they would fly back.

The trip had so far been a poignant reminder to Rogers that he had been this route before. He remembered scenes and places in Jeddah and noted with amusement that the old British Embassy had been converted into a kindergarten, but Jeddah had merely been the appetiser. Climbing the road into Riyadh he was vividly reminded of the descent, on the other side of the city, that he had taken with Whittle, and the numerous wrecks, still liberally scattered along the side of the highway, painted yet more pictures of the man whom he now knew was responsible for eight murders and in all probability a total of twice that number. He had spent many private moments agonising over his inability to detect the signs, but always came to the same conclusion – what signs? Perhaps he should have realised the need to avoid visas in and out of Cairo but if he had missed that so had everyone else and the only other clue he could recall was Whittle dropping a glass at the mention of the name Butterworth. Whittle was drunk and the connection was tenuous. A computer programmed to detect the obscure might have made the connection but a human mind, fallible with scotch, would inevitably miss it. Self-recrimination was over. He knew they were closing in on the truth and he hoped that he would soon be facing Whittle again, in person, this time with proof positive.

Riyadh had changed dramatically since his last visit and Rogers found it difficult to orientate himself in the city. The road system was entirely new; the airport was now twenty miles out of the city, and they booked into a Sheraton that had been built on a street that had not existed on his last visit.

After a good night's rest they assembled for breakfast. Duffield, still bemoaning the lack of bacon, settled for a steak and eggs with a large stack of pancakes; the other two had toast and coffee.

Rogers reviewed the plans they had agreed on the previous day during the long drive. "First, we need to establish that Whittle was in Riyadh on December 10th, 1983. The one avenue to follow is his former office here, on the off-chance that they may still have records on him. If that draws a blank we need a copy of his exit visas from the Ministry of the Interior. If we find that he was in Riyadh then a visit to all the embassies is in order, starting with the British Embassy, to find out if they have any records of a murder around that time. According to the Foreign Office in London there was no incident here in '83 but who believes diplomats? If all that fails we'll resort to the police to find out who he killed."

Duffield wiped his mouth with his napkin, tossed it on the table and stood up. "Right, Sherlock, settle the bill and we're off." He emitted a loud belch and headed for the exit.

"Appetite prodigious, etiquette zero." Rogers commented to no one in particular.

The meeting at the insurance office was unrewarding. The only member of staff left from the Whittle era was an Indian secretary. He could not remember if Whittle was in Riyadh in December 1983 but he did recall that he had left Saudi for good in early 1984 to work in Bahrain and he also remembered that Whittle had gone to Brazil for a holiday in February 1984. Rogers enquired as to why he recalled Whittle's Brazilian holiday. The little Indian laughed and jiggled his head from side to side and said that he remembered because Whittle had been to the carnival in Rio and had come back with many photographs of scantily-clad women which he had shown him.

Rogers and Duffield concluded that the Bahrain information was interesting but that the holiday in Brazil was not relevant. They passed the information to Hayne who, with a pocketful of riyals, set off for the Ministry of the Interior. Four hours later he emerged with empty pockets and the information that confirmed that Whittle was in Saudi during December 1983. In addition he had copies of all exit and re-entry permits that had been issued to Whittle during his stay in the Kingdom. Hayne had never understood the necessity of the exit visa system. To him it showed the true perversity of the country that you had to obtain a visa to leave and in order to prevent you leaving without the requisite permit all passports had to be surrendered to your employer. The system did not affect him as he carried diplomatic immunity, but for the average guy in Saudi, he reasoned, it must be a real pain. However, in this instance he also had to agree that without the system he could not have obtained the information that Rogers and Duffield needed.

The following morning Sam Duffield was dropped at the gate of the British Embassy. Over Rogers' protests Duffield went in alone while Rogers accompanied Hayne back to the American Embassy to check their records. Once inside Duffield had to explain his needs to three separate people before he was finally shown into the office of the Deputy Ambassador, Paul Channing.

"Inspector Duffield, please have a seat. How may we help our American cousins?" Channing extended a thin purple-veined hand and had his fingers crushed by Duffield's vice-like grip. Wincing slightly and caressing his knuckles he listened intently while Duffield explained what he was looking for.

When he had finished Channing picked up the phone and asked his secretary to come in. An anaemic-looking man in his early thirties entered. "Stevens, this is Mr Sam Duffield of the FBI," Channing added as an afterthought, "in America." Stevens nodded in recognition. "Can you retrieve our archives for the months of November and December 1983 and January 1984 and set them up in the library for Mr Duffield to read."

The secretary left and Channing returned his attention to Duffield. "I'm afraid I can't help you personally. I wasn't here in those days and I've never had the luxury of time to go back and find out what happened before my arrival. Anyway, let me show you where the library is."

Channing led him along the corridor and down one flight of stairs. Opening the door of a darkened room he reached out to switch on the light. "If you need anything copied or need any help, ask Stevens and feel free to come and ask me any questions." He went to hold out his hand, thought better of it and left.

Stevens entered a few minutes later carrying the November and December files, saying he would just go and get the January file.

Duffield ignored the November binder and went straight to the

December file. The large ring-binder was made up of press clippings and memos of incidents that had happened that in anyway involved British subjects. In the first week of December there were two reports of deaths, both from automobile accidents; a memo noting the impending release, in January, of a British subject convicted of selling alcohol after a three-year incarceration; and a memo from the Foreign Office in London encouraging the Embassy to ensure that all British nationals working in Saudi were registered with the Embassy. There were no entries in the file for the 8th, 9th or 10th but, turning the page to the 11th, Duffield was greeted by a photocopy of the front page of the local English language newspaper. The banner headline screamed at him: LOCAL GIRL RAPED BY INFIDEL. Duffield felt his pulse quicken. The story was easy to digest and the conclusion was as clear as the newsprint. He quickly read the follow-up reports of the next few days and was amused to note the corner that the local police had painted themselves into. Long before he reached the paragraph concerning the police announcement that the case was closed, he knew they had not found the rapist, who was in fact also a murderer – and Simon Whittle personified.

At that moment Stevens walked back in carrying two more files. "January must have been . . . "

Whatever he was going to say was interrupted by Duffield. "I need copies of all pages from December 11th through to the 19th." He thrust the file at Stevens. "And I need a ride back to the American Consulate all within the next ten minutes."

Stevens took the file and stood holding it. "Move," yelled Duffield. Stevens moved.

Fifteen minutes later Duffield strode into the office at the American Consulate that had been allocated for their use and held up the photocopied headline. He opened his mouth to speak but no words came out as Rogers held up the same newspaper in original form. As Bud Hayne looked from one to the other he was amused that for the first time since he had met them, both Duffield and Rogers were lost for words. The effect lasted for less than ten seconds.

"It's him, isn't it? The arrogant sonofabitch couldn't pass up the temptation. Go for the unobtainable."

"He took me to Dirayh when I was here. It's a few miles out of the city, there wasn't much to it. God knows if it still exists."

"It still exists." Hayne spoke up. "I doubt if the family live there any longer. It's a deserted village restored for the locals to appreciate their heritage."

"Great. We have to talk to this girl." Duffield padded around the room like a caged animal. "Come on, Hayne, prove your worth. How do we find her and her family?"

It took two days but eventually Hayne managed to trace the whereabouts of the family. After the incident they had petitioned the King for money to buy land to the west of Riyadh. The family was still there tending camels and goats on the arid soil.

The directions were suitably vague but with Hayne as guide and interpreter Duffield and Rogers eventually found the track that led them off the main road and brought them to a small, concrete dwelling. The building stood in abject isolation, surrounded by vast empty spaces. The sun beat down relentlessly and, turning in a three-hundred-and-sixty-degree circle, the only sight was a barren tree about one hundred yards from the house. A herd of goats moved aimlessly near the tree and, through the heat haze, you could make out the crouched black shape of a human form.

Hayne stopped the car twenty yards from the house and the three men in shirtsleeves climbed out. The door of the dwelling opened and a short squat Arab in his one-piece under-shirt walked out. A black-clad figure stood behind him in the doorway. He turned and gesticulated at her furiously and the door closed.

Hayne, switching smoothly into Arabic, called out, *"Salaam Alaakam."*

"Alaakam Salaam," the Arab replied and moved closer.

"Que Falliq?"

"Humdillala," came the reply. Rogers remembered enough from his crash course in Arabic, ten years ago, to know that Hayne had merely greeted the Arab and enquired after his well-being.

The Arab was now only a few feet from Hayne; Duffield and Rogers were standing behind him and to his left. Hayne could see from the Arab's eyes that he was wary and had already guessed the purpose of their visit. In his perfect Arabic Hayne explained why they were there. He never got to ask to speak to the daughter; the colour in the Arab's cheeks rose to a violent red hue; he reached into the parched earth and, grabbing a handful of dirt, threw it at Hayne. Screeching in a high pitched whine he began kicking at the ground, sending small showers of dirt over Hayne's legs. Hayne indicated to the other two that they should get back into the car. The Arab continued screeching and the black-shrouded figure reappeared at the door to watch the scene. Hayne started the engine and swung the car around the distraught Arab who still continued to kick the desert soil towards the retreating vehicle.

As they headed back to the road they could still see the silent figure tending the goats under the tree.

"Nice going. Whadaya tell him? We were from the Jewish Defence League?"

"Very funny. I told him we had some information connected with the rape of his daughter a few years back. That's when he gave me the dirt shower. The screaming was his denial that he even had a daughter. They live in total isolation, probably ostracised by the local community. The figure tending the goats was probably the daughter but we ain't ever going to find out."

Rogers, who had been quiet up to this point, simply said, "Fuck. Even when he makes a mistake he gets away with it."

That evening the American Consul General invited the three of them to join him for dinner. His wife was away and the four of them had a pleasant evening shooting the breeze. The talk was mainly about the Giants, Reds and Lakers and Duffield's beloved Knicks; the Consul General knew better than to enquire about the status of the case they were working on.

Rogers felt better for an evening of total relaxation, although his head throbbed the following morning from the whisky. Duffield was one of that rare and enviable breed that did not suffer from hangovers and was his usual jovial self at breakfast.

"Morning, Sherlock. Jesus, you look the colour of vomit. C'mon, let's see some action. I'm relying on your navigational skills to get us to Bahrain, I assume that's where we're headed?"

"It looks like it. Do you have to be so bloody cheerful every morning?"

"Testy, aren't we? If you can't hold your liquor you shouldn't play with the big boys." Duffield signalled a waiter and spent the next twenty minutes wallowing in food.

Hayne arrived just as they were finishing breakfast. He looked worse than Rogers, which made Rogers feel slightly better, but declined all offers of food and drink. "I've booked us on the noon flight to Bahrain and we have –" Hayne sensed Duffield staring at him, "– you have a meeting with the Assistant Chief of Police, in Bahrain, at 9.30 tomorrow morning." He looked up expectantly, seeking praise.

"Us as in we three? Or us as in we two?" Duffield enquired.

"C'mon, guys, you need me. Who else are you going to get to translate for you?"

"I need you like I need piles . . . " Rogers interrupted.

"What the hell, a few days in Bahrain won't hurt him, let him come."

Bahrain, they quickly realised, was the oasis in the gulf. They arrived on Wednesday afternoon to find the capital, Manama, teeming with Saudis. The causeway connecting Bahrain to the Saudi mainland ensured that the bars and nightclubs were well-stocked with the distinctive thobe and ghotra of the Saudi whose subtle approach to picking up Western women was normally limited to the question, "How much?"

Duffield quickly realised that they had been conned by Hayne as English was spoken everywhere. They left him sunning himself by the pool the following morning as they departed to keep their appointment.

The Assistant Chief of Police was a short dapper man in his late fifties. His English had a clipped colonial accent and he held himself with a decidedly military bearing. He was immediately helpful and, after passing pleasantries and providing tea, he settled back to relate what he described as the muddled affair of Guttman Singh.

"Shortly after midnight on December 11th, 1984, the Manama police station received an emergency call from a gentleman reporting that the passenger in his car had suffered some sort of seizure or fit. He said the car, a Rolls Royce, was broken down and his passenger needed an ambulance immediately. I was an inspector in those days and was also dispatched to the scene. I arrived before the ambulance and found the driver, Guttman Singh, in a very distraught state, fretting over the body of a young European lady who was slumped in the rear seat of the car. Once the young lady – a Theresa Evans who worked for the local airline – had been taken care of, Singh told me his version of what had happened. He told me the name of his employer, a prominent local family, and stated that he had been asked to wait and drive the young girl from the beach house by the son of his employer. He told me that several girls had attended a party there that night but all the guests and the hosts, with the exception of the son and the young lady, had left about an hour earlier. The son told Singh that the young lady was sleeping and that he was to drive her home once she woke up. The young lady appeared, about fifteen minutes later, in a distressed state. Halfway back to Manama the car started to overheat. He pulled over to check the engine, discovered that they needed water, and set off to a nearby house to get some. When he returned he found the young lady slumped in the back seat of the car. He called the police and the rest I knew."

The Assistant Chief paused for questions. As none were forthcoming he continued. "The story was very plausible and Singh himself seemed genuinely upset by what had happened. I waited with him until a tow-truck arrived. Although it was a moonlit night there was not enough light to see under the car, so one of the mechanics manoeuvred my car across the road and switched on the headlights. As he swung the car round in a circle the lights illuminated a tree that stood between the road and the sea. There appeared to be a bundle at the base of the tree. I went over to investigate and found the body of Charman Shar, she had been strangled. Singh appeared as astounded as the rest of us at this turn of events but in the light of this development I felt obligated to bring him in for questioning. During the time he was in custody he never changed his story and swore that he had no knowledge of the woman in the bushes.

"Around 8.30 that morning I took a call from the hospital. A doctor informed me that Theresa Evans had suffered a massive stroke and was completely paralysed except for a minimal amount of movement of her left hand. He went on to tell me that she had been sodomized within the last twelve hours and from the bruises and marks on her body he had concluded that the sodomy had not taken place voluntarily. There were no signs of sexual intercourse. I asked him if he thought the act of sodomy had caused the stroke and he replied that it was almost certainly a contributory factor. More tea, gentlemen?" Without waiting for a response he ordered it.

The three sat in silence while the tea was served by a young Pakistani boy. When he departed the Bahraini officer continued. "There is little more to add to the story. Guttman Singh accused his employer's son of the rape and continued with his protestations of innocence in the death of Charman Shar. We of course checked his story with his employers and were told of other incidents with Singh and women. We ultimately felt there was enough evidence to try him and he was found guilty of one charge of murder and two charges of rape."

Rogers found that his mind was in turmoil. The room was excessively warm; there was no air-conditioning, just an overhead fan moving the air very slowly; and he was finding it difficult to focus coherently on any one single fact that had been revealed. Instead, all the information seemed to be running haphazardly through his mind.

Duffield, although confused, was better focused. "What happened to Singh?"

"He was sentenced to death." Rogers head shot up and his eyes rested heavily on the speaker. "The sentence was commuted to life imprisonment, he is still in jail on the island."

"You mean Bahrain?" Rogers had finally found his voice.

"No, Inspector Rogers, we have an island off the west coast

which serves as a prison. Our own Alcatraz. Gentlemen, I feel I have been most patient in telling you about this case. In turn I would appreciate an explanation of your interest in Guttman Singh."

Duffield looked at Rogers who was staring at the floor. He coughed gently before speaking. "We have been following a suspected murderer for some weeks now. There is a quirk in the murders that he commits in that, over a period of years, they have all taken place on December 10th." He paused while the Assistant Chief digested this information. "We are tracing the places our suspect has lived and it appears that he was living in Bahrain in 1984." The words seem to hang in the air between Duffield and his counterpart behind the desk. Duffield was aware of perspiration trickling down his neck and would have welcomed the chance to loosen his tie.

The Assistant Chief in comparison looked pristine and cool and it was some seconds before he spoke. "I see, you believe that we may have made a mistake?"

"At the present time we can't say. The only thing in common at the moment is the date." To placate his feelings he added, "We may just be dealing with a coincidence."

The meeting concluded. The air between them was much cooler, more distant than when they had arrived but it was at least not the open hostility that they had encountered elsewhere. The Assistant Chief promised to have a full copy of the file delivered to their hotel later that morning and offered an invitation for them to return and discuss the case as they saw fit.

As they were leaving Rogers turned to ask one last question. "It may be necessary for us to talk with Singh. Would that be possible?" He knew that he was rubbing salt into fresh wounds but he felt that the question was important.

The answer was an immediate, but resentful, "Of course."

They joined Hayne at the pool and ordered lunch: club sandwiches with real bacon. Rogers was annoyed but he was not sure what at: the inefficiency of the system, the frustration of chasing shadows, or simply the growing casualty list.

Duffield, always more practical and objective, set about analysing the information that they had. "We know an awful lot but there are still huge pieces missing. Who is, or was, Charman Shar? Is Singh guilty of rape and innocent of murder or is he innocent, period? The traits are all in place: the murderer had to be Whittle. The coincidence, the irrelevance, has to be Theresa Evans, she does not fit the pattern. Why would Whittle waste time raping, sodomizing, a girl in the back of a car when he has just raped and murdered, or was just about to rape and murder someone, and sodomy is not his style."

"He somehow gets access to Theresa Evans, she suffers a stroke, he leaves the scene and finds Shar, by chance, and murders her." Rogers knew that it sounded weak but he looked up hopefully.

"Doesn't work, Sherlock, and where does Singh fit into it? Whittle may be a good talker but I can't believe that he could have talked Singh into staying around and taking the rap for him."

Hayne had been quietly munching his sandwich and was attempting to piece it all together from the fragments of conversation that he had heard. He had several questions to ask but was prevented from doing so by the arrival of a policeman at the pool-side.

"Inspector Rogers?"

"Here."

"A package from the Assistant Chief of Police, sir." He handed two large brown envelopes to Rogers and left.

"I can't read in this sunlight, let's go inside." Rogers picked up the envelopes and headed for the door. Duffield rose to follow him. Hayne thought about it but resisted the urge and stayed in the sun.

In the cool of Rogers' room they started to pour over the files. Duffield set about finding the identity of Charman Shar while Rogers tackled the rest of the papers.

They read in silence for about five minutes before Duffield spoke. "Yusuf Bin Alwhary – wasn't that the company that Whittle worked for in Saudi?"

Rogers nodded but added, "Not so much the company as the sponsors of the insurance company that he worked for. Why?"

"Charman Shar worked as a maid for the employees of Yusuf Bin Alwhary."

"In Saudi? What the . . . "

"No, here in Bahrain. She lived at the housing compound on the Janaya road."

"Jesus Christ." Rogers moved across the room and grabbed the phone book from under the phone. In his haste the phone clattered to the ground. Ignoring the instrument at his feet he flicked through the directory and found the entry for Yusuf Bin Alwhary. The typed entry simply gave several telephone numbers but the box advertisement, in the bottom left-hand corner, listed all the services that the company offered and there, nestled comfortably among them, was "Insurance".

Rogers passed the phone book to Duffield and distractedly picked up the phone and placed it on the bedside table. "I don't believe it – he murdered his cleaning lady." Duffield stared at him. Rogers was still holding the phone and his hand involuntarily jumped as the phone rang. Grasping the receiver he answered monosyllabically, "Yes." There was a long pause. "Room 206." He hung up. "We are about to have a visitor, the brother of Guttman Singh."

Rajid Singh was dressed in business attire, although, as was the norm, without a jacket. Damp patches beneath his armpits gave away his agitation and he constantly looked over his shoulder even after the door was closed behind him. He gratefully accepted a glass of water but declined the offer of a seat. Rogers was preparing to speak when Singh placed the glass on the table and began talking.

"I believe, good gentlemen, that you are here in connection with my brother. My brother is innocent. He did not commit the crimes for which he was convicted. He is a kind and gentle man, with a wife and three children back in India. He had no need of women and only agreed to the vile requests of his employers to earn more money and return home a wealthy man."

"You are saying your brother was forced to perform sexual acts with women for his employer?" Rogers asked.

"Oh no, sir, you are misunderstanding. The family that my brother worked for is very influential. They are involved in all aspects of commerce on the island and very close to the royal family. The airline employs many Western girls and the family, the male members that is, make it their business to entertain all of the newly arrived girls. Some girls stay after dinner. Theresa Evans undoubtedly stayed with the youngest son and slept with him. He is, I believe they call it, a sadist. He most undoubtedly performed unnatural acts with her and then insisted that my poor brother drive the unfortunate girl back to her home. That is what I mean when I speak of vile requests."

Duffield looked up at Singh who had remained standing throughout. "The police say that they spoke to the family concerned and they reported other incidents of your brother's indiscretions with women."

Rajid Singh became very angry and his answer was delivered in heated tones. "These are lies. The son framed my brother. To remove the stench from his house he lied to the police. My brother is a good man." There was a pause during which Singh's laboured breathing could be heard. "I am sorry, I do not mean to speak forcibly but . . . " His voice trailed off.

"What about Charman Shar, did your brother know her?"

"My brother knew no one of this name and cannot explain to this day where the body came from. The police are too swift with their justice. My brother is innocent, innocent I tell you." The room fell silent. Neither Duffield nor Rogers knew what to say but it was Rogers who finally broke the silence.

"Mr Singh, we appreciate your coming to see us and we will of course treat what you have told us as confidential. We are not at liberty to tell you why we are here, except to confirm that you are correct in the part of it that relates to your brother. Our investigations have a long way to go and it is possible that at the end we may not be able to prove your brother's innocence on either of the counts for which he was convicted. But, let me assure you, should we find anything that substantiates your brother's innocence we will pass it to the local police."

Singh was concerned but grateful and left.

"Okay, we're getting there. The son of a wealthy Bahraini committed the rape, if it was rape, and Whittle committed the murder. Time to visit Janaya road."

Duffield rose from the chair and followed Rogers outside.

The taxi driver had no problems finding the compound. It was a short, ten-minute ride out of Manama. There was a small security guard box at the front gate, which was empty, and the taxi swung through the gate and parked at the rear of one of the buildings. The compound consisted of two five-storey buildings with three apartments on each floor. The grounds were well-tended and included a tennis court and swimming pool. Another small building appeared to be servants' quarters and there were two areas of covered parking. Duffield asked the taxi to wait for them. Before they could enter the building a figure emerged from the servants' quarters. He was hurrying towards them trying to slip a sandal on his left foot at the same time. The voluminous pants that he wore denoted him as Pakistani.

From the discussion that followed they ascertained that he was the missing sentry. He informed them that he had not worked at the compound at the time of Charman Shar but was familiar with the story of her murder. He told them that they should speak to Taj who had worked there since the compound opened. Taj, it transpired, would not be back until that night as it was his day off.

They were about to leave, intending to return later, when the guard said, "Maybe you should try Mrs McComb. The good lady and her husband have lived here the longest. She is in the second building. Number 310."

Thanking him for his assistance they walked towards the apartment while the delinquent sentry shuffled off to assume his duties.

The door of apartment 310 was opened by a large over-weight woman of indeterminate age. Duffield made the introductions and she invited them in. They explained the reason for their visit and asked if she had known Charman Shar and did she remember who lived on the compound at the time of the murder.

Patricia McComb, "call me Pat", was the compound gossip and relished the opportunity to tell all, or at least all that she knew, about Shar and the compound.

"Poor dear, she was only twenty. She used to clean for me and a few others. Well, I don't know what went on but she was all sweetness and light and had the kind of body that drove men wild, know what I mean?" She placed her hands under her own, not inconsiderable bosom, and heaved it upwards. "Always told me that she was a virgin and was saving herself for the right man in Sri Lanka, then along comes one of them wogs and kills her. Damn shame. If you ask me they should have hung the bastard."

Duffield tried to get her back on track. "Do you recall who lived here in those days?"

"Now let me see, there was Madge and John, Phil, Wendy and Omar – now could I tell you stories about those two . . ." Seeing the look on Rogers' face she continued, "Phyllis and Mike." She stopped, her brow furrowed in concentration. "And us of course. There were only about half the flats occupied then; they were new and we were waiting for people to be allocated to them. Tony and Pat, or did they come later? I can't remember. Oh and of course there was Simon. Who could forget Simon? He was one of the other two that Charman worked for."

"Simon? Do you recall his last name?" Rogers leaned forward, resting his chin on the palm of his hand.

"Now, let me see, Wattle or something like that." Her brow creased even deeper. "Whittle, Simon Whittle, that's it, he ran the insurance office."

They left quickly and it was only after they were gone that Pat McComb realised that she hadn't finished her list and it was odd that the only surname she had given had been Simon's. Oh well, such is life. Checking her watch she poured herself a G & T before settling down for an afternoon nap.

Rogers and Duffield decided that they should visit Guttman Singh in jail and the visit was arranged for the following morning by the ever-helpful Assistant Chief who was far too polite to ask how the investigation was going.

A police car collected them from their hotel at 9.00 and drove them to a jetty at a deserted point on the west coast of the island. A small motor launch was waiting to take them across the short expanse of water to the island. A powerful smell permeated the air as they docked and increased in intensity as they made their way up the concrete path. It assaulted the senses and was almost overwhelming as they entered through a door and were shown into a small interview room. The smell was difficult to describe. It seemed to swing from a urine base to vomit and on to ammonia, occasionally combining all three.

The door opened and a wizened figure, manacled hand and foot, was led in. Guttman Singh looked about sixty but Rogers knew from his file that he was only forty-two. He was frighteningly thin and the manacles looked as if they would slide over his emaciated hands and feet. The door closed behind him. Singh stood in front of the table looking directly at his feet. Rogers rose and pulled out a chair for him to sit on. He flopped onto the chair and the sound of bone striking metal echoed in the isolated chamber.

Duffield commenced the same speech that he had delivered to Andy Simms, which seemed like years ago but was in fact only a couple of weeks ago. "Mr Singh, we have reason to believe that you may be innocent of the crimes for which you were convicted. Inspector Rogers and myself are currently reviewing the case and need to have your version of what happened that night." Duffield and Rogers looked at Singh. His head was still bowed and he said nothing as a tear rolled down his face and landed amongst the multiple stains of his ragged clothes.

It took Guttman Singh half an hour to tell his story and it varied not one bit from the story that he had told eight years previously.

chapter 38

Six years. It is now six years since I was last forced to supplicate to the whim of . . . of what? If I only knew.

The dim anonymous days of 1986 and beyond are mere thoughts on the wind. A recovering drug addict or alcoholic must take it one day at a time, fighting the desires and urges which are ever present, mockingly close.

My own addiction was modified by its content. Even at the height of its destructive powers it was only manifest one day a year. To therefore survive for six years is simplicity itself.

Six days, a mere bagatelle.

In truth it is only five; it is late November and the sixth approaches. Each day has been easy; some easier than others. The voices are stilled but not extinct. I have heard their plaintive wail in the dead of night and in the light of day. Mental weariness sometimes allows them a moment of speech. They are no longer grandiose in their demands; they no longer prey on the susceptibility of physical weakness. They speak as prisoners, begging, no, not begging, but requesting release. They are cunning, shrewd and vindictive, but as the hostage turned captor I am equal to their puny innuendo. I do not know if I can last forever, but four to five to six to seven does not seem hard. Digits of success, digits of confidence.

Life has moved on since Bermuda. We have lived in America now for two and a half years and now we are three. A nine-month-old daughter demands my attentions and unreservedly receives them.

New York has been fun. We have lived it, seen it and are ready to move on. The world of commuting and high finance has extracted its toll. When I found I needed to carry a gun for protection I knew it was not a world for me and I wish to withdraw gracefully, but firmly, from its presence. The

American workplace or, more specifically, the New York workplace is not a rose garden. The work is secondary to the politics and the politics are secondary to nothing. If the time and energy devoted to staying alive and grasping the next rung were channelled into positive areas the result would, I feel sure, be healthier for all concerned.

I have witnessed both sides of the equation: the Arab in the desert, his castles in the sand; the Jew in the city, his castles in the sky. They are of the same cloth, of the same warp and weft. One may be more articulate then the other, one may be more frugal or keener, but I can stop on a Manhattan street, close my eyes, listen, and I hear Jeddah.

Despite its foibles and contradictions we have enjoyed the area's hospitality, savoured the style and delights of American living. It is time to say, "Thank you," and take our leave. A decision not arrived at lightly but one dictated by circumstances, a daughter to protect, educate and nurture.

Where to next? We will return to Bermuda, immigration permitting. The environment in all its manifestations is ideal for raising children. It satisfies our desires to cease our nomadic roaming and establish permanence.

Judith is happy. Besotted with the inexplicable joy of motherhood, she has formed a new career, more rewarding, at least temporarily, than the last one.

In a dark crevice of my mind I know that Bermuda answered once and for all the unanswerable addiction. Once in five years I have been tempted, but the temptation was easily fought; no plan was formulated, no victim selected. Bermuda removes temptation to another time, another place.

This December of '92 looms ahead, obelisk-like in its presence, immovable in its stature, and yet so easy to walk around. I am not the person I was at fourteen or twenty-five. It is trite and convenient to say I have matured. The word is rounded but ineffectual. I feel I have experienced not only life and death but I have eaten from many tables, tasted delights and disappointments, profited in my ventures and exploited my inner self. I would like to be able to say that I have cleansed the inner self but I know that I have simply edited it. I can recall with perfect clarity walking in the woods but I meet no one. I can walk out of a Nottingham night club and simply drive home. I can enjoy the beauty of a Samba dance on Sugar-Loaf and not feel the need to consume it.

Guilt is not a factor. How can you experience guilt without reason and reason without cause? My life has changed. I no longer feel the need to prove myself by drinking to excess or by pushing everyone and everything to the limit. The bull-like charge has given way to a more refined acknowledgement of what I am. It is not maturity, it is curiosity satisfied.

The time of year is fast approaching when I must be vigilant, when I stand and fight alone. You cannot ask for support when the essence of truth will cause the support to crumble before you. I do not look for sympathy. I have enjoyed my life and intend to continue enjoying it in the future.

It is nineteen years since my birthday was forgotten. This coming December I could revisit the man I was then, or I can face the reflection in the mirror on the 11th knowing that I have won again.

Six, six days of abstinence. The choice is simple.

chapter 39

The long flight back to London began on the stroke of midnight. Both Rogers and Duffield were subdued. Tired from the mental exhaustion of the past few days and the heat-sapping environment, they were happy to relax with their drinks and let the plane carry them home.

After their meeting with Guttman Singh they had spent a fruitless two days ascertaining that there had been no serious crime in Bahrain in December 1985, despite the fact that Whittle still lived there at that time. However, they were unable to confirm that Whittle had actually been on the island during December '85 as Bahrain did not operate the odious exit visa system and airline passenger records did not go back that far.

Having decided that the area held no further clues or secrets, they dispatched Hayne back to the monotony of Saudi and spent their final hours in Bahrain rummaging in the *souk*. Rogers bought a small pearl necklace for Cynthia, and Duffield, when Rogers was out of sight, purchased a diamond ring for Heather.

Neither had spoken much about the case in the last few hours but now they were airborne, drinks in hand, Duffield addressed the issue.

"We're tightening the noose around his balls but we still have to nail him." Rogers suppressed the English teacher urge to comment on his mixing of metaphors. "His passport is the key now, we need a copy of it. A break-in at his house should be easy enough to arrange. We could either steal it or at worst have it photographed."

"I agree about the passport but I don't like the idea of the break-in. Can't we just telephone, him, tell him the records in Jeddah have been destroyed in a fire and we need, or more specifically, the British Embassy need a copy of his passport? He could post it to Washington or wherever, and bingo, we get our copy."

Duffield drained his glass and pulled down his tray/table in anticipation of dinner. "Not bad, Sherlock, could work. You don't think we'll spook him?"

"Why should we? To make it foolproof we can rope in the Embassy people in Washington, then if he wants to check the story they'll confirm it for us."

They sat in silence for a while until Rogers let out a heavy sigh. "You realise, of course, that we don't have a case? I don't mean just the missing pages of some passport, I mean we don't have any evidence, not one piece. We have a ton of circumstantial stuff and we both know he's guilty but what we don't have is a case that will stand up in court."

"I know that, Sherlock, I was waiting to see how long it was before you brought it up." Duffield swilled the remaining ice-cubes around in his glass and signalled a passing stewardess for a re-fill. "So what you gonna do?"

Rogers shook his head. "Confront him, I suppose. Tell him what we know."

It took two days of report writing once they got back, to England, plus numerous meetings with the hierarchy, before Rogers was able to convince those involved that Whittle was indeed a psychopathic serial killer, but that hard evidence with which to convict him had thus far proven to be elusive. He received permission to confront Whittle, in the hope that this action in itself would lead Whittle to crack.

The two detectives set about tying up as many loose ends as possible before they left for the States. As there was a British Consulate in New York the decision was taken to route Whittle's passport request there. The fire in the Jeddah office plan was shelved at the last minute when a cursory check by the staff of the Consulate revealed that both Simon Whittle's and his wife's passport had been submitted only two months previously for the inclusion of a daughter. The news of a daughter was added to the growing pile of facts and a new plan was formulated.

On January 16th a phone call was placed to Mrs Judith Whittle. A sympathetic, but bored, Consulate employee informed her that due to a clerical error the details pertaining to their daughter had been added to the passports but not to the Embassy's records. She went on to ask if Mrs Whittle could send the passports to Washington by registered mail. They would be returned within two weeks or, if she preferred, they could be mailed or brought to the Consulate in Manhattan. Judith Whittle took the path of least resistance and decided that Simon could drop them off during the day in Manhattan. The bored voice assured her that it would only take five minutes and that if her husband cared to wait he would be given the passports back again there and then. She concluded the phone call by saying that her husband should ask for Mr John Patterson of the passport section. The Consulate reception staff was supplemented by the addition of an FBI employee to await the passports.

On Thursday morning a woman presented herself at the Consulate reception. She identified herself as the secretary of Mr Simon Whittle and handed over an envelope marked for the attention of Mr John Patterson, passport section. Ten minutes later the FBI employee was heading back downtown with the envelope, and by 3.30 p.m. London time Rogers and Duffield were reviewing copies. A monitor was placed on all incoming calls to the Consulate in New York and the Embassy in Washington for two weeks, but no phone call was ever received regarding the issue.

Rogers was hunched over his desk, his eyes focusing on the papers in front of him. Sam Duffield reclined in an armchair with his feet on the coffee table surveying an identical sheaf of papers.

"Shit, this guy gets around." Duffield turned a piece of paper sideways to read an immigration stamp. "December 2nd, 1986, entered New Zealand. Can't see an exit stamp but his Australian visa is stamped as having entered the country on December 18th. If my geography of the region's correct, there's fuck all else down there so my guess would be that he was in New Zealand in '86." He looked up at Rogers.

"Sounds good and it looks like we have Singapore for '85. From these hieroglyphics he left Bahrain in late November and entered Singapore on December 5th, leaving again on December 11th." Rogers pressed a button on the telephone console on his desk. His secretary came into the room with a notebook in hand. Rogers picked up the file of papers in front of him and handed them to her. "In 1981 this reptile, Simon Whittle, boarded a flight from London to the Middle East. This," he indicated the papers, "is a copy of his most recent passport, and this," he pulled another file of papers out from a drawer, "is the copy of his original passport. All you have to do to win a free weekend at Butlins is produce a chronological listing of where he has been since birth until yesterday." She took the papers without comment and left.

Duffield watched her retreating form. "I like the strong silent types. Where the fuck is Butlins?"

Rogers ignored the question. "Didn't someone tell us in Bahrain that after he left there he travelled the world?"

"Yeah, the Indian secretary, but it was in Riyadh. Remember the guy with the wobbly head?"

"And didn't someone tell us that he moved to Bermuda after that, and when the hell did he get married?"

The rising frustration in Rogers' voice was not missed by Duffield. "He was married in '87, at least that's the year she requested the name change on her passport. Look, Sherlock, he ain't gonna murder again tonight. Let's get out there, go eat the biggest steak we can find and drink till the sun comes up or we fall off our seats, whichever comes first. Whadaya say?"

Rogers looked as if he was going to argue, then laughed, the frustration he felt evaporating with the gesture. "Okay, you smooth talking bastard, let's hit Jimmy's in the Strand on your expense account."

They hit Jimmy's hard and by the following morning Rogers could feel Jimmy's hitting back. Duffield was already in the office when he arrived, trying hard to focus on the type-written sheets he had found on Rogers' desk. For once even he looked under the weather, though he blamed it on the water that they made the ice with in this country.

Rogers picked up his copy, went to the last page and worked backwards. There were numerous entries for Bermuda but since Whittle's move to the States in '89 his travel had come to a virtual halt, apart from one visit back to Bermuda. The only other exits from the States did not show a corresponding entry anywhere. Rogers surmised that these were probably entries into the UK, where his passport would not have been stamped.

Moving on to the Bermuda years Rogers found numerous visits to the States, two to Canada, one to Mexico and several to various Caribbean islands, including five to Barbados. Again there were several exits with no corresponding port of entry. His befuddled brain registered that in 1987 and '88 Whittle had been in Bermuda during December and the same was true for the States for '89 through to '92. They knew about 1992 but what about the other years?

Both men sat in silence studying the list. Rogers looked up several times to ensure that Duffield had not fallen asleep. It was

Duffield who finally broke the silence. "It's no good, I need some food. Kill or cure. Where's that disgusting canteen you have around here?"

Against his better judgement Rogers followed Duffield's example and tackled a full fried breakfast. The first few minutes were not an experience that he would care to repeat on a regular basis but by the end of breakfast he knew he was alive, if not necessarily cured.

Duffield however was cured and, back in the office, set about happily consuming his fourth cup of coffee. "Guess we have two ways of dealing with this: one of us could head down to Singapore and New Zealand while the other one heads to Bermuda; or, more practically, we could utilise the electronic wizardry at our command, pull a few strings, and collect the information that we already know is going to prove the obvious."

"Something's still worrying me." Rogers fixed his gaze on the papers in front of Duffield; he leaned across and with his pen, bracketed the two Bermuda years and then tapped it several times. "Bermuda's a small island in the Atlantic somewhere off the east coast of the States. I don't remember the exact numbers but I do know that it's small – a population of around fifty thousand. I had to run some checks once on one of the banks there, possible money laundering, but it came up clean. It's still owned by Britain. Whittle may be good but I don't see how for two years he can murder people on an island, on the same date, and get away with it."

"You said it, he's good. Let's make that a priority call later this morning; they must be four or five hours behind us. Once we know the details we can set about working out how he got away with it."

"Thank you, commissioner, you've been most helpful . . . No, that's fine. Thank you." Rogers hung up the phone and looked at Duffield. "None, not one. There have only been two murders in the period Whittle lived in Bermuda, both were domestic disputes and both cases are closed. Before you ask, one was in March and the other in August."

"Sonofabitch can't do this to us." Duffield slapped the desk in frustration. "We have him cold then he slips us the curve-ball, little shit. What's he up to?"

The phone rang again. Rogers picked it up. "Rogers . . . thanks." There was a short pause. "Inspector Lee, thanks for getting back to us so quickly . . . Yes." There was a longer pause while Rogers made notes. "Two, both on December 10th? . . . Cause of death? . . . Thanks, that's great. Can you fax the reports? . . . No, just the one where the girl was strangled. Great, thanks again." He hung up the phone. "December 1985, a hotel employee, no one ever arrested for the murder, obviously Whittle. There was another murder, earlier the same day – a transvestite, American, was found murdered in her apartment. He, she, it was beaten to death with a table lamp."

"Anyone ever arrested for that murder?"

"I didn't ask him. It doesn't fit Whittle so I'm not interested.

The faxed report arrived from Singapore thirty minutes later but it was eight o'clock that night before the information arrived from the Wellington police force in New Zealand, confirming the murder of a prostitute on December 10th, 1986. Death was the result of a fractured skull but there were definite signs that the murderer had attempted to strangle his victim. As with the Singapore case numerous people had been questioned about the murder but no one was ever charged.

After Duffield had left to keep a dinner engagement with Heather, Rogers updated the back of the menu that was lying on the desk where Duffield had left it earlier, put it in his pocket, and headed for home.

The following morning Rogers and Duffield spent a frustrating hour trying to fill in the missing years, '88 and '89. At mid-day Duffield called the States and instituted a search for the names of murder victims within a three-day period on either side of December 10th for the two years. The hunt for the information would be an electronic paper chase through the FBI computers in Washington. Since 1968 a permanent central computer record of all murders, solved and unsolved, that happened within the United States, had been held in Washington and it was this store of information that Duffield found himself tapping into.

Duffield was assured that the report would be faxed to him within three hours but it was slightly over four hours later that they sat down to pour over the fifty or so murders for the two years in question. Ninety percent were easily dismissed as they both agreed that it was unlikely that Whittle would change his *modus operandi* at this late stage. In '88 this left only four murders and six in '89. Of the four in '88 only one remained unsolved, the other three having been committed by a person known to the deceased, and that appeared to be as a result of a running vendetta between rival drug gangs in Los Angeles; the victim was a black female who had been strangled. There were two possibilities in the '88 list, although the most likely, a hitch-hiker who was murdered near Atlanta, happened on the 8th of December and Whittle had never been known to strike before the 10th. By the end of their deliberations they had to admit that there was nothing that fitted the well-worn pattern that they now associated with Whittle.

"Either we're missing something, or he gave up '87 and started again in '92."

Duffield's question was rhetorical but before he could answer himself Rogers spoke. "He married Judith what's her name in '88 and he moved to Bermuda in '87. He must have met her in Bermuda, so he falls arse over tit in love with her. All his desires, wants, needs are fulfilled, motive for murder is removed and he enters retirement. Jump to '92, marriage is failing or he has to prove once more that he is smarter then the system so he murders again.

"He chooses New York, easy place to hide for him and his victim. It's a one-off, just like the first one, but who knows, give him eight years or less, then five and hey, we're back where we came in."

"I dunno, I still think we're missing something. As much as I don't want there to be another four out there I can't help feeling there are. We just . . . "

"Dr Terry Carmichael, Christ I'm stupid. Why didn't I think of her before?" Rogers smacked himself on the forehead and called through his intercom for his secretary.

"I agree you're dumb but who the fuck is Dr Terry Michael?" Duffield had to wait for a reply while Rogers asked his secretary to get Dr Carmichael on the phone for him. "Dr Carmichael is my pet psychiatrist. I use her occasionally to try and help put an identity to someone when I'm not really sure what I'm looking for. She'll have a field day with Whittle." Duffield opened his mouth to speak but the phone interrupted him. Two minutes later he was following a fleeing Rogers who was calling over his shoulder that she could see them for a few minutes as she was leaving for a conference in Switzerland within the hour.

Duffield was a lot less fit than Rogers and he spent the next fifteen minutes puffing after Rogers. A cold early-evening drizzle had settled on the city and Duffield found he was constantly dodging pedestrians who were heading for the sanctuary of the tube or bus. The proliferation of umbrellas made it difficult to keep Rogers in his sights and at one time he lost him and swore out loud until he spotted an exasperated Rogers calling to him from the other side of the road.

Eventually coming to a halt at a building on Park Lane Rogers again waited for Duffield to catch up. Duffield was not in a healthy state when he arrived: his clothes were dishevelled and his hair was plastered flat to his scalp; nor was his ordeal over. They climbed three flights of stairs, Rogers bounding up them two at a time.

Duffield coughed and wheezed his way up one at a time. By the time he arrived Rogers was inside the hallway of an open door and was in conversation with a tall attractive woman.

Rogers introduced him to Dr Carmichael. Duffield, unable to speak, simply nodded and wheezed again. "He's American," Rogers explained.

Dr Carmichael led them into a sitting-room which was tastefully decorated and offered them tea. Duffield would have killed for something stronger but, still unable to speak, merely nodded compliantly.

Rogers spent ten minutes giving her a broad brush overview of the Whittle case and finished by posing two questions. "I suppose what we would really like to know, Terry, is one, do you believe that someone with such a set pattern as this could just stop and if so, could they just as easily start again; and two, any ideas as to why he would only commit the murders on his birthday?"

Dr Carmichael moved to pour more tea before she answered. "The probable answer to the first question is contained in the answer to the second. Before you can go anywhere with hypothesis you need to establish the act that triggered the action. In this case we do not know that, so the only thing I can do is make some broad generalisations and leave it to your fertile imagination to see if your suspect fits.

"The catalyst here is the date. We are all affected one way or another by dates in our lives. We revere anniversaries, make special concessions for holidays and remember vividly the dates on which people die. When these days do not live up to our expectations we react. There are many people out there who hate the annual holidays, especially Christmas. The media and shops pump up an inflated view of the bonhomie and good spirit that should be existing everywhere – you don't experience it, *ergo*, there must be something wrong with you. Most people cope with this in a perfectly rational manner but some can't, or don't, cope with it at all. In order to release their frustration they have a binge on food, spend money they don't have, or turn to drink or drugs. In some serious cases they may carry out varying degrees of violence on themselves, or others, potentially culminating in suicide or murder. For Christmas read birthday and you have a boiler-plate schematic of your suspect."

Duffield was not a great believer in this side of policework and the scepticism in his voice came through when he spoke. "If we buy the story, that would account for one year but what about the gaps between the murders?"

"That's the problem with a profile like this – there are far too many unknowns. But take two of the facts that you do know: your suspect is smarter than average and he was married in '88. Based on these facts alone he would appear to be searching for love, a love which was not forthcoming as a child and was noticeably absent on his birthday. Or it could have been one isolated, but serious, incident, that happened on his fourteenth birthday. Guessing further I would go for the latter of these two possibilities as there was a long gap between the first and the second murder. The first could have been an accident." Duffield leaned forward to interrupt, but she held out her hand and explained, "Not an accident in that he didn't mean to kill, but an accident in that the opportunity arose and he acted out of frustrated instinct."

Rogers spoke. "Is there anything specific we should look for around his fourteenth birthday?"

"Well, there are the obvious things, the death of a parent . . . "

Duffield interrupted. "Can't be that, we know they're both alive."

"Perhaps, but it's something like that. Does he have any brothers or sisters?" Rogers and Duffield both looked at each other and shrugged their shoulders. "Of course, it may well be nothing as obvious as that, it could well be something that only he knows about. Returning to the murder itself, remember he was young, immature, probably scared, and it was only after a couple of months went by that he realised he had got away with it. He can now evaluate the act itself. It excites him, it produces a high, it makes him different from his peers. Subconsciously as the anniversary rolls around he looks for an opportunity. None arises for eight years, then five and then, hooked, he begins to create opportunity to ensure that the act will be an annual event. He is an addict, but like all addicts the high wears off quicker and quicker; the dose needs to be stronger. In this case it would appear that the novelty started to wear off. You said the last victim was a prostitute, and yet one of his earliest victim was a woman that he was having an affair with." She stopped to ensure that the impact of her words was sinking in. Both men appeared deep in thought: Duffield resting his fingers under his chin and staring at the wall, Rogers looking straight at her.

Before she could continue Duffield spoke. "And I suppose you would have us believe that his future wife enters at this juncture, fills the void of missing love and he starts to function like the rest of us?"

"It's a simplistically-put notion but yes, that would be my summation of what happened. You said he murdered again last year?" She addressed the question to Rogers who nodded. "That doesn't surprise me. It's the same pull that drug addicts and alcoholics feel. His marriage was a substitute for four years but that was all it was, a substitute; nothing can replace the feeling of superiority that goes with the knowledge of what you are. He was not cured. It could have been four or forty years. The odds that he would murder again were stacked against him from the day he last murdered. Remember, think of him in terms of an addict and it should help." Terry Carmichael stood up and smoothed her skirt. "I would be the first to admit that he doesn't fit the traditional profile of a serial killer but that's exactly what he is. That's the end of the lecture. I have a plane to catch." She walked towards a chair behind Duffield and picked up a fur coat.

Rogers was pulled back from his thoughts. "That's fine. Thanks Terry, you've been a great help, I think. Here, let me take your bag for you."

Walking down the stairs she added, "There is one thing that you said that was odd. You said one year you thought he raped someone and it didn't end in murder?"

"Yes, it was a local Saudi girl. What's odd about it?"

"Remember the addict, he needed his annual fix and he didn't get it. The fix was not sexual gratification, that was secondary. He can have murder without sex but not the other way round. You might want to check, as I would place money on the fact that within a few weeks, a couple of months at the most, he murdered someone else. The date this time was inconsequential; the fix, the emotional release would be everything."

They parted on the street; a swift nod of the head for Duffield, a peck on the cheek for Rogers. As a taxi did a U-turn to pick her up she told Rogers that she would call him when she got back and perhaps they could have a drink. The question awoke Duffield's thirst and, as the taxi disappeared into the London traffic, he asked where the nearest bar was.

The Park Lane hotel was less than a hundred yards away. While they waited for the drinks to arrive Duffield gave his views. "Nice lady, but I'm not sure I buy the story. Recreational murder, that's the term the experts have coined for it back in the good old US of A. It doesn't matter what you call it; these assholes are sick and society at large would be better off without them. So much for philosophy. Seemed to me like she was rather taken with you, Sherlock. She your bit on the side, or as you say over here, your piece of fluff?"

"Chance would be a fine thing. I don't have the time to devote to my own family, let alone have an affair. We're friends, we've known each other for a few years. I thought what she said was interesting – the picture that she drew with a few minor changes fits

Whittle perfectly."

The drinks arrived, scotch for Duffield and a beer for Rogers. They both took a drink before Duffield spoke. "If she's right, then we only have one more year to find and we're there. We'll have stopped at nine or ten and not the sixteen or so we thought it was going to be. What do we do next? Confront him with what we have, or wait?"

Rogers appeared not to have heard the question. "Nine or ten, that's only the surface numbers. What about all the other people the degenerate's destroyed? Andy Simms – twelve years wasted, Guttman Singh seven years; Samantha Strong's parents divorced and devastated; a Filipino executed for a crime he didn't commit. They all had family and friends, and what about Theresa Evans? She's a victim too." Duffield had difficulty immediately recalling who Theresa Evans was and it was only after he started talking that he recalled her as the air stewardess in Bahrain. "Hey, Sherlock, knock it off, we have him cold and he's gonna pay. At worst the rest of his life in jail but hopefully he'll get the chair. It doesn't bring the others back but it sure as hell wipes him out."

Again Rogers looked as if he hadn't heard. "I want to meet her."

"Who? Who do you wanna meet?"

"Theresa Evans – perhaps she saw him."

"She's paralysed for Christ's sake. Even if she saw him she can't tell us."

"If you want to stay here you can. I'm going to drive down to Wales and talk to her."

Theresa Evans' mother had been very accommodating on the telephone and was equally accommodating when they arrived at the small terraced house outside Cardiff later the following morning. Once Duffield realised that Rogers was serious he went along to humour his friend.

Mrs Evans led them into a bedroom and, after announcing who they were to Theresa, left them alone. She had already warned them that they should not expect any response but she had no problem with them talking to Theresa.

Duffield was immediately taken aback by the attractive woman who lay motionless in the bed, her upper body propped up against the pillows. She was immaculately made up and, despite her unanimated countenance, her face radiated beauty; the night dress hinted at a full figure beneath. He had not really thought about Theresa Evans on the drive but whatever he had been expecting it wasn't this.

Rogers took the only seat and sat down by the side of the bed.

"Theresa, I am here as a friend. We have been talking to some of your friends in Bahrain. Do you remember Bahrain?" Her face remained expressionless. Rogers tried again. "Theresa, we believe you may have seen something or someone that night in Bahrain, do you remember? Did you see a woman by the road or maybe a man with a woman?"

Theresa's breathing had been shallow, almost non-existent, but as Rogers finished speaking her chest moved and the tips of her fingers on her left hand moved slightly. Rogers reached out and took her left hand in his. "Theresa, did you see the man kill the woman?" He felt the faintest of pressures on his hand. "Did the man attack you?" Nothing. "Did you know the man?" Nothing. "Do you remember the driver of the car? Did he attack you? Did he kill the woman?" The breathing had slackened and again there was no pressure. "Did the Bahraini kill the woman?" Nothing. "We've found him Theresa, we know who did it." The pressure was firmer and then it was gone. Rogers leaned across the bed and kissed her lightly on the forehead. "And he killed you too, didn't he?"

The long drive back was painful. Duffield had observed what had happened and felt like a heel for doubting his friend's perceptive powers. He tried to turn his attention away from Theresa Evans but found it difficult to remove the hauntingly beautiful image from his mind. "What about the missing piece?"

"I took care of it last night." Rogers stared straight ahead at the road, the iron grey clouds above reflecting his mood. "It has to be Rio. I sent off a fax last night. There should be a reply waiting when we get back." Duffield conceded and they drove the remainder of the way back to London in silence.

As Duffield swung the car into the garage Rogers spoke for the first time in several hours. "It's possible I can use Theresa Evans when I confront Whittle with all the evidence we have and tell him that we have a witness to the murder in Bahrain. He doesn't know that she's paralysed and it may just unsettle him enough to do something out of the ordinary."

Duffield had not yet thought it all through but he was disinclined to argue with Rogers. "Not bad. Let's see if your hunch about Rio is correct and if it is, it might be time to be New York-bound."

A lengthy fax, in Portuguese, with a neatly typed English translation was waiting on Rogers' desk. Eighty percent of the missive, from the Rio police, explained that during Carnival Rio was not only swamped with tourists but that the murder rate also rose dramatically. The year in question there had been sixty-three murders. Most of them were stabbings, run-of-the-mill Carnival activities, but one young Samba dancer had been murdered at a private party on Sugar-Loaf. She had been strangled and sexually assaulted. It had happened in a crowded place but no one saw anything and no one was ever charged with the murder.

"Impressive, Sherlock, let's go get the scum now."

"Just one more call." Rogers pulled a piece of paper from his pocket and dialled the number on it. "Records? This is Rogers over at the Home Office. Can you check a Whittle family for me? Born and resident in Somerset. Mother Olive, father David, one son Simon. Can you tell me if there any other immediate family members, alive or dead . . . yes I'll hang on."

Thirty seconds later Rogers pulled a note-pad towards him and Duffield watched as he wrote, 'Daughter, Karen Louise, born December 10th, 1968.

chapter 40

Standing on the balcony of the hotel room, I stared at the horizon where the two blue lines merged, the sea just slightly darker than the sky. I knew at last that my future no longer lay beyond that boundary. My future was here, within my grasp. I had survived my own personal test and my reward was eternity. I was not just smug. I was ecstatic.

The desire, almost bordering on need, to leave New York had grown dramatically in the last few months, but now that was behind me. I had spent the last two days in Bermuda finalising my appointment as President of one of the offshore insurance companies.

This was my zenith.

The rangy kid in the ill-fitting clothes of a bygone age had come a long way from Somerset. Thought and will had followed spirit to bring me the million miles from there to here. The smaller pieces of the puzzle were as essential as the larger, flashier pieces, for without them the picture was not whole. When I was young, ten or eleven, I announced to my parents that one day I would live and work in New York. The comment was dismissed with laughter. When I started work I wondered how far I could go. I knew now that I was ahead; not just ahead of my peers, I had passed them long ago; but ahead of myself, and I was planning to stay there forever. Like a wine laid in '54 my life had matured and now was the time to witness the fruits of its vintage.

I did not pray, but I silently vowed my love for my wife, my daughter and, looking up, saw only the future.

chapter 41

The British Airways flight from London touched down at Newark Airport in New Jersey. Rogers and Duffield left with the rest of the passengers and were met by an FBI agent who escorted them outside and handed over the keys to one of the two cars that were being watched over by the agent's colleague. The two men threw their luggage onto the back seat and drove off, leaving the agent to drive back to Queens.

They had agreed that it would be better to confront Whittle in his own home and headed straight there from the airport. Duffield drove and apart from one wrong turn they easily found the Garden State Parkway and exited at Edison.

"You okay, partner? You're awful quiet?"

"Yes, I'm fine. Let's just get this over with."

They pulled into a liquor store to get directions to Mount Drive. Heading south across the railway tracks the houses became more palatial. Turning onto River Drive they looked for the third turning on the left which, according to the store clerk, would be Mount Drive. The houses stood in splendid isolation; ornate columns guarded the main entrances while immaculately manicured lawns formed modern day moats. The requisite swimming pools could occasionally be glimpsed at the rear.

"There it is." Duffield had seen the turn and swung the car into Mount Drive. Number twenty-three was situated on a bend in the road and was slightly more prominent than its immediate neighbours. There were no cars in the driveway. Duffield brought the car to a halt against the kerb. The engine died and the two sat in silence. They had both thought about this moment often but had not talked about the specifics of what would happen when they confronted Whittle.

"C'mon, Sherlock, lets go wrap this up." Duffield pulled himself from behind the wheel.

The door chimes announced their presence and after a few moments the door was answered by a petite, attractive woman. Rogers knew immediately that this was Mrs Judith Whittle. She looked slightly quizzically first at Duffield and then at Rogers.

"Excuse us for interrupting you on a Sunday afternoon but is Mr Simon Whittle at home?" Duffield looked behind her as if he was expecting to see Whittle standing there.

"No, I'm sorry, he's away on business. He won't be back until tomorrow."

The answer nonplussed both Duffield and Rogers; they knew that Whittle had been in Bermuda for the past few days but he had been due to return that morning. Before either man could speak a loud cry came from within the house.

Mrs Whittle looked again at both men and then over her shoulder. "I'm sorry, that's my daughter." She turned and left the two men standing on the doorstep. Before Rogers and Duffield had a chance to discuss anything she was back holding a now placated young child in her arms. "Sorry about that. Is there anything that I can do for you?"

Duffield produced his badge and flashed it quickly in front of Mrs Whittle. "We need to see your husband – sorry, I assume you are Mrs Whittle," she nodded in confirmation, "it's a matter involving one of your husband's clients from the office."

"This is a bit awkward standing on the doorstep. Why don't you come in for a minute?"

The two men followed her through a large, spacious hall into an expansive, tastefully furnished living room. A large child's play mat, with numerous soft toys on it, was spread in front of a leather couch. Mrs Whittle deposited the baby onto the mat; she immediately giggled and rolled around, spreading the toys about her.

"Sorry about this. Please have a seat. Can I get you some coffee or a drink?"

"No, not for me thanks." Rogers shook his head.

Duffield waited for Rogers to speak but when it became apparent that he wasn't intending to, he picked up from where he had left off. "As I said, we're making certain investigations into the dealings of one of your husband's clients. We were in the area on another matter and thought we'd take the opportunity to stop by and ask Mr Whittle a few questions."

"I can phone him in Bermuda if you like, I only spoke to him about half an hour ago. He said he would be in the hotel until about seven and then he was going out to dinner." While she was speaking she had risen and was walking towards the telephone.

"There's no need to do that, Mrs Whittle, we're based in the city so we'll visit him at the office. When did you say you were expecting him back?"

"Well it should have been this morning. He went to Bermuda for a job interview. He called me on Friday to say that he had been offered the job and was staying on until Monday to sort out some of the details. We used to live in Bermuda, before Jane was born, and we've decided that we would rather live there than here so we should be moving within the next couple of months."

Rogers had been surveying the room and the furnishings; he was trying very hard not to look at either Mrs Whittle or the squirming bundle on the mat at his feet. He became aware of a tugging on his trouser leg and looked down to see the unsteady figure holding herself up, gripping his trouser leg with two tiny fists. She looked at him, apprehensively at first, and then smiled. Her face lit up, the eyes sparkled, her mouth opened and little gurgling sounds emerged as she rocked back and forth. Rogers stared transfixed. The smiling image was not that of a young girl but of her father. He could see it in the corners of her mouth. Her laughter seemed to mock him for his inadequacies. He felt constricted and stood up abruptly. The child lost her balance and toppled backwards. For a moment she lay peacefully, a look of surprise on her face; it lasted only a split second before she opened her mouth and howled, not in pain but in shock. Rogers was confused and embarrassed by his action. "I'm sorry, I didn't mean to hurt her."

"That's alright, she just got a fright when you stood up." She picked the child up in her arms and rocked her gently. Rogers turned and walked towards the door.

"Thanks for your help, Mrs Whittle," Duffield said, getting up. "Sorry to have bothered you, we'll see ourselves out." As he reached the door he stopped and turned round. "You wouldn't happen to know what time Mr Whittle would be in his office tomorrow, would you?"

"He said he was landing around mid-morning but he has a lunch engagement at a restaurant downtown, the Olive Tree, so he should be in his office after two-thirty."

"Thanks again."

Rogers was already sitting in the car. "Best laid plans, eh? Well,

I found out he should be in his office tomorrow afternoon, so I guess we just meet him there. You don't think she'll call him, do you?" Rogers did not answer. He was staring out of the window. "C'mon, Sherlock, it'll wait for another twenty-four hours, let's go have a drink."

Rogers was sombre and withdrawn for the rest of the evening. After a couple of drinks at the hotel bar Duffield left him and headed off to his apartment in the city.

Rogers did not sleep that night. He lay, fully clothed, on the bed, his mind a cauldron of thoughts and accusations. The constraints of the hotel room finally became too much for him, and at about four o'clock he pulled on his heavy winter jacket, took the elevator down to the ground floor and stepped out into the still morning air.

Manhattan is the original city that never sleeps. The remnants of the night crowd were slowly giving way to the early morning deliveries. The financial district was comatose but as he walked northward he heard laughter and cursing, the sound of metal on metal. The meat-packing district was bustling with activity. Passing the door of a diner he smelt coffee and was tempted to enter and be enveloped in the warmth but he walked on by, his head bent, his stride purposeful. A weary prostitute, her tight, leather mini-skirt displaying matchstick thin legs, bumped his shoulder as she passed. Her eyes met his: they were listless, anaemic-looking. She stopped for a moment, expectant, but the effect of her presence had already passed Rogers by.

He walked for over two hours, oblivious to the biting cold. At 6.30 he found himself outside the door of Duffield's apartment. With a shrug he acknowledged that this was where he must always have been heading. He read the names next to the doorbell, thought about pressing 3B, but instead turned round and crossed the street to an all-night diner. Rogers ordered a coffee; he paid the sixty cents and, taking the quarter from his change, deposited it into a slot by the telephone just inside the front door.

"Hi, Sam Duffield. Please leave your message after the tone. I'll get back to you."

"I'm across the street. Coffee's on me."

Rogers took a seat at the counter and stirred sugar into the steaming black coffee.

Thirty minutes later Duffield fought his way though the bodies at the cash desk and joined Rogers at the counter. "Christ, Sherlock don't you ever sleep? We can't do anything until after lunch so why the rush?"

"I've been thinking."

"Jesus, Sherlock, it's too early in the morning for that."

Rogers ignored Duffield's comments. "I've been up all night thinking."

Duffield looked up to speak but seeing the intense look on the face opposite him he thought better of it.

"It's Whittle . . . "

Duffield interrupted. "We both know the full story, he's as guilty as hell and in due course we're going to prove it."

"But that's the whole point." Rogers' voice had risen and some workmen in blue overalls at the next table looked across at them. Rogers dropped his voice but the edge of anger was still there. "Can't you see what's wrong with Whittle?"

"Sherlock, it's obvious, even to me, what's wrong with the guy. The elevator doesn't go all the way to the top floor, he's a few sticks short of a bundle, in all probability he is insane. But we have from now until December 9th to nail him."

"You're still missing the point. Whittle is not just a murderer. He is evil. He has to die."

Duffield looked at Rogers and realised for the first time what a terrible strain this case had had on Rogers. His face, which had always been thin, was pinched, there were dark hollows below his eyes, and his cheeks were red, almost purple in colour. Rogers was fighting to control his emotions.

"Alan, I know how you feel, but we're only employed to catch him, not judge him. We both know the system's not perfect, but we have to leave justice to the courts."

"Christ almighty. You talk about justice, justice for whom? His victims? Their families? His wife and child? Us?" Rogers' eyes had a wild look about them and he pushed his hand repeatedly through his hair. "I can understand most crimes, they're committed for a reason – for money, revenge, love, hate – they're human. But this, this . . . " he fought for the right word, "this piece of shit has killed again and again. And for what? Because someone forgot his birthday? Because his sister was born on the same day? It will be years before we get a conviction, if ever, and all the while he'll be mocking us. We've beaten him today, but so what? In the end he'll win. He has money and influence, we have paper-thin evidence and morality." Rogers' voice had faded and was little more than a whisper. "He has to die."

The limousine pulled up outside the Olive Tree restaurant, in Little Italy, shortly after 12.30. Simon Whittle stepped out with his overcoat draped across his left arm. He leaned back through the open door and spoke to the driver. Pulling himself upright he moved quickly across the short distance from the car to the door of the restaurant. The door was already halfway open when he heard his name. "Whittle." He turned, expecting to see a familiar face.

Alan Rogers was stood less than six feet away. There was no hint of recognition and Whittle turned abruptly to enter the restaurant; he was forced to take an involuntary step back to allow two people to exit.

"Surely you haven't forgotten me? Saudi Arabia seems like only yesterday. I doubt that Sean Logan has forgotten as quickly."

"Rogers?"

"Why don't we take a walk? I've cancelled your lunch appointment, you are no longer expected."

Whittle remained motionless. The only indication that he was alive was the steady stream of mist that escaped from his open mouth. His eyes, unblinking, remained fixed on Alan Rogers. He blinked suddenly, as if some unseen hypnotist had snapped his fingers.

"This is absurd. You will have to excuse me, I have a very important lunch date. If you wish to talk to me I suggest you call my secretary and arrange an appointment for later in the week."

"Perhaps I didn't make myself clear the first time, you are no longer expected for lunch. We have to talk and it's in your best interest to listen." Rogers turned and walked slowly away.

Simon Whittle hesitated for a moment, then followed. He caught up with him just as he finished putting his overcoat on. "I'm only doing this to humour you and when this farce is over I will give serious consideration to making a complaint of police harassment to whoever it is you work for these days." Rogers remained silent and continued walking.

They left Little Italy and headed for the heart of China Town where the usual throng of people bustled along the narrow streets. Whittle's tone registered both annoyance and exasperation as he demanded that Rogers explain what was going on.

At first Rogers appeared not to have heard but then began speaking, his voice emotionless but firm. "You might have got away with it but for a coincidence, or maybe it's not coincidence, just your natural arrogance and disdain. Whatever it was it's over. I know everything from Tracey Gates to Martha Staples." Rogers became aware that Whittle had stopped walking.

"First it's Angela Logan, who, I will concede, I knew, but who are these other people? I've never heard of them."

They stood about ten feet apart, Whittle defiant, his hands thrust deep into his coat pockets, Rogers simply staring at him. People looked at them quizzically for a moment, then averted their eyes and passed quickly by, anxious not to become involved.

A short distance away Duffield watched as the stand-off continued, neither man speaking. It was Whittle who finally broke the eye contact. Rogers shrugged, turned and continued south through China Town. As Rogers disappeared around a corner Duffield moved forward, his hand resting on his holstered gun. He came up behind Whittle, was close enough to reach out and touch his shoulder, when Whittle moved; he shuffled his feet forward and then, as if propelled from behind, began running. Duffield instinctively went to draw his gun but delayed his action when he realised that Whittle was trying to catch up with Rogers. He followed.

It was a block and a half before Whittle came abreast of Rogers. Rogers did not look at him but began speaking as if he were talking to himself. "I forgot, I don't suppose names are important to you. So if Martha Staples and Tracey Gates were victims without names, let's try some others. I apologise if I don't get them in the right date order: Janice Butterworth, Samantha Strong, Elizabeth McFadden, Angela Logan, a hotel maid, your Sri Lankan cleaning lady. There's more, much more, but I think by now you may understand why your lunch was cancelled." He still did not look at Whittle but was acutely aware of his presence.

"I have to give you credit, Rogers, I didn't think you had it in you. I won't demean the level of our conversation by asking how you put it all together. Like most things in life the details are immaterial, we need to focus on the big picture. We are both men of the world, both realists, and as a realist I know that you are taking quantum leaps to manufacture allegations from flimsy notions."

"Don't push me, Whittle." For the first time Rogers' voice betrayed his anger. "I'm tired, emotionally and physically, this is not some pleasant conversation to debate truth. I'm here to see it doesn't happen again."

They halted on the corner of Broadway and Ann Street, waiting for the traffic lights to change. Around them people clutched at brown bags or briefcases. A young couple – the woman in business suit and fur coat, the man in jeans and a leather jacket – laughed; with his arm around her shoulder he pulled her to him and kissed her quickly but firmly. The lights changed and the mass of people moved in unison across the intersection.

"I'm not sure what's happening here but at a guess I would say that you are on a fishing trip. Having collected a series of names you're looking for a hook to hang them on. You've got nothing on me." Whittle was becoming more self-assured, his own arguments providing the stamina to refute Rogers allegations. "Look around – I can walk away and that would be the end of this farce. If I'm what you say I am, surely I warrant more than the individual attention of one paranoid Englishman in New York?"

Rogers did not respond. He kept on walking until he reached the door of the World Trade Centre. He waited patiently as three people emerged; then, holding the door open, gestured to Whittle that he should go through.

"Look, Rogers, these threats and this conversation are going nowhere. What the hell are we doing here?"

They had arrived at the top of the steps which led to the subway trains, the same steps where Rogers had stood with Duffield a few weeks ago and watched Simon Whittle walk back into his life.

Rogers reached into an inside pocket, pulled out the menu that they had carried from Jeddah and handed it to Whittle. Whittle looked at it quizzically before turning it over; he saw the writing and the colour drained from his face.

Whittle passed the menu back. "I didn't do it."

"The time for bullshit is over, Whittle . . . "

Whittle interrupted. "No, this," he pointed at the last name on the menu, "I didn't kill her."

Rogers looked at Whittle, realising the irony. But it wasn't important now.

"I've got you Whittle, trapped you. You've been good, very good, but you haven't got away with it. I will haunt you. I will destroy you. I will get the evidence if it takes a week or twenty years. You're finished – the top jobs, the nice home, they're all gone. One day I will confront you again, not with some menu reciting facts, but with a warrant." Rogers stopped speaking to let the significance of the words sink in. He saw the flash of anger that shot across Whittle's eyes, and the face contorted as if in pain.

"Nobody dictates the terms of my life, only me, and it's over."

He raised his right hand. The muzzle of a small gun was pointing directly at Rogers' head. Whittle held Rogers' gaze for a few seconds, then suddenly turned the gun, placed it against his forehead and pulled the trigger.

The body fell. As Rogers walked away, head held high, the sense of frustration and anger that had engulfed him over the last few weeks disappeared and was replaced with a smile of satisfaction.